Love is
a time of enchantment:
in it all days are fair and all fields
green. Youth is blest by it,
old age made benign:
the eyes of love see
roses blooming in December,
and sunshine through rain. Verily
is the time of true-love
a time of enchantment — and
Oh! how eager is woman
to be bewitched!

MY LORD ENEMY

A marriage ceremony is cruelly interrupted when news of King Edward's flight from his throne is brought to lovely Elinor and her betrothed, the handsome Lord Cranley. Brutal news indeed, for father and husband stand on opposing sides. As her husband's unwilling captive, Elinor is forced to make the perilous journey over land and sea to Flanders. Yet as she fights her Lord like a wildcat, as she seeks a means of escape, as together they fend off the dangers along the way, a curious love is born . . .

JOANNA MAKEPEACE

MY LORD ENEMY

Complete and Unabridged

ULVERSCROFT
Leicester

First published in Great Britain

'Joanna Makepeace is the pseudonym
for Margaret York'

First Large Print Edition
published 1997

British Library CIP Data

Makepeace, Joanna, *1927 –*
My Lord enemy.—Large print ed.—
Ulverscroft large print series: romance
1. English fiction—20th century
2. Large type books
I. Title
823.9'14 [F]

ISBN 0–7089–3670–9

Published by
F. A. Thorpe (Publishing) Ltd.
Anstey, Leicestershire
Set by Words & Graphics Ltd.
Anstey, Leicestershire
Printed and bound in Great Britain by
T. J. Press (Padstow) Ltd., Padstow, Cornwall

This book is printed on acid-free paper

1

ELINOR sat with her back tightly pressed against the bole of the oak tree. Its familiar feel of gnarled rough bark comforted her, even through the thick folds of her blue woollen gown. Her whole world was changing, frighteningly soon, and she needed this brief escape from Alice's watchful guard to compose herself, to say farewell to the old life, prepare herself to face the new.

He was coming today, perhaps within a few hours, her betrothed, Gerard, Viscount Cranley. Even now he was but five or six short miles from her, with the King camped in Doncaster. Soon, after noon, she would stand with him before Father John in the squat little Norman church to be formally handfasted. Elinor experienced a shiver of fear. Once that short ceremony was concluded she would be bound to him. Only a dispensation from the Pope in Rome could dissolve the contract.

Her father was already talking of an early marriage.

"By Christmas, you will be bedded and installed in your own manor, my child." He had rubbed his hands together in evident satisfaction. "This business could not have fallen out better for us. The marriage has had to be delayed far too long. Now the King is camped so near in Doncaster your betrothed can ride here for the betrothal ceremony. He is eager to claim his bride. Only his need to be constantly by the King's side throughout these recent troubles has prevented him from doing so earlier. You are sixteen, Elinor, full time you were wed. The match was drawn up in 1460, almost ten years ago."

Elinor looked down at her bare feet drying in the warm September sun. Alice, her nurse, would have been shocked to see her, this morning of all mornings, dressed like a serving wench, her hose discarded, trailing her toes in the streamlet, kirtle hitched up almost to her waist, hair streaming free of confining pins and hood, tied back with a length of scarlet ribbon bought from the chapman who had visited the manor only last June.

She bent forward to examine her features in the unsullied depths of the water. Sixteen, a woman grown, ripe for the marriage bed. She did not *feel* a woman, indeed, her cheeks still burned in shame when she occasionally overheard snippets of bawdy talk between the serving maids who, giggling, carried in her bathtub or scrubbed her floor. She was not ignorant of what marriage entailed. Elinor was constantly made aware of the realities of mating by the behaviour of the stallions and mares within her father's stables and of the rams and ewes which were pastured on the broad Beckwith demesne. Indeed, her father's second wife, Isabel, had died only a year ago in childbed. In dreams sometimes still, Elinor woke drenched in the cold sweat of horror, Isabel's dying screams ringing in her ears — and all for nothing since the male child for which her father had longed so desperately had died with his mother.

Yet it was not her fear of dying so which troubled Elinor now, not even the strange wild excitement which made her heart pound or her pulses race at the thought of submitting dutifully to her husband. No, it was the finality of this short ceremony, the knowledge that her dull but safe life on the Yorkshire manor under the gentle bullying of Alice, her nurse, was to come to a sudden end. She must accompany her lord to his Lincolnshire home, or even to London to the dazzling world of the Court at Westminster. She was not ready to face either, unprepared, despite Alice's and the late Isabel's careful tutelage, to assume her position of chateleine of a great house such as she knew Cranley Castle to be, or to face the intrigues and formalities, backbiting and gossip she would find at Court.

Every day of her sixteen years had been spent on the manor at Beckwith. Elinor had not ridden even so far afield as Doncaster. She loved the grey-stone moated house, surrounded by the rolling green acres of sheepland, dry-stone walls, the village, clustering close by the grey Norman church, the sturdy cottages of stone and wood, the cultivated strips of barley and wheat separated by grassy baulks where their villagers laboured, the mill, the noisy welcoming clang of the farrier's hammer as it struck the anvil, the gentle murmur of the little stream which flowed its way through the demesne and widened into the fishpond which provided their food on Fridays and throughout the Lenten fasting. How could she leave it all, and the villagers and manor servants whom she knew and trusted?

Her features appeared pale under the gently undulating water, the face oval, the fire in her chestnut hair quenched. She shook back the heavy waves impatiently, peering still closer. Her eyes were unusual and lovely, golden, almond-shaped, under luxuriant sooty lashes. She had rebelliously refused to allow Alice to shave her equally thick brows in the current fashion. Elinor sighed. If she were soon to go to Court that must be remedied. She prepared herself to do battle with Alice over that again today.

"Mistress Elinor! Oh God o' mercy, there you be, and just look at you! And me exhausting myself searching for you in hall and solar, aye, and kitchens and buttery too, wearing out my old bones. Such preparations to be made. Do you want to kill old Alice?"

Elinor turned, guiltily, as the old woman panted up to her.

"Alice, there was no need for concern. I told Joan . . . "

"That flighty creature? She's no more sense than a green tit. 'Oh, yes, Mistress Alice,' she says, 'the young mistress told me to tell you that she's gone out for a breath of air and you are not to fash yourself.' Mind you, none of it did I hear from her till I'd been calling and shouting all over the manor. Then I had to shake her till her teeth rattled, then she deigned to tell me where you'd gone, or rather where she *thought* you'd gone. Pet," she scolded, more gently, "hadn't you more sense than to frighten the life out of me, like that? Every moment I feared Sir Thomas would come striding up to your chamber to see how we did."

Elinor stemmed the tirade by reaching up to grasp Alice's work-roughened hand.

"I'm sorry, it was thoughtless. I should have asked you, but," she added, smiling wryly, "I knew you would not have

6

allowed me to come and I wanted to say goodbye to all this." She made a wide gesture with her arms, taking in the streamlet, the copse to their left, over which the square, short tower of the church could just be glimpsed.

"Pet, there'll be time yet. Lord Cranley comes only for the betrothal." Alice clucked impatiently, "He's far too busy with affairs, soldiering and such, to be snatching you off to Lincolnshire now."

Elinor joined her, reluctantly keeping pace with her nurse's slow progress for she could see Alice was sadly out of breath.

"Then you think there'll be fighting again, soon?"

"Eh, pet, how would I know? Your father thinks so. If the King weren't expecting trouble why has he marched south from Northumberland in such a hurry? He'd not be here in Yorkshire at all, nor your betrothed expected, if His Grace weren't preparing to face the Earl of Warwick in battle."

"And father will also be off to join Lord Montecute."

"Aye, likely so." Alice sighed as she

wheezed the final distance up the entrance steps. "Not that it need concern you, my pet. War be man's business. Yours is to make yourself eminently presentable for My Lord, who is soon to be your husband." She frowned as Elinor mischievously shook back the thick mane of her hair. "How we're to manage that in time the dear Lord knows. Lord Cranley is expected at any time and your father has commanded you wear your finest gown. Now upstairs and into the tub with you. Do you wish your betrothed to ride in suddenly and see a hoyden awaiting him in the hall?"

"Do you think he might change his mind, Alice?"

"God help us, don't even breathe such a thing. Don't you understand how fortunate you are, you, the daughter of a knight banneret, to wed a viscount, and one close in favour at Court?"

Elinor smiled gratefully at Joan, the serving wench, as they entered her chamber. The girl rose hurriedly from where she knelt by the high-sided wooden tub, adding sweet scented herbs to the hot, steaming water. Poor Joan, one of her

8

ears still looked angrily red and Elinor's conscience smote her, for surely Alice had boxed it soundly in her rage at the girl.

Alice gave Elinor no time to sympathize with the luckless Joan. She was already tugging at the back lacing of Elinor's old woollen gown and sharply ordering Joan to bring forward the wooden screens on which large towels had been draped to allow the young mistress some privacy while bathing.

Elinor stepped carefully into the tub, crouching until the aromatic scented water reached almost to her chin. Alice rolled up her sleeves and gently soaped Elinor's body and hair while Joan waited stolidly nearby, a large white towel in which to envelop her mistress draped over her arm.

"If your hair is still damp under your head-dress," Alice said tartly, giving the curling strands a final squeeze, "you've naught but yourself to blame. All right, Joan, let us have the towel now and the perfumed oil I told you to put ready."

"Alice, that was Isabel's," Elinor chided in a shocked voice as she stepped gingerly out onto the soft, strewn rushes and Joan

9

wrapped her up snugly in the towel's thick folds.

"Aye, that's true enough, but it cannot serve any purpose lying locked in her dower chest now she's gone. Your body must be fragrant enough to please His Lordship's fastidious nose. He'll have been used to the scents of musk and bergamot, ambergris and sandalwood on the Court ladies he's been waiting attendance on over these months past."

Joan dropped the towel and Elinor looked self-consciously down at her body. She was growing tall, was she too lanky, she wondered? Her legs were long and shapely enough, though there were soft brown lines at the ankles where the sun had caught her as she frequently sat without hose near the stream. She blushed hotly as Alice smoothed the scented oil into the soft down of her pubic hair, patting the taut flesh of her buttocks then up and over the silken smooth splendour of thighs, belly and high, youthful breasts, tut-tutting her concern over the brownish sun marks on the neck and shoulders.

"How many times during these past

months have I bidden you stay out of the sun? Cucumber lotion isn't going to whiten this skin before the marriage day. That's for sure."

Joan slipped her fine cambric shift over her shoulders and offered her her bedgown and Elinor sat before her clothing chest while Alice brushed out the dampened curls into feathery tendrils upon her forehead. She peered critically into the new iron mirror, bought, like the scarlet ribbon, from the chapman who'd come to the manor some months before.

"I wish my hair was fair like the Queen's."

Alice snorted. "Yours is true English beauty, the nut brown hair of the minstrels' songs. My Lord'll be pleased enough by what he sees today, my pet. As for the Queen, His Grace wouldn't be spoiling for war with his cousin the Earl of Warwick right now if it were not for this ill-advised marriage. My Lord Earl has never forgiven the King the insult laid on him. Why, hadn't he been sent to treat for the hand of the French princess, and to come back flushed with success, only to be told the King had been secretly wed months before."

"But that was years ago. The Queen has borne the King fine daughters."

Alice sniffed. "But no sons."

"No, poor lady."

"Poor lady, indeed! The Woodvilles have grown too high in the land and My Lord Earl isn't the only man to be dissatisfied."

Elinor sighed. She was no fool. She knew well enough that only the greed for lands and power set lord against lord. Her father was the Marquess of Montecute's man, and her betrothed waited on the Yorkist King. Both expected their loyalty to the White Rose to be fittingly rewarded.

The door latch clicked and Sir Thomas Beckwith entered the chamber. Alice and Joan bobbed respectful curtseys and Elinor half rose from her stool. He waved impatiently for her to seat herself. A strongly built man with the bearing of the professional soldier, Sir Thomas was still in his early forties and not unhandsome. Elinor saw him infrequently as he was often away from the manor in constant attendance on John Neville, Marquess of Montecute. Her heart quickened its beat a little. Though he had never whipped her or punished her over-harshly, she held him in awe. Her father was a bluff, plain-spoken man who would never stoop to flattery. His manor servants did not want second bidding to hasten to his summons, nor did they stint from conscientious service. His broad, square face was weathered and roughened by wind and rain and his hair as brown, even at the temples, as it had been when he'd wed Elinor's mother. His searching gaze passed from his daughter's dishabille to the garments laid out in readiness on the bed. His brows drew together in a frown.

"These are what she is to wear for the ceremony?"

Elinor followed his gaze to the green brocade gown Joan and the serving maids had recently re-fashioned for her from one of her step-mother's, which had been carefully folded away in her dower chest. The colour was becoming to Elinor's fresh complexion and she had been pleased with the effect when she had stood patiently throughout the fittings. Its broad, high belt and heart-shaped head-dress were in cloth of gold like the lining of the wide, dagged over-sleeves which fell fully to the ground when she dropped her hands to her sides. Elinor felt very grand in it, though over-laden by the heavy weight of the cloth with its short train. Alice had pressed her to move about her chamber and up and down stairs in the gown, but she still feared she might stumble while descending the manor stairs or, worse, when proceeding down the uneven flagstones of the church aisle.

Alice's eyes searched Sir Thomas's face for some sign of his approval.

"The mistress looks very well in it, Sir Thomas."

"H'm." He touched the cloth lightly with the embroidered glove he carried. "Hurry. Let me see her dressed in it." He turned impatiently to the window, his back to them.

Elinor's golden eyes rounded in wonder. Her father had never before displayed such interest in what she wore. Most of her life she had been dressed simply,

14

as she had been this morning, in well-cut but warm gowns of fine wool, for the Yorkshire air was keen and chill sometimes throughout even the summer months. When Isabel had become her step-mother, she had, it's true, been anxious that Elinor be dressed more befitting her station and had had two velvet gowns fashioned for her — these Elinor seldom wore. In all events she had only recently emerged from her mourning black and her grander garments been lain aside with those of the dead Isabel. Now, it appeared, her father was determined that she should make a good impression upon her betrothed. Was Viscount Cranley then so very grand? If so, how could she hope to please him, since she had no knowledge of Court fashions or manners?

Sir Thomas walked slowly round her as she stood nervously in her new finery.

He shook his head decisively. "No, it will not do."

"Won't do, Sir Thomas?" Alice's tone was aggrieved if not scandalized.

"Too heavy, ornate, cumbersome. She looks buried in it. No, no, woman, she cannot face Lord Gerard in a gown obviously handed down from another. She needs something lighter, more simple in line. The eye should be drawn to her youth and freshness. My Lord cannot be impressed by ostentation, he is too used to that. His eye must be wooed by simplicity."

"Well, Sir Thomas, Mistress Elinor has little else suitable," Alice grumbled. "There's the burgundy velvet Lady Isabel had sewn for her — "

"Her wedding gown. Is it finished?"

"Why yes, sir, but — "

"Attire her in that, and hurry. I'd not keep My Lord waiting. We expect him soon."

Alice padded off, muttering beneath her breath and Sir Thomas gestured to Joan to assist her mistress from the brocaded gown. He lifted Elinor's chin and scrutinized her pale face thoughtfully.

"Tell Alice to pluck those brows straight and put some colour in her cheeks."

The girl curtseyed. "Yes, Sir Thomas."

He nodded and strode from the

16

chamber. Elinor had been too dumb-founded to exchange one word with him.

Alice hastened in with the wedding gown. Testily she waved Joan aside. "Come then, Mistress, your father must be obeyed to the letter."

When, half an hour later, Sir Thomas returned, he was accompanied by Elinor's cousin, Reginald. She gave a cry of pleasure at the sight of him. They had been constant companions in childhood but, since his years of training in Lord Montecute's household, she had seen very little of him. He was nineteen, a sturdy, brown haired young man, closely resembling her father.

"Reginald, I am glad to see you, I'd not expected it."

He wrinkled his nose at her comically. "Nor I. My duties have been arduous recently but My Lord was only too pleased to allow me leave to attend the ceremony." He sank down on the wooden bench in the window bay eyeing her in mock criticism. "Now I'm here, I cannot say it will be a pleasure to witness this betrothal ceremony."

17

"Why?" She blushed hotly.

"And see so beautiful a vision contracted to another? You expect me to remain unmoved by the prospect?"

"Hush your foolish tongue, Reginald," Sir Thomas snapped. "You'll give the girl airs. Elinor has been gently reared. She knows her duty. This is an excellent match, better than we could have hoped for."

Elinor had heard the tale many times from her mother. Her grandfather had fought beside the present viscount's father at St Albans and Wakefield. Indeed, both men had fallen in that dread battle. Sir William had lived long enough to make his dying wishes known. His heir was to be contracted to his friend's granddaughter. By chance, a knight's child was granted a rare marital prize. She would become a viscountess. If the new Lord Cranley was displeased by a match so hastily made before he had been old enough to either understand or object to it, he had made no attempt to withdraw from the contract over the years. Sir Thomas, flattered by the arrangement, had been equally pleased to grant his only daughter a considerable dowry.

He dismissed the waiting women.

"I wish to speak with my daughter alone."

Reginald bowed his way out in the wake of the women, who scurried hastily to obey the master. Elinor looked longingly after Reginald's scarlet-clad form. She was feeling hopelessly out of her depth, suddenly shy and bewildered in her father's presence. He prowled the room for moments then abruptly took her by the shoulder and led her to stand before her mirror.

She could not contain a faint gasp of surprise at first sight of herself in the unfamiliar short cap covered in gold brocade set well back on her head, with its froth of white veiling framing her face and falling in soft folds to the floor behind her. Alice had skilfully plucked the heavy brows in a fine arched line and lightly touched her pale cheeks with carmine. She looked older, more worldly and, wonderingly, she gazed down at the white velvet over-gown which hugged her form to the waist then fell in heavy folds to the floor, one side drawn up and caught beneath the wide gilded belt to allow her freedom of movement and to reveal the splendour of the undergown of gold brocade. The restriction of the leather belt pushed up her breasts. Hesitantly she laid her hand on the soft swell where the swansdown trimming met in a deep 'V' and where Alice had pinned in the little gorget vest of gold brocade which matched undergown and cap. Her father's voice, unusually softened, sounded close to her ear.

"You like what you see? Good, so will your betrothed. I've been watching you lately, child. You walk and move well with the grace of your mother and the pride of Isabel. God rest both their souls."

She turned from the mirror to face him curiously.

"You are anxious about this match? Has Lord Cranley expressed regret at the thought of it?"

"No, no. I've seen the young man only once or twice over the last months. We've exchanged little more than the common courtesies but — "

"Father?"

He shrugged away her rising alarm.

"Be easy. I've heard nothing to the man's discredit. He's young, scarce above twenty and — personable." His lips twitched. "Though I don't know if your eyes will be pleased by his appearance. A maid's longings are hard to determine. He's no known lecher nor yet monkish in his habits. He's spoken of as a doughty fighter, skilled with sword and lance, and more to your taste, daughter, I understand he is scholarly, reads widely, plays the lute, dances well. You have been well tutored. Do not stand awkwardly silent in his company. Engage him in talk. Show polite modesty but ply him with questions concerning the Court. Young women would be expected to be curious concerning such matters, but, mind, speak no word of the present disagreement between the King's Grace and his cousin, My Lord Earl of Warwick. I cannot stress that point too strongly."

She moved her feet uncomfortably. He was standing close, staring intently into her eyes, impressing the urgency of his need for her co-operation.

"I will do my best, father."

He gave a little sigh of satisfaction then moved hastily to stare down from the window as the noise of arrivals sounded from the courtyard below, jingle of harness, calls of grooms and the frenzied barking of hounds.

"It seems My Lord is arrived. Don't come to the window. Stay out of sight until I send Alice to you."

He left her and she heard him calling urgently to her nurse as he descended the stairs.

Elinor was strangely perplexed. Her father was plainly ill-at-ease. Why? It was so unlike him. Though a simple knight he was no stranger to noble company. His lord, John Neville of Montecute, thought well of him and he frequently took his place at My Lord's table even on the occasion when the marquess had entertained His Grace, King Edward.

She controlled a sudden urge to dash to the window in direct disobedience to her father's instructions, yet she must not be seen gawping like a serving wench to view her betrothed.

She had questioned her father, though shyly, on the subject. Was My Lord tall, thick-set, bearded, dark or fair? Was he gentle mannered? Sir Thomas had been merely irritated.

"Daughter, I have told you, young Cranley is well featured enough. You are fortunate." He'd given a short bark of laughter. "The ladies of the Court think him handsome, judging by their behaviour in his presence. The man is no fool, either. He is nobly born, wealthy, what more could a girl ask?"

All this she knew already, but what did any of it mean to her, Elinor Beckwith, who was soon to become his bride and lie by his side? Hot blood flooded her face at the thought of their public bedding.

Were his person and clothing kept cleanly? Elinor knew only too well that however nobly bred, not all of her father's companions cared strongly enough over such matters for her liking. Would he treat her considerately or beat her if she displeased him? She gave an involuntary shiver of foreboding as Alice hastened into the room to draw her charge to the best light and satisfy herself that Elinor was truly presentable.

"Eh, my pet you are a beauty. Your

father is pleased. I read it in his eyes."

"Alice, did you see him, Lord Cranley? Is he well formed, manly — "

"Now, now, pet, I couldn't tell. There are several gentlemen. Your father wouldn't allow me to linger on the stair. He ordered me to keep you close till you are summoned to the hall. They all say — "

"I know well enough what they all say," Elinor cut in impatiently. "I know all about My Lord's skill with the lance and of his high standing at Court. I must *see* him, Alice, before I greet him before our guests, catch just one glimpse of him from the gallery above the hall."

"It would not be seemly. Your father would be furious — "

"Please, Alice," she pleaded, "I must prepare myself, in case — in case — Please."

Alice capitulated. "Oh, very well. Watch your gown and step carefully and quietly. Pray we are not sent for while we are both from this room."

She stepped cautiously out onto the spiral stair, listening to the noise and

24

talk from below as Sir Thomas's guests passed from the courtyard up the lower steps into the hall. She gestured hurriedly to Elinor that the coast was clear and stood back as her charge preceded her up the next flight, then she followed and the two crept softly along the length of the short minstrels' gallery which ran above the width of the hall facing the high table. The boards creaked beneath them and were dusty, since the place was seldom used.

Two years before, when but newly wed to Lady Isabel, Sir Thomas had summoned musicians to entertain at the Christmas feasting, Elinor remembered. She carefully avoided contact with the cobweb-festooned panels lest the pristine whiteness of her velvet gown be marked when she descended later to the hall.

The high table was set with a fair white cloth for the feasting after the ceremony. Serving wenches were still at work at the table's foot, placing the boards over trestles. Elinor peered over the gallery rail, keeping as far back in the shadows as possible, while affording herself a view of the men gathered below.

A knot of gentlemen was grouped in the oriel window. Her father's elaborate gold chain over his grey velvet doublet caught the light from one of the leaded panes. Besides him, Reginald's bright doublet made a garish splash of vivid scarlet. Impatiently Elinor looked for the guest of honour.

Sir Thomas was in talk with a slight young man whose back was turned to the gallery. He had removed his velvet chaperon and Elinor saw that his fair hair was curled effeminately onto the collar of his brocaded pink and grey doublet. He held his wine cup delicately and moved aside with some grace, as a servant came to refill his cup. Elinor noted the slender elegance of his legs, clad in fine pink hose.

This then was Lord Cranley, this youthful fop? Certainly he was the right age, as near as she could tell, some twenty summers, and more elegantly and expensively clad than any other man in the hall.

Elinor let out a little breath of relief. This man was courtly mannered and though she could not see his features clearly she was sure he would not prove unhandsome. Surely he would treat his promised bride with gentleness and courtesy?

She was about to withdraw and return hurriedly to her chamber, when a movement below caused her to freeze where she stood, one hand tight gripping the gallery rail.

Another guest had turned from the group and looked upwards, alerted, perhaps, by her sudden movement.

Startlingly blue eyes under level dark brows pierced through to her very soul so that she gasped under his scrutiny. He was tall, broadshouldered, older than Lord Cranley, perhaps twenty five or seven years, clad in an overdoublet of blue velvet with a high, stiffened collar, which appeared to accentuate that proud, arrogant stance. The features were fine drawn, dominated by a beak of a nose under which the long lipped mouth curled somewhat contemptuously as he noted Elinor's obvious distress at being seen spying on the company. Slowly he inclined his dark head in an amused courtly bow, then turned abruptly back to the group where he was immediately engaged in talk.

Elinor's heart raced in her breast. Who was he, the imperious stranger, less ostentatiously dressed than the viscount, yet obviously used to instant obedience? Could such a man wait attendance upon the foppishly clad youth without resentment? Elinor doubted it.

She released her tight grip upon the rail and turned back into the shadows where Alice tut-tutted her concern over the impropriety of their behaviour. She had satisfied herself that her betrothed's appearance was not in the least repulsive, though a faint feeling of disappointment remained with her as she regained the shelter of her chamber. He looked so very young, though charming and courtly. A skilled fighter, her father had said. She thought, doubtfully, that his prowess in the tournament lists had been somewhat exaggerated.

She blushed hotly as she recalled the insolent stare of the attendant gentleman. If he were to remain in her husband's household, she would find their future encounters somewhat unnerving, if not alarming. She comforted herself with the thought that her superior position as chatelaine of Cranley would render her distinct advantages in any clashes of will which might occur between them.

2

PAINFULLY aware that all eyes were upon her, Elinor entered the hall, Alice in attendance. Her father immediately came over to lead her forward and she advanced, head lowered, until they reached the great window.

"My Lord, may I present my daughter, Elinor, your betrothed." Her father's voice, but tinged with a very real respect, though more lightly he added, "you will find her vastly changed since the last time you laid eyes upon her."

"'Tis to be expected, Sir Thomas, since, I believe, I was then but eleven years old and Mistress Elinor just six. The wonder of it is that she has changed so gloriously. Allow me, Mistress."

Elinor found herself seized masterfully by the shoulders and a smacking kiss bestowed upon her already crimsoning cheek. Bemused, she found herself released and stumbled awkwardly backwards over the unfamiliar train of her gown. Instantly her future husband caught at her wrist and steadied her. For the second time in less than an hour she was looking into a pair of mocking blue eyes, while one dark, mobile eyebrow swept up in a silent question.

"I trust, Mistress Elinor, you are not too horrified by the changes you find in me."

His voice was deep, a trifle husky. She stared from him to the younger man by his side, resplendent in grey and pink. As if he read her bewilderment in her quick swallow of panic, Lord Cranley said, smiling, "My esquire, Simon Radbourne, who has prepared his wardrobe, even within the limited space of tent equipment, more fittingly than I for today's ceremony. Forgive me, Mistress Elinor, that I appear before you in such simple attire. When times are more settled you will find me as vain a peacock as Simon here."

Elinor was conscious that her father was frowning at her warningly. As yet she had not managed one word in greeting. Lord Cranley must think her lacking in wits. She dropped him a low curtsey.

"My Lord you are very welcome to Beckwith. We are honoured that you can be spared from the King's side." Her fingers trembled convulsively within his hold. She was embarrassingly aware that he knew she had mistaken his squire for himself, for his blue eyes danced mischievously as he drew her closer to the window.

The bantering talk died for moments as Lord Cranley deliberately viewed his future bride in the mellow autumn sunlight which pierced the lozenged panes.

"I am still not answered, Mistress," he reminded her gently.

A pulse beat in Elinor's throat. Was she a heifer to be displayed at market? She saw his bold eyes rake over her face and throat, take in the rapid rise and fall of her chest and pass on to the enveloping folds of the swansdownedged skirts which hid the thrust of her young limbs from him. Was it merely her imagination that she believed those eyes capable of piercing through the heavy velvet pile and delicate cambric of her shift, to see her unclothed before him as she had stepped from her wooden tub only an hour ago?

She matched him stare for stare until his lips parted in slow amusement and he threw back his head and laughed.

"Well, Mistress?"

"I have no complaints, My Lord," she replied stiffly.

"God's Mercy, that relieves my mind. Your daughter has spirit, Sir Thomas, which pleases me."

"My daughter has been gently reared, My Lord, despite the lack of a mother to guide her. Isabel, my late wife, took the matter in hand though briefly. Elinor sews exquisitely, is knowledgeable in kitchen, brew-house and buttery, and has some skill in compounding herbal brews and salves. I believe she will fulfil her role at Cranley efficiently. You'll not find her wanting."

"A treasure indeed." Lord Cranley's strong brown fingers caressed her palm. "Yet we shall not expect too much of you at first, Mistress. My steward's wife is trustworthy and kindly. She will welcome you in all humility to Cranley and I hope you will rely on her for guidance during the early days you rule my household there."

"Certainly, My Lord," she said quietly, "there is much I will need to learn. Our life here is busy but simple. We entertain rarely. My serving maids are all known to me since childhood. I shall find ordering strangers somewhat unnerving."

He had purposely drawn her a little apart so that his next words were soft but meaningful. "And I trust you will learn other, more necessary lessons, Mistress, those I shall delight to teach you personally."

Her golden eyes flashed in anger at his baiting. She was not to be so easily intimidated.

"In those lessons, too, I hope I shall know my duty as your obedient wife, My Lord."

His grip on her wrist tightened, though not painfully so.

"Well said, Mistress Elinor. I believe we shall deal very well together. Now, Sir Thomas, can we proceed to church? I am impatient to have this contract duly sealed."

She walked at his side, outwardly calm,

while her thoughts raced wildly.

How could she have been so foolish? Was it not evident from his very manner that he was the nobleman within this company? It would have been apparent to the merest simpleton had he arrived in worn leathern jack and a footsoldier's metal salet.

The presence of the others faded into the background throughout the brief ceremony in the church while she knelt by his side as Father John gabbled his Latin. The altar candles flickered and appeared to advance and recede before her eyes. The damp chill of the ancient Caen stone pierced through to her flesh and she shivered, colouring as Lord Cranley detected the involuntary movement and glanced at her sharply. The huge uncut ruby felt heavy upon her betrothal finger as she rose and went with him, hand in hand, out into the sunlight.

Back in the hall she sat on her betrothed's right at the head of the table, her father on his left. She ate little, though both Lord Cranley and her cousin, Reginald, who sat on her other side, assiduously plied her with choicest morsels. There had been little time to summon musicians to entertain, yet no expense had been spared at table to honour their noble guest.

Courses followed courses, pottage and broths, fish dishes cooked in rich sauces, eels, pastries, capons, barons of beef, mutton made succulent and savoury with rosemary and other herbs, then the trifles and jellies, candied fruits and cheeses. Elinor smiled politely as her servants and Bobkin, their cook, were roundly praised. She drank sparingly and was glad her betrothed did likewise.

While he was engaged in talk with her father she stole further glances at that dominating face with the jutting chin made even more determined in expression by the deep cleft. Was he truly just twenty? He appeared older. Muscles rippling beneath those velvet-clad sleeves had been made strong at the quintain when he had learned his skills with the heavy broadsword and battle axe. She could not assess even to herself the feelings he aroused in her. Excitement, certainly, tinged with a resentment at his deliberate baiting of her and downright insolent examination of her charms. Beyond him, she noted the younger man, Simon Radbourne, delicately nibbling a damson tartlet. She had prepared herself to wed him. Now she saw him clearly she realized her first assumption had been right. He was indeed weakly handsome and courtly mannered, yet that first disappointment had been acute. He could never have stirred her as Gerard, Lord Cranley, could do.

He turned abruptly towards her and her fingers jerked on the rim of her wine cup, spilling a scarlet trail on the spotless napery. He leaned forward, capturing the hand with which she was endeavouring to right the cup.

"Allow me, Mistress." His strong, brown fingers righted and moved the offending vessel and he signalled to a servant to mop up the spilled wine.

She was trembling with mortification at her own stupidity. The man had only to glance in her direction and it set her behaving like an awkward child. Her eyes sought her father and he gave a slight imperative nod of his chin. He had bid her talk with her betrothed, entertain him, catch his attention. How? She was not practised in the art of exchanging witty, clever remarks. The man flustered and alarmed her. She felt like a trapped bird fluttering in helpless panic as a cat approached its cage. She was close to tears. She had made such a poor showing. What could he be thinking of her?

"Do not concern yourself about the wine, Mistress," he said, his voice become amazingly gentle. "As long as your beautiful gown is unspoilt. It is easy enough to appear clumsy by one unwary movement. I know, only too well. I was once foolish enough to drop a bowl of rosewater near the Queen's jewelled slippers as I was serving His Grace at meat."

"You did that, truly?" Her eyes sparkled with ridiculous tears of relief, she was so grateful for his desire to set her at ease.

His long lips twitched. "The Queen's Grace was gravely displeased, despite the fact that the King laughed, or perhaps because of it."

"I am told she is exceedingly beautiful."

"Very lovely indeed, though languorous and haughty. I have known her keep her own mother upon her knees before her for the space of an hour."

"I think I should never be at my ease at Court," she said falteringly.

"Indeed, I hope you will, Mistress Elinor, since it will be my pleasure and pride to present you at Westminster Palace when this affair between the King and My Lord of Warwick is concluded."

"There will be bloodshed?" She silently cursed her foolish tongue the moment the words were uttered. Had not her father explicitly ordered her to keep silent on this matter?

"Certainly." He appeared not in the least disconcerted by her question. "My Lord Earl has offered his allegiance to Queen Margaret, married his daughter Anne to Edward, the Lancastrian heir. Warwick 'makes' Kings. If they no longer please him he will seek to make others. It's rumoured in Doncaster that the earl has already landed in the West Country."

Elinor imagined Lord Gerard armoured

upon the field of battle. Would he survive to make her his bride by Christmas?

It seemed that he had an uncanny knack of reading her thoughts for he said, "I have already seen service on the Scottish Border and taken part in several skirmishes."

She said nervously, "The King's own brother is arrayed with Warwick against him. How can the King and His Grace of Gloucester face the thought of shedding their brother's blood?"

Lord Gerard shrugged. "George of Clarence is a sapling swayed by any breeze. It's my belief he'll desert Warwick at the first sign of trouble. He can no longer dream of being made King by Warwick. He'll not be fool enough to range himself against Edward of England."

His blue eyes blazed with the enthusiasm of his cause then softened as suddenly. "Forgive me, Mistress Elinor, you fear for your father, naturally."

"For all of you, sir. My grandfather and your father were killed at Wakefield. Is it so cowardly of me to pray that no more English blood be spilled in these wars?"

"No, Mistress Elinor, though I confess to an unholy eagerness to put my own courage to the ultimate test." He smiled. "Will you trust yourself to sit apart with me within the window bay? There will be no impropriety, since we will be in full view of your nurse and your father. There is much I would know about my future bride."

She nodded, her cheeks flushing red, and he rose and offered her his arm to lead her to the padded window seat, after receiving permission from her father. She spread the velvet skirts deliberately, her eyes lowered, still unwilling to meet those piercing blue ones.

"Do you read, Mistress Elinor?"

She was surprised by the question put so abruptly.

"Yes, My Lord. Our parish priest, Father John, taught me my letters."

"Excellent. Wait one moment." He rose and sauntered to his squire's side. Elinor saw the younger man rise and fiddle with the catch on the gilded leather pouch which he wore suspended from his ornamental belt. A silk-wrapped package changed hands and Lord Gerard returned to her side.

"I had little warning of this meeting. The betrothal ring I carried upon my person. But what truly personal gift could I make my betrothed? This troubled me, now I am relieved as I think this will be acceptable to you."

Curiously she took the silk-wrapped gift from his hand, her fingers struggling clumsily with the ribboned knots which secured it. Her gasp of delight was his answer. She withdrew a Book of Hours, bound in tooled leather, each vellumed page revealing a glory of illuminated characters. She stared down at the magnificent gift touching, wonderingly, the bright blues, scarlets and gold of the pictures.

"It is truly beautiful. I shall treasure it always."

"It was my mother's. I hoped you would share my love of reading. I have many more books at Cranley. I am glad my simple gift pleases you. There will be far more splendid ones later, jewels and silks for you, Mistress."

His eyes went to the simple gold and enamelled necklace containing a true relic of the Cross which she had chosen to wear for the ceremony. She possessed few jewels and her betrothal ring made all her other trinkets seem paltry. She flushed and her hand stole to the beloved relic and stroked it gently for comfort.

"My mother's gift on my tenth birthday," she explained. "She died of a fever scarcely more than a month later."

He nodded understandingly. "My mother died when I was sixteen, before she had the joy of seeing me knighted."

"You have known grief and loneliness."

"I have a brother, John, three years my junior. We are close. My sister is a Carmelite in the nunnery at York."

She needed to know far more about him. So there would be no woman to challenge her will at Cranley, though it would soon be necessary perhaps for her to learn to live in amity with any future bride John Cranley chose to bring to the castle.

Lord Gerard looked along the length of the hall, hot and fetid with the stinks of stale food, sweat and smoke from the large hearth which her father had recently had built to replace the old open hearth he himself had inherited from his own sire. The company had drunk well and were replete from the many rich dishes offered. They were becoming openly boisterous and bawdy. Lord Gerard stood up and held out his hand to her.

"It's overheated here. Can we walk in the courtyard or garden? Your maid can bring you a cloak. You'll feel chilled after the warmth in here."

"We have a small pleasure garden near the herb plot," she told him shyly. "It will be cool and flower-scented at this hour of the afternoon."

She signalled to Alice and explained her wish to accompany Lord Gerard out of the hall. Her nurse hastened to Sir Thomas, bent and whispered in his ear. Again Elinor's father's eyes met hers meaningfully over her nurse's bent head. It seemed he was insistent that she continue to do her utmost to impress her betrothed.

Elinor moved with Lord Gerard to the

hall door, her fur-trimmed skirts brushing the fouled rushes near the tables where the dogs fought savagely over the mess of spilt food and bones tossed carelessly to them by the serving men and wenches. Alice hurried up with Elinor's hooded cloak and slipped it round her shoulders, clucking her concern about the chill autumn evenings.

They walked slowly to the gate which led from the muck-strewn courtyard to the yew-hedged quiet of the flower garden which ran from the manor's east wing to the moat. Alice hovered some paces behind them. The air was like wine after the fetid heat of the castle and it was blessedly cool, the scent of honeysuckle and late flowers teasing Elinor's nostrils. Few roses were still blooming but Gerard stopped and broke off one perfect white bud which he presented to her, bowing gallantly. A bright bead of blood sprang upon her finger, despite his care to first remove the thorns from the stem.

"The white flower of York. You embody it for me, my lovely Yorkshire rose in your white betrothal gown. I shall carry this image of you in my heart." He stopped as she sucked at her wounded finger, captured her hand and lifted it to his lips.

"I have hurt you. Forgive me."

"It is nothing, My Lord, just a prick. The bloom is so perfect one forgets about the thorns."

He frowned. "I wish there *were* no lurking fears to threaten our peace. I am so well pleased with my gentle bride that I could wish it unnecessary to ride so soon for Doncaster, and I wish My Lord Warwick in deepest hell that his treachery must take me so quickly from your side."

"I shall pray for your safety," she said shakily. He had drawn so close that she was conscious of the male scent of his skin, fresh from his bath, his breath softly wine-fumed, his garments fragrant, the clean tang of leather over-lading all else. She struggled to withdraw her hand from his grasp, looking anxiously for the reassuring presence of Alice, now hidden from her by a wall of thick yew. He laughed softly and released her fingers, only to cup her chin between strong brown hands.

"Are you afraid of me, Elinor?"

"No, My Lord," then, "yes, a little."

"What had they told you of me that you were so determined to view me for yourself before committing yourself to me for ever?"

"Only that you were brave and courtly mannered, young and — "

"Wealthy," he finished, a trifle drily. "They harp on that too much, it seems. I knew nothing more about you, simply that you were young, chaste — and will bring me a fine dowry. I find I am well pleased with the bargain. What of your feelings now, Mistress Elinor?"

"I am . . . " She hesitated, knowing the hot colour was dyeing her cheeks, betraying her embarrassment, "I am — not displeased, My Lord."

"Not unduly disappointed that your bridegroom is not to be my elegant young squire?"

"Not — in the least disappointed." So he had indeed guessed at her thoughts.

He laughed joyously. "Then, come kiss me, Mistress. Don't be afraid. We are duly bound to each other, the knot so strong that I wait impatiently now for the priest to bless our marriage bed."

His lips captured hers, moving gently at first, then more demandingly, so that her own opened beneath his with a sob of pure panic. He curbed his desire so as not to further alarm her but, already, she had felt he had taken possession of her very breath and with it her soul. Warmth flooded through her and a delight never before experienced. He withdrew, smiling gravely down at her, then drew her close once more, gently this time, pressing his lips to each eyelid.

"Hold the thoughts of me strongly, as I shall mine of you, until we meet again. Pray that I shall be free to claim you by the Holy Season of Christmas."

"I will do, My Lord," she breathed softly.

"We must return to the hall, although I would rather keep you to myself now I know the full splendour of my prize."

Her heart was full to bursting. She had dreaded and feared this day and her first sight of him had filled her with a mixture of excitement and foreboding, yet he had treated her so courteously that she could not doubt his delight in her.

She had steeled herself to go dutifully to the marriage bed. Now the world had become dazzlingly bright with the glory of her response to him. He was everything of which she had dreamed; strong, well-favoured, gallant and loving.

Alice fell into step behind them as they approached the entrance steps to the house. Her father met them at the door and she was relieved to see by his expression that Sir Thomas was in a rare good humour.

"I see you have taken full opportunity to become better acquainted with my daughter, My Lord," he greeted them jovially.

"My pleasure in my future bride grows with each moment I spend in her company, Sir Thomas."

"It is to be hoped, then, the marriage need not be too long delayed."

"That is my most fervent wish, sir."

Elinor stood hesitantly, waiting for her father's instructions. She rarely ate in company and when she had done so under the care of Lady Isabel, she had been dismissed before the behaviour of Sir Thomas's guests had become too unseemly, due to their over-indulgence in wine.

Her father's gaze met hers benignly. "I think it is time you retired to your chamber, Elinor. My Lord, will you honour us with your presence, tonight? A chamber can soon be placed at your disposal and I assure you that your attendants will be comfortably accommodated."

"Thank you, Sir Thomas, but I have been summoned to attend My Lord of Gloucester before he retires and must set out soon for Doncaster."

"Then I'll not detain you. Will you pledge my daughter's happiness in the loving cup before she leaves us?"

Lord Gerard's blue eyes fairly danced as he bowed to Elinor. "Most willingly."

The ornate wooden drinking mazer with the silver rim was brought by Sir Thomas's steward. Nervously, Elinor raised it to her lips and drank sparingly, cautious not to spill the wine in her confusion. Shyly she offered the bowl to her betrothed as the assembled guests cheered and hammered their own drinking cups upon the table to applaud the symbolic gesture. Smiling, Lord Gerard lifted the bowl high in salute and was about to set his own lips on the very spot hers had touched when there was a loud commotion upon the stair, the sound of iron on stone, wild barking of dogs and voices raised in furious argument. The door was unceremoniously thrust open as at first two, then more men-at-arms burst into the hall. The leader halted, his back to the door, his drawn sword in his hand. He was dishevelled and mired to the knees, and panting for breath, as were his men who formed a solid armed half circle, silently menacing the company.

There was a brief, horrified silence while the guests stared in amazement, then the scrape of stools and benches as men sprang angrily to their feet, demanding explanations from the intruders.

Bewildered and frightened, Elinor recognized the Cranley badge of livery on each man's leather jacket. She knew it well, having already discussed with Alice the possibility of embroidering the device upon a silk banner for her husband's use, and later, when leisure allowed, hangings for her future bed-chamber. The golden gryphon with its spread wings seemed to her alarmed gaze to be threatening the company.

Sir Thomas addressed himself haughtily to his guest of honour.

"Perhaps, My Lord, you could explain the meaning of your men's unmannerly and threatening behaviour." His imperious tone silenced the others and they turned their attention from the Cranley men to their lord. It had become obvious to all of them that their escape from the hall was barred and they moved restlessly, murmuring amongst themselves, their eyes wary and narrowed. From outside more clamour and creak of harness told those within the hall that yet other Cranley men had taken possession of the courtyard and stairs. The Beckwith guests were virtual prisoners.

But why? Elinor found the question pounding against her brain. Why should Cranley men invade their hall? It was inconceivable. Her betrothed had sealed a pledge of friendship between her father and himself, yet his sergeant-at-arms had deliberately led an attack on the manor.

Lord Cranley was clearly as bewildered as she, for his brows were drawn together in a frown of fury.

"I'm waiting, Will, for an answer to Sir Thomas's question." He flung the words at his sergeant.

Elinor could see a small tic working on his left temple. He was holding anger in check with deliberate effort.

"My Lord, the Marquess of Montecute has attacked the King's camp at Doncaster. Ranged with his rebel brother, Neville of Warwick, he tried to take the King prisoner. A squire in His Grace of Gloucester's household overheard Neville retainers in the town square raising the rabble against the King's men. He raced back to his master's lodging and warned him. Loyal men held the doors until the King, his brother, Richard of Gloucester, and others of the household rode free from the town. There has been a bloodbath in Doncaster, My Lord and . . . " the man hesitated, passing his tongue nervously over dry lips, "Master John was taken and held by the marquess within the cellars of the King's lodging."

The muttering rose again then subsided as Lord Cranley said quietly, "Was my brother harmed?"

"Not grievously, My Lord, but wounded. We saw him dragged from the stair which he was helping to guard against the King's enemies." The man breathed deeply then his eyes moved warily to Sir Thomas, standing stiffly at Lord Cranley's side. "Our force could do little in Doncaster. The King needed to make for the coast and I rode here to warn you."

"Warn me?" Lord Gerard's chin jerked angrily and again the sergeant's eyes flickered with alarm.

"I've reason to believe you were invited here today deliberately, My Lord. Sir Thomas Beckwith is known to be Lord Montecute's man."

Elinor gave a choked cry. She stumbled and would have fallen had not Alice caught her and stood awkwardly patting her shoulder.

Everything was suddenly made clear to Elinor. Two of Lord Montecute's men had ridden into the courtyard the day before. They had then been closeted for some time with her father. Lord Cranley was known to be expected and he so loyal to the King that he would fight to the death to protect his sovereign! Her father had taken such pains to make his guest welcome and he had impressed on Elinor the need to delay him in talk. She had cold bloodedly been made beautiful for her betrothed's eyes, used to attract and hold Lord Gerard by her side. She straightened, strong white teeth gripping her lower lip to prevent it from trembling. She was disgusted by her father's duplicity. Firmly she put aside Alice's arm.

Her father had not moved throughout the sergeant's accusation, smiling, outwardly calm, making no attempt to refute this slur upon his honour.

Elinor made to speak then choked back the words and turned to her betrothed.

He too was standing perfectly still, blue eyes narrowed and glittering strangely. The long-lipped mouth had become suddenly hard. He looked deliberately from Sir Thomas to Elinor then, abruptly, he reached out and seized her by the wrist in so cruel a grip that she could not stifle a harsh cry of pain.

"Bitch," he said quietly, his gaze travelling from her elaborate, veiled head-dress down the length of her youthful, slender form to her soft leather shoes. "You gilded the flower well, it seems, Sir Thomas. I believed in this maid's innocence. What an arrant fool you must think me, Mistress."

"No," she whispered, "you do not understand."

"*What* don't I understand, that you and your father conspired to keep me here, enamoured, well away from my liege lord's side while treachery had its way? What had you planned for me when the King had duly fallen into the trap? Imprisonment with my brother John, a hasty trial before My Lord Marquess of Montecute, summary execution?"

"Of course not." Sir Thomas's voice had not lost its cool firmness. "You mistake this business, My Lord. Why should you accuse us of gross deception? This betrothal ceremony was planned days ago."

"And Montecute knew that, planned

his attack while my attention was diverted. Perhaps it was hoped that my brother and others of my household would attend me here. My Lord of Gloucester might indeed have so honoured me by his presence, but that His Grace the King had need of him earlier today. Was he, too, destined to fall into this honeyed cage, all unsuspecting? Unfortunate for John that he was prevented from attending the ceremony by his duties." He kept his iron grip on Elinor's wrist and she forced back pain-filled tears. After that first shocked cry she was determined she would not give way to such weakness, he would merely believe that another attempt to trick him, a woman's ruse. "Well now," he continued pleasantly, though those blue eyes of his were blazing with unholy fire, "what are we to do to extricate ourselves from this situation? If I remain here I shall certainly find myself a prisoner before morning."

In answer to Gerard's nodded signal, his sergeant gestured to the men behind him, one gauntleted arm upraised. Four archers instantly ranged themselves to guard the door, two each side. There was a shuffling of feet among the fouled rushes as the guests watched apprehensively those men directly behind the sergeant take their positions on either side of the hall.

Lord Gerard considered, taking his time. Elinor could not contain a gasp of pain as her wrist was twisted sharply.

"My men can ensure my escape but for how long? At the moment we have the advantage of surprise but My Lord Montecute's force will soon be arriving and the countryside hereabouts well searched. You know your own lands too well, Sir Thomas. I would never reach the coast. How can I then prevent immediate pursuit?" His mouth relaxed in a sneer. "By using this lovely pawn as she was used against me. We will ride together, Sir Thomas, you, my betrothed, and four of my men."

"To subject my daughter to such hazards would be unknightly, My Lord," Sir Thomas barked. "My daughter is innocent of any deception. She merely obeyed my orders."

"And *your* conduct towards me? Lord

Montecute's treachery against his liege lord?"

"Lord Montecute has suffered grievous insults at the King's hand. His loyalty is and should be towards his brother, the Earl of Warwick."

"The question of that misplaced loyalty will doubtless lose him his head," Lord Cranley snapped, "and you, yours, Sir Thomas."

Elinor made a moan of protest. He ignored it and, tightening his grip, urged her before him towards the door.

"We lose time in pointless argument. We will go now, Sir Thomas, please step before us down the stair."

Sir Thomas moved forward to directly confront Lord Gerard.

"I am ready to accompany you as hostage. With me in your hands my men will not move against you until the manor is taken by Lord Montecute's force. You will have a head start. To take Elinor would simply delay us. Without the girl to slow us down we can ride hard and fast. When you are clear of this neighbourhood, you can treat me as you wish, release me, or . . . " He shrugged.

"Mistress Elinor will not delay us. I'll see to that." Lord Gerard's tone was ice-cold like his eyes, which had again hardened to chips of sapphire.

For the first time since the untimely interruption to the feast by Lord Gerard's men, Elinor found her voice though a hard lump had formed in her throat.

"Father, I'm not afraid. I'm fully prepared to do as Lord Gerard commands, nor will I fail to keep the pace if — if that will ensure your — safety."

"It might," Lord Gerard snapped, "for the present, at least."

"Then let one of the women come with us, not the nurse, she is too old, but some other wench."

"No woman. That *would* delay us."

"My daughter is not to be taken as if she is some doxy . . . "

"Is she not my betrothed?" Lord Gerard uttered a sharp bitter laugh. "What impropriety can there be in a wife accompanying her husband? By today's ceremony Mistress Elinor became my wife. It wants only the final blessing and the bedding of the bride to complete the contract."

Lord Gerard's sergeant had drawn closer to Sir Thomas, his sword point pressed against his prisoner's back. "Do I ride with you, My Lord?"

"Aye, with Simon and Ralf Brent. A larger company will attract undue notice and make the possibility of capture more likely. Dick Taylor is in command below?"

"Yes, My Lord. There are twelve of us, ten left to guard your retreat."

"Good, then we'll leave. Shout for horses to be made ready."

"Already arranged, My Lord, though no orders were given concerning Mistress Elinor's palfrey. I had not expected . . ."

Again Lord Gerard uttered that chilling, mirthless laugh. "No palfrey. Mistress Elinor rides with me."

Alice, who had kept a shocked silence until the moment of departure, launched herself forward and pulled at Lord Cranley's sleeve.

"The countryside is swarming with armed men. She'll be taken, molested . . ."

"True, old woman," he snarled. "If I'm taken, Mistress Elinor falls victim to that very same company of soldiery, so pray that I remain at liberty. That should keep you well occupied."

"Let me go with you, I beg you, My Lord, please. She needs me. I — "

"She will have the protection of her future husband. That must suffice."

Elinor's heart was thudding wildly and she feared that her legs would refuse to obey her as he urged her nearer the door and the stairs. She saw her father's sudden start of fury at Lord Gerard's harsh jibe to Alice and she feared he would move to attack her captor. A gesture which would surely doom him. An arrow from the bow of any one of the Cranley archers would drop him in his tracks before he could cover the short space between him and Lord Gerard.

"Father," she said quietly, "we must obey. The sooner the viscount is free of the manor, the sooner he will release us. We can only be an encumbrance to him on his journey."

She had realized that her cousin, Reginald, was not present in the hall. Had he already made his escape and ridden towards Doncaster? His arrival at the manor had been unexpected. Had he been dispatched as Lord Montecute's messenger to observe that everything went as planned? Her reasoning told her that was very likely. So reinforcements must be close at hand. Montecute retainers would be even now moving in, confident of taking Lord Cranley, as they had his brother.

The thought was by no means reassuring. The man who held her so brutally would not submit tamely. There would be hard fighting and her father could lose his life, Lord Gerard, his, also. She swallowed hard.

Scarcely an hour ago he had held her close, kissed her passionately, sworn to claim her by Christmas. She had been moved to respond. Now, in the space of moments, everything had changed. The stranger she had come to admire and honour had become an enemy and one to be feared. She tried to check the trembling of her limbs, praying silently that no harm would come to any of them. In her hearts of hearts, she wanted Lord Gerard to reach the coast, make good his escape.

He was urging her forward, his hard

grip on her wrist was agonizing.

"We will follow your father, now, Mistress Elinor, slowly, surely. You will not stop in your walk to the stairs down them or through the courtyard, nor will you stumble. If I suspect the slightest act of treachery from you now or at any time in the future, I shall see to it that Sir Thomas pays with his life. Do you understand me?"

She inclined her head stiffly.

"Simon, close in behind. Will," this to his sergeant, "fall in behind Sir Thomas."

The elegant young squire had dropped his foppishness of manner. He had drawn his jewelled dagger which Elinor did not doubt could kill as surely as any of the more serviceable looking blades within the leather belts of the retainers. His youthful features had become as hard and determined as his master's, as he drew in close, to guard their rear.

Elinor forced her leaden limbs to move. Despite Lord Gerard's grim warning, she stumbled awkwardly over the fur-trimmed train of her betrothal gown, as her captor began her progress with an ungentle push.

64

"Steady, watch yourself," he grated, as she recovered and pressed on. The journey down the spiral stair to the courtyard appeared to be nightmarishly slow and she drew a hard breath as the evening air smote her face suddenly when they drew clear of the house.

Horses were already saddled and drawn to the mounting blocks. Lord Gerard nodded to his sergeant to walk ahead of him with his prisoner, Sir Thomas.

Elinor thought, somewhat incongruously at such a time, that her father's finery would be ruined during such a ride. As for her own — she forced back an hysterical laugh. The mental picture of herself a prisoner, mounted before Lord Gerard in her magnificent velvet gown and cap, appeared ridiculous and humorous. She knew the thought was prompted by sheer panic. At such times of tension one was moved to laugh, to try to keep one's sanity. Now she did not dare. Her eyes roved the courtyard warily. Were all their own men prisoners, wounded, some possibly killed? Even now might not a desperate attempt be made to rescue herself and her father and capture Lord Gerard?

As if to confirm her pricking sense of unease, a snarling, scarlet-clad form abruptly launched itself forward at the split second when Lord Gerard was thrusting her towards his waiting hack. Her cousin had hurtled from his bolthole within the shadows of the smithy. Elinor screamed as Lord Gerard shoved her brutally aside and closed with his assailant. She struggled, sobbing aloud in Simon Radbourne's grasp, as he pulled her hurriedly away from the contest.

Horses neighed wildly and reared. Someone cursed. Elinor was not sure if it was her father or the sergeant-at-arms. The squire was stronger than she had supposed. Despite her frantic struggles to free herself, he held her in an iron grip.

Lord Cranley had uttered only one command before engaging his opponent. "Leave him to me."

Elinor's terrified gaze followed the panting, clawing, scuffling combatants. It seemed to her that each was in too close to use his weapon with good effect without being blooded by the other's. The clang of iron on iron thudded dully on her ears, then came a sudden animal cry of sheer agony.

She half fell against Simon Radbourne's damask doublet, sick and faint with horror, then her wrist was once more harshly seized in a grip she could not but now know, only too well.

"Come," Lord Gerard snapped, "hand her up to me, Simon, but first . . . " He tore her hennin free and hurled it across the muddied, bloodstained courtyard, after first ripping off the veil. "We'll ensure you ride securely and silently." Brutally he thrust her wrists tight behind her back, holding them in a fast lock as he bound them close together then, with the remainder of the silk gauze, he tied a long strip securely round her mouth, expertly gagging her.

She choked and retched as she was lifted and bundled up before him on his saddle bow like so much baggage. The velvet of her gown ripped and she felt her captor's fingers tying the strings of her cloak and pulling up the hood over the heavy masses of her loosened hair. The hood fell forward, impeding her view so that she could not see whether

Reginald still lived or if her father had been similarly bound.

In the few brief seconds as she was being mounted before Lord Gerard, she glimpsed Reginald's huddled form sprawled across the entrance to the smithy. Blood soaked into the mud and dung but the scarlet of her cousin's doublet made it impossible for her to tell where or how dangerously he had been wounded.

Lord Cranley set spurs to his mount and she heard muffled shouts as the iron-shod hoofs of their horses thudded across the wooden struts of the moat bridge.

3

ELINOR could not tell how many hours they had travelled. She only knew that her limbs ached, her buttocks were rubbed sore by the bone-jolting ride, and her misery was further increased by the gag which bit cruelly into her soft mouth and caused her an acute feeling of nausea. Lord Gerard had rendered her incapable of either fighting free or crying out for assistance. Her hood continued to flap unpleasantly about her face and it was almost impossible to know in which direction they were riding. During some part of the journey, she must have fallen into a semiconscious stupor but now she was frighteningly aware once more of her peril and her sufferings intensified.

It was very late for the night sky was star-sprinkled and it had become extremely cold. She shook her head frantically in an effort to free herself from the hood's folds. Despite the cold she felt she was suffocating. Her body was held hard against Lord Gerard's. He rode expertly, one arm, vice-like, around her, the other lightly guiding his horse. Of course he would have been trained to subdue and control his mount by the pressure of knees alone, so that, in the lists, he would have both hands free to handle shield and weapon. Should they be attacked, she was sure he would find little difficulty in controlling her, the horse, and his sword, and yet still be able to use his weapon to deadly effect. She had seen his sergeant hand him his sword belt and broadsword before he had crossed the courtyard, since the elaborate belt he had worn at the betrothal ceremony bore only a gilded dagger sheath. She shivered. With the sheathed bloodstained weapon at his side he had wounded, probably killed her cousin Reginald. She could feel the hardness of the leather sheath jolting against her body.

The men rode silently and in close formation. She was aware of the night sounds even above the jingle of harness and bit and the thudding of hoofs on the soft earth. Lord Gerard's pace slackened and she could now see they were picking their way more carefully through a stand of trees. Her efforts in loosening the hood succeeded and she flung it back and breathed in the sweet night air thankfully. Her hair, pulled painfully free of the confining cap when he had ruthlessly disposed of it earlier, fell softly forward, obscuring her vision.

Abruptly Lord Gerard checked his mount and called imperiously to the men behind him.

"We'll stop here, water the horses."

Elinor fell forward grotesquely like a sack of grain as his grip on her waist was released. She gave a sob of terror and humiliation. Strong arms reached up to grasp her and lift her down. She stumbled awkwardly against the squire, Simon Radbourne, and he guided her slowly and gently towards a log. She could see more clearly now. The party had drawn rein within a clearing. The sound of water trickling nearby told of the presence of a stream, giving the opportunity to rest and water their horses.

Her bound wrists hampered her, together

with the bruised and stiffened condition of her limbs and she floundered her way across the wet grass. In embarrassed silence, Simon Radbourne assisted her to sit and stood awkwardly, a little apart, still clearly on guard over her.

She peered about her. Her father was still mounted and, with a pang of pity, she saw his ankles had been bound beneath his horse's belly, and his wrists were also strapped together in front of him. The man-at-arms, Ralf Brent, was stooping to untie his leg thongs. He dismounted stiffly. He was not gagged and Elinor knew why Lord Gerard had trusted him to remain silent throughout the ride. To have drawn undue attention to the party would certainly have imperilled his daughter and Sir Thomas was aware of it.

Where were they now? Had they ridden well clear of Doncaster? Elinor guessed they had gone east to avoid the main highway. Lord Gerard would make for the coast, either by way of Whitby to the north or, more likely, by King's Lynn in the south-east. If the King had taken flight he must have received word that the men in the vicinity would favour Montecute and the Nevilles, and so at any time in this ride, they might encounter groups of mounted or foot-soldiers, who would challenge and, if dissatisfied about their identity, attack. Yet by now they must be clear of Beckwith Land. Surely, soon, she and her father would be set at liberty.

She glared up angrily as the soft sound of leather shoes on the soaked grass warned her of Lord Gerard's approach.

He dismissed his squire. "See to the horses."

The boy bowed and moved off. Lord Gerard stood regarding her sardonically.

"You look acutely uncomfortable, Mistress. I trust I can rely on you, for the present at any rate, not to scream. If you do so, it will endanger your father. You grasp my meaning plainly?"

She glared at him again over the restricting folds of the gag and then inclined her chin stiffly.

He moved behind her and she felt the touch of his ice-cold fingers as he struggled with the tightened knots on the silk. Oh, blessed relief, her mouth was free at last and she gasped as her taut facial muscles began to relax after the intolerable strain of the gag. For the moment she was too pained and shocked to reply.

He squatted on his heels beside her.

"Ralf and Will have been sent to survey the terrain. I regret we have no provisions, so you must go hungry tonight, Mistress, but it's hoped we'll find some barn or hut where we can at least get you under cover. Meanwhile," he grinned at her, "I've no doubt you will need to make yourself comfortable. Will you give me your word you'll not go beyond calling distance or must I act as both gaoler and tiring maid?"

His meaning was all too clear and her throat and cheeks crimsoned in shame.

"I will do as you demand, My Lord," she replied coldly. It was painful to speak, still. "You will not need to lay hands upon me."

"Good." He stooped and, drawing his dagger, cut free the gauze which tied her wrists. The released blood coursed through her veins and she could not hold back a sudden gasp of pain. "Can you stand? You will have stiffened. Allow me to help you."

She drew back from him angrily. "I can manage to stand and walk without your assistance, *My Lord*."

He bowed, standing back slightly. She rose to her feet and lurched dizzily. The treetops appeared to spin crazily round her. She bit her lip, stiffened her spine, and deliberately moved away from him.

She followed the sound of voices back to the clearing. Staring defiantly at Lord Gerard, she went over to her father. His hands were still bound but he was seated on a jutting outcrop of rock. Lord Gerard made no objection as she stooped to speak to his prisoner.

"You were not harmed in the fight in the courtyard?"

He shook his head tiredly. "And you, child? This exhausting ride . . . "

"I am well enough, father, tired and stiff, that is all. Reginald — " Her voice broke. "Do you think Lord Gerard — killed him?"

"I don't know." Sir Thomas gazed moodily ahead. "Cranley's men couldn't hold the manor for long against Montecute's army. If Reginald lives, he'll be well tended."

Elinor sank down beside him on the grass, ignoring the more comfortable log some yards away to which Simon Radbourne had conducted her earlier. Immediately the young squire came to her side. He offered her, shyly, a coarse woven horse blanket.

"Allow me to place this beneath you, Mistress. The wet will soak through your skirts else."

She rose and allowed him to help her. His grey eyes looked troubled and she understood he was concerned at his master's discourteous treatment of her, yet obedience was strong in him. He would not dare protest.

She waited until he had moved out of earshot.

"Can we hope for our freedom soon?" she questioned her father softly.

He gave a warning grunt as the sergeant-at-arms returned to the clearing and conferred with Lord Gerard. "It's hard to say. Montecute's men will be all round us. Some will have been already dispatched to pursue the King's party.

Cranley will not dare venture onto the main highways. The Cranley arms on his men's jackets will be spotted and reported immediately."

"Have you any idea where we are?"

"Moving south-east, I would guess."

"You think he intends holding us prisoner tonight?"

"Aye, he'll hold us until he's well clear of Yorkshire and safe in his own county of Lincolnshire."

"You believe then that he'll hole up at Cranley Castle?" Her tone was incredulous. Surely she and her father would not find themselves imprisoned in some grim dungeon while Neville men-at-arms besieged Lord Gerard's stronghold!

"I don't think so, though it's possible. He'll be more likely to try to join the King. If he remains in England, his loyalty could be held in doubt."

Elinor had not thought of that. Lord Gerard must indeed be furious, trapped, his honour impugned. She leaned her head tiredly against her father's side, her brain aching with conflicting thoughts.

Apart from the two Cranley men-at-arms they were all badly dressed and ill-equipped for travelling any distance. Neither her father nor Lord Gerard possessed so much as a cloak, jerkin or riding boots. Both were still clad in velvet doublets and fine hose. True, Lord Cranley was now armed with sword and dagger, but the party had not delayed to pack and carry supplies. Despite her utter exhaustion, she was already feeling the keen pangs of hunger. She had not eaten or drunk as well as the others had done at her betrothal feast.

Lord Gerard crossed to speak with them. He stood, regarding them steadily, his feet planted stolidly astride, his thumbs crooked in his sword belt.

"My men report finding a tumbledown hut about a mile and a half away. It's a poor place, more than likely some charcoal burner's hut long abandoned, however it will afford you some shelter from the night air, Mistress."

"I would rather camp in the open near my father," she returned coldly.

"No doubt, but I've no wish to see my betrothed take an inflammation of the lungs. It may well come on to rain later." His white teeth gleamed momentarily. "If you become sick it will delay us. I can't afford that."

She ignored his outstretched hand and climbed stiffly to her feet, pitying her father's clumsy struggles to do the same, hampered as he was by his bound wrists.

Lord Gerard took her by the arm, despite her effort to avoid him, and walked her to the waiting horses. He mounted and Simon Radbourne silently lifted her to his lord's saddle bow. This time she found it easier to endure the short ride, since her hands were now unbound and so she was able to steady herself. She was thankful that she was, at last, free of that sickening gag.

The hut proved to be a dilapidated hovel. Certainly, it had not been used for years. The clearing in which it stood was very small and already the encroaching bushes and shrubs were regaining the ground around it. Elinor was lifted down and she stood uncertainly until Lord Gerard gestured her towards the crazily hanging door.

"If you will please to enter, Mistress, we'll try to find you some dry bracken for a bed. Sir Thomas?" He bowed to his prisoner mockingly and her father led the way into the musty smelling interior.

It was very small. There was scarcely space for more than two or three men to lie comfortably and Elinor leaned wearily against the mud-daubed wall. She was desperately thirsty yet she was determined not to ask anything of Lord Gerard.

Ralf Brent stood guard near the doorway while Lord Gerard conferred with his squire and sergeant.

Sir Thomas slid awkwardly to the ground, his back to the wall. Elinor gazed distastefully round at their prison. There was an ominous rustling in one dark corner and she could not restrain a dismayed gasp at the thought of rats and other vermin crawling over her body throughout the hours of darkness.

Abruptly, Lord Gerard pushed by her, laden with a pile of bracken which he dumped against the back wall, spreading it into a couch with the toe of his shoe, then throwing over it the horse blanket.

"I suggest you make yourself as comfortable as possible, Mistress. The night will seem unendurably long unless you try to sleep."

She regarded him doubtfully. "And you, My Lord?"

"I also intend to sleep, just inside, well in view of both my prisoners, across the entrance." Then he added grimly, "You can hardly want for a chaperone, Mistress, with your own father close by."

She lowered herself onto the improvised bed, huddling beneath her cloak for warmth. Thirsty, tired and aching in every limb she moved restlessly in an effort to get comfortable, the bracken crackling and rustling beneath her.

From the doorway came a brittle laugh. "You will note, Mistress Elinor, how easily I am aware of your every move. I'm an extremely light sleeper when on campaign." There was a little pause before his final comment which chilled her to the heart. "If you attempt to untie your father or escape from me in the night, I shall not kill *you*, Mistress Elinor, I shall kill him."

She lay rigid, staring at the patch of greyness to her left which was the doorway. Her father moved beside her, easing his hips into the most comfortable position, then both men appeared to lapse quickly into light slumber, for their breathing sounded, to her strained hearing, even and steady.

Men, she thought wrathfully, were used to taking their rest when they could, as usual leaving their womenfolk to lie wakeful and terror-stricken through the long hours.

She understood well enough how hopeless it would be to attempt an escape. The three men outside would be taking turn and turn about to guard the hut. Not one of them would dare to relax his vigil, for they understood well enough Lord Gerard's fury would know no bounds if his hostages managed to overpower their guards and escape him. Her only hope would be to crawl out herself. She could not help her father. Even if she could manage to creep by the sleeping Lord Gerard without waking him and escape the vigilance of the men outside, she could not summon help. She had no idea where she was and would soon be recaptured, blundering amongst the trees in the darkness and wearing so unsuitable a gown. If she did manage to reach a village would she be believed? Indeed, it seemed more than likely that she would find herself ill-used by the first band of soldiers she encountered. Better by far to endure the captivity where her gaoler was known to her and she still had the uncertain protection of her father's presence than to venture into a frightening, unknown world outside.

The nearness of her captor made her oddly uneasy. Moving unwarily once, she found her body touching the soft velvet of his doublet. Immediately he stirred and his hand reached out and caught at her gown. A tingle of mingled fear and excitement ran through her and she heard him give a soft laugh in answer to her own fearful apology.

At length exhaustion and despair had their way and she fell into an uneasy doze.

She was shaken imperatively awake. Looking up fearfully, she found Lord Gerard's startling blue eyes gleaming with mockery.

"Good morning, Mistress Elinor. It

seems that you managed to sleep despite the unfamiliar hardness of your bed."

The grey light of dawn was casting long spears between the gaping struts of the hut walls and her father was already struggling to his feet.

She sat up and tried to tidy her hair. The pins had been loosened when Lord Gerard had torn off her cap and long brown tresses fell in tangles upon her shoulders and round her face. She pinned up what she could and without much success brushed down her torn, stained gown. Lord Gerard passed no comment on her appearance. His cold gaze passed over the figure of her father, warning him against any move to escape, before he strode out to his men.

Ruefully, Elinor climbed to her feet and put on her cloak, hoping it would hide the worst ravages to her gown and shift. She pulled up the hood over her badly arranged hair. Without a comb there was little she could make of that, either.

"Did you get some sleep, Elinor?" Her father's voice was gruff with concern.

"Yes, though I was restless for a long

time, tossing about and thinking — "
She turned to look at him closely in
the dim light. "It could not have been
comfortable for you, with your wrists still
bound."

He shrugged. "A soldier learns to rest
when he can on campaign despite all his
discomforts and fears."

"Fears?" Her tone was sharp. "You
think Lord Cranley will harm us?"

"You, certainly not, but if our company
is attacked, I think he would sacrifice me
without a qualm."

"But how can it help him to keep
us prisoner now?" Her voice broke.
"He's escaped from Beckwith. Surely
we have served our purpose in delaying
an immediate pursuit? Would it not be
simpler to leave us here and press on for
the coast?"

"It might," her father said cautiously,
"but it is not a prospect I view favourably,
for you, at least."

"But why not?"

"I've no idea where we are. This
place has been abandoned some time.
We might not be found."

"For days, you mean, or — never?"

Her mouth became suddenly dry.

"I think that unlikely," he reasurred her hurriedly. "It's not slow starvation I fear. We'd be freed in the end, even if he left us bound in the hut, but I'm worried about your safety in this wild country, without an escort. These are no times for a maid to be abroad. Bands of marauding armed men are no respectors of persons and I'm virtually unarmed."

Simon Radbourne paused in the doorway. "I've food and wine, Mistress Beckwith, poor fare, but the best we can do."

Elinor was touched by his rough kindness. He brought her a coarse woven kerchief in which were wrapped two hunks of hard, black bread and a wedge of cheese. He wiped the top of a leather wine bottle carefully with a corner of the kerchief before handing the bottle to her.

"You must be dying of thirst. Lord Gerard thought it unwise for you to drink from the stream last night. It was muddied and brown, swollen from last week's heavy rain."

"Thank you." She drank thirstily and

looked to him for permission to give her father his share. The wine was sour and vinegary but nothing in her whole life had been so welcome.

Simon Radbourne nodded and looked doubtfully at Sir Thomas.

"Lord Gerard says I am to untie your bonds while you eat, sir, if you will give your word not to attempt escape."

"You have it," Sir Thomas grunted.

The squire sliced through the ropes which bound his wrists and Sir Thomas sat with Elinor upon the bed of bracken to share her frugal meal: not a crumb was wasted.

Radbourne explained the sudden appearance of their supplies. "Ralf Brent was sent to the nearest cottage to buy what we needed. If you are ready now, Lord Gerard is anxious to press on."

Lord Cranley's shadow darkened the doorway as his name was spoken. To her surprise Elinor saw that he was now dressed like a mercenary in leather jacket and riding boots. He was carrying a rolled up bundle which he hurled onto the bracken.

"Oblige me by changing into these

87

garments, Mistress. Sir Thomas, please wear this cloak over your doublet. Unfortunately I must relieve you of your gold chain."

Elinor's eyes flashed angrily. "So you play the thief now, My Lord Cranley."

He shrugged. "Sir Thomas knows only too well that we need money for the journey. My men have had to discard their livery and food is dear when peasants guess that we are badly in need. Haggling causes delay and inconvenient questioning. I have no choice."

Sir Thomas handed over the chain without argument, gesturing Elinor to silence.

"Do I have your word that you will obey me throughout this next part of our journey?" Lord Cranley's blue eyes held Sir Thomas's fixedly.

"Aye."

"Then you may ride unbound. Wait by the horses, Sir Thomas, while Mistress Elinor changes her garments."

Her father smiled at her encouragingly and did as he was bidden. It incensed Elinor to see him so subservient.

"I must ask you to hasten, Mistress."

She looked down unwillingly at the garments which had fallen clear of their wrapping. They comprised a rough woollen tunic, brown hose, and ankle-length boots such as countrymen wore.

"I fear I cannot oblige you, My Lord," she said frostily.

"Cannot?" One dark heavy eyebrow arched upwards.

"I will not imperil my soul by acting against the laws of Holy Church. The French maid, Joan, was charged with heresy and burnt for wearing men's clothes."

His cold blue eyes regarded her unblinkingly.

"You must decide, Mistress Elinor, whether to put on those garments of your own free will or to accept my assistance. I make no bones about the matter. I give you two moments to begin to obey me. After that I shall render the gown you now wear entirely useless."

Golden fire flashed from her eyes and he added, "On my head be your sin against Holy Church. I admit I force you to it. It is necessary. You cannot go on dressed as you are. One woman amongst

89

our small party will bring undue notice upon us, which I cannot permit."

Tears sprang to her eyes despite her battle to prevent them but she knew they would avail her nothing. If she did not obey him, he would strip her and dress her himself without the slightest compunction. Her father would be helpless to prevent her utter humiliation.

Angrily she turned her back on him. "Leave me," she snapped.

"I shall count to twenty, Mistress, then come to your assistance."

Frantically she tore at her gown's lacing, unused to coping without Alice's help, then she struggled with the unfamiliar boy's clothes. The tunic chafed her soft skin and the boots were much too large. She was struggling to tie the points of her hose when he re-entered the hut. His lips relaxed in a grim smile.

"You make an attractive lad, but would fool few, I'm afraid. We must see that no stranger comes too close. Despite the avowed shamelessness of your attire, you will find it considerably easier to ride. Now, stand still, and let me look at you.

Good, finish tying the points. I see you'll need to stuff straw into those boots to make them fit, you've a pretty foot and ankle, Mistress Elinor. You have already put up your hair, I see. It should be well hidden beneath this hat."

The brimless brown felt hat he offered her was old and faded but did fit her head close so that most of her hair was concealed. She shuddered at the thought that she would need to rid herself of all the vermin — particularly head lice — when all this was over.

Lord Gerard nodded his approval. "Much better. Take comfort from the knowledge that this will be necessary for only a few hours. There is a gown in the pack for you to wear later and possibly *that* can be repaired." He stirred the discarded betrothal gown with the toe of his riding boot. "You see, Mistress Elinor, your father's chain supplied you with absolute necessities which I doubt he would begrudge you."

She bent and gathered up her torn and stained finery, tying it within the bundle of her cloak. So they were not yet to be released, since Lord Gerard had gone to such lengths to provide them all with disguises. She checked as she emerged from the hut at sight of a sturdy pony held ready for her by Simon Radbourne. Indeed, Ralf Brent had discharged his duty well to acquire so hurriedly all that they required. Ruefully she wondered, as she mounted, if all had been paid for, despite Lord Cranley's apparent need of her father's gold chain.

The air was cold but a fresh wind had sprung up overnight and dried the wet grass. Elinor found a certain delight in the exhilaration of the ride. She was hedged in close by Lord Gerard on her right and Simon Radbourne on her left. Behind came the sergeant, Will Begley, and Ralf Brent, her father between them under close guard. Soon they emerged from the wood and onto a dirt track where Lord Gerard urged his mount to the gallop and they made better progress.

Elinor had no knowledge of their route as they skirted a market town but they pressed on south, this she knew from the position of the watery sun above them. If, as her father supposed, they were making for King's Lynn, they must soon cross the Trent, either by the bridge at Newark, or by some shallow ford. She thought Lord Gerard would avoid the town and was soon proved correct as she was able to see the high towers of the castle away to their right, westwards. Soon they would be safer within Lord Gerard's own county of Lincolnshire.

Again the party spent the night in open country, Ralf Brent having successfully foraged and found for his master and the prisoners a half ruined barn where, this time, Elinor slept soundly, for she was utterly exhausted. From time to time along their journey food was obtained for them by either Brent or the sergeant, presumably from some cottage or inn along the route, barley bread, cheese, bacon, and to wash it all down, cider, sour wine or ale.

On the third day Elinor had become used to riding astride and ignored her aching bones and sore, rubbed flesh. She was allowed few opportunities to talk with anyone and Lord Gerard himself merely issued orders and for the most part remained moodily silent.

By evening it had come on to drizzle and Elinor looked longingly for some sign that they would slacken pace and seek shelter. She was hungry again, a condition she had rarely felt at home on the manor. The keen air and hard exercise had given her a hearty appetite, something she would have welcomed under more pleasurable circumstances.

Lord Gerard barked a sentence to Simon Radbourne which she could not catch and the party suddenly cut once more across open grazing land, splashed across a stream and headed for a building whose vague outline she could see only dimly in the gloom.

Were they, after all, making for Cranley Castle? The party must have reached the Lincolnshire border by now but the small house built of timber and mellow brick before which they drew rein was certainly no nobleman's castle. Elinor peered through the curtain of grey drizzle and could distinguish no other houses or even a church nearby. There were barns and outhouses but otherwise the place was isolated.

A solid wooden door was opened

hurriedly to Lord Gerard's imperative knocking and an elderly man held up a rush dip to examine the visitors more closely. He was tall and stooped and Elinor saw his white hair hung low to his shoulders. Catching a clear sight of Lord Gerard's features in the rushlight, he started and the dip wavered in his trembling hand.

"My Lord, is it really you. Please to come in, sir, come in."

The men-at-arms were already dismounting and Simon Radbourne helped Elinor down. Lord Gerard took her wrist and led her forward, his squire following with Sir Thomas still under guard. The sergeant and Ralf Brent were left to deal with the horses.

The house was small but appeared to be comfortably furnished. Their elderly host was dressed soberly but warmly in a long, outdated blue tunic of finest wool. The company passed from a flagged corridor into a candlelit solar where a woman sat spinning before the glowing log fire in the stone hearth.

Lord Gerard abruptly released Elinor's wrist and went to their hostess, catching her to his chest in a bear hug.

"Meg, my lovely, can you provide us with food and shelter for the night? I know my arrival is unexpected but you need go to no ceremony. My men can bed down in the stables."

The woman was diminutive, birdlike. Lord Gerard could have lifted her easily with one hand, indeed, he had held her clear off the floor in their embrace. She turned twinkling dark eyes on Elinor who stood, suddenly, acutely embarrassed and shamed in her boy's clothes.

"Meg, this is my betrothed, Mistress Elinor Beckwith, and her father, Sir Thomas. The lady is tired and hungry, I suspect, and," he grinned broadly, "extremely anxious to change her clothing. Can she be shown to a bed-chamber?"

"Certainly, My Lord, and at once. Walter will have already set my girls to providing your meal. Now, off with your damp jerkin, you'll take a chill. Have you a change of clothes with you? If not . . ."

Elinor was puzzled by the woman's manner, both affectionate and gently bullying. Like the man who had admitted them, she wore the neat but plain garments of the trusted servant. Her russet wool gown was spotless as was her white linen apron, cap and wimple. She marvelled that the woman could speak so familiarly to the arrogant Lord Gerard.

That question was very soon answered. "Mistress, go with Meg Tyrell, my former nurse. She'll attend you. Your father and I will dry our damp clothes, here, by the fire. We stay here for the night."

So they *must* be close to Cranley. This woman, who led her swiftly up the stairs, had been Lord Gerard's wet nurse so, presumably, the house and plot on which it stood was Cranley land, a gift from a grateful and loving lord to the couple grown old in his service.

Behind her she heard only the tail end of Lord Gerard's command to Walter Tyrell.

"Tell Ralf Brent he has an errand to run for me immediately. Can you provide a fresh mount?"

"Of course, My Lord."

The bed-chamber to which the elderly nurse conducted her was very small. There was a huge wooden bed against one wall and a serviceable oaken chest beside it. To her astonishment Elinor saw that a Turkey carpet had been placed beside the bed. Lord Gerard plainly had special regard for his old nurse, for Elinor did not possess so splendid a carpet in her own chamber at Beckwith.

Simon Radbourne hastened up behind them and, clucking her tongue as Alice might have done in open disapproval, Mistress Tyrell took the bundle of clothing he handed her. As she shook out the offending garments onto the bed Mistress Tyrell sniffed audibly.

"My, Mistress Beckwith, these have seen a mort of travelling. If you will get out of these wet things I'll bring you some hot water and towels."

Elinor tore off the hated boy's clothes. It was wonderful to wash herself all over in the herb-strewn water and she was especially grateful for the container of soft soap. She scrubbed her skin and hair free of the filth and vermin which she was sure had infested the rough garments Lord Gerard had forced her to wear. Mistress Tyrell provided a clean shift and a comb. There was no mirror and Elinor gladly accepted the old woman's assistance as she donned a gown of soft green wool, waist and sleeves tight fitting, so that for the first time in days, she felt warm, clean and comfortable. Mistress Tyrell pinned in the gold brocade vest from the ruined betrothal gown and handed Elinor the gilded belt of soft leather.

"Now, Mistress, you'm be quite presentable again. 'Tis a pity I've no head-dress to lend you, but your hair is so pretty worn loose and free on your shoulders and just as it should be tonight."

Elinor flashed her an enquiring glance but the old woman shook her head, smiling.

Downstairs, in the fire-lit solar, a meal had been set and Lord Gerard rose courteously to lead her to a stool near the hearth. Elinor raged at his duplicity. No one observing his courtly treatment of her would believe that he had only recently forcibly abducted her from her own home. He had once more donned the blue velvet doublet and hose in which he had set out on his ill-fated visit to Beckwith. Even within this homely setting he made a commanding presence.

"Thank you, Meg, you've done well," Lord Gerard smiled warmly as the old woman basked in his praise. "I am more than pleased. Does Walter understand fully . . ."

"Everything, My Lord. All shall be done as you wish. Your men will lie safe and snug in the stable, never fear."

"And Ralf is not yet back?"

"Not yet, My Lord. He cannot be long now and Walter will bring him straight in here. Now, eat hearty." She clearly adored him. "You'll be needing your strength, that's for sure."

Despite her weariness, Elinor enjoyed her first hot meal in days. There was pottage and fish and fowl in plenty to follow. Meg Tyrell's household seemed well run. The two young serving maids who scurried in with the dishes were deft and efficient, though much in awe of Lord Cranley. Elinor, who normally ate sparingly of most courses at home, saw her way through to the beef cooked in wine, a venison pasty and finished with syllabub. Looking up, she encountered Lord Gerard's amused gaze and castigated herself for revealing such obvious enjoyment. She had behaved like a greedy child. He poured wine for her and proffered a linen kerchief so she could wipe her greasy fingers. The wine was excellent and she relaxed, despite her irritation, under the mellowing influence of good food and the comforting warmth from the fire.

Sir Thomas sat slumped forward, his fingers gripping his wine cup tightly. She saw he was frowning and her feeling of well-being vanished.

Tomorrow they must set off again and the nearer they drew to the ports, the closer the watch set for them, the greater their peril.

4

WHEN the heavy blow sounded on the outer door Old Meg, who had seated herself in the inglenook with her distaff, looked up anxiously. Sir Thomas's head had jerked up, then he grunted and poured himself more wine. Elinor's eyes sought and found those of Lord Gerard. He merely signalled to Simon Radbourne, who rose and left the chamber. Subdued voices were heard from the corridor, then the squire reappeared in the doorway, ushering in the rotund form of a black-clad priest.

Lord Gerard instantly rose and went to greet the man, his hand outstretched.

"Father Robert, I am grateful you came so promptly. I trust Ralf did not find you in bed."

The priest's double chin wobbled delightedly as he threw off his wet cloak and hood, turning a round, red, good-humoured countenance to Elinor's view.

"No, no, My Lord, and had I been so, I would gladly have risen from it to ensure that yours, tonight, will be greatly to your liking." He beamed in Elinor's direction.

"Is this the maid, My Lord?"

"This is Sir Thomas Beckwith's daughter, Elinor, my betrothed, Father, and here, by my side, to witness I speak the truth about the contract, is her father, Sir Thomas, and my squire who was present at the ceremony."

Elinor sat frozen to her place, despite the heat from the glowing apple logs sizzling and spluttering behind her. She was much too quick witted to ignore the significance of the priest's sudden arrival. She allowed Lord Gerard's words to flow over her while she tried to come to terms with the imminence of the fate which threatened her. She came to herself with a jerk as she heard him address her directly.

"Mistress Elinor, I regret that our marriage cannot be celebrated in so grand a manner as I had planned, nor with the splendour your father contrived for your betrothal, yet it will be as binding and as blessed as any other, and I would not take you to Flanders unwed. That would not be seemly." The final remark mocked her.

She tried to answer him firmly but her voice emerged as a hoarse-sounding croak.

"I will not marry you, My Lord, now, not ever. I cannot." She fought to subdue the tears which were thickening in her throat. "You have become — my enemy."

There was a short silence. Lord Gerard moved his right hand in a commanding gesture. The priest looked questioningly at Elinor, his eyes half hidden under mounds of fat, yet for all that unusually moist and concerned. Mistress Tyrell curtseyed and withdrew to the door. The priest moved after her awkwardly, looking anxiously from Lord Gerard to Sir Thomas, who remained silently slumped on his stool, then once more at Elinor's set, white features. Murmuring an unctious apology, he followed Mistress Tyrell from the chamber.

Simon Radbourne rose without a word and closed the door on them, then stood with his back to it.

"Leave us," Lord Gerard ordered.

"My Lord . . . "

"Leave us."

Lord Gerard's blue eyes were fixed unblinkingly on Elinor as the squire inclined his head in bewildered obedience and left them. Elinor struggled against the torpor induced by outraged shock to rise to her feet, but her father leaned across the table and pushed her gently back on her stool.

Lord Gerard addressed himself to Sir Thomas.

"You will understand, sir, that my marriage to your daughter will ensure that her good name and honour will not be in any way besmirched when she returns with me from Flanders. His Grace King Edward will undoubtedly defeat the Kingmaker and take his seat once more in Westminster. Also, you will see the advisability of doing your best to ensure that, for her sake if for no other, the castle, manors and estates of Cranley are not sequestred or over-run by Lancastrian forces."

"And if I am unable to prevent that happening?"

"It would prove unfortunate." Lord Gerard's tone was clipped but even. "Also," he smiled deliberately, "with the knowledge that your daughter is in my hands, I am convinced that you will do your utmost to safeguard the comfort and well being of my brother, John."

A slight hiss of fury escaped Sir Thomas's lips, but he met Lord Gerard's gaze with a long, cold stare.

"It would seem I have little choice but to do as you request, My Lord."

"Mistress?" Lord Gerard turned and those bright blue eyes bored into Elinor's.

She caught back an anguished sob. "I cannot, I tell you. It would be a sin against God to force me to the altar."

"Bah, Mistress Elinor, you will be forced to the altar eventually, whatever you may say to the contrary. Your father will wed you to some man of his choosing and," Lord Gerard's tone became sardonic, "he'll not ask if the man pleases you, only if his lands and title are sufficient to advance his interests. Well, it seems, this time his interests are to wed you to me, for if you do not consent, I shall be forced to carry you and him with me to Flanders to King Edward's camp where he will undoubtedly reap his deserts as a traitor."

Her eyes sought those of her father and he shrugged uneasily, unwilling to meet her gaze.

"And — if I do consent?"

"Your father will be released very shortly after the ceremony, that I swear."

"You have been very free with oaths, My Lord," she said wearily. "Not three days ago you swore to love and cherish me, protect me from all those who would seek to harm me."

"And will do so again," he said cheerily, "aye, and keep that oath. I am not the one who turned traitor, Mistress. I trusted your father as companion and future kinsman. How do you think I would have fared had I been taken by Montecute's men?"

She recognized the truth of it. This was war. Had he not taken Sir Thomas and herself as hostages, Beckwith men would have seized and held the viscount and she was in little doubt that Lord Montecute would have ordered his execution. He had had no course but to take her in the need to extricate himself. Her father had betrayed him and she must pay the price.

"Then I must consent," she agreed, dully.

"Well said, Mistress." He threw open the door and called in the priest.

"You may proceed, Father. We have Mistress Elinor's consent and the blessing of her father. Now tie the knot swiftly and tightly."

The plump little priest regarded her worriedly. She judged him to be a kindly man, a gentle shepherd of his flock. He was doubtful about marrying a maid against her will, even on the direct command of his imperious young lord.

She smiled to reassure him, blinking back tears of impotent fury. "I am willing, Father. Lord Gerard and I have been betrothed since childhood."

"That I understand, Mistress. It is merely that this unseemly haste disturbs me."

"Father, I go into exile. I want my wife

with me. Should I leave her to become prey of some marauding baron? These are unsettled times."

"That is certainly true, my son." The priest sighed heavily.

Elinor stayed close to her father while the men removed the trestle table and a prie-dieu was brought in and placed before the hearth. It was of carved oak, she noted, the cushions of dark red velvet, another gift from Lord Gerard to Meg Tyrell, whom he had held in such affection. She exchanged no word with Sir Thomas, knowing instinctively that he was enduring agonies of shame and repentance that he had brought her to this.

Obediently she took up a kneeling position by Lord Gerard, their bodies touching close, since the prie-dieu was meant for Meg's devotions alone. Elinor felt the warmth of him through the soft velvet of his doublet against her own icy-cold flesh. As if she was hearing someone else repeat the vows Father Robert pressed on her, she spoke the words mechanically. Lord Gerard's voice was clear and firm and the hard kiss he bestowed on her frighteningly real. His signet ring, with its gryphon device, burned on her finger beside her betrothal ruby. She rose shakily to be kissed by her father. His lips, unlike those of her husband, were ice-cold, merely brushing her mouth.

"Be loving and dutiful, my child," he exhorted her.

Now she saw that the marriage had been witnessed by Meg and Walter Tyrell, Simon Radbourne and the two men-at-arms. She had not been aware of their presence throughout the brief ceremony, only conscious of herself and Lord Gerard.

The room emptied swiftly, the men withdrawing after husky words of congratulation to their lord and his lady.

Mistress Tyrell was close beside her, beaming her delight.

"And now, My Lady, if you will come to the bed-chamber, I will help prepare you to receive your lord."

Elinor's limbs trembled beneath her and she was unwilling to betray any trace of the stark fear she felt at the ordeal ahead. At last she threw back her head proudly, acknowledged her lord's nod with an inclination of her own chin and preceded the old woman out of the solar and up the stairs.

Meg undressed her, exclaiming at her beauty, though with due deference. Elinor was made aware of her new position as Viscountess Cranley. As such she must be treated with the ceremony befitting her rank.

Lord Gerard's nurse drew back the scented sheets and removed the heated brick which had warmed the bed in readiness to receive the wedded pair. Elinor slipped naked into bed and sat rigidly against the far wall, for the chamber was so small that the bed was sited right against it, and her hostess drew up the coverings.

"I wish you all joy, My Lady." Mistress Tyrell curtseyed low, her old eyes moist with joyful tears. "I have so looked for this day and My Lord could not be blessed with a lovelier bride."

Nor a more unwilling one, Elinor thought, as the old woman withdrew, leaving a candle burning brightly upon the oaken chest by the bed. An extravagance.

It was unlikely that wax candles were ever burned in this house outside the solar, and there rarely.

How different this chamber was from the room where she had expected to spend her wedding night. It would have been at Beckwith most likely, or in the splendour of Cranley Castle. There would have been feasting, musicians and the revellers would have burst into their chamber to see them bedded. At least she was to be spared their bawdy encouragement to the groom.

She waited in a daze of terror. Three short days had upturned the course of her life. Throughout the whole of this year she had thought and dreaded the moment when she would lie like this in her husband's bed, waiting. Under normal circumstances that would have been hard enough, but now she could scarcely believe this was actually happening to her. This man who had brutally abducted her, threatened her father's life, forced her to dress immodestly in boy's clothes, would at any second open that door, come close, climb naked beside her and take what was his right. Their union had been blessed by Holy Church. To attempt to prevent him, to resist, was a sin against God. She closed her eyes, sick and faint with horror, striving to still the frantic trembling of her limbs.

She gave a quick catch of the breath as she heard his slow, firm tread on the stair. Her fearful eyes saw the latch move, then the door was thrust fully open and he was framed in the entrance, the rush dip he held flickering over his tall, blue-clad form.

He came in, closed and bolted the door against intrusion; then came to the bedside, smiling as he noted Meg's thoughtfulness in providing the candle in its serviceable pewter holder. He extinguished the rushlight between strong brown fingers and stood regarding her.

She lay rigid, the coverings drawn up completely to her chin. It seemed to Elinor that only her eyes had power to move as they followed every move he made. She knew she should speak, greet him politely if coldly, that he would put down her silence either to fear of him or to sullenness, but her tongue clove to the roof of her mouth.

He undressed quickly for one who was used to the services of squire and servants, tossing aside his velvet garments carelessly upon the Turkey rug. The candlelight flickered gloriously on his splendid masculinity as he came naked to join her. There was not a spare ounce of flesh on him and the taut muscles rippled under smooth brown flesh. Silky dark hair glistened in the light upon his chest and upper arms.

He reached out and caressed the long thick tresses of brown hair which Meg had brushed so lovingly. She shied away from his touch.

"Come now, I'd not have you play the martyr, *Lady* Elinor." Chuckling, he emphasized her new mode of address and she shivered at the finality of it. "Haven't you been taught there is joy in bed-sport?"

"My — my nurse and — and my step-mother, Lady Isabel, tried to prepare me for my wifely duties." Elinor was furious with herself that her hesitation betrayed her nervousness still further.

"Ah," he gave a rueful sigh. "That word, 'duty'. What a wealth of distasteful experiences that conjures up."

Angrily she retorted, "You cannot believe that I could ever do aught but *endure* your love-making?"

"I had hoped I could teach you better things," he said mildly, "though not, perhaps, tonight."

She froze once more. What did he mean? Did he intend *not* to consummate the marriage tonight? Her hopes rose, only to be dashed again as she caught sight of his amused expression. No, he had not meant that. This marriage *must* be consummated, otherwise it would not be binding and Lord Gerard had no intention of leaving the slightest loophole by which her father could evade the issue and repudiate this ceremony performed so hastily and under duress. Then he had implied that she would not enjoy the experience. Pain was to be expected, she knew that, but they had told her it was soon over and, later, there would be pleasure in the act if she could only bring herself to the right frame of mind to submit.

She had dreamed of the courtly lover who would woo her to surrender with gentle kisses and intimate caresses. In his arms she would find true bliss.

At Beckwith she had allowed herself to believe that it would be so with Lord Gerard. He had spoken courtly phrases of love, kissed her sweetly, tenderly.

Within hours of that he had torn her brutally from her home, gagged her, tied her wrists cruelly. Could she hope he would be patient with her now, furious as he was at her father for his duplicity and suspecting that she had been a willing pawn in the game?

Her trapped gaze sought to avoid his proud, eager manliness, as he put back the coverings and slipped into bed beside her. She moved from his proximity, seeking to escape from the touch of his naked thigh against hers and, again, he laughed softly deep in his throat.

"The wall cannot give further, Mistress. You are fairly trapped and in my power and I advise unconditional surrender if you hope for mercy."

She choked back a sob and he took the covering firmly from her tightly clutching hands and surveyed her fully in the mellow light from the candle.

"Yes, indeed, I was not deceived by the skilful cut of that gown. You are as beautiful as I hoped," then, "gently, gently," he murmured as one hand cupped her chin. "There is no haste. If you are sensible and trust me, this need not be so terrifying an experience." He kissed her tenderly, as he had in the garden at Beckwith, while his free hand caressed the soft waves of her hair again. Despite her rigid control and determination to endure without struggling against the inevitable, she was fearful of her own response to his touch and, involuntarily, she jerked her head sharply back. Again he murmured, "Gently, I say," and eased her back against the pillows.

Her eyelids pricked with unshed tears of shame and bewilderment as he continued to lean and gaze down at her. Instinctively she moved to cover her breasts with her hands and he instantly prevented her, his fingers tightening warningly on her wrist.

"Don't fight me. That is not the way. Your skin is as fine as that white velvet gown which hid so much delight from me and just as soft to the touch."

She was further angered. He had married her against her will, taken her to suit his own purposes. Need he now keep up the pretence, flatter her, speak words of love which were all meaningless, after what had happened between them?

His fingers lightly stroked her throat and then her breast. She felt a tingle throughout her body and quivered with excitement and desire, as her nipples tautened and stood up rosily. Then his hands were caressing her belly and rounded thighs and he stooped his head to kiss the pulse which beat in her throat and sent it racing wildly.

She controlled her need to keep her legs tight closed. If he had need to force her, she could not prevent it and she knew she would suffer badly. His hands were gentle, persuasive, and she accepted his heavy weight on her body without complaint, willing herself not to cry out at the moment of taking.

There was pain, certainly, a moment when her body seemed torn apart, but with it a wild longing which swept through her and took possession of her utterly so that she heard herself moan against the enveloping sweetness of his lips on hers.

Later she lay back against the pillows again, her hair and body sweat-soaked, only partially aware of the pain between her legs and the ache of the bruises on her upper arms where he had caught and held her to him.

He extinguished the candle and gathered her once more to his heart.

"I'm sorry, sweetheart. It is always so the first time, but you are truly mine now and will learn, in time, the full delights of love."

She made no answer, turning her face to the wall while the slow tears coursed down her cheeks.

She cried for her own need, her longing to respond, and her unwillingness to melt with love under his arousing caresses. She could have loved him so, had he not used her so ruthlessly in his game of power with her father.

She realized too that he had taken her gently, tenderly, slowly. Had he thrown himself upon her, thrusting hard before her child's body had been roused by his skilful touch, it would have been excruciating, horrible. All this she knew instinctively, and it was little comfort.

Yet how could it be that she longed for his kisses and hated and feared him at the same time, for, despite his restraint now, she was aware that she *did* fear him? If she angered him, denied him, endangered him or his men, he would take steps to subdue and punish her.

She was now his, his chattel, his possession. There was no escape for her. He would take her with him to Flanders and she would become his hostage for her father's subsequent conduct. Should Sir Thomas act against his son-in-law in these coming months of trial by seizing or agreeing to the seizure of his lands, or worse, agreeing to the trial and execution of Lord Gerard's younger brother, John Cranley, she would be the one who would suffer for it.

His arm tightened compellingly around her waist and he turned her to face him in the darkness, his finger tracing the slow trickle of moisture upon her cheek.

"Tears? You can dry them now. It is

over. I shall not be too demanding. I can wait." She saw his mouth break into a smile in the shadowed dimness. "I am a patient man, though I do not expect you to believe that yet awhile. Rest now, sleep, for you will need your strength. We must ride hard and fast again in the morning."

5

ELINOR woke to find herself alone in the bed. It was still early but the room was veiled in grey dawn light. She turned her head to the indentation on the pillow beside her where her husband's head had lain and a little shudder ran through her body. She moved cautiously. She was stiff and there was a dull ache and soreness between her legs which brought a crimson flush to her pale cheeks. She sat up abruptly as voices could be heard outside her window, from the stables most probably, then footsteps ascending the stair. She remained huddled against the wall, facing the door fearfully.

Mistress Tyrell entered, smiling, and dropping a low curtsey.

"Give you good day, My Lady. I'm sorry I must disturb you so early but My Lord gave instructions that I was to help you dress, serve your breakfast quickly, since he is anxious to be off. The rain has stopped. It is a fine morning for you to resume your journey . . . "

She chattered on, as one of the serving girls hastened in with a pitcher of hot water for washing, fine linen towels draped over her arm.

"Will you eat in the solar with your father, My Lady, or shall I have breakfast served here in your chamber?"

"What?" Elinor stared at her hostess uncertainly. The woman seemed determined to act as if this was a perfectly ordinary morning, a joyful occasion for a young, willing bride, yet surely she must have known of at least some of the strange circumstances which had made necessary this hasty, ill-prepared ceremony.

"Thank you, Mistress Tyrell," she said hurriedly, "I — I'll come down to the solar. My husb — has My Lord already eaten?"

"Oh yes, My Lady, and is overseeing arrangements for departure."

Mistress Tyrell dismissed the serving maid who was wide-eyed with curiosity and went to help her mistress out of bed. Elinor was relieved by the girl's exit from the chamber. It seemed that every tongue in the household would be wagging on the subject of My Lord's wedding night and the behaviour of his young bride.

She rejected Mistress Tyrell's offer to help wash her, wishing that she could, without discourtesy, dismiss her too. She needed to be utterly alone. She averted her eyes as the woman swept up the stained sheets for laundering. They at least gave evidence that this marriage had been duly consummated. The fact would be noted and remarked on by the kitchen staff. Elinor scrubbed at her body fiercely, as if she would erase all memory of her husband's skilful caresses and the enforced intimacy which had given her entirely into his hold.

Mistress Tyrell helped lace her into the warm green gown and provided a white linen hood and wimple.

"My Lord wishes you to dress as a simple merchant's wife, My Lady," she said regretfully. "Such a small company travelling to the coast should not then arouse notice. There is a palfrey being saddled for you, unless you would prefer to ride in a litter. That could be brought from Cranley if you wish."

"No, certainly not. I shall ride, Mistress Tyrell."

Elinor descended to the solar where her father was taking breakfast with Simon Radbourne. She was disappointed that she had not found him alone. There were things to be said between them before parting, for Lord Gerard had promised her that her father would soon be freed.

Sir Thomas acknowledged his daughter's entrance by rising, drawing her close affectionately, and kissing her upon the forehead. Simon Radbourne also rose and bowed low. It was another tacit reminder that she was now his mistress, Viscountess Cranley.

"Elinor, my child, is all well with you?" Her father's question was softly uttered as the squire turned aside to carve meats for her.

"Yes, father." Elinor took her seat, eyes lowered, unwilling to meet the speculation in Sir Thomas's gaze. "And you, did you sleep well?"

"Yes, here in the solar, snug and warm with young Radbourne."

She thanked the squire as he set

a tankard of ale before her. She was unusually thirsty but not hungry. She forced herself to eat.

Her heart thudded as Lord Gerard entered and, stooping, kissed her cheek in careless affection.

"Good morning, my wife. I'm glad to see you eating heartily. We've a fair way to go before the next meal. Ale please, Simon."

His squire poured for him and he hooked a stool forward with the toe of his riding boot and seated himself.

She saw that this morning he was wearing a longer, less fashionable doublet of brown wool and a low brimmed felt hat of the same colour. Elinor wondered if this drab clothing would fool anyone if they were stopped and questioned. Whatever he wore, Gerard, Lord Cranley, would look the soldier and one accustomed to giving orders and being instantly obeyed. However, from a distance, their merchants' clothing might deceive.

"Now, Sir Thomas," her husband was saying, "to business. Have I your word that you will not try to prevent us from leaving the country?"

"Since my daughter rides with you, I could only endanger her. I shall do nothing to hinder you. You have my sworn oath on it."

"Good, then I suggest you remain here as Master Tyrell's honoured guest for today at least. You will then be free to ride into Grantham and make whatever plans you wish."

Lord Gerard's tone was cordial but dry. It was made plain that whatever was said to the contrary her father would still be ostensibly a prisoner here until Lord Gerard and his party were well free of the county. Elinor suspected that, already, Cranley retainers had come from the castle to ensure that their lord's commands were obeyed.

Sir Thomas was perfectly aware of the situation. He nodded brusquely.

Lord Gerard turned again to his wife. "Elinor, my love, I suggest you take leave of your father and join me quickly in the courtyard. Meg Tyrell has provided you with a bundle of necessities, clean linen and such, which is already loaded upon the packhorse."

He drew Simon Radbourne from the solar still issuing instructions, and Elinor and her father rose and faced one another.

"God keep you, my child." Sir Thomas's voice was husky with genuine emotion. "If — if anything should go wrong on this part of your journey, make quite sure that you are known to be my daughter, and an escort will be provided to bring you home."

"You will not break your word to him?" Her voice trembled a trifle.

"I'd not widow you, yet awhile," his tone was bitter, "at least until I'm sure you would be safer from the direr consequences of any skirmishing."

He kissed her with more outward show of affection that she was used to receive from him. Elinor believed that he was blaming himself for her plight.

"Give your husband no cause to deal harshly with you."

She swallowed back salt tears. This was the moment she most dreaded. She was to be alone with her father's enemies and the thought terrified her.

She forced a smile so that he would

not continue to be alarmed for her and then she hurried into the corridor where Mistress Tyrell waited, Elinor's hooded cloak folded neatly over her arm.

"It is sunny this morning but there's still a chill wind blowing. You'll need to wrap up warmly, My Lady."

Lord Gerard was waiting by the mounting block, Simon Radbourne by his side. The two men-at-arms, dressed plainly as serving men, stood ready by the packhorse loaded with supplies, so it would no longer prove necessary for them to forage for their food and drink along the way. Lord Gerard put his two hands round her waist and lifted her lightly to the palfrey's saddle. She turned to catch a last glimpse of her father, hoping he would have come to the door to watch their departure, but there was no sign of him and she wondered if he had been prevented from doing so.

She leaned down to murmur a last word of appreciation to Mistress Tyrell for all her care of her, and then they were off down the track on the next stage of their journey.

After the brief spell of poor weather

which had bedevilled their departure from Beckwith, the final days of September were mellow and sunny. Had Elinor not been so anxious concerning her father and Reginald and afraid that Lord Gerard's small company would be challenged and attacked, she would have greatly enjoyed the journey, for this part of the countryside was entirely new to her. The grass was green again after summer's drought, the leaves still bright gold, copper and brown on the boughs, and her eyes searched eagerly for each fresh sight on the road.

Lord Gerard now took to riding openly upon the highway, trusting to their merchants' clothing to stand them in good stead against questioning by groups of Lancastrian men-at-arms, and they made leisurely progress, through the flat, fen country. The inns where one of the men bespoke accommodation for them were small, their fare meagre and standard of hospitality poor, but at first sight of Lord Gerard's stern expression innkeepers and serving wenches, grooms and ostlers instantly put themselves out to make their guests comfortable. Had she been in any state of mind to appreciate the situation, Elinor would have been vastly amused by the flurry and haste to bring clean if patched linen and the vigorous wielding of brooms on their behalf.

The first night at Bourne, Elinor was unaccountably shy in her husband's presence. The innkeeper and his wife had moved out of their own bed-chamber in order to accommodate their wealthy merchant guest and his young wife. Lord Gerard treated her with due consideration not, this time, pressing her to accept his love-making.

"It's late," he commented in his habitual peremptory tone. "You must get to sleep at once. I'm well aware that the pace of this journey is hard and may be more so later."

She lay awake for hours despite his command, listening to his steady, even breathing beside her. His nearness filled her with dread and she was hesitant to move and ease her cramped limbs for fear of waking him. She thought he would not press her again until they had reached their destination. The consummation of their marriage had been absolutely necessary upon their wedding night, now he was more concerned that she would not prove over-tired by their long hours in the saddle and delay him.

At Holbeach the innwife sniffed audibly when she saw that Elinor was not accompanied by a maid, but was soon checked by My Lord's frown of black fury. She hurriedly curtseyed and stumbled from their chamber. Later, her redoubled efforts to please amused Elinor.

She had little conversation with her husband. She was too timid to question him about his plans, nor did she feel it incumbent upon her to speculate about her father's welfare nor the success of Lord Montecute's bid to back the Lancastrian cause. Lord Gerard's forbidding manner prevented her from discussing the state of affairs in the country at all.

He satisfied himself by asking frequently after her comfort and well-being and contented himself with that. Each night he continued to sleep soundly beside her while she lay wakeful, her thoughts and emotions strangely confused and unhappy. She could see no immediate future beyond the point of their possible escape from England. What would happen to her if her husband were captured and imprisoned? Could her identity as Sir Thomas Beckwith's daughter shield her from any molestation by her husband's enemies? Her father was no great noble. Who, in this part of the country, would even be aware of his name or his allegiance?

If they managed to reach the coast safely, how would they get passage to Flanders? Surely King's Lynn would be well watched and all vessels leaving port under surveillance by the earl's men, who would be anxious to catch the main prize, the King himself, and members of his party.

To Elinor, totally unused to travelling, the highway fairly crawled with traffic. At regular intervals Lord Gerard's party was delayed by the ponderous, iron-wheeled farm carts creaking along at a snail's pace. Villagers plodded stolidly from their stinking hovels to their cultivated strips and their work on the lord's land. There were also fellow merchants, hedge friars in their sombre grey robes, a doctor in his long gaberdine tunic, travelling teeth pullers and chapmen laden with heavy packs. The one sight Lord Gerard's men looked for warily, the glint of sunlight on metal salets and bills, which would warn of an approaching troup of mounted men-at-arms or company of foot soldiers, did not materialize.

At Long Sutton, Lord Gerard held a brief council of war with his men before retiring for the night. The innkeeper had agreed to place his smoky parlour at their disposal and Elinor sat by the hearth supping her tankard of mulled ale thankfully, since the warmth of the autumn day had now turned suddenly chill. The men gathered round the rough trestle table, their heads inclined to catch Lord Gerard's quietly spoken comments. He waited deliberately until the landlord had withdrawn.

"From now on we shall be travelling uncomfortably close to the coast and the roads will be well watched by Warwick's men. Once we have crossed the river we must leave the highway and ride across country again. It won't be easy, a roundabout road avoiding drainage ditches and marshland." He leaned across to address his sergeant. "Will, you ride ahead and discover the situation in the port."

Will Begley nodded soberly. "All ships' masters will want bribing and heavily, if they're to take us on board in secret. The King's party is likely to be ahead of us. That will make matters more difficult, My Lord."

"I'm well aware of that."

Begley glanced awkwardly towards Elinor. "Wouldn't it be wiser, sir, to send Lady Cranley back to Doncaster where she would be under her father's protection? Young Master Simon could escort her."

"No," Lord Gerard snapped and the men exchanged concerned glances.

"Damn it, Begley, are you suggesting I'm incapable of protecting my wife?"

"No, My Lord, simply that — " Begley shrugged helplessly. He could see well enough that no advice from him on this subject would be acceptable and drained his ale tankard mournfully.

Elinor lay nervously in their bed-chamber later, her eyes troubled as she watched her husband restlessly prowl the small space left in the room.

At last he came close and stared down at her. "I must demand that you give me your ruby betrothal ring and the enamelled necklace," he said at last, his voice made overharsh with embarrassment.

Obediently she withdrew the heavy ring from her finger and handed it to him. Her eyes clouded with tears as he nodded brusquely and waited for her to unclasp the jewelled relic from about her neck. She had never once removed it since their departure from Beckwith. The touch of the worn gold and enamel had comforted her throughout the worst moments of her ordeal.

"You — you cannot ask it of me," she said at last in a choked little whisper. "I told you it was my mother's last gift to me. I treasure it above all my possessions."

"Yes, I know. I regret the need, but sentiment will avail us nothing if we cannot obtain passages from the port.

I have little ready gold. I have no alternative but to insist. You can blame your father and cousin, Mistress, that they have forced this action on me."

"I would willingly part with my marriage ring," she retorted bitterly and, snatching off the Cranley signet, she hurled it across the room.

He stood impassive, his blue eyes like cold Northern seas.

"I don't doubt that, but that is quite impossible."

"Because it is yours and must not be sacrificed."

"No, because it is yours and binds you to me."

"I would to God it did not."

He made no reply but stood, his hand outstretched, his fierce eyes never moving from her pale, furious little face. Blinking back anguished tears, she tried to obey him, but her fingers were shaking so that it took some moments for her to undo the clasp and hand the necklace to him. His fingers closed over the beloved trinket then, abruptly, he bent and retrieved the signet.

"Put it on."

She turned defiantly from him, her shoulders hunched.

"Put it on, I say."

Still she did not turn and he said sharply, "Must I force obedience?"

She twisted round then, to meet his furious scowl. Her lips trembled. She was deeply afraid of him. Checking a storm of angry tears, she reached out for the ring. He seized her hand before she could do so, and thrust it firmly onto her marriage finger. She snatched her hand away and he stood for a moment holding her gaze with his own, then turned and strode from the chamber.

She lay for hours afterwards, trembling and cold, waiting for his return. It was the first time she had resisted any order given by him since their marriage. She knew well enough that she had angered him by her defiant rejection of his marriage ring, and, worse, she had also insulted his house. It had been a foolish, childish act and one for which he might punish her.

Gradually the sounds within the inn were silenced and she lay miserably watching the intermittent glare of the lighted brand from the courtyard reflected in the grimy horn window of their bed-chamber, until that, too, burned itself out.

He was not coming. He had found accommodation somewhere outside with his men, the stables, probably, or he had drunk heavily in the parlour and fallen asleep by the fire. She told herself fiercely that she was glad of it. Tears came unchecked now that she was sure she would remain alone. He had taken from her the one thing he knew she treasured. The final memento of her mother's love, her last link with the manor at Beckwith. And for what? To ensure himself passage aboard some ship which would take her further from all she held dear. Turning, she sobbed out her despair into the harsh, straw-filled pillow.

If Lord Gerard was still angry with her after her outburst of the previous evening, he gave no sign of it when they breakfasted early next morning. Neither did he make reference to the fact that for the first time since their marriage, they had slept apart. Elinor, knowing him anxious to make an early departure, finished her meal quickly and prepared to enter the courtyard. Since she had been deprived of the services of her nurse or any other maid she had had to struggle awkwardly today with the back lacing of her gown. On all the other mornings since they had left the Tyrell house in Lincolnshire, Lord Gerard had fulfilled that task for her.

As Simon Radbourne helped her into the saddle of her palfrey, she saw that Will Begley was missing. So he had gone ahead to arrange passages as Lord Gerard had commanded, waiting only for his lord to provide him with the means to bribe the ship master. Elinor's lips tightened mutinously at the thought.

Lord Gerard mounted up and rode in silence beside her. She stole a glance at his set features and gave an inner sigh. The issue between them had undoubtedly touched his pride. He smarted against the necessity of taking her jewels from her.

He was less relaxed now his eyes roving the road restlessly. From his instructions to his men the previous evening, she understood that he feared ambush. Every mile they rode nearer to the port of King's Lynn brought them nearer to danger. It was necessary to be constantly on the watch lest they ride straight into a trap set for the King or his followers.

He rode in close behind as they clattered noisily over the wooden bridge which spanned the Nene. Soon they had struck off left from the highway across great desolate wastes of salt marsh, where nothing stirred but the marsh fowl and sea birds which rose into the air ahead of them with a great flapping and shirring of wings. Their mournful screeching seemed to Elinor a grim omen for what lay ahead. She drew her cloakstrings tight about her neck. This place was alien and frightening, the very air chill and dank with a coastal mist rolling in from the sea, heavy and foreboding. Elinor had never seen the sea. The thought of venturing onto a vast emptiness of water terrified her but this dread she could not disclose to Lord Gerard. As it was he held her in sufficient contempt. He would consider her an arrant coward.

They appeared to be riding in circles for hours, their horses stepping warily on the coarse marsh grass along the banks of seemingly endless drainage ditches. No animals grazed here and there were no houses or barns in all this desolation of wasteland.

Then, abruptly, the landscape changed and Elinor was relieved to see ahead of them cultivated fields and water meadows reclaimed from the fen. Now they were riding along quiet woodland paths through ploughed fields, copses and villages. Simon Radbourne explained to her that the tall wooden structures with sails were windmills.

"The sails rotate and turn wheels which keep the water flowing into the ditches to drain the ground, My Lady. You will see many structures like them in Flanders where the land is also very flat."

But Lord Gerard gave the windmills scant attention. He urged the tired little party to greater speed.

It was now well past midday and Elinor longed to dismount, stretch her legs, make herself comfortable, answer the call of nature and satisfy her hunger. As usual she had become extremely thirsty for the dust and seed from the dry grasses caught at her throat.

Lord Gerard cast her a hasty glance

and, reading utter exhaustion in the drawn lines of her face and slumped posture on the palfrey, he drew rein within a small copse, his hand uplifted.

"We'll withdraw from the main path, dismount and hobble the horses. This way." He leaned across and seized Elinor's bridle rein. She was only too willing to obey him. Though they had not ridden so hard or fast as in the early days, that damp and cheerless country had greatly depressed her spirits.

The copse was dense and their progress was slow as they blundered through the overhanging trees so that she was forced to bend almost double in the saddle. Their trail was blazed by the noise of their horses' hoofs, the upthrust of birds on the wing disturbed by their passage and the scuttering of wood creatures in the thickets. Lord Gerard had no intention of allowing the party to camp near the path where they might be seen by some passing villager.

Obviously he was following the sound of water, for the bubbling of a small brook ahead seemed to hearten their mounts and they pressed on with renewed determination, ears pricked forward eagerly.

It was then that the silence of the copse was abruptly shattered by a sudden blood-curdling yell. Instantly Lord Gerard pulled up his mount and jerked at the lead rein of Elinor's palfrey.

"Keep absolutely still all of you."

The first horrifying yell was followed by others. Elinor sat, one hand clutching at the reins as her palfrey moved restlessly beneath her. Harsh oaths sounded, savage cries and the clang of iron on iron, the ominous panting breaths and thuds of men engaged in mortal combat. Lord Gerard was leaning forward in the saddle, frowning, listening intently. Simon Radbourne drew abreast of them and Elinor saw that his face was pale, almost greenish in the shadowed sunlight filtering in through the trees.

Ralf Brent said softly, "Off to the right about two hundred paces, I'd say, My Lord."

Lord Gerard nodded impatiently.

The sounds of battle intensified. There were hoarsely muttered grunts and a hastily cut off scream. Elinor could distinguish no words or names. She knew her husband was trying to decide whether the fight was merely a casual encounter between a group of footpads, who'd set upon some company of travellers and met more resistance than they'd bargained for. On the other hand it might be something far more sinister, the presence of an armed company which he must avoid at all costs if he intended to reach the port in safety. She tried to gauge his expression. Would he risk their safety by going to the help of the threatened travellers? If he left them to their fate, he might be ignoring a plea for assistance from some of the fleeing Yorkists ahead of them on the road.

He straightened and nodded brusquely to his squire.

"Stay here with My Lady. Guard her with your life, boy. Ralf, let's investigate."

Elinor knew it was pointless to protest. She looked uneasily at her youthful guard as her husband and Ralf Brent rode off.

She swallowed hard. "Simon, does My Lord fear an attempt from Warwick's men to prevent — "

"Aye, My Lady. Whoever they are, they sound well armed and efficient fighting men. This is no place for robbers to waylay unwary travellers. Any band intent on robbery would lie in wait nearer the path, or better still, the highway."

"Then who?"

He grimaced, a warning hand steadying her mount which, alarmed by the sounds of conflict ahead, was pawing the ground more nervously now. "In these uncertain times we could encounter any company of warring nobles or their retainers. This could merely be a settling of accounts between two knights with a grudge held for their neighbours, or travellers like yourselves, intent on escaping the country and beset by enemies."

"You mean Yorkists?"

He nodded.

"But surely involving himself could endanger all of us."

"Trust Lord Gerard, My Lady. He'll not disclose your presence in the copse unless he thinks it wise to do so, nor will he enter the fray unless he is sure he is needed."

She felt suddenly sick, her mouth

dry with apprehension. True, there was no love lost between Lord Gerard and herself, and she had declared him her enemy to his face, but now she feared for him in the coming engagement.

She tried to tell herself that these fears were natural enough. He was now her only protector. If he were killed how would she fare? Her father had warned her of the dire consequences of falling into the hands of a company of undisciplined soldiery, yet she knew her feeling was stronger than that. He had left Simon Radbourne to guard her and the squire would do so, with his life if need be. She was safe enough. No, she could not bear the thought of Lord Gerard dead or mortally wounded, lying untended in this copse, that magnificent body sprawled awkwardly, those piercing blue eyes clouded and dull.

The fight was continuing though it seemed that the opponents were tiring. There were fewer shouts and taunts and the movements the men made were slower and more blundering, arms tiring of wielding those heavy two-handed swords or battle axes. Soon one of the sides would claim the victory and her heart raced at the thought. What if neither Lord Gerard nor Ralf Brent were to return to them? Had Simon Radbourne been given instructions earlier by his lord that in such an event he was to continue their journey, or could she persuade the squire to escort her home to her father? Impatient to know the outcome, she impulsively jerked her lead rein clear of the youth's hold as he was caught off balance, his attention fixed firmly on the noise of battle.

Her palfrey neighed sharply as Elinor drove her spur into the animal's fat side. It reared and almost unseated her. She leaned forward in the saddle, clinging on grimly. Behind her she could hear Simon's startled yelp as she blundered her way through the trees towards sounds of battle. Suddenly the clamour stopped. Elinor halted in her tracks and wrenched at her palfrey's bridle to bring her under control. For moments the sudden hush which fell on the wood was eerie, unnatural. She pressed forward again determinedly.

She was free of the trees now and into

the clearing. Her vision blurred oddly, then she saw men grouped together, six or eight of them. More men were down, some lying ominously still, others moaning or struggling to rise.

Elinor pulled her mount up short and jumped down. She gave a great sob of relief as her husband's familiar form in the unfashionable merchant's clothing withdrew from the group and bent over one of the huddled forms on the ground. She bit back a cry of sheer horror. The sunlight glimmered on his dagger as, ruthlessly, he dispatched his fallen opponent. There was a horrible choked cry from the dying man. Lord Gerard rose to his feet, wiped his dagger on a handful of plucked grass and prepared to return to the group of knights pressed tightly against their leader. He checked suddenly as he saw Elinor. Angrily he strode towards her as Simon Radbourne rode up, his young face red with embarrassed shock and the desperate urgency of his hectic ride.

Ignoring Elinor, Lord Gerard turned furiously on his squire.

"I ordered you to guard her. How *dared*

you disobey." Even from this distance Elinor caught the low note of outrage in his voice and she saw the squire quail and draw back slightly. His lips writhed in terror of the rage he saw distort his lord's features.

"My Lord, I — "

"It was no fault of Simon's. I took him completely by surprise and tore away from him. He was powerless to prevent me."

Elinor shuddered, averting her eyes from her husband's bloodstained hand as he sought to take hers and draw her towards him.

"Fortunately, the affair is ended. There is no further danger. Come."

She allowed herself to be led to the small knot of men who were gathered around a tall, golden-haired giant.

"Well now, Cranley," he said genially as he sheathed his huge, two-handed sword, "you came upon us most opportunely." He indicated with a contemptuous movement of the hand the wretch Lord Gerard had dealt with so uncompromisingly. "Is the fellow dead?"

"Aye, Your Grace. I saw out of the

corner of my eye that he had managed to retrieve his weapon. He could well have hamstrung My Lord of Gloucester as he walked by him."

"He'll fight no more. God rest him." The fair-haired man crossed himself. He stared at Elinor in undisguised curiosity. Nervously, she drew her cloak more closely round her.

"Your Grace, may I humbly present my bride, the former Mistress Elinor Beckwith."

The man standing on the King's right gave a hearty laugh. "Faith, Cranley, you never cease to amaze us. I thought it was merely a betrothal ceremony which had so delayed you. No wonder you were in no hurry to extricate yourself from Yorkshire."

A burst of amused laughter greeted the sally and Elinor felt her cheeks crimsoning. The speaker was a brown-haired man, well built, dressed in a green velvet doublet which was muddied and besmirched with the recently spilt blood of the combat. He was floridly handsome and Elinor guessed him to be a great favourite with the Court ladies.

"I think you forget yourself and the presence of Lady Cranley, Lord Hastings." A cold, clipped voice rebuked the man. "Lady Elinor must be both exhausted and greatly shocked by these sights. This is an ill time to make jests concerning My Lord's need to bring her here."

Elinor turned to face her defender. He came up to join the group who respectfully gave way before him. The King smiled and placed an affectionate hand on the newcomer's shoulder. He was smaller and slightly built with a dark, narrow, clever face. Elinor supposed that his stern expression made him appear much older than his years. He sheathed his dagger and bowed to her courteously. She inclined her chin in answer, curtseying as she had done to the King. She was still bemused to find herself in the presence of His Grace. The meeting had come about so unexpectedly.

The brown-haired man assumed a suitably chastened expression. "My pardon, Lord Cranley, you must excuse my foolish tongue, and you, I beg, Lady

Elinor. I assure you I meant no disrespect. The relief of the victory after this affair prompted me to jest where I certainly had no business to do so."

"You're an idle fellow, Will," the fair man said, his lips twitching with amusement. "It's as well you also prove a doughty fighter. I must urge My Lord Cranley and his lady to forgive you your discourtesy, for I would find it hard to manage without the loyal service of any of my gentlemen left to me."

The King stooped and, taking Elinor's fingers, kissed them gallantly. "Forgive My Lord Hastings, My Lady. I swear your beauty touched his heart and bade him speak what must be in all our thoughts. Had we stood in Lord Gerard's place we might well have found ourselves tempted to remain at Beckwith with you for ever." He smilingly turned to the dark young man who had come to a defence of her honour. "My younger brother, Duke Richard of Gloucester, reminds all of us of our duty to you. Cranley, is there some place where My Lady might rest in safety while we count the cost of this encounter?"

"I would greatly prefer that my wife remain well within my sight, Your Grace. It seems that my squire cannot be trusted to keep her within his control and there could well be other companies of armed men in this vicinity."

"Very true, unfortunately." The King beckoned to one of the younger members of his party, possibly a squire to one of his household nobles. "Piers, stand with Lord Cranley's squire some yards distance from this unpleasant scene. The two of you find a log or saddle on which My Lady might be seated and see what food and wine we have is placed at her disposal."

Elinor shuddered at the merest mention of food. Her first excitement and alarm over, her stomach churned at the signs of carnage within the nearby clearing.

There were four men lying on the ground, one of whom had been killed by her husband. The grass was trampled and slippery with spilt blood. One of the fallen men moaned in pain. She turned to look at him, compassion stirring.

"One of you, see what you can do for that fellow," Duke Richard commanded.

"John Rampton is slain, Sire, and Lord Rivers has sustained a wound in the sword arm, but for that we appear to have come well out of this. Two of the ruffians fled when Lord Cranley and his man erupted so suddenly into the clearing. They made so much noise I imagine the enemy believed at least a whole company of men was coming to our assistance." A smile relaxed his grim expression. "I have you to thank for my life, Gerard."

"Your Grace would have been equally prompt in acting so for me had I been in peril."

Lord Gerard nodded coldly to Elinor and was clearly waiting for her to obey the King and accompany Simon and the other young squire some way apart from the clearing. She knew he was still furious with her.

Reluctantly she allowed herself to be escorted, picking her way awkwardly over the mired and trampled grass.

A tree stump was found for her and Simon Radbourne spread a blanket for her to sit. She did so thankfully. Now this affair was over she found herself cold and trembling. The other young man, Piers, moved away to the horses and returned with a bottle of wine, bread, cold meats and cheese. She shook her head as he offered to serve her.

"Thank you, sir, but — I couldn't — not — just yet."

The two exchanged glances of sympathy and Piers said, hesitantly, "You have no need to fear. It is all over, My Lady. Now Lord Gerard has joined us we shall be well guarded against any repetition of this attack, I can assure you."

"I am far more concerned for the dead and wounded," she said coldly and he hung his head.

"I'm sure His Grace will be merciful," he said at last, unhappily.

Elinor was by no means convinced. In these last few days she had seen savagery unleashed, and before her eyes Lord Gerard had dispatched one man without mercy and badly wounded another.

Her husband returned to her side an hour later.

"His Grace is concerned that you should have to spend the night without shelter, but I am more alarmed about

156

going into the nearest village. We must all stay together tonight. The men who attacked the King's party might well have been missed from their own camp and others sent to enquire after them. We could quite easily be caught in such a trap, and the King with us. We are too close to the coast now for me to allow anything to stand in the way of accompanying the King and seeing him safe to Flanders. Our men will try to fix up a temporary shelter of boughs for you. I hardly think it will rain tonight."

She accepted his decision without protest, but was less agreeable to eat with the company. He insisted.

"It would be an act of gross discourtesy to His Grace the King for you to refuse to join us," he said shortly.

It would have been useless to point out to him that since her father had now allied himself with King Henry she could not, in all conscience, accept Edward of York as her King. Ruefully she saw the wisdom of holding her peace on that subject.

She was treated with the utmost courtesy as she took her place in the clearing round the improvised table. The King granted her the honour of placing her upon his right side. He was charming and solicitous, offering her the choicest morsels of food with his own hand. Elinor was embarrassed and uncomfortable, feeling the bold dark eyes of the handsome Lord Chamberlain, Lord Hastings, constantly upon her.

On her return to the clearing she found that the bodies of both wounded and slain had been removed, either to hastily dug graves in the copse or been carried off by the Yorkist knights to some place nearer the path where they might be discovered later by some villager and conveyed to the nearest monastic infirmary.

A rough shelter had been erected by the two squires. Boughs had been placed over cut down tall poles to protect her from the wind and allow her some privacy from the gaze of other men in the company. As on the previous occasion during her journey from Yorkshire, a bed of dried bracken and leaves laid over with blankets formed a reasonably comfortable couch. When Lord Gerard joined her in the early hours of the morning and gathered her into his arms she was nervously aware of the nearness of his companions lying close by them.

He eased his hip into a more comfortable position, apparently unaware of the reason for her discomfiture.

"I'm sorry I woke you. I was taking my turn on watch."

Outside the makeshift shelter she could hear the crackling of the camp fire and the monotonous tread of the sentries' feet as the guards passed to and fro near their resting place.

Lord Gerard's arm tightened abruptly round her waist and she stiffened. She could not rid herself of the vivid image of him as she had seen him rising from his feet after killing the Lancastrian soldier, his hands and dagger blade blood-stained.

Irritably he whispered, "What is it? Are you afraid still?"

"No."

"We cannot be observed from the camp fire where the nobles are sleeping and the sentries dare not take their attention from their guard duties."

His lips caressed the tip of her ear and the old, wild excitement she had experienced on her wedding night began to race through her being. He felt her quiver under his touch and gave a yelp of suppressed laughter.

"The King showed you much honour at supper, Lady. Is he more to your taste than your husband?"

She did not dignify the question with a reply and he continued. "I can see I must keep a wary eye on Hastings. The man is insatiable."

Fuming she said tartly, "My Lord, I assure you you have no need to fear that I shall cast as much as an admiring glance at any man within this company, not even His Grace the King. I find all Yorkists equally detestable."

She heard him chuckle in the darkness as his free hand fondled her breasts.

6

WILL BEGLEY had apparently come back to the copse during the night and inadvertently stumbled upon the King's camp, where he was immediately challenged and finally accepted as Lord Cranley's man. Early next morning he reported what success he had had during his scouting expedition in King's Lynn.

"My Lord there is a Dutch ship in port whose master expressed his willingness to take us on board. Surprisingly he did not prove as rapacious as I feared. He is to sail on the evening tide."

"What's the situation in the port?"

"I saw no mounted or liveried men near the waterfront, though I imagine some of the earl's men are quartered in the town."

"Could the Dutchman take other passengers?"

"I reckon he could, My Lord, at the right price."

Lord Gerard nodded brusquely and signalled to Elinor.

"I regret that it will again prove necessary for you to change into your boy's clothing."

Without waiting for her to answer, he strode off to report to the King.

★ ★ ★

It was difficult to make the change in the restricted space the shelter allowed and she was in no easy temper when she emerged to encounter Lord William Hastings leaning easily against a tree bole nearby. Sweeping off his velvet hat, he made her a gallant bow.

"I give you good day, sir. Will it please you to allow me to escort you to the clearing for breakfast?"

"Thank you, My Lord," she replied stiffly and was not unaware of Lord Gerard's hard, uncompromising stare as she took her place on the tree stump where Lord Hastings had squired her with some show of formality.

The Duke of Gloucester acknowledged her presence courteously but seemed preoccupied with arrangements for departure from camp and the young squire, Piers, was busy dressing the wound in Lord Rivers's arm.

It came on to rain heavily by the time they were ready to ride into Lynn. Since it would have proved unwise to coddle the supposed apprentice in cloak and hood Elinor was forced to endure the discomfort of soaked garments and rain-water cascading in rivulets down her neck. The over-large boots she had stuffed with straw became soggy and difficult to manage and she was so wrapped up in her own misery that her first view of the sea failed to register on her as heavily as it might have done under more favourable conditions.

The wharf was littered with great bales of wool and linen — wrapped packages, coils of tarred rope and rusting ironware. Elinor walked gingerly in Lord Gerard's wake as he navigated the cluttered stonework of the quay. The rain was an impenetrable grey curtain through which she could scarcely distinguish the lines of the round ship with its square sail and castles fore and aft.

163

They had encountered no difficulty in reaching the quay. At the city gates Lord Gerard had been stopped and questioned by a sergeant-at-arms. Elinor could not hear what was said but the man appeared satisfied by their explanations for he waved the party on. From a waterfront tavern they heard the sound of drunken revelry and judged Warwick's men had risked lowering their guard during such foul weather.

They were hustled swiftly aboard the Dutch vessel, Elinor wrinkling her nose against the strong stinks of bilge water, tar and greasy wool. The crewmen all looked villainous and she shrank closer to Lord Gerard and Simon Radbourne. The ship's master, a pot-bellied lard-tub of a man with greasy hair and beard, conducted them to the foul-smelling cabin in the forecastle. Lord Gerard gestured to Elinor to seat herself on the hard wooden bunk and called the man closer. She watched as the two conferred, heads close together and a leather bag which exuded a distinct clink of coin changed hands. Since Elinor had concluded that their passages had already been paid by Will Begley, she assumed the gold was to provide passage for the King's party. Edward and Gloucester had been persuaded to remain outside the port, while the squire, Piers, had come on with the Beckwith men to discover if it would be safe for His Grace to proceed further. She had seen both the King and the duke hand the youth their gold chains and rings, an action soon followed by the other gentlemen of their party. Like Lord Gerard none of them possessed anything but those jewels he had been wearing during their escape from Doncaster.

The captain moved off with that distinctive rolling gait of the seaman to some duty about the ship and Lord Gerard summoned the squire to the cabin.

"Inform His Grace that passage has been obtained for him and all his gentlemen. Exhort him to take special care, particularly when passing through the city gates. That massive physique of his and brave yellow hair cannot easily be mistaken for any other than Edward Plantagenet's."

The youth hastened off and Lord

Gerard frowned with distaste as he surveyed the cabin. The place was lit only by the flickering glow of a tallow candle set in a horn lantern suspended from a hook over the cabin door.

"This is a poor place, the captain's own cabin. His Grace and the duke must stay on deck with the other gentlemen throughout our passage, which won't be pleasant in this weather. You, at least, will have shelter from the rain. I suggest you get out of those wet clothes and into the bunk. Try to get some sleep. We don't sail before midnight."

She was startled when she heard him lock the door from the outside.

"I feel happier knowing that no member of that villainous-looking crew can get near you while I am gone."

On this point she could not but agree. Once she had assured herself that she could not be overlooked from the high ox-horn-covered porthole, she stripped and, placing her cloak carefully over the grimy palliasse on the bunk and wrapping herself in the blanket which had formed her bundle, lay down and tried to rest.

That wasn't easy. The vessel rocked

at anchor and she found the motion distinctly unnerving. The stink of the fetid place caught at her throat and turned her sick. She tried, desperately, to quell her rising fears. Soon all possible contact with her father and kinsmen would be lost to her when this terrifyingly delapidated tub set forth onto the high seas. At last boredom and exhaustion took their toll after the excitement and strains of the last few days and she slept.

She woke to a more horrible rolling and grinding about and above her. She sat up, striking her head upon the timbers of the bulkhead.

Overhead the ship's timbers creaked and moaned. So they were underway! One moment it seemed to the terrified Elinor that she was being tossed aloft to some great height, then the vessel wallowed downhill and her stomach plummeted with it. She scrambled up in the bunk, her gorge rising, as the howling of the wind could be heard even over the noise of the ship's passage and the staccato rattle of rain against the ox-horn covering of the porthole.

The lantern swung and heaved and the sight of it made Elinor's plight far worse. Before she could set her bare feet over the edge of the wooden bunk rail, she was unbearably sick upon the cabin floor. She sobbed with fear and disgust at her own weakness. They were adrift in a gale and would never reach Flanders. The ship plowed the furrow of the waves and the vessel shuddered throughout its length. Once more she retched and vomited, then scrambled fearfully back onto the palliasse. Would this nightmare never cease? Would she die alone in this coffin of a cabin?

There was a noise of feet stumbling and awkwardly attempting to navigate the length of planking outside the cabin door. Whoever it was could scarce stand upon his feet. Elinor was too far gone in her own misery to care if the newcomer were some member of the crew intent on ravishing her. If her life had depended upon it, she could not, at that moment, have summoned up the strength or inclination to drag on some clothing.

She cried out in terror as the door was

fumblingly unlocked, wrenched open and someone entered, breathing heavily in a frantic struggle to close the door again against the overpowering force of the gale which threatened to prevent him.

Elinor felt herself seized and held down firmly upon the bunk.

"Holy Mother of God, I've never known such a gale. You must be terrified half out of your wits and sick too, I see. Lie still, sweetheart, if you try to move you'll roll from the bunk and hurt yourself. We've all been involved for the last hour in trying to strap down anything which is liable to move in this rotting hulk. If only that fool of a master would turn her into the wind."

She sobbed her relief against his shoulder and he sat on the bunk side, holding her close.

"Will — will we all drown, My Lord?"

"Nay, sweetheart, there's little fear of that. The ship's taking in some water but she'll hold. I called her master a fool just now but I've been watching him. He knows his business, right enough. We'll weather the gale and land safely. The man knows these waters." Lord Gerard made a sharp exclamation as his questing hand discovered the bleeding wound on her scalp. "You're hurt."

"I hit my head on the timbers as the ship rolled. I was so frightened. I'd been asleep and suddenly awoke to all that roaring and plunging — I tried to get up to find out what was happening." She gulped back sobs of panic.

"Let me look." He grunted, as he felt the wound gently. "It doesn't appear to be too bad, but it's still oozing. I'll wipe it with my kerchief. I'd fetch water if I dared venture upright on deck but wait while I make you more comfortable and mop up this mess."

He was tender as any woman as he wiped her body clean of slime and sweat, dabbing the cut on her head very carefully. It seemed that she had rid herself now of the food in her stomach or else she was already becoming accustomed to the movements of the ship, for she wasn't sick again, but her head ached and she felt deathly cold, shivering under his ministrations. From somewhere he had managed to find another blanket, rank-smelling of unwashed fleeces and tar, but cleaner than either her own cloak or the blanket from her bundle. Both were now unbearably soiled by vomit. The rough texture of coarse wool against her naked, chilled flesh was comforting as she huddled beneath it, gritting her teeth as the ship plowed relentlessly on. She was still terribly afraid, but she struggled to hide her panic from her husband.

Lord Gerard moved cautiously about the cabin and she whispered, "Are the others all safe, My Lord? Where are they?"

"Clinging together for dear life forward on deck. The boy, Piers, is greener than you are, and our Simon looks little better, but they are all safe enough and the King is in excellent spirits now we are on our way to freedom."

He came back to the bunk, stooped and touched her cheek. "You're still very cold."

"I'm — I'm frightened," she admitted. "Think what it would be like to drown in that grey waste of water."

"Hush, there is no great danger. It's miserable for landlubbers like us, but our captain would not have put to sea had he thought there any likelihood of risking this ship of his." He laughed grimly. "To hear him talk, you'd think this hulk more precious than rubies, so it is, to him."

"Is the King — not sick too?"

"He won't admit it, but I think he feels no more comfortable than the rest of us. So far he and young Gloucester have managed to keep a hold on their stomachs and save their dignity." He chuckled.

Elinor gave another moan as the vessel shook from bows to stern and it seemed that the very timbers would split apart under the fierce buffeting of the winds against its sides. She stuffed her knuckles hard against her lips to prevent herself crying out. Lord Gerard would think her poor spirited indeed.

"Elinor, my poor love." He was lying beside her in the confined space of the bunk, holding her close to his heart. "Come, let me warm you." His arm cradled her waist, straining her ever closer, gentling her as he would a frightened animal. He was again, the gentle, considerate courtier who had wooed her so tenderly, a lifetime ago, it seemed to her, in the garden at Beckwith. His lips brushed her tangled, sweat-soaked hair, then moved softly to her throat and the soft white coldness of her breast. She clung to him tightly, giving little whispered sobs of fear which gradually quietened. Her body arched against his. He had hurriedly stripped himself before stretching out beside her and the warmth of his thighs scorched her.

Suddenly, miraculously, she felt herself free of this heaving, leaking colander, aloft somewhere, high, safe, protected. She relaxed utterly in his hold, surrendering herself as she had not dared to do in their marriage chamber at Grantham. He murmured her name, whispering soft endearments, waiting, as he had that first time, until she was ready to receive him. There was no pain, only a release, an ecstasy of joy, and afterwards a supreme experience of well-being, unconditional trust in him and his ability to keep her safe. She lay cuddled against him, cocooned in warmth and bliss until her eyes closed and she no longer cared that the ship continued to blunder on across the turbulent North Sea.

She woke to find pale golden sunbeams in play across the coarse brown weave of the blanket which covered her. The ship was still moving clumsily beneath them but the convulsive heaving and wallowing had ceased. The mountainous grey waves had subsided into greyish green rolling hills.

Lord Gerard was struggling to tie his points. Elinor sat up shivering, for it was still cold.

"The worst is over." He smiled down at her. "You're feeling better?"

She managed a watery smile in reply.

"Good. I'll get up on deck and find out if last night's gale blew us much off course. If not, we cannot be far off the Dutch coast. Are you hungry?"

She shook her head ruefully.

He grinned. "You will be the moment your feet touch dry land again. Come and dress now. Put on your warm green gown. I'll lace you up the back. Don't I always prove myself an excellent tiring maid?" He shook his head at her puzzled air.

"The ship's master knows who you are. It was only in the port that we needed to keep up that deception."

She was delighted by the touch of his hands on her body and, as he completed his task, he stooped and kissed the nape of her neck, so that a sudden thrill passed through her.

"Turn round and face me."

She obeyed him, blushing.

He reached up and cupped her chin in his hands.

"That's my brave wench. You're still a mite pale and green about the gills but practically yourself again. How is the wound on your head? Let me feel."

She bent her head and his fingers gently probed the cut through the soft waves of her hair. "It appears to have stopped bleeding. Does that hurt badly?"

She winced under the gentle pressure of his fingers but shook her head.

"You deserve a reward, for your endurance, say?"

She was unaccustomedly shy and struck dumb before him. To what was he referring, her endurance of the storm's terrors, or his love-making?

His fingers were cool about her throat and she gave a little gasp as, glancing down, in the watery sunlight which filtered greenly through the grimy ox-horn of the porthole, she saw that he had again placed about her neck the enamelled necklace.

Before she could recover her wits sufficiently to thank him, he had left the cabin.

She sank down upon the bunk, her thoughts in chaos. She was afraid of this man, had called him her enemy to his face, yet, last night, in the worst transport of her fear, she had turned to him for comfort and reassurance. He had not failed her. She had slept in his arms, replete with love and an utter sense of wellbeing.

Could it be that despite all that had happened she loved him? Or had her response to him last night been purely her body's answer to her most dire need?

Despite his contempt for the trick she still believed she had played on him with her father's connivance, he had been kind, loving.

And he had returned to her her

mother's gift, knowing how greatly she prized it.

She sighed. What had the future in store for her when this ship landed them all upon Dutch soil?

7

ELINOR found the city of Bruges both bewildering and fascinating. Their party had entered by one of the eight gates the city boasted.

At Alkmaar Edward of York had been welcomed by the governor of Holland, Lord Gruthuyse, formerly Duke Charles of Burgundy's ambassador to the English Court. Since the duke was married to King Edward's sister, Margaret, it was only to be expected that the Yorkist party would be offered a refuge in his territory. The bedraggled little company was received graciously. They had all stumbled ashore, more dead than alive after the rigours of that hideous crossing, exhausted, wet and hungry, most of them suffering from the aftermath of sea sickness. Immediately horses and supplies were provided, as well as accommodation overnight.

Elinor retired thankfully to her spotless little chamber with its benison of clean sheets, and a bed warmed by heated bricks, while the inn wench chattered in her unintelligible tongue. Lord Gerard did not join her until it was almost dawn and she concluded that he had been closeted with the King's council in exile. It was vital for Yorkist interests that the duke be persuaded to provide money for the buying and outfitting of ships if a successful attempt was to be made to regain control of the English throne.

Now as she rode by his side she looked eagerly back at the gigantic enclosing walls to Burgundy's greatest trading city. Behind her she glimpsed the windmills Simon Radbourne had promised her she would find in Flanders. There they stood, tall and gaunt, erected on the rising ground near the new fortifications. Not only was this city protected by the usual method of erecting tall, well-guarded walls, but also by huge ditches and ramparts.

Soon they were riding through the principal streets towards the ducal palace. Elinor had never visited a town before. She had often dreamed of accompanying her father to Doncaster or York but this town was overwhelming in its wealth of splendid churches and buildings, its paved streets near the famous Waterhalle, which Simon Radbourne pointed out to her, the shops and offices of the Hanseatic League, that most powerful organization of merchants which controlled much of the commerce in Northern Europe.

Lord Gerard was faintly amused by her expression of wonder.

"Yes, it's an amazing city. I remember I sat and stared like a witless child when I first came here in attendance on My Lord Earl of Warwick on one of his visits to the Duchess Margaret. You'll hear all tongues spoken in these streets, German, French, English, Danish, even Portuguese, Spanish and Italian. The Hanse merchants deal in wool, silver, metals, silks, dyes from Hungary, wine from Gascony, cloth from the length and breadth of Flanders. Duke Charles can well afford to make substantial contributions to our cause."

Elinor had expected noise and confusion, even the unpleasant stinks from the kennels running the length of the streets, but she could have imagined nothing on so grand a scale. The bustle and flurry was continuous, the racket of iron wheels over cobbles as bales and packages were conveyed to the canals, the raucous cries of apprentices and gabble of foreign merchants. Everything caught her attention and held her wrapt in wonder so that Lord Gerard was forced to call to her to watch where she rode.

Ruefully she reined in, narrowly missing a beggar in tattered rags who sat on the pavement's end, whining his lament to passers-by to be generous to a poor blind man in his misfortune. Since he spoke in the French tongue Elinor could catch the gist of it for Father John had taught her the language.

The cavalcade ahead slowed and Lord Gerard leaned to catch at Elinor's bridle rein. Now they passed through ornamented iron gates into a vast court where liveried grooms ran to their assistance. From nearby came the noise of the armourer's hammer as he repaired the mail and weapons of the duke's household knights, the baying of hounds, fluttering of wings and rasping cries of hawks in the mews.

Open-mouthed with wonder, Elinor found herself brushed close to her husband, as the King's party was ceremonially greeted by the duke's steward, his white wand of office brandished high, and they were escorted into the palace.

Lord Gerard, with the other nobles, was kept cooling his heels within the high raftered hall, larger and far more imposing than the one at Beckwith and seemingly crowded with notaries, clerks and clerics in their sombre black, as well as gorgeously clad courtiers and pages. Elinor strained back against the wall on the bench where Lord Gerard had seated her, ashamed of her plain green gown now sadly dust-stained and muddied at the hem.

At length they were escorted by a twinkling-eyed young page to the apartment put at their disposal. Elinor exclaimed at the splendour of the tapestries and carpet. Lord Gerard grunted approvingly.

"Well, it seems we are highly honoured. I had thought we would have had to find our own lodgings, and, as you know, my purse is almost empty. Our men will be accommodated in the guardrooms and Simon can sleep in the hall."

Elinor lowered herself carefully upon the splendidly covered bed with its embroidered silk spread. She was anxious to avoid marking it with her travel-stained gown.

"Will we — be expected to attend the duke and duchess?" The thought terrified her, and she had no suitable gown in which to be presented.

"Certainly we shall eat in the great hall." Lord Gerard frowned. "I think you will find that Meg Tyrell provided a change of clothes for you in the supply baggage." At her expression of horror he added, "We can't be expected to shine amongst these peacocks in Duke Charles's retinue."

"I am unused to mixing with the nobility," she faltered.

"Nonsense, you have been presented to His Grace and have managed to entertain Lord Hastings."

She glanced at him sharply. It was a decided rebuke and undeserved, since she had not once encouraged the Lord Chamberlain's attentions and had taken every possible opportunity to avoid them.

Already Simon Radbourne was supervising the disposal of their baggage.

Lord Gerard bawled in French for hot water, towels and wine to be brought. There was a scurry to obey him. Illclad or not, this was not a man to be ignored with impunity.

"I'll take myself off to Lord Hastings's apartment." He looked imperiously at one of the Flemish girls who was toiling up the stair to their chamber, burdened with a heavy copper ewer of hot water. "Get this girl to help you wash and change."

The maid appeared willing enough and though she understood few French words Elinor managed to convey to her requirements by smiles and gestures. She washed and stripped. It was the first time she had experienced such luxury since her marriage night in the Tyrell household.

To her delight she discovered that Meg Tyrell had somehow achieved a miracle in repairing her sadly torn white velvet gown and also provided her with a new cap and silk gauze veil. The Flemish girl was plainly impressed by the gown's splendour and, viewing herself in My Lord's iron travelling mirror, Elinor was somewhat reassured about her appearance and fitness to appear in the great hall with the other courtiers, as she waited for her husband to escort her.

Lord Gerard had once more attired himself in his blue velvet doublet which Simon had managed to brush and press, and though neither of them wore jewels or gold chains, with the exception of Elinor's treasured necklace, they made an imposing couple when, later, they swept into the great hall.

Already the vast place was packed with gorgeously dressed courtiers though the high table, under the cloth of estate, was not yet tenanted. A black-clad steward, flaunting a magnificent gold chain and gold-tipped ivory wand of office, received Lord and Lady Cranley and escorted them to their place at table well above the salt.

Lord Gerard scowled when he saw that Lord Hastings had been placed on Elinor's right. The man's eyes narrowed appreciatively at sight of her in Court attire, the broad gold leather belt encircling her waist tightly and revealing the glory of her youthful breasts under the expert cutting of the soft white cloth.

Elinor ate and drank of the rich dishes and wines, bemused, in a golden daze. When the duke and duchess entered and took their places with their princely guests, Elinor could not have believed such grandeur possible outside the pages of one of her French romances. King Edward positively glittered in a doublet of scarlet and cloth of gold while his gold chain with its uncut rubies and pearls glimmered sombrely on his chest. Surely the duchess had provided such fine borrowed plumes for her brothers! Beside his magnificently clad brother, the youthful Duke of Gloucester looked slight and pale in a doublet of olive green velvet which did nothing to enhance the paleness of his complexion or compliment his plainly cut dark hair, yet his jewels were no less regal. An emerald glowed darkly in his velvet cap and another was suspended from the massive gold chain which sat heavily upon his youthfully narrow shoulders. Duke Charles of Burgundy, their host, was clad in black and silver while the duchess bloomed at his side in carmine samite edged with some costly dark fur.

Hastings smiled mirthlessly at the sight of the glittering array on the high table. "It seems our worthy Charles has been persuaded to at least make a show of good feeling. How will it prove when he is asked to contribute hard coin for our enterprise?"

Lord Gerard shrugged. "The Duchess Margaret can surely be relied upon to make her husband see the necessity. It should delight the duke to flout Louis of France who is playing host to Margaret of Anjou just now, at Amboise."

Hastings sipped his wine thoughtfully. "Ah, but the Duchess Margaret is known to dote upon George too and he is ranged with Warwick and the Lancastrian party."

"But for how long?" Lord Gerard replied lightly, as he raised his wine cup in a salute to his King, who bowed from his seat beside the Duke of Burgundy.

"So you still believe George of Clarence can be persuaded to return to his allegiance?"

"By the right person and for the right reasons."

★ ★ ★

Elinor was relieved at last to withdraw to their chamber. As the Flemish maid was not in evidence Lord Gerard helped her to unlace her gown and when she stood in her shift he drew her close and cupped her breasts in his hands.

"You looked very lovely tonight, I'm a fortunate man."

She was alarmed by the thickness of his voice. He had drunk deep during the meal. That was excusable. The good wine had relaxed him after the stresses and strains of the journey. He was regarding her owlishly and she tried to break from him and reach the bed. He continued to hold her, tightening his grip on her wrist.

"I see My Lord Hastings was very much aware of your beauty. The fellow scarce took his eyes from you. Heed my warnings. Don't allow yourself to be caught with him alone." He gave a harshly yelped laugh. "The man's a true lecher, experienced. I know, I've been with him on his adventures too often not to know the score."

It was pointless to explain that she had no liking for the handsome Lord Chamberlain. Lord Gerard was too far gone in wine. She said nervously, "He would not dare insult me, knowing me to be your bride — "

"That wouldn't stop him. He's the King's favourite, companion in whoring. They've been known to share a mistress or two in their time. Watch yourself with both of them."

He released her and stumbled towards a joint stool where he hastily slung his gilded leather sword belt and dagger sheath.

She stayed by the bed, shivering incontrollably. His fingers had bitten cruelly into the flesh of her upper arms and then her wrist. His suspicions disturbed her. How could he believe, even when in his cups, that she would play the wanton with any Yorkist, even the King himself?

He undressed hurriedly, climbed into bed and drew back the covering invitingly.

In order to divert his attention from Lord Hastings's apparent interest in her, she sought desperately for another subject.

"The King seemed cheerful and confident but I thought the Duke of Gloucester was unaccountably withdrawn and troubled. Didn't you think so?"

"Dickon?" Lord Gerard leaned back against the pillows, his head resting upon his clasped hands. "Poor Dickon. He's suffering the pangs of unfulfilled love."

"Dickon?"

"Young Gloucester. He loves his cousin, Lady Anne Neville. They were childhood friends. She was close to him even when he was training for knighthood at Middleham. It was his dearest hope that Lady Anne would be given to him in marriage."

Elinor knew that the younger of the Kingmaker's daughters had been wed to the Lancastrian Prince of Wales, doubtless to further her father's ambitions.

She could believe completely in Richard's loyalty to his brother. He was entirely honourable. How different had been his chivalrous attitude to her throughout their journey to that of both the King and the Lord Chamberlain. Both had made no secret of the fact that they found her attractive, despite the presence of her lord. Her cheeks burned at the thought. Doubtless her situation, her arrival amongst them without the services of maid or nurse, had left her open to some discourtesy. It would be difficult, if not impossible, for Lord Gerard to call his sovereign to task for his lack of chivalry towards her.

Lord Gerard's voice called to her sleepily, "Come, sweetheart, you must be wearied to the bone."

As he clasped her in his arms, Elinor's thoughts winged to Duke Richard's love, the Lady Anne. Was she trapped within the web of intrigue? Did she, too, lie trembling by her young lord's side, waiting apprehensively for his caresses as, she, Elinor, was doing now?

As on their wedding night her husband sat up and drew back the bedcovers to gaze on her.

"You are so very beautiful." His voice was low, his breath wine-fumed, fanning her cheek. "And growing daily more so. These harrowing experiences of the last few days have served only to spur my admiration for you. The other night, on the ship, I felt you were beginning to accept your situation, to turn to me, as I hoped. Was it so, Elinor, or were you merely too frightened and sick to be aware of what you did?"

She swallowed nervously. "I — I was grateful for your loving care of me, My Lord."

"Grateful? Is that all?" He gave a sharp bark of laughter, harsh, jarring at her senses. "So, I'm still married to an icemaiden who'll melt only for some man who bears a Lancastrian device on his banner? Your cousin, perhaps, Montecute's faithful hound?"

His mocking words again conjured up for her the sight of Reginald lying mortally injured or slain in the mud of the courtyard at Beckwith. She shuddered and turned instinctively from his slayer.

The movement, slight as it was, infuriated Lord Gerard.

He caught her to him, his fingers forcing hard into the small of her back. "I can *make* you love me, respond to me. I'll prove it tonight on your body."

192

She felt the full weight of him and the hot, scorching touch of his thigh against hers as he bore her backwards against the pillows. Horrified by the wild passion she sensed she'd aroused in him, she fought doggedly. His arms were like steel bands, forcing her to submit and she thrashed beneath him helplessly, her face twisting vainly from side to side to avoid his kisses. His lips found and held hers despite her frantic efforts, bruising them, smothering her in that fierce heat of desire which made her moan, partly with a matching and incomprehensible longing, and partly with sheer terror.

Suddenly he pulled himself free with a muttered oath and she struggled up, sobbing, clutching at the sheets to cover her nakedness.

Head averted, he said hoarsely, "Forgive me, sweetheart, too much wine. I'd not meant to force you, let alone terrify you half out of your wits. It's too soon to have you surrender as I wish you to. Tonight, in the great hall, I saw those other men looking at you. Naked desire was there plain for all to read and it raised the devil in me. Your reaction when I spoke of that cousin of yours revealed that there was more between you than cousinly affection."

"No," she said sharply. "You're wrong. Reginald was a good friend as well as a kinsman. We played together as children. Lately, since he entered My Lord Montecute's service, I have seen little of him. Yet you murdered him. I cannot forgive or forget that."

"*Murdered* him?" Again that half strangled laugh. "The man betrays me, seeks my life. I defend myself with cold steel against cold steel and you accuse me of murder? You've much to learn about the hard facts of war, my wife. In all events I doubt if the fellow is dead."

She gazed at him wonderingly and his brows drew together in a black scowl. "I read in your eyes that the truth of your feelings for the man belies your words to me just now."

"You wrong me," she said stiffly through bruised lips. "I would pray for the life of any man, Lancastrian or Yorkist, and Reginald is my kinsman."

"See that he remains nothing more to you," Lord Gerard snarled. "If I ever have cause to suspect otherwise, I'll make very sure I complete the work I began at Beckwith."

She turned from him. There was a cold ferocity to his tone which she could not doubt.

Impatiently he put back the covers and stood up. "I think it wiser if I sleep in the hall tonight. There is too much hatred between us for me to take you as considerately as you have come to expect." The words were almost a sneer. "And take you I must if I remain near you much longer."

Elinor watched fearfully as he tugged on his clothes and slammed out of the chamber, then she eased her bruised body back into a more comfortable position. She *should* be feeling profound relief at his going. Why was it she felt nothing but a sense of bitter frustration?

Lord Gerard appeared his normal, courteous self next morning when he presented himself in her chamber to escort her to breakfast in the great hall. Certainly his manner was still coolly distant and his paleness and angry frown gave her to believe that he had, as he had claimed, drunk too deeply at the previous evening's feasting.

As they concluded the meal, he said, "I've been ordered to present you to the Duchess Margaret. Apparently she was greatly intrigued by the tale of your adventures and wishes to see you."

Elinor glanced at him timidly. She had once more dressed in her plain green gown which the Flemish serving wench had cleaned and pressed for her. It was more befitting a merchant's wife than a Court lady. "I — I have nothing suitable in which to appear before Her Grace. Should I change into the white velvet gown?"

His blue eyes surveyed her coolly. "No, this one will do. The duchess knows full well that all of us landed here without baggage." He paused and looked at her keenly. "I doubt if she is aware, however, of the full details concerning *your* arrival."

"You mean she does not know I was abducted from my father's house against my will?"

He smiled grimly, amused by her

defiant tone. "Exactly, and I would prefer that she should not know."

"Then you do not think that the King has told her?"

"I did not see fit to inform His Grace that I pressed you to marry me."

She gave a great gasp of breath. "Then he — they all — believe that I was so besotted with love that I eloped against my father's wishes."

"Something of the sort."

"But why," she said furiously, "did you allow him to continue to believe such a thing?"

He shrugged as he drained his wine cup. "For your own safety I deemed it wiser that no one should know how I was tricked at Beckwith — and with your connivance."

She was on the point of protesting her innocence, then thought better of it. Let him think what he wished. It rankled that her own father had used her so, worse still, that Lord Gerard had used her even more ruthlessly as hostage.

★ ★ ★

She curtseyed low when presented to the Duchess Margaret in her private chamber. The King's sister resembled him. She had that fair Neville bloom, yet there was something in the duchess's features, a sensitivity, a directness in the steady gaze of those grey-green eyes that reminded Elinor of her younger brother, Richard of Gloucester, too.

Elinor was ruefully aware of her own shabbiness when she saw how splendidly the duchess was dressed today in a gown of peacock blue samite trimmed with vair. Even the tall Burgundian steeple cap with its froth of white veiling falling completely to the floor could not disguise that Queenly height.

"Lady Cranley, I am pleased to welcome you to my Court. Please, sit close to me. I wish to hear all the news of England first-hand, my brothers talk only of war and politics."

She waved to Lord Gerard in imperious dismissal.

"Pray, go and find my brother, the Lord Edward, sir, and leave me to talk with your lady."

Lord Gerard made her a low bow and

withdrew. The duchess signalled for her attendant ladies to continue their work at a huge tapestry frame some distance from them and drew Elinor down to the padded stool near her chair.

"Now, child, tell me how you managed to endure the discomforts of the journey. Some of the dangers I have heard from Dickon but I would hear the truth from you. Men understand so little of what a woman suffers when she forsakes her family and home." Her gusty sigh brought forth a pitying response from Elinor. Great as her position was, the Duchess Margaret was merely another unfortunate pawn in the game of power played by her male relations. Keeping her account of her abduction purposefully vague, Elinor proceeded to tell what had befallen the company since leaving the Tyrell house in Lincolnshire.

"Then you were present when my brothers' party was set upon near Kings Lynn. Did you witness something of the killings?"

"Yes, Your Grace." Elinor's voice trembled and the other woman reached out and took her hand.

"My dear, how much you must love that rogue of a husband of yours. Dickon tells me your father is the Marquess of Montecute's man."

"He is, Your Grace," Elinor replied uneasily.

The Duchess clucked her tongue against her teeth in sympathy. "And who would suspect that the man would turn traitor? So you are now in the position of having deserted your home without adequate baggage. Don't distress yourself. We can soon remedy that. I shall be delighted for you to attend me during your stay in Bruges and it will be my pleasure to provide you with a wardrobe in keeping with your position at Court."

"Your Grace, I am deeply honoured, but I could not accept — "

"Of course you will accept." The duchess's tone 'was suddenly haughty, then she dispelled its coldness by giving a warm little laugh. "I have told you, it will delight me to hear the English tongue spoken again in my presence. Did you bring a maid? No, I imagine that wasn't possible. No matter, one will be provided."

"One of the girls who has served me since we arrived has been most willing and helpful, Your Grace."

"Good, then we shall release her to wait on you alone."

The duchess questioned Elinor about her family. Hesitantly, she confessed that life at Beckwith had been secluded and uneventful until the arrival of Lord Gerard Cranley on the scene.

"I miss England so," the duchess confided, "the cold and the rain and the wonderful greenness everywhere, especially in the Dales."

* * *

The duchess was as good as her word. That same afternoon a chest was delivered to Lord Cranley's apartment which Elinor found to contain six gowns, probably drawn from the duchess's own wardrobe, for they were all of the finest quality.

Two were in velvet for the colder months ahead, one soft brown, trimmed with some light coloured fur, the other in deep blue. The second two were in

201

heavy brocade. One in crimson and silver, the second was green woven with gold thread. The two remaining gowns were of lighter silk and could be worn as the weather became warmer, one a soft shell pink which enhanced Elinor's fresh complexion and the one which pleased her most of all, in yellow, the soft, delicate yellow of primroses.

The young Flemish maid, Beatrix, proved an excellent needlewoman and spent most of the time she was not attending her mistress in taking in and adjusting the fine new gowns and fashioning veils and head-dresses to complement them.

During the day, Elinor saw little of her husband while she waited personal attendance upon the Duchess Margaret. Simon informed her that Lord Gerard was busied with My Lord of Gloucester making a tally of what men and supplies the King would require to furnish his fleet for the future invasion of England. Though Duke Charles had not as yet given his sanction to the venture, or promised monetary support, the duchess told Elinor she was confident that sooner or later she would persuade her husband to back her brother.

The Burgundian Court was agog with the news from England. On 6 October, the Earl of Warwick, with many attendant English nobles, had entered London. Edward's Queen, Elizabeth, had retreated to the sanctuary of Westminster with her daughters. She was already big with the King's child. Lord Hastings openly sneered at the news that poor, mad King Harry had been paraded through the city streets, blinking in the light after his long imprisonment in the Tower, and scarcely aware of what was happening.

"It's as well that the earl ordered his squires to bathe him, else he'd stink like a midden. It's well known he doesn't even take care of his person."

Elinor wondered if her father's hopes of advancement had borne fruit now that the Marquess of Montecute would rise high in the kingdom with his other, powerful kinsmen.

Despite all the bad news about the success of their enemies, the King's party was cheered by the announcement of the birth of a baby prince to the Queen in sanctuary on 2 November. The exiled Yorkists toasted the child joyfully.

Christmas was celebrated splendidly at the ducal palace and Elinor was positively bemused by the reckless abandon and sheer extravagance of the feasting. The music especially delighted her, composed in honour of the duchess, for Margaret was a renowned patroness of the arts, but Elinor was less impressed by the drunken revelry and the frolics devised by the chosen Lord of Misrule, most of them bawdy, tasteless and sometimes alarming to a girl brought up in the strict seclusion of a Yorkshire manor. Once she caught an expression akin to her own disgust mirrored on the youthful features of Duke Richard of Gloucester as he watched his brother cavorting with Hastings, flushed scarlet with wine and the exertions of the dance.

Louis of France unequivocally declared war on Burgundy in the New Year even before the twelve days of Christmas feasting were concluded. Black with thunderous rage, Duke Charles swore an oath to put fifty thousand crowns at Edward's disposal for the hire of ships and the recruitment of Flemish gunners. So the enterprise would soon be launched. Elinor fretted in private. What would happen to her when Lord Gerard embarked for England in the King's company? Would he take her with him, or leave her behind in the duchess's service until the matter was decided?

During the bitterly cold days of January, Elinor saw less and less of her husband, as he spent every waking moment in helping to supervize and assemble Edward's battle fleet. At night he would come exhausted to bed though, on those occasions when he required submission of her, Elinor dutifully performed her wifely duties without protest.

Throughout these last hectic months she had undergone a period of bewildering adjustment. She had only to see her own face in the mirror or reflected in men's admiring eyes to know that her beauty had matured magnificently. Her fashionable Court gowns now revealed the full splendour of her woman's body, the slim proud posture, the glory of those firm young limbs, no longer lanky or colt like, subtly revealed beneath the rich silks and velvets. Her eyes were haunted, liquid gold and amber, in which men read the wealth of her hidden desires and longings.

Simon Radbourne worshipped her. She could not be unaware of the fact, though she made a conscious effort to allow herself few occasions to be alone with him. Hastings was quite another matter. He laid deliberate siege to her and it became a considerable embarrassment that whenever she turned a corner of the palace corridor, the handsome chamberlain would be somewhere close, solicitously anxious to offer her gallant attentions and fulsome flattery.

Her attitude towards her husband continued to be both perplexing and disturbing. Now that he had so little time for her, she found herself often lonely, even when surrounded by Burgundian nobles and her companion ladies who waited attendance with her upon the duchess. She found her French sufficient to allow her to converse with them freely and they soon accepted her, but she felt she had little in common with any of them and she feared Lord Gerard's wrath if she were seen to be openly welcoming the attentions of the English, Yorkist nobles.

Her eyes yearned for sight of him and that strange mixture of delight and fear which surged through her at his entrance to their bed-chamber filled her thoughts to the exclusion of all else — except her longing to receive news of her kinsmen in England.

It was the duchess who brought her the news she was most anxious to hear. She was seated close to Margaret one morning sorting through skeins of embroidery wool for the tapestry frame when the duchess said softly in English, "I imagine you have not heard that your cousin, Reginald Beckwith, is at present at King Louis's Court at Amboise in attendance upon Queen Margaret."

Elinor's chin jerked in spite of herself, betraying her delight at the news and her eagerness for more information.

"There is a fondness between you?"

The duchess's question was searching and her grey eyes curious, but Elinor did not fear her mistress's anger nor a betrayal of her trust to Lord Gerard.

"We *were* close, as children," she admitted, cautiously. "He — he was badly injured in Lord Gerard's escape from the manor and I feared him dead. Your Grace, you are certain that this news is reliable?" She coloured hotly at her temerity in questioning the duchess so roundly.

"Oh, the information is from a reliable source, a trusted spy in my husband's service. He is closeted with Duke Charles and my brother Edward at this very moment."

"And this man, he — he will return eventually to Amboise?"

"I imagine so." The duchess regarded her closely and Elinor again felt the hot blood stain her cheeks, then Margaret said mildly, "I imagine it would also be possible for you to confide some personal message to the man, it could do no harm, provided it was just that, a personal message to reassure your family about your health and happiness. Your husband's squire, Radbourne, could doubtless be trusted to help you."

"Your Grace would not consider such behaviour disloyal?"

"My dear, we women must retain some control over our natural family desires. The behaviour of my brother George in deserting Edward has hurt me deeply but it cannot destroy the affection I have for him, nor does it prevent me trying to communicate with him. I trust you with my confidence."

Elinor nodded, tears pricking at her lashes. How kind the duchess had proved to her, and truly understanding.

Back within her own chamber, she pondered for hours over the risk to them all of following the duchess's suggestion. Would the spy refuse to carry a letter for her to Reginald and could he be trusted not to betray her to her husband? Dared she approach him personally? No, that would be most unwise. The duchess had put her finger squarely on the one man at her disposal who might agree to bribe the French spy for her. Simon Radbourne. He would do anything for her. But could she ask it of him? Suppose Lord Gerard was to discover the truth? Her cheeks paled as she recalled his dire threat. "If

I find this man is any more to you than kinsman I will take steps to complete the work I began at Beckwith." Feeling as he did about Reginald, his fury would know no bounds if it were to come to his ears that Elinor had tried to communicate with her cousin. Yet she needed to assure her father that she was well, not unhappy, and, if humanly possible, receive from Amboise some news of Sir Thomas and all at Beckwith. There could be no possible harm in it. The duchess had said as much.

She rose and fetched the small wooden portable writing desk her husband had bought in the town, blessing Father John who had taught her to write, an accomplishment few girls of her age and position possessed. Thoughtfully she dipped her quill in the small ink bottle and began.

Lord Gerard was absent from Bruges. He'd ridden to Flushing with Lords Gloucester and Rivers. Work had begun on victualling the fleet and equipping the mercenary army. Elinor was attended by Simon Radbourne in the great hall and, as he held out the basin of rosewater for her to cleanse her greasy fingers at the close of the meal, she whispered to him that she wished to speak to him privately within her chamber.

He nodded, his fair face flushed with ill-concealed delight and the basin shook in his hands.

While she awaited him, Elinor suffered a sudden rush of conscience more strongly intensified when the squire presented himself. His eyes shone with his eagerness to do her some practical service. She motioned him to come close, after first ensuring that the door was firmly closed and that no one was hovering in the corridor within earshot.

"Simon," she said hesitantly playing with the fringe of her leathern girdle, "I wish to request a favour of you. Before I state what it is, I assure you that I shall be in no way displeased or hurt if you refuse me."

"Lady Elinor, you know that I can refuse you nothing." The words came out jerkily in a youthful rush. "I — I would die for you willingly."

She gave an embarrassed little laugh. "I hope I shall never involve you in so dangerous a mission, Simon. I — " She paused and looked away from him. "You understand how much I miss my home and family and, under the circumstances of my departure from Yorkshire . . . "

"I do, My Lady, and my heart bleeds that you should have suffered so at My Lord's hands." There, it was out, his outspoken criticism of his master.

"I cannot ask you to disobey your lord, Simon." She paused. "It has come to my notice that there is a man presently at Court who will soon be returning to France." She fidgeted nervously with the skirt of her gown. "I understand he is in close contact with Lancastrians at the Court of King Louis."

"Aye, My Lady. Raoul Dupont, a former barber to the Spider King, he is known to be a spy in Duke Charles' pay."

"I — I need to have news of my kinsmen, especially my cousin, Reginald Beckwith, who was injured, you remember. He is at Amboise in attendance on Queen Margaret." The rest came out in a sudden rush. "All I want is for this spy to deliver a letter to my cousin.

The contents are purely personal." She held out the unsealed parchment for him to examine. "You may read it, if you wish. I have merely informed my father of my position here and in particular of the kindness of the Duchess Margaret."

"I understand your need, My Lady." Simon looked steadily back at her, shaking his head at her offer to allow him to scrutinize the letter. "If you swear there is nothing in this message that could harm or compromise my master, I will find some way of bribing the Frenchman." His lips twisted wryly. "I have to confess that I have nothing of value to offer the man."

She hesitated then unclasped the enamelled necklace and gave it into his hands. "This is all I have in the world and I would not part with it but my need is desperate. It's of little value but it should be enough. The service is only a small one and involves no risk to the messenger."

Simon knelt and kissed the tips of her fingers. "Trust me to see to it, My Lady."

She called him back from the door. "Simon?"

"My Lady?"

"Take care. I would not have you incur My Lord's displeasure."

He gave a little fearful shudder and grinned back at her. "Nor would I, My Lady. Lord Gerard is a hard man to cross."

Her husband was absent from Bruges for several days. For once Elinor was glad of it.

Simon Radbourne presented himself to her next day and assured her that everything had been satisfactorarily concluded.

"The man, Dupont, made no objection, My Lady. You need not fear that he will blab of the matter. He left this morning for Amboise at first light."

"You were extremely — discreet?"

"Oh yes, My Lady. Have no fear of that."

He gazed at her adoringly but she was not afraid that he might expect more from her than her gratitude. By no look or gesture could she fault his behaviour over the next few days.

The duchess made no further reference to their conversation. Elinor wondered, privately, if the Frenchman was also carrying personal messages from Margaret to her errant brother, George of Clarence, advising him to return to his former allegiance.

Elinor was woken suddenly on the evening following Lord Gerard's fourth day of absence by the sounds of night arrivals. There was a clatter of hoofs in the courtyard below, a muffled shout for service, the flare of torchlight brought hastily by a sleepy groom illuminating her window. Beatrix, the Flemish girl who had slept on a truckle bed within her chamber since Lord Gerard's departure, struggled up drowsily as Elinor rose and, donning her nightrobe, went hurriedly to the window to look down into the courtyard. The girl had still little French or English and Elinor smiled at her reassuringly.

"It is perhaps Milord returning."

Beatrix understood the one word 'milord' and her face brightened. She was now fully awake and shrugged on her clothing.

Peering close to the opened casement, Elinor could just distinguish the murrey and blue livery of the Yorkist House although the colours were indistinct in the flickering torchglow. So Duke Richard had returned. Was Lord Gerard with him? She could not be sure for already the nobles had entered the palace.

Elinor shivered, even within the comforting warmth of her furred bedgown, another gift from the Duchess Margaret. Hastily she drew to the casement. The February air was bitter and there had been talk of a threatening snow fall all through the day. It had not yet materialized but the weather was certainly cold enough to warrant it.

Her chamber door was burst open unceremoniously and she drew in her breath at sight of Lord Gerard framed within the circle of light cast by her hurriedly kindled candle. He had obviously ridden hard, for his cloak and boots were caked with mud and his hose stained. His blue eyes glittered unnaturally and she saw at once that he was in an ice-cold fury. Her limbs trembled uncontrollably beneath the heavy brocade bed-gown. He knew! Yet how was that possible?

She moistened dry lips while she gazed

from him to the Flemish girl who stood waiting for his orders.

"Get out," he snapped.

The girl could be under no misapprehension as to his meaning. She shot Elinor an anxious glance, bobbed a hurried curtsey and scuttled into the corridor. Lord Gerard slammed the heavy door shut and advanced towards Elinor. She found herself unable to move a muscle, her limbs refusing to obey her. She was quivering as if stung by a whiplash when he suddenly opened his gloved hand and displayed to her horrified gaze the enamelled necklace.

She opened her mouth to attempt some explanation. The words would not come.

He continued to stare at her stonily.

"Well?" he said at last, and again she cowered back from the menace unleashed with the single word.

"Well, madam," he repeated brutally, "have you no word of gratitude for me? Again I return to you the relic you assured me so tearfully you treasured above all your possessions?"

She shook her head dumbly. Tears

pricked at her lashes and she jerked her head in a seeming gesture of defiance, at least she judged he would think it so.

He seated himself on the bed stool, leaning towards her, his riding whip swinging rhythmically, so that she found herself following its movements to and fro, as a rabbit trapped by that strange, hard stare of a stoat.

"I'm waiting, madam." The swing of the whip caught the hem of her bedgown and she stirred, whimpering uncertainly.

"Then if you'll not talk to me, I'll tell you how I came by it. A French spy of Duke Charles', Raoul Dupont, presented himself to the Duke of Gloucester just as we were returning from Flushing. He carried letters from the duchess to her brother. As the man sat with us at the inn I saw the relic around his throat. I could hardly mistake it. I know it too well, madam. Do you recall our conversation on the subject at Long Sutton? It seemed to me then that you were very anxious not to part with it so the inference I drew was that there had to be some extremely pressing reason for you to sell it now."

She swallowed as his mocking tone

continued. In her mind's eye she could imagine the scene at the inn. Lord Gerard's amazement, his chagrin, his natural desire that the duke should not know of his humiliation.

As if he read her thoughts he said quietly, almost pleasantly, "I think this is yours too."

Reaching within the embroidered purse which he wore suspended from his sword belt he withdrew her letter, its bloodlike seal now broken. Deliberately, carefully, he placed it upon the bed where her trapped gaze was drawn inexorably to it.

"Now it remains for me to deal with the person who communicated with the Frenchman." He smiled grimly, his expression belying the artificial pleasantness of his tone. As she caught the sound of booted feet in the corridor outside he said, "I think here is our man now."

Again the door was jerked open and Ralf Brent stood framed in the opening. He was gripping Simon Radbourne by the elbow. At Lord Gerard's nod the youth half fell, half stumbled into the room as the man-at-arms released his grip. Simon remained crouching, his eyes fearfully surveying his lord.

"Thank you, Ralf. I shall want you later. Remain on guard."

Brent closed the door and Lord Gerard turned his attention to his squire.

"Good evening, Simon. I trust Ralf did not wake you too ungently in summoning you to My Lady's chamber." His tone was even, courteous.

Simon scrambled awkwardly to his feet, his eyes deliberately avoiding contact with Elinor's. He was struggling to find the courage to outface his master.

"My Lord?" The greeting was half respectful, half defiant.

Apparently Lord Gerard considered it the latter, for his eyes glittered with blue fire and his whip snaked across the distance between them and cut the youth across the right cheek, leaving a livid wound from eyebrow to mouth. Simon uttered one shrill cry like a woman's scream and Elinor covered her ears in torment.

Almost immediately she realized her own responsibility to defend the squire. Forcing her frozen limbs to obey her, she launched herself between Simon

Radbourne and Lord Gerard.

"Don't do that." Her golden eyes flashed at him with a fire as deadly as his own. "You know well enough none of this is Simon's fault. I begged him to bribe the Frenchman for me."

Simon put up his hand to the wound wonderingly and bright blood dripped through his fingers and splashed onto the brave splendour of his damask doublet.

"I don't doubt that for a moment. Though Dupont was not aware of the fellow's name, his description was unmistakable, not that I needed any description. I'd already drawn my own conclusions. Who else but Simon Radbourne could be persuaded to commit treason for you? Do you think I have been entirely blind to the moonstruck glances of love my squire has been giving you?"

Simon had found his voice and his courage. His head was thrown back proudly as he faced his tormentor, his hand still vainly trying to staunch the bleeding which poured from the fearsome gash.

"My Lady is innocent of any impropriety, My Lord," he said hoarsely. "I did the service willingly and — and without hope of reward."

"Ah." The single syllable was hissed out through gritted teeth.

"And now you have read my letter," Elinor put in sharply, her fury aroused by his deliberate cruelty to Simon Radbourne, "you know that there was nothing in the message to my kinsman which could possibly be interpreted as treason to King Edward's cause. I made no mention of troops or movements or even of Duke Charles' attitude to His Grace."

"In my book there's nothing to choose between treason and disloyalty. That he showed disloyalty to me is clear enough, and he must take the consequences of his actions."

Elinor's heart missed a beat. "Consequences? What can you mean, My Lord? Simon has already been terribly punished. He will be fortunate if he does not carry the mark of that punishment with him all his life."

"The thought of that need not concern him, nor you madam, since there'll be little of that life left to him."

Her lips parted in a soundless gasp. He could not mean it. He would not doom his squire for a youthful indiscretion.

"We are at war, madam," Lord Gerard informed her coldly. "Radbourne is guilty, on his own admission, of treating with the enemy. His Grace the King must hear of it and, undoubtedly, the boy will hang. He's fortunate we are not in England so that he won't be called upon to pay the price of treason at Tyburn."

Elinor saw Simon's face had paled and her own heart lurched within her breast. Even the mention of such barbarity, the partial hanging, castration, the tearing of the heart from the living body, the butchering of the limbs, held her in the same grip of terror as the boy's.

She threw herself at Lord Gerard's feet, her fingers catching at his riding boot. "My Lord, you *cannot* do this. I spoke to my cousin only of myself and my need to hear news of my family. Not one word was said concerning His Grace's plans for the expedition to England, nor the numbers of his men and ships. Indeed I do not know them. Please, I swear to you it's true."

"And Simon read the letter, knew its contents, word by word?"

"No, My Lord, I did not. I trusted Lady Elinor."

"Naturally." Lord Gerard's lips curved in a sneer. "Ralf," he called imperiously and the soldier instantly opened the door.

Behind him Elinor could see the burly form of Lord Gerard's sergeant-at-arms.

"Master Radbourne is to be confined in the Duke's dungeons until the matter of his disloyalty to the Crown can be judged by His Grace, the King. See to it."

He moved to avoid her clutching fingers and Elinor crawled some paces after him. "Please, I beg you to listen to me. *I* am the one solely to blame, the one who must bear the punishment. You cannot allow Simon to suffer for my fault."

"Make no mistake, My Lady," her husband said coldly, "you won't escape punishment, either."

Simon straightened his shoulders and went with his guards without protest. He managed a glimmer of a smile in

224

Elinor's direction and her heart went out to him. She had judged him immature, even effeminate, she had been wrong. He accepted the threat of his horrifying fate bravely enough now.

She rose and staggered to the bed as the door closed on the men, her fingers gripping blindly at the silken coverings. She felt sick and deadly cold. *She* had doomed Simon Radbourne, for she'd little hope that he would escape from this coil with his life. Some instinct warned her also that to plead his cause further would infuriate Lord Gerard and that he would take steps to ensure that the King acceded to his wish to see the young squire hang.

She was not aware of her husband's nearness until she felt his hot breath fan her neck.

"And now, madam, we have a reckoning, you and I." The voice was thick, as if he had taken too much wine, yet she could sense no smell of it on his breath.

She tried to turn to face him but he was too quick for her. In a daze of horror, she felt and heard the stuff of her bedgown rip under his impatient fingers. She choked back the first scream as white hot pain caught her across her bared buttocks as he plied his riding whip with restrained but devastating effect, not so much to leave lasting scars but to deal excruciating pain. Again the agony scored through her, this time higher, across the small of her back, then again across her buttocks. This time she could not prevent herself from calling out. Again her fingers groped and caught at the silken cloth of the bed covering. It ripped as she thrust handfuls of the costly material tight across her mouth in an effort to prevent herself from screaming aloud, begging him for mercy. She would not give him the satisfaction of witnessing her shame and terror.

The pain stopped. She could hear Lord Gerard's hard breaths, as if he, too, was fighting to regain control of himself. There came a harsh slithering sound, as if he had hurled the whip from him, then he moved away from her.

She lay crying softly, weakly, face down on the bed, unwilling even to pull herself forward onto its length and uncertain if, even now, he had done with her. She dared not lift her head to see where he was or what he was doing and she stayed still, blindly listening, in an attempt to distinguish his movements within the shadows.

At last she managed to drag herself painfully onto the bed, drawing the torn coverlet around her as if it could afford her some protection. Now she could see his tall, unyielding form limned against the dark square of the window. The candle revealed fully the hard line of his shoulders, the sheer bulk of him, and she caught her breath in a fearful gasp. He was in a white heat of fury. He believed that yet again she had betrayed him to treat with the enemy.

He turned and came towards her, unbuckling his belt. She gave an instinctive whimper of fear. If he heard it, he paid no heed. She waited, her body tensed in an agony of suspense, while he undressed, throwing his discarded garments heedlessly to the floor. He loomed over her and she saw the hard glitter of his eyes, the bitter set of his mouth, the harsh jutting line of his chin.

He said no word but took her brutally. For the first time in their coupling he had not waited until she was ready but treated her with as little consideration as he would some whore from London's South Wark brothel. She was a chattel on which he slaked his lust, coldly, savagely.

She submitted at first, then when outrage took over from terror, she fought him wildly, doggedly. Without a single word he forced her to his will, his arms jerking her wrists high above her head, locked in a cruel grip, his free arm holding her body to his with a grasp of steel around her waist. She cried out then, pummelling at him when she managed to wrench one hand free, but he took absolutely no notice. The blows from her clenched fist raining hard on his body appeared to have no effect whatever. He simply gave a fierce, animal grunt and recaptured her hand again, holding it so tightly she feared her wrist bones would snap under the pressure of his fingers.

Her strength failed and she could do nothing but endure while her breath came like his in harsh, rasping gasps.

Suddenly it was over and he released her. She lay still, bruised and aching, while he settled himself immediately to sleep.

The hours stretched out to eternity. Unwilling to move a muscle which might rouse him once more, she continued to wait out the night in a cold sweat of torment. She was no longer dazed. Every nerve in her body screamed for attention and she suffered not only bodily but mentally. Her foolishness had doomed Simon Radbourne and after this display of Lord Gerard's chilling ferocity, she could not clutch at the faintest straw of hope. She could not save him. In this thought lay her most terrible punishment.

8

WHEN grey light filtered into the chamber, Elinor moved her cramped muscles cautiously as Lord Gerard stirred at her side. She bit down savagely upon her bottom lip, sweat dewing her forehead. As she moved the agony of her torn flesh sent waves of fire through her whole body. He woke quickly and completely as he always did, sitting up to gaze broodingly down at her. She felt herself cower beneath his fierce stare then, abruptly, he thrust aside the coverlet and stood up.

"I'll send your maid to you, madam," he said coldly. "It might be best if I send some excuse to the duchess for your failure to attend her this morning."

She nodded, slow tears forming, and she fought to prevent her lips trembling.

She watched him dress and longed to speak to him of Simon Radbourne, yet did not dare do so. He said nothing more and strode out of the chamber.

Beatrix looked alarmed and unhappy when she came to wait on her mistress. Elinor turned away from the pity she read in the Flemish girl's eyes. Embarrassed though she was, she gave herself to Beatrix's ministrations. Though peasant born and not expected ever to serve as a tiring maid, Beatrix's fingers were gentle as she bathed Elinor's hurts and she hastened off to the kitchen for warm water then she applied aromatic salve to the whip cuts and bruises. The first touch was fiery and painful but the salve eventually took the worst of the sting from the wounds and Elinor felt able to move more comfortably.

Peering at her reflection in the mirror Elinor was relieved to see that Lord Gerard's passion of the previous night had not revealed itself too obviously to the curious gaze of others, but her lips were bruised and swollen, her eyes dark-shadowed in a face drawn and pale with anxiety and suffering.

The Flemish girl spoke softly in her own language. Though understanding little Elinor was comforted by her gentle sympathy and at last fell asleep, reassured by the soothing presence of the girl's nearness and her promise to keep out intruders.

For the present she was safe. Lord Gerard would be unlikely to approach her for hours yet. He would be closeted with the King and the duke, as Gloucester reported what progress had been made in Flushing for the departure of the invasion fleet.

Just before supper time, Lord Gerard swept into the chamber and ordered Beatrix to dress her mistress for the feasting in the great hall.

Elinor stammered, "If you would excuse me this one time, My Lord — "

"No," he retorted brusquely. "Duke Charles has thrown this feast to honour King Edward. It would be the height of discourtesy and a source of gossip within the Court if my wife were not present at such a gathering."

Beatrix withdrew while he changed into a fine new doublet of murrey coloured velvet. The chain he wore across his breast with its enamelled suns and roses had been a gift from the Duchess Margaret in reward for his services to her brothers. He had accepted the costly thing reluctantly since, secretly, he believed the gold would have been spent more fittingly on the purchase of extra supplies for the English expedition, but it would have been both unwise and churlish to refuse.

Elinor watched him fearfully from her bed. How handsome he looked and so stern. Today that unnatural glitter had faded from his eyes and he had himself under rigid control but she knew he was still furiously angry. She dared not press further excuses upon him, but she dreaded her entry into the banquet hall upon his arm while her whole body inwardly flinched from his touch.

He withdrew, pausing briefly in the doorway to admit the waiting maid and to exhort her to hasten.

"We must take our places at table well before the royal party enters the hall."

Beatrix suggested the white velvet gown but Elinor shook her head. She was far too pale and drawn this evening to wear white. After hurried consideration, it was decided she should wear the brown velvet gown which enhanced the golden glow of her eyes. Its warm hue would soften the pallor of her complexion. Beatrix finally persuaded her to accept a touch of carmine on her cheeks and the soft veiling on the gold brocade cap shaded her face admirably. She scrutinized herself carefully again within the mirror. Only a close observer would note the increased pallor or the violet shading beneath her eyes. Lord Gerard would have no cause to criticize her appearance.

When Beatrix informed him, curtseying low, that Elinor was ready, he paused in the doorway, frowning, his fierce eyes taking in the rigidity of her tense-held form. His eyes narrowed, then his chin jerked in a brief gesture of approval, and he offered her his hand. Her fingers felt icy and trembled in his grasp. His were warm and strong as he led her out of the chamber.

The feasting was extravagant, even for this Court, and prolonged. Fearing her husband's eyes upon her, willing her silently to make no gesture or sign which could cause the slightest suspicion that all was not well between them, she ate and drank mechanically. The rich dishes appeared tasteless and had to be forced down. The wines coursed through her, giving her courage and determination to endure the lengthy ordeal. One part of her being longed for the feasting to end, so that she might return to the seclusion of her chamber, the other, dreaded that terrifying moment when she would be once more alone with her husband.

Dancing began and Elinor watched as the duchess, splendidly gowned as usual, took the floor with her handsome, elder brother. Laughing, he swirled her high into the air and she joined in the spirit of the dance, flushed and merry-eyed, clutching at his strong arms as he guided her through the lively steps to the sound of pipe and tabor.

Lord Gerard excused himself and left Elinor's side as a liveried page summoned him into the Duke of Gloucester's presence.

Elinor's head ached and she found it hard to sit still on the uncushioned wooden seat, despite the voluminous petticoats which partially padded the form for her. She blushed as she recalled her humiliating punishment, the weals Lord Gerard had raised on her back and buttocks still causing her acute pain. She sighed and momentarily closed her eyes to shut out the glare of candles and torches, the glitter and gold of the bejewelled and painted company. She was free of Lord Gerard's hated surveillance for some time, at least.

A familiarly pleasant but irritating voice roused her from her reverie and she looked up into the bold, handsome features of Lord Hastings.

"Forgive me, Lady Cranley, I see you were lost in your own thoughts. I trust you are not feeling unwell, you look very pale, tonight."

She was alarmed by his concern. Lord Gerard would be furious with her if it should come to his ears that Lord Hastings had guessed at the reason for her discomfort. Already rumours must be circulating through the palace. Lord Cranley's squire was in disgrace, lodged in a dungeon, My Lady had pleaded indisposition and not attended on the duchess today. Had their bitter words been overheard? She knew neither of the Cranley retainers would gossip but there had been other servants and pages within earshot.

She forced a smile.

"No, My Lord, I'm overcome by the noise and heat, that is all. I fear I've eaten and drunk too well."

He laughed heartily. "The duke has certainly spared no expense tonight, and rightly so. It is good that we Yorkists should celebrate the birth of our prince. Soon London will ring with the King's triumph."

Elinor made some non-committal remark. Privately she considered that it would not be so simple to achieve, this victory. Warwick had proved himself a formidable foe. Many good men would die before King Edward would take his place once more in St Edward's chair, if, indeed, he would ever do so.

Lord Hastings remained by her side and she was forced to make polite conversation. He was charming and solicitous, but she was always uneasy in his presence, knowing Lord Gerard's opinion of his character. The last thing she wanted was for her husband to return and find her in close talk with the Lord Chamberlain. Hastings's voice droned on and she allowed her attention to wander.

Where was Simon Radbourne being held? Forcibly she was struck by the thought that the squire would normally have been close by, refilling her wine cup, protecting her from unwelcome attentions such as this. Was he at this moment chained in some damp dungeon? Lord Gerard had commanded his men-at-arms to conduct the squire to the duke's dungeons. Worse, had he already been judged, condemned and executed? No, she was convinced that had that been the case, Lord Gerard would have taken pleasure in informing her of his fate. Yet it could not be long delayed. Simon would hang and she was powerless to prevent it.

She swayed in her seat, overcome by the horror of the situation. Lord Hastings rose instantly, his expression concerned.

"Lady Cranley, I see you are suffering in this overheated atmosphere. Won't you allow me to conduct you nearer to the door where the air is purer?"

She was feeling more and more unwell.

The flare of the torches swirled round her in some hellish dance. She would faint if she remained in the room. Nervously, she allowed him to lead her. Few noted their passage to the main door. The duke's good wines had already had their effects on the guests and many had subsided beneath the table. Couples openly fondled mawkishly and the dogs fought for the food scraps, when not being kicked from the trestles. They snarled and snapped at the irritated revellers.

Outside, within the duchess's garden, more torches flared in their iron sconces. Elinor was aware of the muffled giggling and chatter of those around her. Many were so far gone in wine that they'd thrown discretion to the winds and were finding heady delights in their lovers' arms. The chill air hit her squarely in the face and she checked in her walk, realizing the utter foolishness of venturing from the hall with her rakish escort.

"I must — thank you for your kindness, My Lord," she stammered awkwardly. "I am recovered now. I — we — should return to the hall — to our places."

His hand was over tight on her arm.

"There is no haste, My Lady. I noted earlier that Duke Richard had sent Lord Gerard from the hall on some errand. We shall be unobserved here, at least by anyone who would report on your conduct to your husband."

Elinor shivered and vainly attempted to pull free.

"My Lord," she said icily, "there will be nothing anyone could find to report to my husband. We will go in — now."

"Of course not," he returned, soothingly, "you were indisposed and, naturally, I conducted you from the hall in search of fresher air."

"And I have thanked you for that service. Now we will return."

He pressed in closer, reaching for her free hand, so that she was drawn close to his body. She struggled ineffectually, revolted by his easy assumption that she would welcome his attentions. William, Lord Hastings, was a flamboyantly attractive man. Elinor judged him to be in his late twenties, tall, well built, though shorter by several inches than his golden giant of a sovereign. His face was well-featured though fleshy, the mouth good humoured but somewhat slack. There was nothing about his presence to repulse her, his person was clean, and his hair well groomed and scented with bergamot, but she recoiled from the thought of that sensual mouth pressed upon hers. That he would kiss her, despite her objections, she was sure, and she struggled more frantically to free herself. His wine-scented breath came hot on her neck as he drew her inexorably close, one hand cupping her breast beneath the soft fur of her bodice trimming.

"Let me go, My Lord," she snapped, her voice purposefully low despite her undoubted anger. "Your behaviour is unknightly, an offence against your vows and your high rank."

"Indeed, My Lord, were you not far gone in wine, you would see the truth of Lady Cranley's assertions clearly enough for yourself."

The cold, youthful voice stopped Lord Hastings short in his tracks. Immediately he released his hold upon Elinor so that she stumbled and half fell. A steadying hand was placed at her disposal and she looked up into the grey, green eyes of

Duke Richard of Gloucester. The cool stare of them expressed contempt and Lord Hastings had the grace to look ashamed.

"You may leave Lady Cranley safely within my care, Lord Hastings, and return to the hall."

The Lord Chamberlain's dark eyes narrowed dangerously and, for one moment, Elinor thought he would object, but the younger man was imperiously dismissing him from his presence and the royal duke must be obeyed. Lord Hastings stood back, bowed low and took himself off. Elinor shakily noted the rigid set of his back and knew how humiliated and resentful he felt at that peremptory command from the younger man.

"Your Grace, I do not know how to thank you," she said huskily.

He frowned slightly then courteously put one hand round her waist to gently help her back towards the hall. She gave a sharp cry of pain, hastily suppressed, and he stopped and stared gravely down at her.

"Forgive me, Lady Elinor. I seem to have hurt you."

"No, no — it — it is nothing, Your Grace — I — "

"Lord Hastings did not harm you?"

"No, Your Grace, it was not Lord Hastings — " Too late Elinor heard herself blurting out the fatal words.

He continued to regard her steadily. At last he said quietly, "I think I should conduct you to your chamber, Lady Elinor. I take it you have no wish to return to the merrymaking in the hall?"

"No — but — my husband will be displeased if — "

"Lord Gerard will accept my opinion that you should rest, Lady Elinor. Of that I am quite certain."

Tears threatened to fall and further discomfort her. The duke's kindness and understanding had so disarmed her that she was guilty of betraying her dread of angering her husband.

"I — I would be grateful to withdraw, Your Grace, if such conduct would not be judged discourteous to His Grace, the King."

The tight held mouth relaxed into a smile. "I think His Grace will be unlikely to so much as note your departure, Lady

Elinor, nor, for that matter, mine."

Her legs were still shaking beneath her, but he walked slowly, his arm supporting her. At the door of her chamber he released his hold and stood back, bowing politely.

"I will inform Lord Gerard that you are not feeling well, Lady Elinor. It has been insupportably hot in the hall and I am sure you will find him understanding."

Her eyes silently implored him and he smiled again. "Have no fear, I would not dream of telling him of your encounter with My Lord Hastings. Quite apart from being unmannerly, such conduct on my part would prove gravely unwise. We Yorkists must remain friends throughout these next critical months at least."

She dropped him a deep curtsey. He bowed again and turned to descend the spiral staircase. How grave and stern he was for one so young and already carrying almost the full weight of responsibility for the invasion preparations. Yet he had found time to note the departure of Lord Hastings and Elinor from the hall, deemed it indiscreet and followed hastily in order to protect her from the consequences of her own folly.

Wearily she leaned against the door to her chamber, wiping away large drops of sweat from her brow. Until now she had not fully realized how the whole ordeal of her presence at the feast had taxed her strength.

Beatrix was waiting for her return. Murmuring sympathetically, she helped her mistress to undress and climb into bed. Elinor sank back with a grunt of pain. Her buttocks and lower back seemed on fire and she tossed and turned restlessly in an effort to find relief.

When a knock sounded at the door her heart beat quickened. Lord Gerard? No, obviously he would not stop to knock for admittance at his own door.

There was a mutter of talk then Beatrix, round-eyed with excitement, returned to the bedside.

"Milady, it is Her Grace, the duchess, she asks to see you."

"The duchess?" Elinor struggled up, confused and bewildered.

"Beatrix, how do I look? Are there signs — " Distractedly she gestured towards the mirror on her dressing chest, then realizing that the maid did not understand her, also that she was having the temerity to keep the duchess waiting, she said hurriedly, "Ask Her Grace to be pleased to enter."

The Duchess Margaret entered the chamber in a swish of stiff brocade. Immediately she dismissed Beatrix and Elinor glimpsed an attendant lady waiting just outside the door before it was hurriedly closed.

"No, child, don't attempt to get up. You are in no state to rise from your bed." The duchess's perfume enveloped Elinor in a fragrant cloud which reminded her of summer roses at Beckwith. She came close and seated herself upon the bed stool.

"We can speak quite freely, Elinor. Richard has promised to engage Lord Gerard in talk until he sees me re-enter the hall. He informs me that he believes you to have been mistreated. By Lord Gerard?"

Elinor bit her lip uncertainly. She bowed her head before the steady, unyielding gaze of those grey eyes and wept unashamedly.

"I — I deserved it, Your Grace. He deemed me disloyal and punished me as he had the right. But worse than this by far is that his squire, Simon Radbourne, is disgraced and accused of treason — because — because of me. My Lord has threatened that he will see to it that Simon hangs."

"This treason you speak of? He carried a letter, as I suggested, to your kinsman in Amboise, to be delivered by the spy, Raoul Dupont?"

"Yes, Your Grace. I — I gave Simon a necklet, a reliquary, containing a sliver of the true Cross. It is well known to Lord Gerard. I treasured it but I lacked any other means to bribe the man. Unfortunately Dupont was wearing it when he presented himself to the Duke of Gloucester on the way from Flushing. Lord Gerard recognized my necklet."

"Ah." The duchess grimaced and beat a hasty tattoo upon the silken coverlet with one shapely finger. "As I feared, all my fault."

"Oh no, Your Grace, how can that be?"

"I should not have gossipped of what

I knew concerning your kinsman nor should I have advised you to disobey your husband. But there, I have a tendency to meddle. Where is Simon Radbourne now?"

"My Lord commanded him to be imprisoned within the duke's dungeons until the King can judge the extent of his offence."

"Yet I have heard no word of any hanging." The duchess's eyes narrowed in thought. "So, the young man still lives."

"Your Grace, will you plead with your brother, King Edward?"

"Lord, child, that would do no earthly good." Those cool grey eyes surveyed her compassionately. "Do you imagine Ned would listen to my pleas on such a matter? No, if we are to save the boy, we must take matters into our own hands."

"But how?"

"Leave that to me." The duchess patted Elinor's hand reassuringly. "I have my own methods and my own trusted servants. Naturally Radbourne must leave Bruges, leave Burgundy, if he values his life."

"Your Grace, I have wracked my brains for hour after hour believing there was no hope. Lord Gerard is so angry — "

"Which brings us to the subject of his treatment of you. How badly are you hurt?" It was a blunt question and Elinor could not evade it. Timidly she told of her humiliating beating. She made no mention of her husband's brutal assault upon her body, but this she was sure the duchess had already surmised, for her lips compressed angrily.

"Please, Your Grace, you will not tax Lord Gerard with his harshness — "

"Certainly not, child, since that also would be pointless. It is a man's right to chastise his wife, I wish it were not so." She rose. "Trust me, Elinor. I will send you word as soon as possible concerning Simon Radbourne's fate. In the meantime dry your tears and behave as if you have nothing of which to be ashamed. I've found by experience that this is the simplest and most effective way of humbling one's opponent, especially if that opponent is one's husband and the battleground one's bed-chamber. You understand me?"

A glimmer of a smile brightened Elinor's golden eyes. She inclined her chin.

"Good. I will keep you at my side as much as possible over the next few days and I shall appear concerned that you look so pale and drawn."

"But, Your Grace — "

"I have said, trust me." The duchess bent and impulsively brushed her lips on Elinor's forehead, then she was gone. Elinor lay, hearing the soft rustle of her garments and the murmur of talk as she descended the stair, her lady in waiting close behind her.

It was several hours later that Lord Gerard came to bed.

Elinor started up as he moved cautiously towards her, the candle light revealing his naked form. Although his breath, like that of Lord Hastings, was wine scented, those blue eyes had completely lost their furious, unnatural glitter. Was she mistaken that she read something akin to shame in the way he avoided her gaze?

"Did I wake you? I'm sorry." His harshness of tone, she was sure, was to cover his embarrassment.

She could not prevent a shiver of apprehension running through her as his naked body touched hers.

"You need have no fear," he said sharply, "our reckoning was made last night. I am sure you will not repeat your offence."

"No, My Lord." She hoped she had managed to keep the whispered words steady.

"Then we'll say no more on the matter." There was a pause while he stretched out his long limbs beside her. A tingle ran down her spine at the nearness of his thigh to her own. Her mind was a confusion of conflicting thoughts and fears. She had tasted utter delight in his arms, that night on the ship when he had so tenderly nursed and comforted her, yet he had used her so roughly last night that she could not believe that any feeling but contempt and disgust existed in his heart for her. She was terribly afraid of him, yet when he was away from her she was forlorn and lonely. Her heart yearned for the gentle, courteous lover of her dreams, the man who had made her the gift of the illuminated Book of Hours, yet some glimmer of instinct told her that such gentle consideration was not what she craved. Nor could she believe that she truly loved him, yet if not, why did her traitorous breasts and loins ache for his caress as they did now?

He settled himself for sleep without attempting to take her. She stared beyond him into the darkness. His very hesitancy when he had approached her spoke of his regret for having allowed his fury to strip him of all control. He had punished her with his whip. It was not that which lay between them, she sensed. The pain and the marks upon her body were well deserved, by his reckoning. No, it was in his forcible taking of her, his rape, for that was what it had been. In that he had revealed his passionate hatred and jealousy of Reginald Beckwith. Elinor sighed. How could they continue to exist together with this barrier between them? And should the duchess manage to achieve what she had promised, Lord Gerard would be still more angry and he could not fail to suspect Elinor's involvement in the squire's escape. In his grim determination to see Simon Radbourne pay with his life for his devotion to her, did she glimpse a very real jealousy of the squire, too?

She told herself fiercely that she did not *wish* to love Lord Gerard. He was her enemy still. Nothing could alter that. Passionately she wished that they had never met, that she had not known the bitter-sweet delight of his kisses nor his most intimate caresses.

Elinor was somewhat embarrassed when the Duke of Gloucester's young squire, Piers Langham, came to her chamber next morning early with a polite request that she wait upon his master. The duke had proved himself her friend both when he had rescued her from the importunate attentions of Lord Hastings and when he had informed his sister, the Duchess Margaret, of Elinor's plight. Yet she felt nervously uneasy about this coming interview. He had been a witness to her struggle with the Lord Chamberlain and though none of the blame for the affair was hers, she was shamed by the incident. Lord Gerard had already left their chamber on some errand and she was glad there was no need to invent some excuse which would account for the duke's summons. She sighed. Undoubtedly Duke Richard had sent for her to enquire courteously after her welfare. She did not dare to hope that he might have been able to plead successfully with his brother for Simon Radbourne's life.

The duke rose politely as the squire ushered her into the apartment. The room was luxuriously appointed but bare of all personal belongings, no hawking gloves, jesses, bells, books or lute lay discarded upon the table or chests. Like all of the King's party, Duke Richard was bereft of his most cherished possessions by their sudden escape to Burgundy. He was dressed today plainly in a serviceable green doublet and brown hose.

"Lady Elinor," his voice was gentle, solicitous, "I trust you are feeling much better this morning. Forgive me that I summoned you so early, but my need is pressing." He urged her to sit in a padded chair near the fire.

"Your Grace, I must thank you again for your help last night and for the gentle care of your sister, the duchess."

He nodded. "We conferred together later as to what was best to be done for young Radbourne. At last we decided that he must be freed before Edward got wind of his treachery. He is now at the inn The Golden Fleece. The young fool refuses to leave Bruges until he has seen you and assured himself that you are unharmed. He fears, understandably, that Lord Gerard has wreaked his fury on you."

Elinor smiled faintly at the impatience revealed in the duke's tone. Young as he was, Gloucester was unused to having his will thwarted by underlings.

"He must go, and at once." She was alarmed despite the warm glow that coursed through her at the knowledge that Simon still remained faithful to her needs. "*I* must go to the inn, convince him of the necessity of instant flight. Your Grace, how — how did you manage it — to accomplish his release?"

His lips twitched. "There was only one way, Lady Elinor. I went myself and exerted my authority, so you will understand that it is now vital that

Radbourne leaves Bruges immediately."

Her hazel eyes were troubled. "Your Grace, you have placed yourself in a difficult position by this act. If the King is angered — "

"Better that his anger fall on me than on any other, Lady Elinor. His Grace has dire need of my services and also he has a very deep affection for me. I can stand the force of his anger, I do assure you."

She smiled wanly. "I am even more in your debt, My Lord. I hope that one day I may be of service to you. In the meantime I can do no more than pray constantly for Your Grace's health and happiness."

He smiled. She wondered as that stern young face took on a sudden radiance. "That is indeed the greatest service anyone can render another, Lady Elinor."

He rose and she knew herself dismissed. As she curtseyed, he said, "I have to tell you that, unfortunately, as Lord Gerard and I were crossing the hall this morning, some fool was gossipping about your exit from the hall on Lord Hastings's arm. I am sure that Lord Gerard heard, though he passed no comment."

She went pale to the lips.

He was immediately concerned for her. "Do you require an escort to The Golden Fleece? Piers is most trustworthy."

"Thank you, Your Grace, but no. Better far if you are not compromised further by this business. My Flemish maid will go with me. She knows the town well. I shall be . . . " she hesitated, "very discreet, and I will make very sure that Simon takes your advice. I am grateful for the warning concerning — the other matter."

Outside, in the corridor, she dismissed the squire who was eager to attend her. She leaned weakly against the dark wood panelling, as drained of strength as she had been last night after her distressing interlude with Lord Hastings.

Simon Radbourne was out of immediate danger but he must be made to see the need for instant flight. One of the pages glanced at her curiously, almost insolently, as he passed along the corridor and she forced herself to move. Her limbs were cold, frozen with the shock of realization. Lord Gerard *knew* she had left the hall with Lord Hastings, apparently quite willingly. There had been others in the gardens and courtyard. She had heard their laughter, their murmured comments. She had been recognized. The Court was a sink of malicious, bawdy innuendo. Lord Gerard could be under no misapprehension about Lord Hastings's intentions. He knew the man too well and he had warned her . . .

Within her own chamber, she paced the floor distractedly. How could she bear a repetition of the scene he had made the night of his return from Flushing? He would be insane with fury. She had disgraced him. The matter of the letter stood some chance of being kept from common knowledge but already her name was a byword in Court circles.

Should he discover that she was about to disobey him yet again and go to Simon Radbourne . . .

A terrible shudder passed through her. Lord Gerard terrified her when in a mood of such frenzied jealousy. She could not bear to face him. Her body trembled at the thought of further pain and humiliation.

She started nervously as Beatrix stole quietly into the chamber, two of Elinor's gowns draped over her arm. Obviously she had been hard at work sponging and pressing them.

"Milady?" The Flemish girl was aware instinctively that her mistress was upset. She quickly came and knelt beside the stool where Elinor was sitting.

"Beatrix help Milady. Milady trust her?"

Elinor forced a smile and reached out to touch the girl's hand.

It was difficult. The Flemish girl understood hardly any English and little French but, at last, Elinor was able to make her understand that she wished to be taken to The Golden Fleece and that that visit must be kept secret from Milord Gerard.

Beatrix nodded her head determinedly and touched first her own gown and then Elinor's.

"You are saying I should wear one of your gowns to go to the inn? Yes, Beatrix, of course. I should stand far less chance of being noticed when we leave the palace."

The girl looked puzzled and Elinor smiled and nodded at her. "Beatrix, we must go at once." She rose and began to undress. The Flemish girl jumped up eagerly to help her.

An hour later the two women approached the inn, a busy hostelry popular with the droves of foreign merchants who flocked the city. Obviously it had been suggested to Simon as a place where his presence would be unlikely to attract undue attention. Nor would he be easily remembered by potboys or serving wenches.

Beatrix had done her work well. Elinor was now dressed in a peasant skirt of russet wool, a coarse holland blouse and brown fustian cloak. The maid's eyes had widened when she saw her mistress make up a bundle of necessities, her green woollen gown, clean underclothing, what gold she possessed, for Lord Gerard had given her a little from his slender store so that she might reward pages and serving men.

As they were about to enter the

building, Elinor put her hand gently on Beatrix's arm. "Go back," she said softly, pointing away up the street, "say that you lost me in the market." She repeated the word as the Flemish girl stared back at her perplexed. "'The market', Beatrix, nothing more." She pressed one of her precious store of gold coins into the girl's hand. Only this morning before leaving her Lord Gerard had put four gold florins upon their dressing chest. Now she felt a sudden pang of distaste that she needed to betray him again and with his own coin. Beatrix shook her head violently and tried to push the coin back into her hand but Elinor insisted. No, if there was trouble — later — the girl would need the money. Fortunately Beatrix could not easily be questioned by Lord Gerard, and even if an interpretor was found, her story would be incoherent, she knew little or nothing of her mistress's intentions. Elinor waited until the maid was lost to sight in the busy street, then she entered the inn.

The tap room was packed to the limit and steamy with smoking tankards of mulled ales and the wet smell of greasy cloth, for it had rained earlier. Brawny arms reached out for her hips, her waist, even in clumsy attempts to paw at her bosom, but she shook them off, looking impatiently about her. A tavern slut, her blouse low cut and torn further to reveal her grimy breasts to the nipples, stared at her resentfully and demanded to know her business. Elinor ignored her, though she understood, since the girl had spoken in French. She flounced off in a pique. A burst of coarse laughter greeted their exchange. Elinor gritted her teeth to hide her feeling of panic. Never before had she braved such low company without an escort, yet it had been essential that she dismiss Beatrix *before* she met Simon Radbourne. If the girl had seen him she might have been forced to tell of their meeting. But suppose he had already left? Elinor took a hard breath and prepared herself to be subjected to further insults.

Then she saw him, seated in a dark corner, picking moodily at a knot in the begrimed and ale-stained wood of the trestle table. How unfamiliar he appeared in that grey wool jerkin, so unlike the elegant squire she had first seen from the minstrels' gallery at Beckwith and mistaken for her future husband. He turned his head towards the fire and she held back an instinctive scream at the sight of that jagged scar which marred his handsome face. Hurriedly she pushed her way towards him. He looked up curiously as her shadow darkened the table top, then recognition dawned and she saw relief and gladness register.

"My Lady, Sweet Virgin be praised, I had thought . . . " his throat worked, "feared . . . "

She sat down beside him on the hard bench, her head close to his.

"Simon, you must leave this place at once. Don't you understand how greatly you stand in danger?"

"Oh yes, My Lady, I know." He smiled and her heart failed her as she saw how his mouth twisted to one side, puckered by the ugly red wound. "I have lived very close to death during these last hours. My only real fear was for you. My Lord — he — he did not hurt you?"

"Of course not," she lied, "but we cannot linger here, Simon. I need you to escort me to France, to Amboise."

It took a while for him to fully register what she was asking. His blue eyes peered at her uncomprehendingly. "My Lady — "

"Do I ask too much of you?" she demanded brutally to impell him to urgent action. "Will you be safer travelling alone, unhampered by a woman companion?"

She read instant reproof in his eyes. His hand shook on the handle of his leather drinking jack.

"My Lady, I would go with you to Hell itself. Can you doubt that? But I would not have you run into danger, regret that — "

"I shall have no regrets," she said briskly. "What I ask is for my sake, not yours. I must escape from Lord Gerard."

"Then he *did* punish you cruelly." Simon's voice was low, hoarse with anger.

"No more, I suppose, than I deserve, yet I cannot fall again into his hands." She gave a little rasping sob. "I cannot bear to go on being his prisoner, the butt of his hatred for all Lancastrians — And there is something else. I will not speak of that, cannot. You must help me, Simon. I have to reach my kinsman at King Louis's Court." She saw his facial muscles stiffen. "I understand your natural distaste for such a journey. I — " She hesitated then plunged on. "I would not ask you to treat with the enemy. If you will take me safely within reach of Amboise, that will be enough."

He regarded her gravely. "You know that His Grace of Gloucester saved my life?"

She nodded.

"I will take you wherever you wish, My Lady, but I will not serve Margaret of Anjou nor My Lord Earl of Warwick. That would be an act of foulest treachery directed against Duke Richard and — and against Lord Gerard whom — " he groped boyishly for words, "whom I still respect and admire. I — I failed him and he has punished me. That was his right. He is my lord. He trained me to arms and I owed him my loyalty. I make no complaints nor do I whine for sympathy for what has — " He averted his marred cheek from her. "I think *you* know what prompted me to betray him, My Lady."

She did not answer and he turned that scarred face back to regard her sternly.

"I can promise you nothing but my profoundest gratitude, Simon," she said at last, her tongue awkwardly cleaving to the roof of her mouth. "You *do* understand?"

He nodded slowly. "Aye, My Lady, only too well. You can trust yourself to me — utterly." He rose, offering his outstretched hand to help her to her feet. "And now we should go. Will you eat first?"

"No, we must be on our way."

"You have means?"

"Three gold florins, some silver, necessities for the journey. Do we buy mounts? Have we sufficient? I can walk if need be."

"There is sufficient but we shall not be able to lodge comfortably." He grinned suddenly, a boy again. "We are not unused to such hard conditions, My Lady. Your maid, Beatrix, will she betray us?"

"I don't think she will. Beatrix is a

266

good girl. I have paid her, not as a bribe, but because she may well be dismissed after this. She does not know what I intended, even if she guessed."

"My Lord of Gloucester?"

"He, too, will guess, though — " she hesitated, "he will know the reason and I think he is unlikely to betray us, at least he will play for time for, undoubtedly, he will have to account to the King for his unauthorized freeing of you and Lord Gerard will suspect that I am with you."

"Then we must avoid direct routes into France for some time at least. We are both suitably dressed for our journey. One of the duke's grooms supplied this jerkin and hose and you do not now resemble the proud Lady Elinor Cranley who walked in the duchess's train. We have a fair chance of evading capture."

Elinor scrambled up and followed him from the tap room. No one appeared to notice. The comely wench had met her lover as prearranged, they'd think, and gone with him. What was there in that to excite attention or curiosity?

Simon set a good pace and Elinor had

some ado to keep up with him, her feet slipping on the mud and refuse of the street.

"Horses?" she queried, panting hard.

"Not yet. We'll get clear of the city first. All stables and inn ostlers will be questioned."

He was right, of course.

As they set their faces into the grey veil of rain, Elinor said, "*If* we are captured, together, it would go very hard with you, Simon."

He grunted but forbore to answer her.

9

ON the third night of their journey and miles from any village or inn, the snow began to fall, not in gentle, feathery flakes but in a maelstrom of needle-sharp particles which froze and near blinded them. Simon drew in his horse and reached across for Elinor's lead rein.

"I think I can just see some building over there." He was shouting above the noise of the wind but she had trouble hearing him. He pointed to his right over the length of a hard, rutted field already disappearing beneath a covering of white. "A barn, possibly deserted, for the roof needs repair. We must make for that, My Lady."

She nodded, blinking back the cold flakes from her lashes, the wind catching away her breath before she could reply. Her horse stumbled awkwardly on the rough ground. Poor brute, it had looked half starved when Simon had bought it from a farmer some six or seven kilometres from Bruges and they had pushed their mounts hard in an effort to avoid pursuit.

Simon had advised avoiding Lille and Elinor had left the decisions to him. He appeared to have gained a new maturity during his nerve-racking imprisonment in Duke Charles's dungeon. She had been surprised by his determination and his firmness in haggling with the peasants along their way.

The two previous nights he had obtained a bed for her in an inn and reasonably cheaply, for their stock of coin was fast dwindling, while he himself had slept beside the horses in the inn stable.

At the last place she had had to share her chamber with a loud-snoring merchant's widow who was making for Chartres. The woman had been coarse-spoken but friendly enough, nor had she asked awkward questions, her button black eyes passing from Elinor to her escort and back again, an intimation which had brought a flush of shame to Elinor's pale cheeks. It had been hard to rest on the vermin-infested mattress but at least she had been sheltered from the wind and rain which, from the first, had made their travelling almost unbearable. It seemed she would be denied even those creature comforts tonight.

A barn the ruin appeared to be and, thankfully, the two dismounted and made for the poor shelter it offered. Simon tethered their mounts to a ring constructed for the purpose at the rear. The barn's projecting roof would offer some protection for the animals from the biting wind. Elinor shook her cloak free of the snow and withdrew from the doorway into the building. The wind still howled through its rough wattle daub and the snow filtered in powdering the hard-packed dirt floor. At least the place was not foul smelling, it had been open too long to the elements for that. She laughed as Simon paused in the doorway, he so resembled a snowman, covered as he was from head to foot by the dense flakes.

He wiped his forearm over his face as he approached her and she saw he was frowning anxiously. "My apologies, My

Lady. I'd hoped to reach Amiens by nightfall but I don't think we should try to get further in this. We could fall and be lost in a deep drift."

"You're right. The horses need a respite. They'll die under us if we press on in this."

"I've given each of them a nosebag, not that there's much for them." He shook his head doubtfully. "Very little for us either, My Lady, just some rye bread and hard cheese left over from dinner. I'd hoped to order a hot supper for you tonight. Amiens is a large enough town for us to have risked staying at some inn."

"It's unlikely that any pursuers could have made more progress than we have in these conditions. I think even Lord Gerard will have given up by now. Lay out the food, Simon. Did you bring in the saddlebag?"

He produced it and she busied herself in dividing the bread and cheese into two equal portions. There was a half filled wine skin and she was glad of its comforting warmth coursing through her half frozen body as she set it to her lips. They ate in silence, and she forced herself to talk to cover his uneasiness at their close proximity.

"Perhaps it would be as well to avoid Amiens, as we did Lille. With luck, if the snow storm dies down, we could press straight on for Paris in the morning."

He looked at her gloomily. "If we do not keep to the main highway we could be lost, My Lady. Who knows how deep the drifts will lie in the fields? I see little likelihood of our being able to cross into France for two or three days yet."

She sighed. It was essential for her purpose that they press on as soon as possible. Reginald would not wait for ever in Amboise. If he had already left the castle she must find some other way of reaching her father. She would beg Queen Margaret to allow her to travel in the Lancastrian party when they embarked, but if the Queen refused to receive her, then she must become a camp follower, use any means to take ship for England. She shuddered at the prospect for she was not ignorant of the kind of existence she would be forced to endure, a dogged fight to preserve her very life and body from the determined assaults of any footsoldier who dragged a pike in the Queen's army. She set her teeth. If the worst happened, why then it must be faced! Could any fate be worse than seeing the contempt and fury in her husband's eyes?

Yet she was still Gerard Cranley's wife. The fact was inescapable. Even should she reach the haven of Beckwith, sooner or later the Church would insist that she be returned to her husband. Her vows bound her to him till death should part them. 'Death' — she shivered at the thought, not this time from the icy cold.

When Simon moved to go outside the hut she forbade it.

"You would die within the hour of exposure. Where would I be without you to help and protect me? No, Simon, you must stay inside the hut, within call. I — I trust you — "

He lay down as far from her as the limited space permitted. His voice came, a little hoarse. "I have sworn a solemn oath to preserve your honour, My Lady. You — you have nothing to fear from me."

She lay huddled against one ruined wall, listening to the wind howling outside. Her thoughts returned to the first night of their flight from Beckwith. Then Lord Gerard had been within call, well within the touch of her fingers.

At first light, Simon hastened out to discover how their horses had fared through the night. He came back quickly to report that they had survived the rigours of the bitterly cold night, but that the snow had continued to fall through most of it and he doubted if they could make their way to the road, let alone to Amiens.

"The poor brutes would break their legs in one of these treacherous drifts, My Lady. It has stopped snowing now, but I advise that we stay within this shelter, for today, at least."

Elinor agreed soberly. "We can go without food for one more day and there is frozen snow to refresh our thirst, but the horses should be fed if they're to carry us any further. They were an ill-nourished pair when we bought them."

"Aye, My Lady. The moment I think the snow hard enough to bear my weight

I'll set out on foot and find some farm or tavern and return with food for us and fodder for the horses."

Now that it had ceased snowing and the wind had dropped it was not so bitterly cold, yet the two huddled within their woollen cloaks, their teeth chattering miserably.

"There's one crumb of comfort to be had, My Lady. As you said last night, Lord Gerard's pursuit can hardly be successful now."

By late afternoon a watery sun had made its appearance and Simon pronounced the crispness of the snow suitable for his foray for supplies. Elinor knew he had lingered longer than he should have done, being reluctant to leave her unprotected. She too had dreaded his going but managed to put a brave face on it.

"I'll be safe enough, Simon. What could happen to me in the short time you will be gone? The sooner you leave, the sooner you return."

He kissed the tips of her frozen fingers and set off, looking back many times to see her standing by the hut door. Soon he was lost to sight beyond the dip in the ground and she turned back to the dubious shelter of the dilapidated building, swinging her arms and blowing on her fingers. She tried to force a cheery imagining of Simon's return. Retreating to the back of the hut she sat down again on the pile of mouldy hay which had formed her bed last night. If only they had been able to find some wood to start a fire, yet she doubted that in these wet conditions that would be possible. Despite her brave words to Simon, she began to wonder if they could survive another night of such terrible privation.

She longed to lapse off to sleep but knew that would be unwise. She had heard of men who had fallen and slept on the Yorkshire moors in deep snow and never opened their eyes again. To her relief, after a shorter period than she could have believed possible, she heard Simon's call and dashed to the crazily hanging door to greet him. He staggered, bent almost double under the weight of a bundle of fodder and a goatskin bag which she assumed contained food.

He slithered to a halt, easing his burden to the ground in front of her.

"I was lucky. There's a tavern less than a mile beyond where I hit the highway," he informed her joyfully. "They were pleased to supply us, though the landlord charged us dear."

Elinor eagerly took the wineskin he offered and swallowed. Instantly she felt warmer and considerably cheered that they were not, after all, so far from habitation.

"Well done, Simon. Was walking very hazardous?"

"Not good, My Lady, and death for the horses, but considerably better on the highway than the frozen fields. There are bad drifts there. If it freezes tonight the going should be hard enough for the horses in the morning. I'll see to their needs first. We shall owe our lives to them so they must be preserved at all costs. There's bread in the bag and goats' cheese; no meat, I'm afraid, it was a poor place."

"This will do very well." Elinor broke the bread and ate ravenously. "Did you see any other men in the tap room? Was there news of — of other travellers?"

He shook his head. "I made cautious

278

enquiries. There have been no other travellers on the road, not for days. We are safe hidden while this weather holds."

He went out to tend the horses. When he came back he was jubilantly brandishing some split logs.

"These must have been stacked at the back near the horses. One rolled clear so I rummaged and found some others. We missed them last night as they were well under the snow. They'll be damp, of course, but I've tinder and flint. I can try to kindle a fire in one angle of the wall where's there's shelter from the wind."

She watched as he stacked the dampened wood and tried clumsily to strike a light. His fingers were blue with cold and she took the tinder and flint from him. "You come and eat now. Let me try."

Over and over again she managed to produce a spurt of flame only to see it die down as quickly. Within a short space of time she was almost crying with frustration.

So intent were they both on their task, for Simon soon joined her, his mouth crammed with bread and cheese, that they were not aware of footsteps crunching through the snow near the hut until a man's voice, coarse-accented, in French, drew their attention. He sounded distinctly amused by their efforts.

"What have we here, Henri? Hermits, deliberately subjecting themselves to the bitterness of the elements, to test their spirits? But there, it's far more likely they're runaway lovers, eh?"

Elinor sprang to her feet to face the intruders.

There were two of them, the speaker, a huge mountain of a man wrapped in a tattered fustian cloak that showed bare flesh through the rents and rude patches. He wore a greasy woollen cap which was pulled so low on his forehead that she could not see his features clearly, apart from his thick mane of black beard. He lounged insolently against the crumbling doorpost, arms folded. His very inflection and the mocking nature of his question warned her to beware. She gestured Simon to keep silent while she tried to assess the extent of their danger.

The second man who sidled up to his partner was dressed like the first, in tattered filthy clothing which had been made for a much smaller man, and he tripped over his trailing cloak in his haste to elbow close to his friend and peer at her. He looked wiry enough but over the years or months of their association he'd been beaten into subservience by his companion, for he hovered slightly behind, his sharp, ferrety features sniffing out the possibility of profiting himself at the expense of the two in the hut. He gave a nervous, high-pitched laugh which jarred on Elinor's fears more terribly than the bigger man's overt insolence had done.

"What is it you want, sirs?" she asked in French, her eyes passing over them in an effort to discover if either or both was armed. She half turned, appealing silently to Simon to allow her the initiative in her dealings with these two. He was too impetuous, inexperienced. She recognized his danger.

"My brother and I are sheltering here from the wind. We've food we can share." She pointed to the opened skin bag and the wineskin. "You're welcome, sirs, to eat, then — " her voice quivered slightly "to go on your way. My — my brother tells me there is a tavern nearby. He can direct you."

The little man watched his companion avidly. The tip of the big man's tongue was passed over bearded lips and Elinor's heart leapt in her breast. She sensed his feral nature, his brute needs, and she knew he would never be satisfied by the gift of food or money, certainly not the few coins they had left.

"Ah, *oui*, mademoiselle," he said at last, indolently moving further into the hut and stretching out his hand for the wineskin.

Elinor felt the tenseness of Simon's body close to her. He was quivering with fury.

Sulkily he handed the wineskin to the Frenchman, who drank deep. He wiped his lips on the back of his hand and passed the skin to his fellow, then jerked his chin towards the unlit fire. "Henri, light the fire for our friends here."

Elinor did not take her eyes from him and she was conscious that Simon was still bristling with anger which could explode into action at any moment.

Such a move would be fatal. She was sure that the two beggars were more than a match for a young squire armed only with a dagger. To have travelled fully armed would have attracted undue notice.

With practised skill, Henri took tinder and flint and soon had the fire going well. His shifty eyes darted to Elinor then away again, as he took his seat by his companion. He had not yet spoken and Elinor wondered if he could be dumb. Her silent appeals to Simon to be cautious appeared to have had the desired effect, for he sat beside her, watchful, as she further divided the food and the two French beggars fell upon it and noisily consumed their share.

"So, mademoiselle," the bigger man purposefully addressed her, his mocking tone confirming that he had not believed her explanation of the relationship she had assumed for herself and Simon, "it is a bad time to be travelling. Some trouble, perhaps, which has brought brother and sister from the comfort of their house in — " His bushy eyebrows swept up in interrogation.

Adroitly forestalling Simon, she said, "We are from Lille sir, orphans. Our father has recently died and we have been cast out of our home. We are travelling to Tours where we hope a cousin will take us in."

Almost immediately she realized her mistake. Now the Frenchman would know they were unprotected and could be robbed and attacked with impunity. The very stink of the two warned her of her danger. Had she saved Simon from death by hanging only to plunge him into the likelihood of having his throat cut by footpads?

As if he read her thoughts, the big Frenchman leered across at her and, as she moved to retrieve the empty wine skin, he placed an immense hairy-backed paw over her hand. She gave a little hiss of fright and, before she could warn Simon, he rose and hurtled upon the beggar, knocking him backwards. Elinor wrenched free her hand but before she could withdraw from the fray, the smaller beggar, Henri, had seized her shoulder in a paralysing grip and pulled her to her feet. She fought with him but his thin

284

wrists had the strength of toughest steel and he caught her close to his stinking body. The stench of his filthy rags turned her sick and she wrestled to get one hand free and claw at his face. He drew a hard, gasping breath and slapped her against the side of the jaw. She reeled under the blow but he held her fast with his other hand, his fingers biting into the flesh of her shoulder until she thought her bones would be crushed.

Dimly she was aware of the animal-like snarling and scrambling behind her as the big Frenchman and Simon Radbourne were locked in desperate combat.

Soon she was forced to give her whole concentration and efforts to her frantic struggle with Henri. Inexorably he pulled her once more tight to his body and she found herself screaming aloud.

Simon's opponent was mouthing obscenities but though her captor made gasps and grunts he called her by no filthy names and she became more and more convinced that he was dumb. While he still held her by the shoulder and wrist she bent and bit savagely at his hand. He gave a hoarse inhuman cry but, for precious seconds, she had one hand free. Reaching out blindly behind her for anything she could use as a weapon, her clawing fingers found and identified a weakened strut. The splinters tore at the smooth tips of her fingers but, panting and sobbing, she wrenched wildly at it, never truly believing she could detach it from the crumbling mud which held it in place. Those final moments while she fought doggedly with the last of her failing strength seemed unnaturally lengthened, as if they would stretch out to eternity. The man would recapture her hand, knock her senseless, brutally rape her — it would happen now — soon — and afterwards . . .

She screwed her eyes tight shut against the ghastly image of the man's rat-like features, the blackened stumps of teeth, as his mouth opened in a ghastly grin of pain. The strut tore free and she grasped it tight in sheer desperation. As the beggar came at her again to wrench at her hand she swung it with all her might. It caught him full on the face. She heard the terrible crunching of nasal bones, felt the horrifying spurt of blood on her hand

and breast. He reeled, freed her shoulder. She staggered back sobbing wildly.

She watched as he stumbled, blood flowing freely now between the hands which he'd put up unbelievingly to cover his face. Momentarily he was blinded and at her mercy. She had to render him unconscious before he recovered and came at her again. She crawled closer, searching for the bloodstained strut which had fallen from her fingers. She found and secured it, just in time, before the man launched himself at her with a savage scream of pure fury. The impetus of his lunge carried him offbalance. She side-stepped and, lifting the strut high, hit him again on the temple. He gave a moan, surprisingly soft, considering the extent of his frustration and animal hatred. She found herself battering again and again at his head until he dropped at her feet then, panting with exhaustion and reaction, she turned to where Simon was engaged with his own grim battle for survival.

Locked in a deadly hold with the big Frenchman, he was rolling across the hard-packed earth. Their hoarse, panted grunts were growing slower and weaker. Elinor sobbed aloud as the ashes of the fire were scattered by the flailing bodies and the beggar's tattered cloak caught fire. He uttered a shrill scream of mortal terror and Simon, in a final effort, pounced and thrust his dagger cleanly between the man's ribs. The beggar's body arched obscenely and Elinor choked back a cry of horror. The dying Frenchman looked full at her, his mouth working aimlessly in a call for help or a defiant final oath. Blood frothed his lips. There came a hoarse rattling within the windpipe and he collapsed like a pierced corn sack. Simon half crouched and half lay, too exhausted to make sure his enemy was truly finished.

Elinor approached warily. The Frenchman's eyes stared with the blind terror of the corpse who has perished violently and cannot believe his own dread fate. She shuddered.

"My — My Lady?" Simon's right sleeve was soaked in blood and there was a purple bruise on his temple. He tried to stand, wincing back little moans of pain.

"Keep still, Simon." She raced to his side. "It's over, the man's dead and the other — the other — he's unconscious. He might be dead as well. I — I can't tell but, for the moment — he can't harm us."

He collapsed at her feet and she knelt and cradled his head on her lap, tearing at her bloodied kirtle for bandaging to check his bleeding.

Wildly she looked from the injured Simon to the other beggar, the one the dead man had called Henri. He lay where he'd fallen and she had no way of knowing if he were dead and, if not, how long before he regained his wits and came at them again. Simon had lapsed into unconsciousness and she feared that the head wound was serious. The fire would soon go out. Without help the squire would die in the night. How could she even manage to keep him warm? His arm was now only oozing blood and she could see no other wounds. She had stemmed the bleeding for now, but Simon had to have skilled care. She held back a sob of despair. Even if she managed to find a monk or physician she could not be sure his life could be saved. She shuddered throughout her being at the sight of the big man's sprawled body. He was evil, as his companion had been. If she *had* killed him she couldn't find it in her heart to regret it. It had been necessary, if she and Simon hoped to survive. Bleakly she reviewed her situation, her hand gently smoothing back the sweat-soaked hair from Simon's brow.

Could she reach the tavern on the Amiens road and bring help? If she left Simon helpless, would the other man recover sufficiently to attack him again? It was a dilemma she had no way of solving, but at last she moved Simon's head gently from her lap and rose stiffly. She had to go, reach the road. It was their only chance. She removed her cloak and wrapped it round the boy's body. He was breathing stertorously and her alarm at his condition grew. Casting one terrified glance at the man she had felled, and with a murmured prayer that he would remain insensible, or at least sufficiently weakened to be no danger to Simon, she went out of the hut and began to follow the firm tracks the others had left in the snow.

It was obvious to her now that Simon had been sighted and followed when he had first left the tavern. He had been laden with food and fodder. It had been the beggars' intention to kill whoever they found in the hut and steal the horses. The discovery that Simon's companion was a woman had inflamed their lust.

She stumbled and slipped on the icy track. It must be well past noon now. Already the watery sun was setting and it would soon be full dark. Haste was impossible in these dangerous conditions. She did not feel the loss of her cloak for the strenuous effort needed to keep her footing on the treacherous surface was more than sufficient to keep her in a heavy sweat of fear.

At last, the ditch which marked the highway came in sight. Elinor gathered her failing strength to scramble across it and heave herself onto the flatter road on the far side. She was now at the end of her tether. Her breath was coming harshly and there was a nagging pain in her side. Gamely she struggled on, taking her direction from the setting sun. The tavern could not be far now, yet could she persuade the proprietors to help her? It was so late and she had no money. It had not occurred to her in her panic to fetch help to search Simon who carried their coin in his purse. Even if she were believed, few men of this peasant community would have either the courage or the inclination to risk the danger from other beggars in the vicinity to accompany her back to the hut.

Then it was she heard wheels behind her on the road, a slow creaking, accompanied by the utterly bewildering sound of bells on harness. She could not believe that her ears were not playing her false. She paused for a moment, until, round the bend of the road, appeared a little cart drawn by a donkey whose harness was, indeed, decorated with small silver bells which jingled pleasantly in the cold air. On the driving seat was a man, strangely and garishly clad in a ragged doublet of bright purple velvet and striped hose. His cloak was thrown back and he wore a purple felt hat adorned with a tall, curling feather.

Elinor's first instinct had been to plead

for a ride to the tavern but the dubiously rakish appearance of the driver alarmed her. She had never seen a travelling musician, had heard of the celebrated Trouveres of France, though many had perished when their brotherhood had been persecuted for heresy a century or more ago. Now she recognized this man as one of their number. Her father had frequently scoffed at her love of the old French romances, declaring that all jongleurs and troubadours were little better than vagabonds and robbers. If she appealed to this one for help, would she be falling into the hands of yet another disreputable traveller who would be more likely to steal what was left of their gold and their horses than to aid her?

She looked frantically for some place of concealment but there was not so much as a tree or bush within view. The roadside drainage ditch offered the only possible hiding place and she made for it with all speed. Her headlong rush proved her downfall, for she slipped on a patch of ice and fell sprawling.

The pain in her foot was indescribable and tears streamed down her cheeks as she struggled weakly to climb to her feet. The cart's wheels had stopped creaking and she knew she had been seen by the occupants. Her efforts to put weight on the injured foot caused her such agony that she was forced to fall back again.

"No, no, demoiselle, do not try to get up."

Elinor's whole body was trembling as a woman's voice exhorted her to remain where she was. The French was pure yet strangely accented. A hand pushed her gently down on the ground and the speaker dropped to her knees beside her after jumping hastily from the cart and running lightly to the ditch.

"Let me feel, demoiselle, a bone may be broken." Skilful fingers probed the injury and Elinor gave a sharp hiss of pain. "*Non*, not broken, I think, but badly sprained. Allow Blaise to carry you to the cart."

Elinor had no more strength to fight against the strong arms which lifted her. The troubadour's woman companion padded her way beside them to the covered cart where the patient donkey was standing quietly. Elinor was placed down upon a feather-filled mattress while the woman climbed up beside her. The two had held a muttered conversation which Elinor could not catch and, as the woman bent her head once more to tend the injured ankle, Elinor caught at her strong brown hand.

"Please, I need help urgently. My squire — my brother," she corrected herself hurriedly, "is lying badly injured in a ruined barn back there." She indicated the direction and the woman followed her gaze. "I was going to the tavern. Simon said it is not far along the road." She appealed to the troubadour who waited near the cart's tail. "Will you please go back to him, monsieur? I cannot and he will die there alone. For the love of God, monsieur."

"For the love of God, I will go, demoiselle," the troubadour replied calmly without a hint of hesitation. "If he is as badly hurt as you say, we must take the cart and carry him."

"The track is difficult, monsieur. If your donkey is injured, you will be in bad straits," she warned.

The woman laughed and the sound

was melodic in the silent, snow-covered waste. "Phedre is used to difficult ways, demoiselle. Trust Blaise. He will guide her safely."

"But there is the ditch — "

"*Oui*, demoiselle, we know that."

Once again Elinor was pressed back firmly against the softness of the mattress and the woman bent back to her task while the man drew some sturdy wooden struts from the rear of the cart and carried them to the side of the road near the ditch. Presumably he would use them as a sort of bridge to guide the donkey across into the field beyond.

There was a splash of water in an earthenware bowl and the woman was gently removing her shoe in order to bind a soaked cloth round the swollen ankle. Instinctively Elinor rested back, content to trust the woman to tend her. She gave a great gasp as the icy water touched her flesh, biting down hard on her bottom lip. There was something in the attitude of the strangers, in their calm acceptance of her need and their duty to serve her, that she found both touching and comforting.

The woman deftly replaced her stocking over the cold bandage and drew up a woollen blanket to cover Elinor's chilled form. It was well she did so, for Elinor was shivering, her teeth rattling together, partly with the intense cold but mostly from the shock of her recent, terrible adventure.

She saw that the woman was not in her first youth. The face was thin, the cheekbones high, the mouth unusually tender and quite beautiful. It was her hair which caught Elinor's notice, thick, luxuriant and fiery red in which one or two silver threads rather enhanced its loveliness than detracted from it. Elinor had never before seen a respectable woman with her hair uncovered and her cheeks burned as the woman's lips parted in a smile of amusement, completely discomfiting her.

"My name is Jeannine. I am Blaise's woman, as you surmise, but no harlot."

"I did not think — that is — "

"Like him I am a lute player and a singer of songs. We are on our way into France, first to Amiens then to Paris. We travel the roads at will. Recently we were at the Courts of Duke Charles in Bruges and Lille."

"I am Elinor Cranley. My — " Elinor hesitated for a moment then pressed on, "I, too, am on my way to France escorted by my husband's squire, Simon Radbourne. We sheltered last night in a ruined barn and today were set upon by two footpads. We fought them — but Simon is unconscious. In this bitter cold I knew he could not survive and — and — one of the men — I am not sure if he is dead. Even now he could recover and finish Simon." Agitatedly she tried to struggle up into a sitting position.

Jeannine nodded thoughtfully. Elinor registered that her eyes were green, reflecting the grey light of the winter sky. It was difficult to guess at her age, perhaps she was in her thirties or even older. The lute player was tall and slender, as supple as a maiden, but there were little lines around her eyes and mouth which belied her youthful appearance. Like Blaise, she was dressed garishly in a scarlet skirt of peasant weave, a faded but once splendid laced bodice of green velvet and a rubbed and mended cloak in the same colour and fabric.

She said softly, "Trust Blaise. If the gods will it, we will be in time to save your young friend."

It was an odd phrase and Elinor quickly looked away, fearing the woman would think her unmannerly for her undue curiosity.

Blaise was now leading the donkey very slowly. Once over the ditch, he gathered up the struts and resumed his place on the driving seat. Soon they were crossing the field track. Elinor marvelled at the skill with which the sturdy little animal, encouraged by words and strange sounds from Blaise, picked her way across the waste of frozen snow. Elinor leaned forward anxiously to peer through the opened canvas back of the cart for a first view of the ruined barn. She was afire with impatience, though she knew well enough that for Blaise to urge the donkey to greater speed would be hazardous in the extreme. If Simon could be carried to the tavern in the cart it could well prove his salvation.

The barn could now be seen black

and stark against the whiteness of snow. Blaise gave a little clicking sound and the donkey made in that direction. The moment he drew up the donkey near the ruined door Elinor made to jump down. Jeannine put a cautioning hand on her arm.

"Let Blaise help you. If you put weight on the injured foot now, it will heal less quickly than I should wish."

Elinor obeyed her, though as Blaise lifted her down, her heart was thudding painfully in her impatience and dread to discover the worst for herself. Leaning on the arm of the troubadour, she approached the crazily hanging door, calling loudly to Simon.

"It's I, Elinor. Simon, answer me, if you can."

There was a trail of blood near the door. She slipped in it and almost fell full length. Excruciating pain ran from her sprained ankle right up her leg. The troubadour and Jeannine came running to her assistance.

"Not me, go to Simon, please — "

He had fallen face-down this time some yards from them. At the sound of Elinor's well-loved voice he strove to rise, but weakly fell back again. Jeannine hurried to him while Blaise walked steadily to the bodies of the two robbers. The smaller one, Henri, was no longer lying where Elinor had left him. He sprawled on his back, one hand stretched towards Simon's body. The squire's dagger had caught him full in the throat and it did not need the troubadour to confirm to Elinor that he was dead. She turned away, horrified, not at the man's dreadful end, but at the danger he had proved to Simon. She should have bound him before going for help but her courage had failed her. Believing him dead, she had not been able to steel herself to touch his body. But for a supreme effort on the squire's part, they might well have arrived too late. Gritting her teeth against the pain of her hurt ankle, she hobbled to where Jeannine knelt by Simon.

"Is he — is he going to die?"

The lute player pursed her lips. "He has lost much blood, and is terribly weakened, but we must trust to God and the boy's determined will to live, which must be great, for he exists but to serve you. Is that not so?"

Elinor nodded in dumb agreement. The lute player was perceptive.

She swallowed. "We have little gold, but — but if you would carry my squire to the nearest tavern, I could, perhaps, reward you more fittingly later. I — we — go to Amboise, to — to my kinsman there."

Jeannine turned from her patient to smile at Elinor. "There is no need of coin nor thanks nor reward between you and us. *Certainement*, we will do what we can for the boy. Blaise will carry him to the cart where I will tend him."

"There was a wound in the arm which I bound and another on his temple. Are there further injuries? Did the man — "

"I cannot tell yet, Milady Elinor." Jeannine pronounced her name in the French manner. "It is the head wound which gives me most concern. First he must be made warm and comfortable in the cart."

Much later, Elinor remembered that she had not told the lute player that her husband was a lord, yet Jeannine had known how to address her once she had been told her name. Elinor was content to allow the two musicians to handle the situation as they saw fit. She was utterly worn out and confused by all that had gone before. Blaise carried Simon to the cart as tenderly as any woman and placed him on the mattress. Jeannine jumped up beside him and busied herself with her medicines. Elinor watched, uncertainly, by the cart's tail. First the lute player laid bare Simon's wounds and cleansed them thoroughly with water into which she poured some greenish liquid from a dark coloured phial. From a similar container she forced some cordial between the boy's lips. His wounds duly cleansed and bandaged, she wrapped him warmly in blankets, and replaced the medicines in a small wooden chest.

"He must sleep now, Milady Elinor. That is his only chance of recovery. He cannot be moved today, so we must stay here in the barn. Have no fear. Blaise will dispose of the corpses and he will rekindle the fire. Phedre cannot carry all of us. She is a game little animal but she must rest now, and you, Milady, will not be able to walk yet on your injured foot."

"But there are *our* horses tethered behind the barn."

"Ah, good. Blaise will attend to their needs as he will to the donkey's."

When Elinor re-entered the barn Blaise had removed the two bodies. He had already cleansed the floor of blood as best he could and the fire was again blazing brightly.

For the first time he spoke. Like Jeannine's his voice was deep and musical.

"Trust to Jeannine's skill to help the boy, Milady, no woman is more knowledgeable concerning herbs and unguents. If the young messire is to be saved, she will do it."

She sank down by the fire and they were soon joined by Jeannine. Blaise brought food and wine for them all.

"The young man sleeps now. Nature performs her own cures. He may continue unconscious for some hours, even days."

Jeannine's words were so confident that Elinor could not but feel deeply comforted. She ate of the bread, cheese and onions.

Jeannine explained. "Blaise and I do

not eat of animal flesh but meat can be provided for you when we reach some convenient tavern."

Elinor stammered, "There is no need. This food is good."

She was watching the sure, deft movements of the troubadour. Like Jeannine he was tall and thin, almost to gauntness, his face brown and deeply scored with lines by exposure to wind and weather. Elinor realized, intuitively, that both of her companions had experienced danger and suffering throughout their lives. They bore the marks of it in their calm acceptance of fate. They had found the squire and Elinor in dire need and instantly put themselves at their disposal. After the frugal meal, Blaise took himself off to the cart to sleep beside the injured boy, after first bringing blankets for the two women and making up the fire for the night.

When they were alone, Elinor hesitantly told the lute player her story. It was as if she felt compelled to do so. To have continued to lie to Jeannine was simply not possible.

"I had to — to leave my husband," she

said shyly. "I was so ashamed at what had transpired in the palace gardens and he would have been so angry. Also, there was Simon. I do not think he would have left me friendless in Bruges."

Jeannine held Elinor's gaze with those green eyes of hers. "The boy loves you, *oui*?"

"I — I believe he does." Elinor looked away to the darkness beyond the opened doorway. "We are not lovers, Jeannine. He has treated me with the greatest courtesy, but my husband is jealous of his honour. He would hound Simon to his death."

"So." Jeannine gave a heavy sigh. "And you fear you will be followed?"

"It is possible, yet I believe Lord Cranley will have turned back by now. The expedition to England is imminent. My Lord will not swerve in his loyalty to the Yorkist House, not even to have me in his charge again."

"He has ill-used you." It was not a question and Elinor felt the hairs lift at the nape of her neck. She had not revealed to the lute player Lord Gerard's punishment of her treachery nor of his later, brutal attack upon her body, though she had told of her abduction from her home in England and her fears of retaliation against Simon for the squire's complete and utter devotion to her.

Jeannine's eyes were dreamy. "You fear him, this husband of yours, yet you love him with every fibre of your being. You may not be aware of it yet, but it is so."

Elinor's eyes pricked with sudden tears. How could she have been so stupid as not to recognize that all-consuming love for Gerard Cranley? She had told herself fiercely over and over again that the aching longing she felt was merely the reaction to her vulnerability. He had snatched her from home and kinsmen. In Bruges he had been her one link with England. She had leaned on his strength. Hadn't he nursed and comforted her on the ship, when she had shivered in an agony of fear? Her traitorous body had responded to his and she had denied the truth of it. He was her enemy, always she had to remember that. Finally she had come to fear him and had accepted her responsibility to Simon Radbourne. Because the boy cherished a hopeless love for her, he had imperilled himself and her one thought had been to extricate him from the consequences of his folly. She knew now that if she had not felt guilty about involving Simon in her schemes, she would never have fled from Bruges. She would have faced Lord Gerard's accusations, endured the punishment which would have undoubtedly followed.

What had she done? She had turned her back on her one hope of happiness, there could be none, she knew now, without Lord Gerard beside her. This terrible war, which ravaged the land and divided cousin from cousin and brother from brother, had made them enemies, and she was powerless to halt what she had set in motion. He would not forgive her defection, for she had shamed him further. How would all this end; in the death of one or all of the men she held dear, her father, Reginald, Simon — or her husband?

"Have no fears, Madame la Vicomtesse, all will go well with you. I know it."

Jeannine had known of her love, had felt it flow from her. The lute player's simple statement uttered so confidently, caused Elinor to wonder yet not to doubt. Jeannine was a seer, a sensitive. All her life Elinor had been taught to fear and distrust such powers in mortals. Gifts of prophecy were heretical and could come only from the devil, yet Elinor recognized no evil in the woman who faced her, only a deep compassion and true wisdom. She reached out for the older woman's hand.

"Will you stay with us until Simon is out of danger? I have no right to ask so much of you, yet I believe that you alone can save him."

"We have already decided. We shall go with you to Amboise. In our company you can travel safely through France. Who would recognize La Vicomtesse Cranley and her squire in the woman and youth who accompany the travelling musicians? It is possible that we shall receive news. Men talk to travellers such as us freely enough. You will reach your cousin in time, before he leaves King Louis's Court, yet — " Jeannine lifted her shoulders and let them fall in a little enigmatic shrug. "There, Madame la Vicomtesse, you can safely leave the problems of the journey to us."

"But we shall take you from your way."

"No, it was our intention to attach ourselves to the wagon train of Queen Marguerite of England. It is becoming dangerous for us to remain here. We would be safer out of France for a while at least."

"You, too, are threatened by enemies?"

"Not immediately." Again Jeannine uttered her little sigh of resignation. "You have already guessed at the truth, Madame la Vicomtesse. We are heretics. We carry the truth of our mysteries to all our brotherhood along the way. Our fellowship was almost destroyed centuries ago, yet the Ancient Mysteries cannot die and those of us who remain true to our beliefs continue to practise our faith and to minister to those who have need of us."

"You are not true believers in Holy Mother Church?" Though she had partially guessed at it, Elinor was visibly shocked by Jeannine's confession.

"So you have heard the ugly rumours; that those of us who harbour heretical beliefs practise witchcraft, sacrifice children in our rites, worship idols? I see the doubt and fear in your eyes. You have been well taught, madame. Tell me, do you believe that the God you worship created the whole earth and everything and everyone in it?"

Elinor crossed herself devoutly. "Of course I do."

"Then can you believe that what gifts I have do not come from him? My knowledge is not bought from some imp or devil at the price of my immortal soul, but truly learned after much seeking and meditation and the purifying of the flesh. The priests of Rome seek our lives only because we challenge their authority. We know that salvation is for the spirit to achieve after much suffering and the experiences of many lives."

"Lives?" Elinor echoed the word doubtfully. "Do you not pray that you will die and after the pains of purgatory enter the perfect happiness of God's heaven?"

"That, too, surely, in God's good time, for we shall have then become perfect, as our Father in Heaven is perfect."

Elinor had some vague remembrance of Father John's teaching. Hadn't some godless sect in Southern France centuries ago suffered persecution for their heretical beliefs? The Pope had preached a Holy Crusade against them and many had perished. Albigensians, the believers had been called, since the city of Albi had been the centre of the cult, or Cathari, the Pure. Their priests had been termed 'the perfects'.

So the beliefs of Jeannine and Blaise were akin to those 'doomed ones', yet she could not find it in her heart to consider them evil. She would not speak again of the matter. They had trusted her. Their lives were in her keeping and she had implicit faith in their ability to bring her and Simon safely to King Louis's Court.

10

WHEN Elinor rose next morning, Jeannine had already made up the fire and was laying out food for the meal. She smiled reassuringly.

"All is well, madame. The young man is better this morning. There is no fever. He is weak and confused, but it will be safe enough for him to travel in the cart. We should not stay here too long."

Elinor shuddered in agreement. Even now she was afraid that her husband might be following and she could not rid herself of the vague dread that the two footpads who had been killed might have had companions who would come looking for them. Jeannine had heated water for her to wash and for this she was grateful. After her terrible adventures of the previous day Elinor felt positively unclean. She made a hurried toilette and when Blaise came to the fire she ate with the two musicians.

Jeannine flashed Blaise an enquiring

glance and he shook his head, doubtfully.

"The young messire has eaten the gruel. He seemed hungry and has fallen asleep again." He looked meaningfully at Elinor and added quietly, "He still does not appear to remember what happened to him."

Elinor's golden eyes widened in alarm. "Simon has lost his memory? But — "

"Not entirely, madame. He asked after you, knows he is responsible for your safety and would not eat until I told him you were well and he would see you soon. But he does not appear to remember his fight with the beggars or what has caused his injuries."

"Such a condition is not unusual following a blow to the head," Jeannine explained. "He must sleep, let nature do its work. His memory will return, in time. For the present try not to worry him, madame. Provided he sees you are well and that you put your trust in us he will accept the situation."

Elinor nodded doubtfully. She *did* indeed trust the two musicians, though she couldn't explain even to herself why she did so.

"Your mounts have been fed," Blaise told her. "If you will take my advice you will allow me to sell them, madame. If you are to travel with us, as one of us, you must walk beside the cart. Can you do that?"

"Of course, whatever you think best. I do not want to be a charge on you. As I told Jeannine last night, I have no gold until — "

"You need not think of payment, madame." Jeannine rose and went to the cart.

"Where will you sell the horses, monsieur, in Amiens?"

Blaise nodded. "I think it best if we buy food for the journey at some tavern on the way. You say your squire spoke of a place nearby?"

"Yes, he brought back food and fodder for the horses. I think it was there he was followed — "

"Quite likely, madame. We must take care, but they will think it pointless to warn footpads of troubadours on the road. We are known to be poorer than peasants. There will be no danger for us or for the boy. Trust us."

Jeannine returned with a bundle of clothing. This time Elinor did not scruple to adopt the disguise. Jeannine's bright skirt of scarlet wool and coarse peasant blouse were scrupulously clean and faintly aromatic-scented.

The lute player surveyed her, lips pursed. "The skirt is long, but not too long. It will serve, but you are very pale, madame. No one would believe you've travelled the roads with us. I'll rub some dark coloured salve into your cheeks. It will not smell pleasant, but it will darken the skin temporarily. Do not concern yourself. It will wash out simply enough when needed."

Elinor put herself unreservedly into Jeannine's hands. She tied a peasant kerchief over her loosened hair, though the lute player scorned to do so. A coarse woven fringed shawl completed the outfit and Jeannine declared that she would pass for a jongleur and could help them at performances by collecting coin and possibly accompanying either her or Blaise on the tambourine. She laughed at Elinor's rueful expression. "It is not so difficult, madame. I can instruct you very simply. Your beauty will attract our audience. It is frequently done. A troubadour will employ some young gypsy girl to do such work for him."

Simon was drowsing in the cart, in a kind of stupor. He did not stir when Blaise made that strange clucking sound to the stolid little donkey and, with the two horses tied to the cart's tail, the little party set off. Jeannine insisted that Elinor ride in the cart on the first leg of their journey.

"Your ankle is still weak," she declared, "though healing well. When we pass through the villages you must walk with me, but rest now, while you can."

The tavern on the Amiens road was a poor place as Simon had told her. Blaise left the two women in the fetid and smoky tap room, the only one the place boasted below stairs, while he went off into the town, presumably to sell the horses. Jeannine carried out broth to Simon and reported he had woken briefly and eaten it.

"He has fallen asleep again," she said as Elinor rose to go to him.

Elinor hesitated. She suspected that the lute player had drugged Simon but those green eyes regarded her steadily and she sank back on the bench, prepared to continue to trust her new companions. Their own meal was ill-cooked but hot and nourishing and Elinor was thankful for the rough comfort the sulky peat fire offered.

Blaise was soon back and they waited only until he, too, had eaten, before continuing their journey into the town. Elinor blushed hotly when the troubadour handed her a leather bag of coins.

"I could not get their true worth, madame, but I thought it best not to haggle. Better for you and the boy if we attract as little notice as possible."

Elinor insisted that he accept the money to compensate the two in part at least for their care of herself and Simon. Jeannine took the leather bag without further argument and stowed it with their supplies within the cart.

Blaise had arranged lodgings for them at an inn some way from the town. It was not their usual practice, but Jeannine was still concerned for Simon.

"He should not spend another night in the open," she said. "If he takes a chill now, in his weakened state, it could prove fatal."

What story Blaise had told the landlord, Elinor could not guess, but he stayed beside the cart in the stable, Simon well wrapped and comfortable on the feather-filled mattress, while Elinor shared with Jeannine the one bed the inn possessed. The mattress was grimy and scratchy, but she was too exhausted to care and slept without dreaming or waking.

She woke to find the room empty. For one terrible moment she entertained a fear that her companions had deserted her, then rose and dressed hurriedly in the bitterly cold room. Jeannine was waiting in the tap room and silently offered her a cup of mulled ale.

"I have already tended your squire. We must go quickly, madame."

"How is Simon?"

"Improving."

"Does he remember?"

The lute player's shoulders rose and fell in a regretful shrug. "It will be some time yet, madame. I have told you."

319

They had travelled some distance and stopped to water Phedre when they were overtaken by a pedlar's cart. Elinor had seen the swarthy little Frenchman pass them on the road the previous day and, since he hailed Blaise familiarly, she guessed they often met on the road. She could not tell what passed between the two men but when the pedlar's cart lumbered off, Blaise returned to them, his face grave.

"Marcel says there was a stranger asking questions at that first tavern, about a woman and a young man, a *scarred* young man."

Elinor gave a little frightened cry. Jeannine hushed her with a commanding gesture.

"And the landlord saw the messire in the cart?"

"I think he did."

"Ah." She considered, green eyes narrowed. "Then we must turn aside from our road, approach Paris a different way."

Blaise nodded slowly, though his expression was concerned.

"If we reach Amboise too late — if

the Queen's army has left, what then?"

Again Jeannine shrugged. "Then we must take a separate way to the coast. The presence of Madame and the squire will give us added protection. We are known to the priests as two troubadours. Who will suspect us, especially as we must take extra care that we minister to no member of our brotherhood, for their sakes as much as our own."

Elinor obeyed Jeannine when she ordered her to jump up quickly into the cart as Blaise turned Phedre and led the patient little beast painstakingly through the rough copse onto a less frequented road. The man at the inn near Amiens? Had Lord Gerard himself followed her, or had he sent Ralf or his sergeant? Simon stirred and looked up at her wonderingly. She bent and wiped his brow.

"There's nothing to be afraid of, Simon. We are taking another way. Does your wound pain you?"

He shook his head and, again, she wondered if Jeannine had administered some herbal brew in his food to keep him quiet and dull his pain.

"You are quite unharmed, My Lady?"

"Yes, Simon. These people have been very good to me. They are taking us to Amboise."

"Amboise?" He looked at her doubtfully. "The French Court is at Amboise."

"Yes, my kinsman is there. You offered to escort me. Don't you remember?" She saw him struggling to recall, but he was gazing at her with that dumb devotion he always afforded her. "Hush," she said softly. "Jeannine has said you must sleep. You'll soon be well again and my champion."

He nodded, smiling, and settled to sleep again.

Over the next few days his injuries healed well, but despite all Jeannine's skill his memory did not return and he spent long hours drowsing in the cart. Eventually he recovered sufficiently to be able to walk with the others, for the stolid little donkey trotted manfully under the weight of their supplies, costumes, musical instruments and household equipment. Simon accepted Elinor's account of the fight with the robbers but he appeared to remember nothing of his ordeal in the dungeons of the ducal palace at Bruges. Elinor allowed him to assume that he had acquired that disfiguring scar in the fight. When Lord Gerard's name was mentioned, he appeared to believe Elinor's journey was with her husband's approval, or at least he did not question her reasons for wishing to leave Bruges. Soon both came to accept their wandering life and lack of creature comforts as if they had never been used to any other.

Blaise and Jeannine performed in many of the villages they passed through and Elinor fell completely beneath the spell of their artistry. They were no common, vulgar jongleurs whose humour was suited to coarse and low tastes, but true poets. Both were proficient on several instruments, including the mandola, the viol, the psaltery and tambourine. Blaise occasionally also performed upon the reed pipes and the kettle drums. It was a delight to Elinor to sit at the cart's tail and listen to the wonderful tales of lovers, of Tristan and his tragic passion for Iseult, of Arthur, Lancelot and Guinevere and, more dramatically, of Parsifal and the Quest of the Holy Grail. Jeannine had kept her promise and taught Elinor the rudiments of rhythm so she was sometimes allowed to play the tambourine while Blaise sang and Jeannine danced. She was becoming aware of the inner truths of the legends and her admiration for her companions grew, though she was also afraid for them. The sight of a brown or black priestly habit amongst the spectators kept her on thorns of apprehension that their inner purpose might be recognized and the pair hauled before some ecclesiastical court and charged with heresy.

Their relationship puzzled her, for never once during the journey did Jeannine sleep with Blaise, though always she referred to him as 'her man'. Dressed in the vibrant scarlets and greens, golds and tinsels of her performing costumes, Jeannine was an excitingly beautiful woman and Elinor could not believe that the lute player was not as passionate a lover as she was herself.

Once, timidly, she broached the subject. They were sitting alone by the camp fire, the men busied with Phedre's needs and the checking of supplies for the next day. Elinor had been silent all day, her concern for Simon's fate when they reached Amboise and her bitter sense of loss and longing for her husband occupying her mind to the exclusion of everything else. Even Blaise's beautiful voice had failed to win her from her feelings of melancholy.

"You are thinking of Milord, your husband," Jeannine said gently, "wondering if he has yet sailed for England."

"Yes, and worrying about Simon."

"Simon is improving day by day, in fact the open air and hard exercise have been good for him. His inner wounds are healing."

Elinor looked at her sharply. "You mean he does not remember what Lord Gerard did to him, because it is too painful for him to bear?"

Jeannine inclined her head. "I have noticed that does happen sometimes. I think perhaps he loved his lord dearly until — " she shrugged.

Elinor looked away over the drifting smoke of the fire to where the squire stood in earnest talk with Blaise.

"Until he saw and came to love me?"

"That is not your fault, Madame la Vicomtesse."

"Yet I feel responsible, Jeannine. I came between Simon and his loyalty both to his master and to the House of York."

"Yet you gave him no encouragement."

"No, none, yet I could be the cause of his death." She gave a little shiver of remembrance. "I think My Lord would have seen him die a barbaric, traitor's death without lifting a finger to save him and all because he believed I had seduced Simon from his duty."

"Your lord must then have great love for you."

"Oh, no, Jeannine," Elinor gazed at her blankly. "He married me simply to safeguard his interests. It was an arranged match. He — I — there was no love between us." She broke off, confused by the steady regard of those strange green eyes.

"Yet love can come very quickly, an exchange of glances across a room, an unexpected meeting." Jeannine fed the fire with fresh kindling.

"And your love for Blaise?" Elinor stammered. "Was your . . . " she groped for words to cover her embarrassment for she did not know if the two were wed in the eyes of the Church, "your association planned by your parents? I mean — as mine was?"

"Not by our parents, but destined for all that, as true lovers always meet by predestination."

"Yet you do not make love — " Elinor was horrified by her own temerity as she blurted out the question.

Jeannine laughed, shaking back the thick masses of her lovely red hair. "While we are on the road I must remain chaste. As you see, not only do I sing, but tumble and dance for the crowds. Men call us strumpets, yet all tumblers are more chaste than other women. When we are safe, in England, then Blaise and I will become true lovers and, if I am blessed, I shall bear his child."

★ ★ ★

If Bruges had proved a revelation to the country bred Elinor, it paled to

327

insignificance beside the splendours of Paris and Chartres, where the towers and gargoyles of the Gothic cathedrals dominated the mean streets which clustered below them. The glory of the stained glass windows caught her breathless in admiration, but she was also saddened by the sight of maimed and deformed beggars who harassed the worshippers, their hands outstretched, imploring them for alms, near the porches of both great churches. In Paris, the troubadours gave one performance in an inn yard on the isle of the city near the cathedral of Notre Dame. Students and scholars flocked to hear them and they were given rapturous attention and applause. Here their poetic artistry was understood and recognized as it could not be within the villages and hamlets where they had played along the way.

Once in the valley of the Loire the weather became milder and travelling pleasant. Here were the fruit orchards bordering the long stretches of yellow muddy river. Further South vineyards were cultivated in terraces and the river widened and islands could be seen in its centre, despite the heavy rains of winter. In this lovely valley, the greatest nobles had built their castles and, amongst them, high placed on the left bank of the river like an illustration from one of her favourite romances, stood Amboise itself.

Blaise pulled up the cart in a wood just outside the town walls while they decided how best to proceed.

Elinor was concerned for the safety of her friends. "The King is in residence and it might be dangerous for you and Blaise. There will be many priests in attendance, even members of the Inquisition. Will travelling musicians be suspected of heresy?"

"Blaise and I have already made provisions for that. We hoped to join the baggage train of the English army. My skills with the healing herbs would have been useful to the soldiery and Blaise is a fair cook, and provided he sticks to the common, bawdy songs of the jongleur we should not be suspected. But now matters are different. You should not go to the palace unaccompanied by a serving woman. It's true that since the trial and burning of the Maid, Jeanne d'Arc, there has been a revival of persecution of people like us who perform and travel the roads, especially since I have the gift of prophecy, though naturally I make no mention of that to strangers." She laughed. "I have the colouring of the accredited witch, have I not, the red hair and green eyes of the cat? If I dispose of my colourful gypsy clothing and go dressed soberly as your maid, Blaise can join the wagon train as we originally planned. It might be best if, at first, he is not known to be connected with Madame la Vicomtesse Cranley."

Elinor's eyes were troubled as she looked up at her friend.

"You are thinking that we might need a means of escape?"

Jeannine's eyes danced. "I think it necessary always to have means of escape from any fortress, madame, and Amboise is a grim one for all its outward beauty."

Simon refused even to consider Elinor's suggestion that he stay with Blaise.

"It is my duty to stay close by your

side, My Lady, even in the camp of the enemy."

Within the cart, Elinor dressed with care. She had in her bundle only her green woollen gown and simple head-dress. Jeannine helped her to once more braid up her hair and pin it securely beneath the silk covered cap. Her cloak had been carefully sponged and brushed. Jeannine had already whitened her complexion again by the application of a different salve, but the harsh winds and cold had roughened and chafed her skin and Elinor knew she would appear more peasant than lady when she presented herself at the castle gate. Jeannine, dressed in the skirt and blouse Elinor had herself taken from the Flemish girl, Beatrix, made a passable waiting woman, her bright hair hidden by wimple and veil. Simon wore no livery so his plain garb could not attract hostility from the Queen's men-at-arms.

For all that, Elinor's mouth was dry with apprehension when the three approached the outer ramparts of the castle on foot. Blaise had already led Phedre into the town and would find a tavern where he could lodge until he was able to approach some sergeant inside the castle and obtain employment with the army.

Viewed from a distance, the fortress had assumed a fairy-tale appearance with its ornamented high turrets and shining white stone, now the huge walls and gate house towered above them menacingly.

Simon halted for a moment and gazed upwards. He frowned and she saw him touch fleetingly the scar which ran from brow to the corner of his mouth. He turned and looked full at her and she was aware that he was once more fully knowledgeable about his service with Lord Gerard. He had spoken haltingly of fragmentary glimpses of the past during these last days of the journey. It was as Jeannine had said. The sight of this massive fortress had jarred his memory. He drew a hard breath, his expression stern and she touched him gently upon the arm.

"If you wish to do so, find Blaise, Simon. I shall be safe enough with my kinsman. Your work is done. I would not have you treat with the enemy."

"I will not leave you, My Lady."

His chin was set in a stubborn line and she sighed faintly. There would be no moving him. Proudly he advanced and challenged the sergeant of the guard.

The man rubbed his chin doubtfully as he looked from him to the shabbily dressed and ill-attended lady who was demanding admission but, noting her haughty manner and the insistence of her squire, he passed them through the gatehouse into the outer courtyard. The place, like the ducal palace at Bruges, was ahum with activity and the three found themselves the object of many insolent and curious stares from men-at-arms wearing both the French royal livery and those of the nobles who had exiled themselves to serve Queen Margaret. Elinor continued to hold her head high as she walked towards the inner gate, but inwardly she was nervous of her coming meeting with Reginald. Would he greet her thankfully or had she placed him in an awkward position by escaping from her husband?

Within the great hall a supercilious steward, brandishing his ivory wand of office and clad in the blue and white silk of Louis's household, his tunic ornamented with the device of the fleur-de-lys, accosted them.

"My Lady Cranley has journeyed here from the Burgundian Court to see her kinsman, Messire Reginald Beckwith." Simon addressed the man in English with lordly disdain for the possibility of the official's inability to understand or communicate in that language.

The man conferred with his underlings. Covert glances were cast at Elinor as she stood aloof, unbending, Jeannine in close attendance. A shabbily dressed clerk in rusty black rattled out an interpretation of Simon's demand and himself addressed Elinor.

"In all humility I beg Madame to pardon my seeming impertinence, but it is necessary that we have proof of her identity before we dare to trouble Messire Beckwith."

Convinced that arrogance was the best attitude to assume when dealing with Court officials, Elinor surveyed the steward with the same haughtiness that Simon had adopted. She addressed him in French and ignored the clerk.

"I am the wife of Viscount Cranley and the cousin of Messire Beckwith. Is he still in the castle in attendance upon Queen Margaret or has he already left for England?"

"Messire Beckwith is still here, Madame la Vicomtesse."

Removing her wedding ring bearing the Cranley signet and the necklace returned to her by Lord Gerard, she offered them to the steward. "My cousin cannot fail to recognize these jewels. My squire will accompany you into his presence." The inference was obvious and the man's pale cheeks flushed dark red with anger. So he was not to be trusted with tokens so paltry! He bowed frigidly and signalled to Simon to accompany him from the hall. The clerk, bowing obsequiously, conducted Elinor and her maid to a seat in one of the great window bays.

Elinor forced herself to sit still and rigidly upright, knowing herself to be the subject of speculation by many of the pages and squires who flocked the hall, some lounging on stools, others occupying their time at chess or with dice while they waited to be summoned by their masters. Firmly she controlled a tendency to tap her foot nervously on the elaborately tiled floor. This situation was intolerable. Even the officials were better clad than she was.

A door was flung open at the far end of the hall and a young nobleman attended by several gentlemen impetuously burst in.

He was dressed in a sleeveless green silk tunic richly embroidered, over under-tunic and hose of scarlet wool. Elinor shivered inwardly as she noted the unnatural glitter of those dark eyes as his gaze lighted on her. Eyebrows twitched together imperiously as he turned to an older man, more soberly dressed, behind him.

"It seems King Louis's Court is to house more well-born beggars than those in my mother's train." His voice was high, excitable.

The older man smiled faintly and bowed regretfully towards Elinor, guessing that she had heard.

"It would be discourteous, My Prince, to assume so much without knowledge."

The whisper carried to her and Elinor flushed. Though plainly dressed the man was well spoken, obviously no servant.

Anxious to resolve the embarrassing situation, the older man attempted to draw the nobleman's attention from Elinor, for he was continuing to stare at her offensively. "The grooms will have Your Grace's horse ready. Your mother could, even now, send to call us back. You know how anxious she is to keep you in her sight."

The youth was handsome enough, though she read a lack of resolution in that receding clean-shaven chin and the mouth was held in a pettishly drooping line.

"That's true, De Vere. God's blood, she treats me like a child. My cousin Richard is scarcely a year my senior, yet Edward of York trusts him with the command of an army and the victualling of his troops." The dark eyes flashed impatiently. "When we are quartered in Westminster palace again, I'll prove to them all how much a man I am, especially that bitch of a wife of mine." He uttered a harsh laugh and strode past Elinor, the older man hard on his heels.

There came a hurried patter of boots on the polished tiles and another man entered the hall. The two near the outer door swung round to face him. Elinor gave a little gasp as she recognized her cousin, Reginald, the steward puffing in his wake.

He glanced hurriedly across at the two English lords and bowed low.

"My Lord Edward, I had not known you were here."

"Then my mother has not sent you to forbid me to go hawking?"

"No, Your Grace, I came in search of — " He had by now seen Elinor who half rose from the bench to greet him. She was reassured by his smile of welcome. "Forgive me, sir, if I seem lacking in true respect. I forget myself when I see my dear cousin, safe at last with her own kinsmen."

He hastened to her side and bent to kiss her fingers.

"Allow me to present Lady Elinor Cranley, Your Grace. Her father, Sir Thomas Beckwith, is one of Lord

Montecute's gentlemen."

The youth bowed stiffly, his dark eyes passing over her shabby attire with ill-concealed contempt.

"My mother will be pleased to receive you, Lady," he said coldly. "We have heard of your plight, married to that traitor, Cranley, against your will, we understand. Come, de Vere, let us go while we have opportunity."

Elinor curtseyed low. It needed no explanation from Reginald for her to realize that she was in the presence of Queen Margaret's son, Edward Prince of Wales. Poor Lady Anne, wed to this discourteous youth whom Elinor had heard talked of little but the proposed executions of his enemies!

The heavy door swung to as the two men left with their attendants and Elinor lifted troubled eyes to look full at her cousin. He laughed joyously, despite his expression of utter astonishment.

"Elinor, I hardly dared believe the truth of this fellow's tale, yet he carried Cranley's signet and then, of course, I recognized his squire and got confirmation from him that you were truly here and waiting for me."

Elinor looked to the far door where Simon stood uncertainly.

"I was afraid that you might already have left for England."

Reginald shook his head. "I wait to go with the Queen, but it cannot be long now before we leave. I must present you to her. As His Grace Prince Edward said, she will welcome you royally."

"But more sincerely than her son?" Elinor whispered so low that only he could hear.

Reginald's eyes twinkled at her. "He is a somewhat unusual young man, as you will learn, but we must humour his whims if he is to be our future King. Come." He drew her quickly from the hall, signalling to Jeannine and Simon to await their return.

In the corridor he checked, his expression grave and anxious.

"What has happened, Elinor? Your husband has not threatened . . . harmed you? How did you escape him?"

Elinor glanced round uncertainly. She felt bereft now that Jeannine was not close.

"There were reasons — " she broke off uncertainly. "Simon helped me and my maid, Jeannine. Can't we go somewhere more private to talk? I need to know so much. How is my father? Does your wound still trouble you?" She touched Reginald's arm gently. "I feared you were killed till I heard word at the Court at Bruges that you were here in attendance on Queen Margaret."

He gave a little harsh laugh. "As you see, cousin, I'm very much alive still and your husband will learn that, to his cost, and very shortly."

Elinor went icy cold. This deadly hatred between her kinsmen and her husband would bring them all to disaster.

He nodded understandingly and drew her along the corridors of the palace to a wing less richly furnished and decorated. In a small, bare room which overlooked the tilt yard, he gestured her to seat herself upon an uncushioned window seat. There were one or two older ladies present, but some distance from them, so they could not be overheard. One looked up curiously and whispered to her companion. A young page was half asleep on his feet. Elinor supposed this to be the antechamber to Queen Margaret's apartments.

Reginald was elegantly dressed in blue velvet and she thought he had not had to flee his home without baggage or jewels as his King and Gerard Cranley had had to do. He was frowning at her thoughtfully and she shifted nervously under his scrutiny.

"Your father described to me how you were forced into this shameful marriage. How are things with you, Elinor? I swear by all I hold sacred I'll seek out this husband of yours and free you from this hateful match. Set your mind at rest on that score. I wait only for the opportunity in battle — or after. It can't be long now."

She looked down at her hands, tightly clasped upon her knee. Now was not the time to talk with Reginald about her husband.

"Then my father is well and with Lord Montecute?"

"Yes, he reached Doncaster only two days after your marriage at Grantham. I was still in bed at Beckwith recovering from my wounds. The infirmarian was sent for from Roche Abbey and he tended me. We realized we could do nothing for you at that stage. Indeed, to have tried to prevent him from sailing from England might have endangered you. But how have you managed to get free from him and travel from Bruges and in such bad weather?"

She told him briefly how she had quarrelled with Lord Gerard, and about the message she had attempted to send to Amboise. Deliberately she omitted to tell him how her husband had punished her.

"I had put Simon into danger. The Duke of Gloucester obtained his release but he had to leave Flanders. He was willing to escort me to France and I seized the opportunity to escape from Bruges. But we were attacked on the road and Simon badly injured." She filled in hastily the story of her struggle for life in the ruined hut. "He suffered a blow to the head and until now has remembered very little of what happened to him before the fight. He's devoted to me and will do whatever I ask." She looked up searchingly at her cousin. "I feel responsible for his safety now that he is in the hands of Lancastrian nobles."

Reginald nodded brusquely. "He'll be safe enough in our company. I'll see to it."

"So now the Queen's army is ready for England? I had hoped that I could travel in her train to join my father."

Reginald's frown returned. "I'll send a messenger to your father the moment we land in England. He's still in Montecute's camp. My Lord will be pleased to hear the news. With you a hostage in Cranley's hands we could not deal with young John Cranley as we wished. Now we're free to dispose of one more Yorkist viper."

This was a Reginald she had not known before, ruthless, determined and lustful for land and power. Her blood ran cold as she thought how she had sealed John Cranley's doom by her escape to France.

Reginald was continuing to talk and his words filled her with horror.

"As things have turned out, your marriage should prove a blessing in disguise. When Cranley dies your dower rights should prove substantial." He looked at her keenly. "Unless he has already sown his seed in you, in which case it will be a simple matter for us to obtain control of the estate until the young heir comes of age."

Her cheeks flamed. It was far too soon to be sure yet. She had noticed Jeannine regarding her closely several times during their journey. True, she had not seen her expected course, yet that proved nothing. It could come late. That coupling in Bruges could not have brought about conception! She shied from the possibility.

If Reginald noted her distress at his brutal comment, he did not allow it to disconcert him. His eyes raked over her as hotly as Lord Hastings's had done. He reached out and took her hand, squeezing it tightly. "You cannot be ignorant of my feelings for you, Elinor. We have been childhood companions. Lately I have been tortured by the thought that you were promised to Cranley. Now this could turn out well for us. You will be a wealthy widow and I a loving and eager bridegroom. Our kin is not so close that we couldn't petition His

Holiness the Pope for a dispensation for our marriage."

Her flesh crawled. She suddenly felt sick, as if she could no longer bear such close proximity to this man. It was as she had suspected all along. Her father and cousin had used her shamelessly to trap Lord Cranley and further their own ends. Had Reginald hoped from the beginning that her young husband would be killed and he would be free to marry his rival's wealthy widow? It seemed that his love for her had not been strong enough for him to risk a declaration without the assurance that he would gain in gold and lands from such a love match.

Yet she had to have confirmation of such dreadful suspicions against the honour of her own kin. She swallowed hard and withdrew her hand from Reginald's grasp.

"Then — my betrothal ceremony was set as a deliberate trap for Gerard Cranley?"

"Aye, it was, and we hoped to net bigger fish than he. We thought Gloucester would attend, he and Cranley have always been friendly, or even

Edward himself." He shrugged. "That would have been a great catch but things went wrong. Cranley was warned and I was horrified when he made off with you as hostage. Still, as I've said, it appears that things have turned out even better for us though, naturally, I would not have had you suffer as you did, Elinor. I'm relieved you have come to us now, safe and well."

She turned away to hide her contempt from him. So, he had actually felt some fear for her. That was indeed kind of him! He and her father had put her in danger and had the grace to be concerned for her safety! Should she be thankful for some crumb of comfort, at least? This bluff, jovial young man, whom she had liked and trusted, had revealed himself to her in a totally new light.

Now she faced her plight bleakly. She had again put herself into the hands of men whose only interest in her was as a pawn in the high-staked game they were playing.

She would now be guarded most rigorously. She had wished only to be free from this conflict of interests, free to wait quietly at home for the outcome under her father's care. Now she knew that was impossible. Whether her husband lived or died in these coming battles, her father and cousin would try to use her against him. Her limbs trembled with shock and she leaned back wearily against the cold leaded window pane.

Reginald came instantly close to her side. He put a supporting arm round her shoulder. She stiffened instinctively at his touch. "Elinor, you're not ill?"

"No, just exhausted by the journey and — afraid that I would not find you or that I would not be admitted." There was no escape from his closeness. The window seat was too narrow for her to move further from him. His breath fanned her cheek. She felt physically sick.

His tone thickened and he leaned towards her. "You have suffered much, Elinor, but it's all over now. You are safe with me again."

"Yes," she murmured breathlessly, "but I'm very tired, Reginald. Can you find some place for me to rest and there is my maid, Jeannine — "

"You must first be presented to Her Grace, Queen Margaret. I'll ask her to place you amongst her ladies. Certainly she will offer you her protection."

She put up a hand to push him gently from her. "Then if you would see to it — "

He totally misunderstood her action or chose to do so. He drew her up and into his arms, his lips crushing hard upon hers, one hand fondling her breasts beneath her cloak so that she writhed under the touch of his fingers.

"Please," she entreated him, "remember, cousin, I am still Lord Cranley's wife in the eyes of Holy Church and — "

His lips were wet and hot on her own. "Not for long, Elinor," he muttered hoarsely, "I promise you that."

She felt herself about to faint when, thankfully, she heard a door opening somewhere behind them. Reginald muttered an oath beneath his breath and hastily released her.

Embarrassed, Elinor stumbled and almost fell. Looking up, confused, she encountered the hard stare of a pair of shrewd black eyes. She curtseyed low, knowing herself to be in the presence of Margaret of Anjou. King Henry's French-born Queen was dressed in an outmoded gown of emerald and silver brocade, belted high under her breasts, and with loose flowing sleeves lined in emerald silk and dagged at the edges. Her heart-shaped head-dress, which surmounted a jewelled caul over her dark hair, had also been out of fashion at the Yorkist Court for many years, but despite the rubbed shabbiness of her gilded leather belt and the tarnishing upon the caul's gilt mesh, she made an imposing and somewhat frightening figure. Elinor could well believe how her former beauty had stirred the hearts of English nobles when she had come from Anjou as a child bride for King Henry.

Slightly behind her stood another lady Elinor judged to be about her own age. She was dressed in a blue gown trimmed with white fur. Her head-dress was simple, the veil framing a heart-shaped face, gentle in expression. Deep blue eyes regarded Elinor gravely but there was no hostility in their steady gaze. Elinor read in it a genuine longing for true companionship and understanding. She smiled back timidly in answer. Was this truly Duke Richard of Gloucester's love, the Lady Anne, the Queen's daughter-in-law?

Reginald was presenting her. Again the Queen's unwinking dark eyes were fixed upon Elinor and she waited for some moments before addressing her. At last the greeting came, harsh with the hint of French intonation and utterly without warmth.

"So, Master Beckwith, this is the cousin who was married against her will. So she looks for refuge at our Court. You are welcome, Mistress."

Elinor bowed her head. "Thank you, Your Grace."

Reginald was continuing. "My cousin hopes she may have the honour of serving you, Your Grace. She is naturally anxious to return to England in your train."

The Queen did not reply immediately and Elinor felt herself flushing dully under that chilling stare.

A soft, low-pitched voice broke across the hostile silence.

"I understand Lady Cranley to be a

Yorkshire-born lady like myself. It would give me great pleasure to have her serve me, Madam, if you would grant it. We should have so much to talk about."

The Queen's dark eyes flickered spitefully as she turned them upon her daughter-in-law. She shrugged, spreading her hands wide in an expansive gesture. "It can matter little to me whom the lady serves," she said coldly. "If you wish to have her by you, Anne, why, so be it."

She turned majestically towards the elderly serving woman who waited by the door, nodded coldly to Reginald and swept from the anteroom.

Elinor turned nervously to her new mistress.

Anne smiled again, courteously dismissing Reginald. "You can safely leave Lady Cranley in my charge, Master Beckwith. She can sleep in my chamber tonight, and then we must find her lodgings close to my own apartments. Will you send her attendants to wait upon her there?"

He bowed low. Elinor read the frustrated fury in his eyes as he withdrew.

She drew a thankful sigh of relief. Here in this alien Court she was sure

352

she had found one person who could offer her protection from her cousin's importunities and, later, it would be possible to speak to her mistress of Richard of Gloucester.

11

LORD GERARD reined in his hack and pushed back his cloak hood. Ralf Brent grunted in admiration as he peered up at Amboise castle, its fine white building stone shining in the February sunshine. It dominated the left bank of the Loire, its turrets fancifully adorned yet, for all that, he did not doubt that the French King's castle was effectively guarded and its dungeons as noisome as any in Flanders or England.

Ahead lay the town gates and Ralf sighed as Lord Gerard advanced his mount at a walk. He was dressed as he had left England, in merchant's garb, but his military bearing and proud tilt of the head could betray him as a man more used to issuing commands than haggling over current prices.

Once in the shadow of the mean streets which clustered below the castle, Lord Gerard made for the nearest inn whose sign bore the badly executed painting of a grey cat. Ralf followed him into the tap room, taking his place at table by Lord Gerard when his lord beckoned him. The room was packed with a motley assortment of humanity, liveried men-at-arms, clerics, townsmen and apprentices. Lord Gerard's steely blue eyes examined all badges of livery. A buxom serving wench eyed him covertly as if she were willing and eager to provide him with more than the district's finest wines. For once Lord Gerard did not so much as notice her.

His impatience had mounted since leaving that tavern on the Amiens road. The innkeeper's description of the travelling musicians and the younger woman who had limped beside them had at first held no interest for him until the man spoke of the injured man lying within the cart, a youth whose face had been badly scarred in a recent encounter with thieves on the road. Surely that could be none other than Simon Radbourne, yet how had he come to be injured? The ice round his heart had thickened on his terrible fear for Elinor. Was she now a prisoner of these itinerant jongleurs and

Simon powerless to protect her?

His instincts told him Elinor would make for Amboise. He ground his teeth in impotent fury when he thought how she would turn to her kinsman Reginald Beckwith, who was in attendance on Queen Margaret.

Now he must enter that nest of traitors and extricate her before the Queen's train embarked for England. He met Ralf's concerned brown eyes with his own level stare. The man was as true as tried steel and as efficient in service, yet he balked at placing him into jeopardy. Beckwith knew him and so did other nobles in the Queen's service. To enter the castle precincts was to invite arrest and imprisonment. His mouth twisted wryly. Elinor might well betray him after his treatment of her. Could she be blamed?

Edward had released him at once from his duties. "If you find your wife on the road, bring her to Bruges, man, if not, join me in England when you can. I don't doubt your loyalty to York."

Lord Gerard fretted to be with his liege lord on this most vital of expeditions but he would not leave Elinor within the hands of a man like Beckwith. She had no knowledge of his true nature. She would blindly trust herself to him. As her husband, it was his first duty to ensure that she was returned to the protective custody of the Duchess Margaret until this business with Warwick was concluded. He sweated, despite the February chill, at the thought of how Beckwith might use her for his own purposes.

His eyes narrowed as he searched the room for the man he sought. Raoul Dupont had once mentioned that he frequented Le Chat Gris inn and Duke Charles's French spy was the only man who could get him safely into the castle.

Ralf Brent grunted and laid a warning hand on his lord's arm.

"By the door, just come in."

Lord Gerard inclined his chin.

Dupont was a thin, seedy-looking man in late middle age, though he could be younger, since that lined, comical countenance could be deceptive. He served King Louis as barber, amused him by his wry witticisms and so became knowledgeable concerning all who flocked to the French King's Court. Doubtless Louis was shrewdly aware of the man's secret occupation and it pleased him to have about him a man who had a foot in both camps, his own and Burgundy's, yet could Lord Gerard trust him to admit him secretly to the castle?

After what seemed an aeon of time the little Frenchman sidled over to the bench where he sat with Ralf and smiled down at them.

"Strangers to Le Chat Gris I bid you welcome messieurs. I, Raoul Dupont, its most celebrated and regular customer."

"Thank you, monsieur. I welcome the friendship of one who knows a town well. Will you drink with us?"

Dupont ordered and waited while the wench served them. Jovially he applied the flat of his hand to her ample rump and she slapped him back, archly.

"Do you bring Duke Charles's message, milord?" Dupont's eyes darted around the room, his voice lowered.

"No, my need is personal. I have to get into the castle without being recognized by any of the English lords. The Queen is still at Amboise?"

"*Oui*, milord."

"Has she recently acquired a new lady-in-waiting, a slender young woman who . . . "

"Madame la Vicomtesse, your wife, *Oui*, milord."

"I must have talk with her."

"I could carry a message — "

"Not enough, I must see her myself."

"Difficult, milord, since she is well attended by her kinsman, Messire Beckwith."

Lord Gerard reddened with anger. "Can you get me in, man?"

The barber regarded him mildly. "The question is, milord, can I get you out again afterwards?"

"I can get myself out."

Dupont shrugged. "There is a water gate. The innkeeper will guide you. I trust him — for a price. You'll come dressed in a footsoldier's jacket. I'll provide badges of livery. Milord the Earl of Oxford's men are camped within the inner courtyard. You must seize an opportunity to contact Madame." The sloe-black eyes flickered thoughtfully to Ralf Brent. "Does your man enter with you?"

"No." Decisively Lord Gerard quelled Ralf's objections by a glance of command.

"*Bon*, then he must be lodged here in the inn. We may have need of him later."

"When do I meet you?"

"Tonight, after vespers."

"Good, the sooner the better. You'll be well paid."

"Then wait, milord, while I make the necessary arrangements with the innkeeper. He'll provide the clothing you'll need."

★ ★ ★

Lord Gerard wrinkled his nose against the sour stink of stale wine which emanated from his guide as the two squatted low in the boat beneath the bare branches of an alder which overlooked the river close by the castle's water gate. The vesper bell had sounded some time earlier and he was cramped and chilled. What could be keeping Dupont? He moved restlessly and saw the landlord's eyes gleam at him reproachfully.

There was a bark of command above them, then the creak and grind of gate mechanism. The innkeeper sent their boat gliding towards the gate. Grimly Lord Gerard noted the man's efficiency. Clearly this wasn't the first time he'd aided and abetted Dupont in his dubious occupation. The boat grounded on shingle and Lord Gerard leapt out lightly, his hand ready upon his dagger hilt.

"*Doucement*," Dupont cautioned him, "you'll find no treachery here, Milord." He led him unhurriedly beneath the raised iron portcullis into the castle precincts then to the guard chamber. He chuckled. "The sergeant will be about his rounds for some time yet." Throwing back the heavy lid of a rough-hewn chest, he drew out a rolled up surcoat bearing the star device of the Earl of Oxford. "Now it will be unwise to be seen talking to me. Many of the English nobles and men-at-arms suspect that I'm a spy for Burgundy. As for the French, they care nothing, so long as I pay well. In this livery you should be able to move freely about the castle and leave by the gate.

If you need me, contact me at Le Chat Gris. I'll see to it that your man stays well out of sight."

Lord Gerard belted on the liveried surcoat. "When I do, I shall be escorting a lady. Can you arrange for a palfrey?"

Dupont's black eyes widened in surprise. "If the lady is willing, milord."

"Willing or not, she comes with me."

Again Dupont shrugged expressively. "Wait for some moments before you follow. *Bonne chance*, milord."

As expected Lord Gerard found the castle tightly packed with men-at-arms, some wearing the royal badge, others the liveries of the English Lancastrian nobles who supported Queen Margaret. It was a simple matter to move about the courtyards without being challenged. Some men saluted him in English which he returned, keeping his head purposefully lowered or averted. He avoided the places where torches in sconces lit up faces too clearly. Others of Oxford's company might know him as a stranger and challenge him to account for his presence in the castle.

It was the hour before supper and

ladies with their attendant nobles were beginning to descend to the banquet hall. He concealed himself in an angle of wall where he might observe the corridor clearly. He had already discovered that this wing housed the exiled Queen and her attendants.

A man paused momentarily beneath a lighted flambeau. He was dressed in red velvet and Lord Gerard recognized the doublet and hose worn by Sir Reginald Beckwith for Elinor's betrothal. He considered, grimly, that after their fight in the courtyard the garments must have required considerable repair.

A door opened and a woman dressed in the sober grey gown and white wimple of a serving maid emerged and curtsied. Lord Gerard stiffened as Elinor appeared behind her. She was dressed in the familiar green gown and the torchlight flickered over her slender form and the folds of her gauze veil billowed in a draft which swept down the corridor. Her face was shadowed and Lord Gerard leaned to watch more closely as her cousin bent to kiss her hand. She appeared to try to avoid him, quickening her step, but Beckwith deliberately delayed her. She backed nervously against the wall, putting out a hand as if to ward him off.

It was impossible for Lord Gerard to hear what was said. Beckwith leaned too close, whispering urgently, and Elinor's reply sounded high and breathless. She was giving hunted glances around her and, abruptly, she wrenched free her hand and moved imperiously ahead of him down the stair.

Lord Gerard's fingertips were torn by the rough stone as he forcibly kept himself in check. To go to her now would doom his chances of winning free later. A page hurried by on an errand. The boy flashed him an astonished glance, as if questioning his loitering in this part of the palace. Finally the wing settled into silence as its chief inhabitants gathered in the hall. Lord Gerard knew now which was Elinor's door but did she share her room with some other lady? Very likely, as the palace was packed to overflowing by courtiers of both royal houses. Yet it was now or never, before the nobles began to leave the feasting and returned to the privacy of their own chambers. Below he heard the sound of reed pipes and viols, interspersed by bursts of laughter. Now, whilst the Court was being entertained, he must deal with Elinor's waiting woman.

He beat a tattoo upon the door and withdrew to one side where he was in deep shadow. The woman emerged and, not immediately seeing the caller, moved further into the corridor to investigate. He slipped inside while her back was turned and as she re-entered, perplexed, he sprang, his hard hand effectively silencing her instinctive cry of terror.

★ ★ ★

Elinor was grateful that the Lady Anne had drawn her to her side as she and Reginald entered the hall. It was becoming more and more difficult to hold him at arm's length. Warwick's daughter had recognized in Elinor a sister in misfortune. Both had been used ruthlessly by their fathers as pawns in the game of power. Both were Northerners, once taught to be loyal to the House of York, now bewildered by the turn of events which made them traitors to their former companions and loves.

It had been hard to hide her fears from Simon. The squire had still not fully recovered from the head wound sustained in her defence. Jeannine's skill had restored him to bodily health but he remained confused and remembered nothing of his punishment at Lord Gerard's hands or indeed little prior to his fight with the robbers. She was concerned that she had involved him in the Lancastrian Cause. He would not leave her and, devoted as he was to her interests, he would recklessly challenge her cousin to combat if he believed the man was forcing his attentions on her. Now she studiously ignored her cousin and gave her complete attention to the musicians. Blaise had been invited to sing and received rapturous approval for his rendering of the sad tale of Tristan and Iseult.

After that frigid reception by Queen Margaret, Elinor had had little or no conversation with her and was grateful for it. The cold ferocity of the Queen's nature was obvious to all who came in contact with her. Since Elinor feared that Reginald might intrude upon her even within her chamber she was glad that the Lady Anne had sometimes requested that she sleep within her chamber on night guard.

The musicians concluded their dance and King Louis left the hall.

"Conduct me to my chamber, Simon, please," Elinor said hastily as Reginald rose at once to escort her. "Stay and enjoy the rest of the dancing, cousin. I have a headache and will retire early unless the Princess of Wales has need of me."

Anne Neville's blue eyes clouded with genuine concern. "Of course you must try to sleep, Elinor. I'll send my maid with a posset for you."

"You are kind, My Lady, but Jeannine is very skilled in preparing herbal potions. I shall be much better tomorrow."

She withdrew thankfully, having no wish to endure Reginald's possessive clutching hands on her body during the intricate and energetic movements of the Court dances. At her door Simon stooped to kiss her hand. "I'll stay on guard in the corridor, My Lady."

She was glad of his shrewdness. If Reginald came to her chamber she would have warning, for he must first clash with Simon.

The squire opened the chamber door and stood back for her. The interior seemed darker than usual. Only one candle was burning on the bed chest. Elinor stood for a moment, accustoming her eyes to the gloom.

"Jeannine?" It was unlike the lute player to be careful with candles and rushlights.

As there was no response, Elinor turned hastily to the shadowed recess behind the door. At first she could not believe her own senses, then the couple huddled there moved into the circle of light, the man impelling his captive forward. Elinor saw Jeannine's green eyes flash warningly over the man's hand which covered her mouth. Elinor's heart leapt in her breast at sight of him.

He said softly, "Cry out and my dagger finds its mark in your maid's back. I trust you have some regard for her."

"I have." Tears blurred Elinor's vision, though her voice was steady. "Please let Jeannine go, My Lord. She is sensible and will not betray you."

"And you, madam?" There was an edge to his tone.

"I am your wife, My Lord. It is a wife's duty to preserve her husband's life."

He laughed softly as he released hold on the lute player. She staggered then righted herself, her anxious gaze passing from her mistress to the intruder.

"You endanger yourself. Why are you here and not in attendance upon the King?"

"It is a husband's duty to ensure his wife's well-being." The tone was mocking but there was also a steely note behind the raillery.

Elinor gave a little sob of despair. "They will take you."

He took her into his arms, regardless of Jeannine's presence, his mouth hard on hers, demanding.

It had been so long for she had steeled herself against all Reginald's blandishments. Her lips parted beneath Lord Gerard's and she experienced the bewildering sweetness and weakness of surrender. He released her so that she could breathe again. His lips brushed the nape of her neck, his fingers impatiently pushing back the gauze of her veiling.

"The woman, can she be trusted?"

"Yes."

"Then send her away."

"Simon is outside the door." He stiffened and she added hurriedly, "He will accept that she goes on an errand for me." She turned to the lute player. "You will speak no word of My Lord's presence?" Her tone was half imperious, half appealing.

"Then you truly wish me to leave you with him, madame?"

"Yes." The single word was whispered tremulously.

"Then certainly, madame. I will go to Blaise. If Madame the Princesse should send for you?"

"That's unlikely. I pleaded indisposition as an excuse to leave the hall early."

"*Oui*, madame." Jeannine withdrew and Lord Gerard stood listening to her muffled conversation with Simon then the light tap of her heels as she moved off down the corridor.

Elinor gave a little helpless movement of her hands as he turned to face her. "Oxford, Reginald and the others, they can all recognize you. You must have known what peril you faced . . . "

"I thought it might be deeper than it is."

Her eyes widened in horror. "You thought *I* would betray you?"

"You have a score to settle."

Again her vision blurred oddly and to cover her sudden embarrassment and fear for him, she turned to the bed.

"You will be safe within my chamber tonight. You must go at first light when the gates are opened."

"*We* must go," he corrected.

"I should merely hinder you in your escape."

"I did not notice that you did on our flight from Beckwith." His tone had softened. She had not spoken of her determination to remain.

"How did you get in, and in de Vere livery?"

"The French barber, Dupont, provided it. You will remember him?" Her cheeks flamed at the flagrant reminder of her attempt to bribe the man to carry her letter to Reginald. He continued, "He appears to have an arrangement with the sergeant-at-arms in command of the castle water gate. You could leave the same way. Will your new maid accompany us?"

She did not answer immediately and, as she struggled ineffectually with the back lacing of her gown, he hastened to her assistance, chuckling. "I'm becoming experienced in the duties of a lady's maid. What if your chamber is invaded. Palaces are plaguey public places!"

She slid between the sheets, sitting up to let free her hair from its braids. "Yet the one place where my right to invite a lover to my bed is unlikely to be remarked upon or questioned. It will ensure your safety tonight, My Lord." This time the hard note was evident in *her* tone.

He threw off his clothes and pulled back the bed coverings, glorying in her loveliness. "And Beckwith will accept that? I saw how he pawed you just now in the corridor." His blue eyes hardened as he noted the shudder which convulsed her.

"Simon will refuse to admit him. A loud altercation could prove an embarrassment to Messire Beckwith. The Queen would be gravely displeased and already she has no great love for him or any of Warwick's gentlemen. She remembers past humiliations." She put back the hand with which he sought to discover if the weals he had raised upon her buttocks had healed. "I am prepared to shelter you, My Lord and — and to submit to you dutifully, but it was foolhardy of you to risk your life and the success of the King's Cause merely to repossess an erring wife."

"I shall take you to Margaret, in Bruges, until this business is over. If victory goes either way you would still be safe with the duchess. She has genuine affection for you."

"You have risked the King's anger, for me?"

"I was prepared to. As it was, the King gave me leave to ensure your safety." He had joined her in the bed, his arm encircling her bare shoulder. "If you prefer, I'll take you to England, send you with Ralf, to your father."

Again he felt that tremulous shudder run through her form. "No, not to my father," then, stiffly, "I will go to Margaret, as you wish."

He drew her down so they lay close, hip to thigh. Her capitulation surprised him. He had expected obstinacy, rages even. Had Beckworth shown his hand too freely? It was a changed Elinor who lay beside him, no longer an innocent victim, but a mature woman, who was fully aware of her body's needs and of how shabbily she had been used by all of them. His conscience pricked him as he thought how harshly he had dealt with her and of Simon Radbourne's scarred face.

Feeling the rigidity of her body beside him he handled her very gently. As he caressed her, she gave little hard breaths. As if a dam had burst within her she gave herself freely, her body arching to his, her fingers pressing so tightly into his back that he knew there would be violet bruises by morning. He gave a grunt of satisfaction and pulled her yet closer, his mouth nuzzling her cheek and throat. At last she relaxed her pent breath in a little sigh of contentment and he touched her closed eyelids lightly with his finger.

"Then you will trust yourself to me?"

"Yes, My Lord."

"Elinor you have been hurt, by Beckwith?"

"No, not bodily."

"Then — "

"Please, I do not wish to talk of it. I should not have deserted you and I'm prepared to return to my duty."

The words were sharp, abrupt, as if already she regretted her surrender to him and her body moved from his in the bed.

Moonlight silvered the brown splendour of her hair, spilled onto the finely chiselled line of nose and eyebrow, for her face was turned partially from him.

"I should be able to leave the castle by the gate tomorrow without being challenged. I must see Ralf at Le Chat Gris. Will Beckwith stay too close to your side throughout the day, and what about your duties as lady-in-waiting? Could you manage to join me at the water gate after supper?"

"I think it best if I tell the Lady Anne what I intend, though I'll not reveal your identity despite the fact that I do not believe she would have you arrested. Her heart lies with York although her father, like mine, has turned to Lancaster."

"You say that you sometimes sleep within her chamber. What of the Prince, her husband?"

"I do not think the marriage has been consummated. Margaret hates Warwick. She will try to repudiate the match once he has put Lancaster in control again."

"Poor Anne. Has she spoken of Gloucester?"

"Only once, when we were alone together and we were talking of the old days at Middleham. When you leave this room you must keep well clear of the nobles. If Reginald should see you — and — there is Simon."

"Yes, Simon, he too has a score to settle."

"He does not remember clearly what happened in the dungeons at Bruges." She told him of her encounter with the robbers and how Blaise and Jeannine had come to her help. "We travelled with them through France by Paris and Chartres. They performed and Simon and I walked by the cart."

"It has been hard for you."

"Not the journey. It was cold and the walking rough but Jeannine has been like a mother to me."

"Then she will come with us?"

"She and Blaise are anxious to leave France and go to England."

"Oh?"

"I — I believe they are heretics," she said hurriedly. "You would not bring them to harm, My Lord, hand them over to the priests — "

"A man's faith is his own business. If the troubadour would join us it would prove excellent cover for us all to make for the coast, but what of Simon?"

"I — I don't know," she faltered. "I feel responsible for Simon. I would not leave him here in the Lancastrian camp yet — "

"He is hardly likely to wish me well," Lord Gerard finished grimly. "Leave Simon to me."

"As you leave he is bound to recognize you. He may call the guard."

"Aye." He lay back, head resting on linked hands. "I've no wish to kill Simon, not now, but I may need to render him unconscious unless — "

"I'll call him in now and we put our lives in his hands."

"It seems the wisest course. If he proves stubborn, I'll deal with him, tie him up and hide him, though it poses considerable problems. Dupont is hardly likely to look on me favourably if I saddle him with a prisoner to smuggle out of Amboise."

She sat up and reached for her bedgown. "Stand in the shadows, behind the door, as I open it. The moon is full."

He pulled on hose and shirt and waited while she went to the door and opened it a crack.

"Simon?"

"My Lady?"

"Come in a moment, I want you to go on an errand for me."

"My Lady?" He sounded doubtful but she drew the door open further.

He hesitated, then entered. "Is anything amiss?"

"No." She closed and latched the door beckoning him further in.

Lord Gerard stepped from his hiding place to confront him. Simon's grey-blue eyes widened in shock and astonishment and Elinor thought his face drained of colour, though she couldn't be sure of that because the pale moonwash silvered everything.

"Do you hate me still, Simon?"

Elinor saw surprise give place to full remembrance and the youthful mouth hardened. Lord Gerard said, "Your mistress wishes to leave the castle and return to Bruges. Will you help us?"

Simon's eyes besought Elinor's for guidance. She nodded, her teeth worrying her under-lip.

"We were wrong to come here, to our enemies. Would you stay and fight against York, Simon?"

He shook his head though there was a sullen cast to his features that she misliked.

"I punished you, I'd do so again if you

prove disloyal." Lord Gerard's tone was not concilitary.

"What do you wish me to do, My Lady?" Simon turned deliberately from him.

"Find some way of keeping my cousin away from me after supper until I have left the castle, then join us on the Paris road, if — if you've a mind to."

"I'll join you, My Lady. I am devoted to your service, come what may." His gaze shifted almost insolently to his former master. "I'll serve you while you are true to her, My Lord."

"Then our interests are identical. There is much between us, Simon. We must settle our account when all this is over."

"Aye, My Lord."

"Simon, will you see the way clear for My Lord?"

As the boy moved out, his shoulders still stiff with resentment, Lord Gerard drew her to him, tilting up her chin with his finger. "Come to me at the water gate as soon as you can after vespers. Dupont will arrange for mounts for you and the maid. Can she ride?"

Elinor smiled faintly. "I'd be surprised to hear she couldn't, Jeannine is quite a remarkable woman. She can ride pillion if necessary."

"Tell the troubadour to leave the castle when he can without arousing suspicion and join us at the tavern on the Blois road, Simon too."

Simon's head appeared round the door. "All clear, My Lord. Everyone in the hall is fast off. You would be best to sleep in the stables. There'll be no one there on such a cold night."

Lord Gerard kissed Elinor, reached for and donned jerkin and surcoat, then nodded to his squire that he was ready.

As they came out into the inner courtyard the wind blew in icy blasts. The stableyard looked black against the silvered moon glow.

"Get back and guard your mistress," he ordered Simon.

He waited until the sentry had passed this section of the ramparts then walked quickly over and pushed wide the stable door. Horses trampled restlessly in their stalls and the straw rustled ominously some feet from him. Two tousled heads bobbed up and peered at him sleepily; a serving wench and her admirer seeking privacy from their crowded sleeping places in the hall and kitchens. He grinned and waved at them, then moved to a more sheltered spot in an empty stall.

At first light the lovers scrambled from their straw bed and made for the door. Lord Gerard waited a while longer, then, as the castle woke to noisy life, stood up, shook off the wisps of straw which clung to his hose and jerkin and went out to the kitchens in search of bread and ale with his fellow men-at-arms.

No one challenged him and he ate and drank hurriedly, watching his fellows cautiously over the rim of his leather ale jack. No one here was wearing Oxford livery and he had mingled with this group of Frenchmen deliberately.

As he made for the main gate the watery sun glinted into his eyes, though it was still bitterly cold. Wenches, potboys and scullions scurried about emptying pitchers and buckets, fetching water from the castle wells; the farrier's hammer could already be heard striking the anvil, men-at-arms stamped feet and blew on their hands to warm them as they hastened to and from their duty watches.

He was almost at the entrance to the inner bailey when an English voice commanded him to halt.

"You, fellow, I need you."

He stopped, uncertain how to proceed. He knew the voice, William Crompton's, an esquire in Montecute's household. They had met many times when Lord Gerard had been in the North on border patrol. He cursed his illfortune in encountering a former companion now. He decided to walk on as if he had not heard.

Angrily Crompton bellowed a second order and men turned and stared. Lord Gerard stopped, keeping his head averted.

"I'm on an errand into the town for My Lord Earl, sir."

"Good, you can do one for me whilst you're about it. Come here."

He was fairly caught, and would not make it to the outer gate. He waited until Crompton strode up and swung him round by the shoulder.

"What do you mean by forcing me to come to you? Such insolence deserves a sharp lesson. A flogging might teach you respect, fellow."

Lord Gerard turned and looked full at him. Crompton's infuriated gaze became first puzzled then recognition dawned. For moments each stood his ground, outstaring the other.

"By the Mass, Cranley, you here?" Crompton blustered. He was a big man in his late thirties, whose countenance had long since set into lines of sullen acceptance of his failure to receive royal favour and the long hoped for knighthood. Lord Gerard's thoughts raced. Could he take the man off balance and make a run for it? It might yet be possible to convince Crompton that he, too, had changed his allegiance. That hope was dashed when a second man strode to Crompton's side.

Reginald Beckwith's brown eyes were pebble-hard as he surveyed his enemy. "It seems that, after all, we have caught a Yorkist rat in our trap. My Lord, it might have saved you inconvenience and trouble had you accepted our hospitality and stayed with us longer at Beckwith."

Lord Gerard did not need to turn to be aware that he was ringed by a company of men-at-arms. Bowing ironically, he unsheathed his sword and, ignoring Beckwith, he offered it deliberately to Crompton.

★ ★ ★

Elinor explained the situation to Jeannine when she came to dress her.

"Jeannine I can no longer take sides in this business. All I want is for it be settled so that I can go home, but not to England yet, to my father who is determined to use me further against my husband's interests. I am almost sure I am with child. The Duchess Margaret will shelter me until after the birth and I will fight to ensure the child's inheritance if — if My Lord is killed."

"Then I must stay with you, madame."

"But you were anxious to reach the safety of England."

"Blaise must go. Lord Cranley will, perhaps, offer him protection. While you eat I will arrange for him to leave the castle and make for Blois. What about Simon?"

"He will follow when he is sure I am clear, tonight. Oh, Jeannine, I have never feared anyone as I do my cousin. Why was I so foolish as to trust him? If he should learn about the coming child — "

"There's no reason why he should, not for months yet."

The moment Simon came to her she read the worst in his strained, pale face. He was breathless after his frantic run upstairs.

"My Lord has been arrested. By ill luck Master Crompton was crossing the inner bailey and summoned him. To confound matters further Sir Reginald was nearby, I saw My Lord dragged off to the guard room in the west turret."

"Was he hurt?" Elinor put up a hand as if she could still by an effort of will the wild hammering of her heart. She had lain sleepless throughout the night, dreading and fearing this would happen.

"He went docilely enough, offered Master Crompton his sword with that bow of mocking courtesy he often makes."

"They will torture him; he knows so much about the King's plans."

Simon's eyes darkened. "The dungeons beneath Amboise are well equipped with implements guaranteed to extract information from the most obstinate prisoner."

Elinor rose and prowled the chamber. "This barber, Dupont. You had contact with him before in Bruges. Will he help us?"

"He'll be unwilling to risk himself, My Lady, yet he might find himself implicated if Lord Gerard talks. The fear of that might outweigh his unwillingness."

"Then find him and inform Ralf Brent at The Grey Cat. Men must be bribed. I have so little left of the funds I brought. My wedding signet is too easily recognizable and my necklet not valuable enough."

Simon waited and she impelled him to the door. "Do as I say. Promise the barber what you must."

"But, My Lady — "

"Do it, I say."

Jeannine's green eyes narrowed in consternation when Elinor told her of Lord Gerard's peril.

"You will appeal to the princess?"

"If I have opportunity to be alone with her, though how she can help me I do not know. Jeannine, I need ready gold and we have none." She tugged off the ring and handed over her precious relic. "See what you can get for these in the town."

"*Oui*, madame. Blaise will hold himself ready to do anything he can to help. It would be best if he takes Phedre and the cart and waits in the town."

Elinor was fortunate to find the Lady Anne attended by one of the younger French maids, whom she dismissed at Elinor's whispered request. She listened, her eyes troubled, to Elinor's account of Lord Gerard's reckless entry into Amboise and subsequent arrest.

"The Earl of Oxford is in Blois," she said. "They will do nothing without his authority and since Sir Reginald and Crompton are both Neville retainers the Queen is not well disposed towards them. I think it unlikely that they will approach her. Lord Gerard will not be put to the question until the earl returns. He must be freed by tonight."

"He told me Dupont had an understanding with the sergeant in charge of the water gate, but the man will demand gold . . . "

"Bring me my jewel chest."

"My Lady — "

"Hurry, before my ladies return."

Elinor hastened to place the leather covered casket before her. Lady Anne unlocked it and drew out a necklace studded with rubies and seed pearls. "This was given to me by someone who is now absent from my father's side, so it will not be noted that I have lost it."

Elinor took it wonderingly. "My Lady, it is a beautiful piece and you must treasure it greatly."

"The giver would not cavil at its use to save Lord Gerard."

Elinor flashed her a questioning glance and the Lady Anne inclined her chin. "Yes, the giver was His Grace of Gloucester. Now take it, Elinor, and put it to good use. Keep me informed."

Elinor bent and kissed the princess's

hand. "I will, My Lady."

Simon's eyes rounded in astonishment at the sight of the costly bauble. "I found Dupont and Ralf. The barber is outside. Shall I smuggle him up?"

"Yes, at once. Simon, have you heard if My Lord has been transferred to the dungeons?"

"Not that I know of. The arrest has caused no general stir. Only the English men-at-arms are concerned."

The Frenchman darted Elinor curious glances from beneath scanty lashes as he obsequiously made his bow. Those snapping eyes gleamed avariciously as she showed him the ruby necklace.

"That should prove sufficient for our purpose, Madame la Vicomtesse."

"Can you get my husband out?"

A meaningful shrug was her answer. "We can try. If Milord is injured and must be carried or supported, our task would be more difficult."

Elinor caught her breath in a dismayed gasp.

"The Englishmen on guard, it will be necessary to dispose of them. That — " He spread his two hands wide in a gesture of regret, "will make it awkward for me to continue my work here. You understand?"

Jeannine said quietly. "These men are served wine or ale whilst on guard?"

"*Oui.*"

"You will drug them, Jeannine?"

"It could be done but it will entail the complicity of the serving men."

Dupont's eyes again moved to the sombre gleam of the rubies in Elinor's hand. "That should prove no problem, madam."

Elinor surrendered it. "Then go about your business. Remember you stand in peril if My Lord is tortured beyond endurance and reveals your part in this affair."

Dupont smiled thinly. "I have already considered that, madame. His man, Brent, will wait with the horses on the right bank of the river some miles from the town, though if milord is unable to walk he can be carried some distance in the boat. You should meet us at the water gate an hour after vespers if you still intend to go with your lord."

Simon said firmly, "I shall go with

your men to the guard room."

Dupont looked questioningly at Elinor and she nodded.

"Good, then come armed and carrying food and funds necessary for the journey."

The long day stretched out cruelly. Elinor fretted against the need to attend the Queen and Lady Anne, to sit passively stitching, unravelling silks, while her whole being burned to know if Lord Gerard was being mistreated. She suspected that he would be made the butt of Reginald's spite and despaired that he might be too badly injured to escape with his rescuers.

Simon came to escort her to supper though she declined to go down. She was too anxious to eat. Food would choke her.

"My Lady, one of the de Vere retainers told me the prisoner has been put in chains. Sir Reginald dealt him several blows about the head and body. The man said Lord Gerard made no outcries."

Elinor found the knuckles of her right hand ivorysmooth and hard as she caught at her chair arm.

Jeannine had prepared her travelling

cloak and a bundle containing bare necessities. It was an iron hard frost but Elinor was shivering more with apprehension than cold as she waited to make her own way to the water gate. The moon was full. That would not help them. Simon had already gone to join Dupont and the French sergeant. The squire had carried a small green phial which was to be emptied into the mulled ale served to the English foot soldiers on guard in the west turret. Elinor had avoided Reginald throughout the day. She was shocked by the realization of the hatred she held for him.

She started at the knock on her door. She had pleaded indisposition. The Court had already assembled in the banqueting hall. She exchanged glances with Jeannine and the lute player admitted Sir Reginald.

"Elinor, I heard you were still unwell and I was anxious about you. Should I call a physician?"

There was a dew of sweat on her upper lip. "There's no cause for alarm, my headache is still troubling me, but Jeannine's herbal brews do help. I shall be better by morning."

"But you should eat. You were not at dinner."

"No, I — " she felt his eyes rove her chamber. Did he detect some change in her, a fever of impatience? As yet no one had informed her officially of Lord Gerard's detention in the castle. If Reginald guessed that she knew, that her husband had spent last night in her chamber —

She made up her mind on the instant. Only she could ensure that her cousin paid no more visits to the guard room tonight. She could keep him by her side, if necessary, pay the price she most dreaded. Yet surely, the Lady Anne would see her need and relieve her of that sacrifice.

She forced a smile. "It is good to know your devotion to me, Reginald. There must be more pressing business for you than dancing constant attention upon a sick kinswoman, and more pleasurable company than mine."

He lifted her hand gallantly to his lips. "You know that to be untrue, Elinor. There is no one with whom I would sooner occupy *all* my hours. I hope, soon now, to be in a position to give you my undivided attention."

Just that one, chilling hint that he intended to see that her husband was dead. She forced back a shudder of revulsion.

"Then of course I *must* make an effort to eat and drink for your sake. The merriment may do me good, after all. If you will escort me?" Her expression was deliberately arch.

As they crossed the inner bailey she forced herself not to look towards the west turret. Simon would go with his master, for her sake, and Ralf was waiting and stolidly loyal. If Lord Gerard was unable to walk the innkeeper would carry him by boat to where Blaise waited with the cart. They *must* win free. He had risked life and honour to extricate her from danger. Now she must use all the means in her power to keep Reginald's attention on her until well into the small hours.

★ ★ ★

Dupont was waiting in the shadow of the water gate, slapping his crossed arms across his chest against the piercing cold of the night air. He grunted curtly as Simon joined him and gestured the squire into the guard room. A bearded sergeant-at-arms sprawled full length above the arms chest, a leather wine cup in one hand. His liveried coat and woollen hose were stained by wine and dropped food. Simon's lip curled in contempt. Had Dupont put his trust in a drunken sot? They sorely needed a man with his wits about him for tonight's work.

"Have you brought the phial of drug, messire?" The barber held out his hand for it.

Simon nodded, but kept the stoppered container safely hidden beneath his doublet.

Dupont's lips parted in a thin smile. "You do not trust us?"

"I trust no one until my master is clear of this place, not even then. It might be to your greater advantage to betray us."

The French sergeant sat up and gave a great bray of gusty laughter and Dupont's dark eyes flashed at him angrily in warning.

"Messire Radbourne, you mistake this matter. I am pledged to the service of the Duke of Burgundy. If Viscount Cranley is retaken, he will divulge my identity as a spy. Can I risk that?" In a softer voice he added, "I have been well paid. You may not approve of my work, but you must believe I will remain loyal to my paymasters. Now, the drug, if you please. The man who serves the guard will be here for their wine soon."

Simon glanced doubtfully at the sergeant who was still chuckling as he drained his own cup.

Dupont shrugged. "You can trust him too. He works well for gold, as I do."

Simon handed the phial to the barber, who unstoppered it and sniffed cautiously. "Is it dangerous?"

"Jeannine says it is potent. It would be unwise to use too much, unless you wish to silence the men-at-arms permanently."

The sergeant rose and stretched, his arms high above his head, and yawned. Standing feet astride he grinned at Simon. "See how they eat up each other, these

Englishmen of Lancaster and York. You are bloodthirsty, young sir, too much so for your age."

Simon glared back at him. "I care for no one but my own master and mistress."

"Be quiet, Lavaliere." Dupont emptied some of the powder from the phial into a leather wine tankard he lifted down from a shelf above the arms chest. "It would be stupid to kill them. When they are discovered, after our escape with the viscount, it will simply be believed that they became drunk on duty. There will be an enquiry into their misdemeanour rather than an ardent and vengeful search for their murderers."

"But after they are rendered helpless, if the drug does work, how do we get into the dungeon?" Simon snapped.

"Our friend here has copies of the keys." He laughed at Simon's astonishment. "The Englishmen's keys disappeared from the nail where they were left hanging, only for a while, but long enough. Our farrier is a reasonable locksmith, at least he is when he is paid to be."

"But My Lord is in chains."

"That should cause us no problem. Our real anxiety is to know how badly hurt he is."

Simon's face paled. "If he has to be carried — "

"Then he will be, young sir, but let us hope that will not prove necessary."

There was a timid knock upon the door and the three fell instantly silent. A ferrety-faced individual insinuated himself forward, into the guard chamber, his eyes darting nervously from the burly figure of the sergeant to the other two. Dupont handed him the wine tankard and he slunk off without a word. The sergeant settled himself once more upon the chest, his head resting comfortably upon his clasped hands. Dupont seated himself on a joint stool below the high arrow slit and gestured to Simon to sit down on another by him.

"We wait now for the wine to do its work for us."

Simon prowled the chamber, unable to settle. He was shamefully aware that he was terribly afraid. Bitter tasting bile rose at the back of his throat and burned him. His breathing had become fast and shallow, so much so that he feared the other men would hear it and have contempt for him. This waiting was intolerable. Every moment that he was from Lady Elinor's side he feared for her. Reginald Beckwith waited only an opportunity to press his attentions upon her. These days Simon hardly dared to leave her side. He fingered his dagger in its sheath, wishing he were better armed for this business with broadsword or even bow and arrows, yet his position as constant attendant upon Lady Cranley, so near the person of the Lady Anne, forbade that. Even tonight, in the courtyard, it was imperative that other Englishmen should not suspect his errand in the west turret.

The sergeant rose and buckled on his own sword belt. "I go now and make my rounds," he announced. "Afterwards we set off."

He strode off, banging to the door. Dupont leaned his head wearily against the dark wall behind him. "You would be best to harness your restless energy, Messire Radbourne."

Sullenly Simon slumped down upon

the arms chest while they waited for the return of their accomplice.

A hoarsely uttered summons brought them to their feet.

"*Bien*, all is as it should be. We go now." As they crossed the courtyard, the French sergeant threw a beefy arm round Simon's shoulder, haranguing the barber as they went. No one challenged them. Simon only half heard what the two men appeared to be arguing about. He felt so jittery now that he was glad of the sergeant's physical support.

The west turret loomed up before them blackly. The sergeant released Simon and nodded to Dupont. There was no one about.

"Wait here with the Englishman while I go up."

A sentry in the royal livery patrolling this section of the courtyard appeared on the battlements. The sergeant summoned and questioned him. A moment later the man was moving off again to patrol the curtain wall.

Dupont drew Simon into a shadowed recess by the opened doorway where two torches set in iron sconces were blowing wildly in the icy wind. He drew apart from the spy, unwilling for the man to detect his fear for this, the most dangerous part of their mission, by the trembling of his limbs.

The sergeant reappeared in the doorway and signalled for them to follow him. Simon's heart leapt into his mouth as he stumbled over the sprawled form of a man who had fallen half across the first step of the stair. Dupont urged him on impatiently. He was conscious that his foot had slipped in blood as he mounted, though it had been too dark to see the injured man. So this guard at least had not fallen victim to the potion concocted by the lute player, but more than likely to their ally, the sergeant.

A single torch gave fitful light to the first landing. From it a recessed guard chamber led off into a dungeon beyond. Two men-at-arms were slumped across the rough wooden table where they'd been dicing. One hand dangled a wooden dice cup in which the ivory dice still rattled. Both men wore de Vere livery.

The sergeant was struggling with the

key in the lock of the dungeon. Dupont stooped and searched the guards for the original. He stood up, spreading his two hands wide in a regretful gesture. The sergeant swore roundly and bent again to his task until the key grated at last and the door swung open, whining loudly on its hinges.

The place was so dark that Simon could see nothing until Dupont wrenched the smoking torch from its sconce on the landing and held it high in the doorway. Lord Gerard sat upon filthy straw, his back to the wall, wrists enclosed in iron manacles, secured to an iron bracket above him. He stirred warily at their intrusion, blinking at the sudden torchlight.

Simon hurried to him and dropped to his knees. "My Lord, how badly are you hurt?"

Blue eyes narrowed and Lord Gerard tried to hide them from the sudden glare, turning querulously from his squire. "Simon?"

The voice was unfamiliarly weak and stirred Simon's compassion.

"Yes, My Lord. We've come to free

you. Keep still while we get these irons off."

Dupont bent closer to reassure the prisoner.

"Be very quiet, milord. We must be quick. Your guard is drugged. Can you manage to walk?"

Simon saw the tight line of Lord Gerard's mouth and the purple bruising round the eyes and brows. That swine, Beckwith, had vented his spleen on his helpless prisoner. The sergeant, grunting, bent to release him and Simon reached down one hand to help him up. Lord Gerard ignored it and struggled to his feet unaided. Simon heard him give a half concealed gasp of pain and guessed that his ribs were bruised, possibly broken from repeated blows or kicks to the body.

"My Lord," he urged, "you must let us help you down the stairs. My Lady is waiting by the water gate and Ralf is ready in the boat. The troubadour has already driven his cart outside the castle walls. He can drive you to Blois or further until you're fit enough to ride."

Lord Gerard leaned back against the

wall, his breathing laboured.

Dupont said hurriedly, "Milord, we must go at once."

Lord Gerard's hard blue eyes flashed at him imperiously, then he looked full at Simon. "*Can* I trust you, Simon Radbourne?"

"Yes, My Lord."

The eyes continued to bore into him, then it seemed that he was convinced of Simon's sincerity for he nodded and took his arm. "Come then, help me out of here. Dupont, give me a weapon."

The Frenchman hesitated then stooped and drew a dagger from the sheath of one of the guards. He handed it over silently.

"There should be no need for more killing, milord."

"*More* killing?" Lord Gerard's brows rose in interrogation and his lips twitched in a wintry smile. "I see you have already been busy over my affairs, messieurs."

The journey down the steep stair seemed a lengthy one to Simon who was supporting his master's heavy weight. The sergeant and Dupont sped on ahead to spy out the dangers. The barber lingered in the shadowed doorway and gave a warning hiss for the Englishmen to stay where they were. Simon softly cautioned Lord Gerard not to stumble over the corpse on the bottom step. There was a sharp command from the courtyard then a steady tramp of booted feet moving away from the west turret. Still Dupont waited before giving the signal for them to come on. The sergeant took his time before coming back to the door.

"Come, it is safe now, messieurs."

Lord Gerard pushed Simon from him and straightened. Once clear of the building, in the cruelly revealing moonlight, Simon caught back a cry of horror. Lord Gerard's mouth was swollen and broken as if from the cut of a whip or the corner of a signet ring, beside the heavy bruising and distortion of the features but, obviously it was his ribs which were causing Lord Gerard so much pain for, despite his effort to put aside his suffering, he clutched at his chest with a clawing hand. The effort to breathe was difficult enough, let alone the need to move fast and silently.

Simon hastened once more to his side

and reluctantly his help was accepted. Now the sergeant had dismissed the guard the courtyard was once more deserted. When they emerged into the outer bailey they were hailed by a company of English men-at-arms. Simon returned their salute and grinned at their bawdy comments on the slumped condition of his companion. He indicated his own amusement with a scornfully upraised thumb.

There were good natured comments and advice to water their wine, then the men had passed on and into the main hall ahead. Simon felt a sudden spasm pass through his master's body.

"Not far now, My Lord," he whispered huskily, "once we're clear of Amboise we'll get your ribs bound and supported. Movement will be easier then."

"Get on, man," Lord Gerard hissed at him.

Dupont led them into the guard room near the water gate and Simon helped Lord Gerard down onto the arms chest.

"Wait here while I check that the boat is ready." The barber slunk off and Simon was left anxiously watching the door for his return and fearing to anger

Lord Gerard further by offers of help or useless assurances. All colour had drained from Lord Gerard's features and Simon was afraid he'd sustained some wound.

"Where are you hurt, My Lord?"

"I'm well enough, a couple of broken ribs, splintered by the feel of them, catching at every breath I take. I'll manage till we have Lady Elinor clear of this place. How long since you saw her?"

"An hour ago, My Lord. She was anxious for you, otherwise well."

"And the lute player, her maid, supplied the drug?" There was a trace of humour in the hoarse whisper.

"Jeannine? Yes, My Lord. She assured us it was no poison — "

"I could hardly complain if it were," Lord Gerard chuckled sardonically, "yet Heaven defend us from women, Simon. Their weapons are infinitely more dangerous than any of ours."

Dupont appeared in the doorway and signalled to Simon to approach him. He threw a doubtful glance at Lord Gerard as he bent and whispered, "There is no sign of your mistress. The boat man is anxious to be off. We should get him away — now."

Simon stared at him wonderingly. "My Lady not there? We must wait for her."

In his panic his voice had carried to Lord Gerard who struggled up from the chest.

"What's that you say? My wife not at the meeting place?"

Dupont moved towards him, walking confidently despite his alarm. "Not yet, milord, but there is no cause for fear. The Queen or perhaps Madame la Princesse has sent for her. We should get you across the river and return later for Madame la Vicomtesse."

"Certainly not. We wait. Simon, you get back to her side."

"My Lord, she would wish me to stay with you."

"Obey me." The words were snarled with such intensity that Simon gazed at Dupont helplessly. He was sick with desperation. The barber was right. It was imperative that Lord Gerard be rowed across the river immediately. At any moment the guard in the west turret would be relieved and the hunt for the prisoner begun. Yet he knew Lord Gerard in this mood. Nothing would persuade him to leave without Lady Elinor.

Dupont shrugged and said soothingly, "*Bien*, then we wait, milord. There is time. You rest and gather your strength." He nodded smilingly to Simon. "I think it unwise for Messire Beckwith to change his plans now. Milady and he could miss each other and delay us further."

Astonished, Simon watched him move nonchalantly across to the shelf where the wine jugs were stored. His back was to Simon then he turned and came back with a filled tankard.

"Drink, milord. The wine will give you strength for the journey."

Lord Gerard reached for the tankard then, abruptly, drew back his hand. "After you, Monsieur Barber."

There was a pause. Simon stared at Dupont imploringly and the Frenchman's shrewd black eyes danced with amusement.

"*Alors*, if you wish, milord, *certainement*." He took a deep swallow and held out the cup once more to Lord Gerard. "As you see, there is no cause for you to distrust me. The drug was for your jailors, no one else."

Still Lord Gerard hesitated, his eyes narrowed, watching the Frenchman intently, then he took the tankard and drained it. Simon saw him lean back exhausted against the wall.

Dupont walked jauntily to the doorway and, after a moment, Simon followed him. The barber looked anxiously towards the water gate.

"Find Sergeant Lavaliere. He will help you carry Milord to the boat. You must hasten, messire, or it will mean the deaths of all of us."

"Then — the wine *was* drugged?"

Again Dupont's eyes danced with merriment. "*Mais certainement*, I could see that he would not leave without Madame la Vicomtesse."

"But you — "

"I swallow a very little, *n'est ce pas?* But already I feel how do you say in English, dizzy? This drug, it is strong."

"But — "

"Have no fear for me, *mon ami*. Lavaliere will take good care of me and I shall lie well hidden until morning, but

Milord must be got away without delay." He staggered and reached clumsily for the doorpost to support himself. "Leave me here, just outside the door. Milord must not suspect he was tricked — not yet."

Simon's throat thickened with fear. He looked behind him into the guard room where Lord Gerard sat slumped against the wall. It was impossible to tell yet if Jeannine's potion had taken its toll. Simon knew Lord Gerard. He would fight its effects to the utmost of his strength.

"I'm going to look out for Lady Elinor, sir." His voice came out in a nervous croak.

There was no answer so he set off at a stumbling run to search for the sergeant-at-arms.

Dupont was still conscious when they returned and the sergeant bent and whispered to him then hastened to Lord Gerard's side. The viscount lay prone across the arms chest, his breathing stertorous.

"So," Lavaliere nodded briskly, "now we can go. Help lift him to my shoulder,

412

messire, then go before me to the gate. The innkeeper of Le Chat Gris will wait for only a short time then he will push for the further bank. We have little time."

Lord Gerard muttered thickly in his sleep and stirred but did not wake. Simon hurried before the sergeant, burdened with the viscount's heavy weight, his eyes alert for any sign of the returning sentry to this section of his patrol beat.

Under the frost-rimed branches of an alder, a figure unbent from the dark recesses of the boat and the innkeeper's voice was impatient. He addressed the sergeant in French so rapid that Simon was unable to get the gist of his argument. Lord Gerard was laid carefully down on the stern seat.

"Where is Ralf Brent, My Lord's man?"

There was another hasty interchange between the two Frenchman.

Lavaliere explained. "The man-at-arms, he goes to Blois to hire horses. The troubadour waits along the far bank. He will carry Milord in the cart to Blois. You must get into the boat quickly now, messire, before we are seen by the sentry."

Simon was trapped and he knew it. He feared for Lady Elinor, was deeply apprehensive as to why she had not come to be at Lord Gerard's side. How could he abandon her to her fate, distrusting her cousin as he did? With Blaise gone, there would be no man to guard the two women, yet neither could he trust Lord Gerard to this Frenchman who was prepared to fulfil any task if well enough paid.

Drugged, weakened by the cruelties and indignities heaped upon him by Reginald Beckwith, Lord Gerard would be entirely at this man's mercy. He could be murdered and his corpse disposed of without trace beneath the river if it suited these men to betray them and pocket the proceeds from the sale of Lady Anne's necklace. There would be no threat to themselves whatever, in fact Lord Gerard's death would make matters infinitely safer for them all.

Lady Elinor would wish him to go with his master. There was no help for it.

The innkeeper clucked his tongue

against his teeth impatiently. Sergeant Lavaliere shrugged. Simon was unable to read the man's expression. His features were shadowed by the alder branches which met above their heads.

He jumped down into the boat and ordered the innkeeper to push clear of the bank. The castle's high curtain walls menaced them, the river water lapped in black, oily waves against the boat gunwale. Simon sat huddled forward, in the prow, his eyes fixed resentfully upon the unconscious form of his lord.

12

ELINOR sat in a shaded corner of the convent kitchen. From the abbess's parlour she could hear the Queen's voice, sharp and waspish with anxiety. The Lady Anne had sought the refuge of one of the cell-like rooms the convent allowed its guests. Only a few miles from them, near Tewkesbury, the Yorkist and Lancastrian armies were engaged in mortal conflict for the second time.

Elinor turned, wearily, from her memories of that exhausting journey from Weymouth. Soon after they had landed they received the news of Warwick's defeat at Barnet. Elinor's heart had stirred in pity for the Lady Anne. Her father and uncle, Montecute, slain. The Queen had been anxious to return to France. She had no wish to risk her darling Edward in a battle for the throne, but her commanders had persuaded her and she had made all speed to cross the

Severn. It was 4 May. Yesterday the exhausted Lancastrian army could go no further, the King hard on their heels. Camp was made near Tewkesbury. Elinor knew that her father and Reginald were fighting in this last desperate struggle. Sir Thomas had escaped the debâcle at Barnet and managed to join the Queen. There had been a restraint between him and his daughter, though, thankfully, she was aware that his presence prevented Reginald from pressing obvious intentions upon her. The Lady Anne's insistence on her nearness had prevented what Elinor most feared while they were still in France. Now she wearily awaited the outcome, her heart sick with dread. There had been no news of Lord Gerard. She had not dared to enquire of her father. Had he reached England in safety? The French spy, Dupont, had informed her that he and Simon had been conveyed by river to where Blaise waited with the cart.

"He is a strong and brave gentleman, madame," he had said comfortingly. "He will soon recover from the indignities heaped upon him by Messire Beckwith."

Jeannine, too, waited patiently for news of Blaise. Elinor was sure that if Lord Gerard *had* reached the King he had fought at Barnet, and had he survived that, he must even now be near Gloucester's side. If he died today he would never know that she carried his child. Deliberately she had kept her condition from her father. After Reginald's shameless revelations at Amboise, she no longer trusted her kinsmen.

Jeannine came soft-footed to her side, her expression concerned. "You should be lying down in this appalling heat."

It was a surprisingly humid day for early May. Elinor's blue silk gown was plastered to her body with sweat. Rivulets ran down between her breasts and she wiped her brow with her lawn kerchief. "Is there news?"

The lute player sank down beside her on the rushes of the flagged kitchen floor. Her billowing skirts swirled up the sharp acrid odour of crushed herbs, tansy, lavender and rosemary.

"It's said the Queen's army has the advantage of numbers but the King's men will be confident, after their victory at Barnet." Her face was averted and, with a sudden pang, Elinor wondered if the lute player had some premonition of disaster. There had been times when Jeannine had known beforehand what was to happen. Elinor had never pressed her to divulge her thoughts and fears, for the woman's own safety. Now she was afraid to ask. She would not be able to bear certain tidings of Lord Gerard's death.

A frightened young novice approached them soon after noon.

"Lady Cranley, there is a man at the portress's gate very insistent that he must speak with you and with your attendant."

Elinor's heart missed a beat. Lord Gerard come to claim her? Was the battle already over? Yet how could he know where she was? Common sense told her that could not be. Then if not Lord Gerard, who? Were there grave tidings from the battlefield? Had her father fallen?

"This man, mademoiselle, would you describe him?" As usual Jeannine had remained calm and practical.

"A tall man, not young, strangely dressed in a ragged velvet doublet with a tall feather in his cap. I do not think he is a soldier."

Blaise then. Elinor and Jeannine exchanged glances. So they were right, Lord Gerard was fighting for York and Simon and Blaise with him. They waited to hear no more but lifted their skirts high and ran towards the portress's gate.

Blaise was waiting outside, his face grave and set. He drew the two out of earshot of the elderly portress who was obviously consumed with curiosity.

"Blaise, thank God we see you safe. How goes the battle — and — and how is My Lord? Is he with you?"

Blaise made no move to embrace Jeannine. It was not their way to be demonstrative in public but Elinor could see by the lute player's shining eyes that she was overwhelmingly thankful to see him again, safe and well.

"It is over," he told them hurriedly in French. "The Queen's Cause is lost. The banks of the Avon are slimy and red with the blood of the Lancastrian slain.

But it is Milord Gerard, madame. His standard is down. Simon was with him, *naturellement*, but one of the Cranley men-at-arms came running to me near the baggage train. Simon guessed you would be with the Queen at the nunnery and that — that you would be unguarded."

It seemed to Elinor that her over-heated body had been drenched in iced water. "How bad is it? I must go to him — at once."

Blaise shook his head. "The man did not say. He was confused and incoherent. All Hell has broken loose, madame. The Yorkist knights are pursuing the enemy across the meadows. No one concerns himself about the wounded and later — " his expression was grave as he prepared her, as gently as he could, for the horror to come, "later, there are those who prey on the dead and injured."

"I will come. Jeannine, fetch me a light cloak, I must cover this gown. Once the sun goes down it will get chill and the field will be dark — " She shuddered at the image Blaise's words had conjured. The field would become a place of horrendous shadows, the realm of the dead and those ghouls who prowled like jackals, stealing from the bodies and often murdering those who tried, weakly, to prevent their gruesome pickings. She had to find Lord Gerard, discover the fates of her father and Reginald. She prayed they had both fled the field, for she could not trust them to the King's mercy. He had been foully betrayed at Doncaster and her kinsmen had been involved in that treachery.

The neighbourhood of the nunnery was deserted. The townsfolk had either rushed to view the proceedings near the abbey, where men would run for sanctuary, or barricaded themselves within their houses, fearing pillage and looting. Elinor fretted until Jeannine returned and the three, unobserved, made their way into the town. A crowd had collected near the abbey's west door. Elinor addressed herself to a soberly dressed woman standing next to a butcher, whose brawny figure exuded a greasy smell of fat and blood. Blaise would not be heeded, his foreign accent a source of instinctive mistrust.

"I've menfolk in the fighting. Please can you tell me what's happening here?"

"They're bringing the prince's body to the abbey." The woman crossed herself. "The Virgin comfort his poor mother, even if it's true what they say of her, that she's a terrible hard woman."

"The prince, slain?" Elinor repeated the words wonderingly. "Is there news of the King and — of his brothers?"

The woman shrugged uneasily. "Fugitives have been pouring into the abbey since noon. My man says King Edward'll not let them rest there, he'll drag them out."

"Break sanctuary?" Elinor's hazel eyes widened in shock.

The butcher turned and grinned at her, showing blackened stumps of teeth. "Aye, sounds bad, mistress, I know, but there'll not be peace in this land till all they Lancastrians be killed. Stands to reason." His expression sobered as he recognized her obvious distress. "You'd be best to head for the nunnery or get clear of the town. There'll be further bloodshed when the Yorkist princes ride in."

"I have to reach the field."

The couple stared at her curiously. She read their doubt in their faces. She didn't appear to them to be a drab or camp follower so what was she doing with the army?

"My husband be right, young mistress," the woman said awkwardly, "it can't do no good for you to be molested. If you've kin out there, it be best to wait for news at the abbey guest house, the only safe place, I do reckon, and that's not to be relied on."

She turned from Elinor as a new ripple of excitement went through the crowd and there was a surge backwards which almost knocked Elinor from her feet. She stood on tip-toe, hoping for a view of what was happening. It was difficult but, over the heads of the crowd, she glimpsed the glint of iron salets worn by a company of soldiers. There came a sound of weeping from some of the watching women and Elinor deduced that the body of the prince was being borne into the abbey, laid upon some hastily constructed bier. She turned away, shuddering. So he would not now have his heart's desire and see the heads of his enemies fail before him. She hurried back to her companions.

"They're carrying in the prince's body," she said, looking significantly at Jeannine who nodded gravely.

It was a hard fight to press through the crowd of bystanders who were blocking the Gloucester road but Blaise managed to clear a way for them. Elinor was jostled almost off her feet and stumbled several times, then they were through the worst of it and Blaise gestured towards the bank of the Avon.

"We must go that way, Madame la Vicomtesse. The baggage train was set up by that stand of trees. I left the cart there. I'll bring it as close to the river bank as I can, but the ground will be badly churned by the horses — "

She knew only too well what he implied. "Thank you, Blaise. I'll try to find Simon."

Jeannine put a detaining hand on her arm. "Madame, you should stay close to Blaise. Let me search."

Elinor shook her head decisively. "No, Jeannine," Elinor's lip trembled but she was beyond tears or any show of weakness. "I must go."

Men-at-arms were now trailing in from the field, some mounted, many more on foot wearily trailing pikes, their leather coats ominously stained with blood. Some were already jubilantly laden with spoils, leather riding boots, helmets, weapons, parts of armour. Others stumbled, trying desperately to staunch bleeding from wounded limbs or bodies. To Elinor's profound relief none of them made any attempt to molest them. All were intent on the possibility of looting within the town where pickings would be greater, and some had that wolfish look which told of a determination to further hunt down and destroy their enemies. Many wore the murrey and blue colours of York.

The three were constantly thrust aside and forced to move off the highway by mounted men, knights and nobles, some reeling in the saddle, others proud, impatient men less hurt but weary, their visors up, peering out for fugitives near the abbey, squires riding by on urgent errands for their masters.

The sun was just beginning to set,

casting a lurid, red light across the land. Soon the grey twilight would fall and, with it, would come the despoilers of the dead. Elinor stumbled on, pulling her cloak about her. Already the noise from the crowd near the abbey door was fading in the distance and there were fewer men passing them on the roads. Those they did see were slinking along between the trees and beside the ditches, hoping to escape notice. Obviously these were defeated men who were hurt and had not fled the field in the first mad rush for sanctuary. They would be well advised to throw down their weapons, tear off their liveried coats and salets, which could identify them to their enemies, melt into the wooded land which surrounded the battlefield and lie low for a while. The red glow over the river made Elinor swallow hard, its likeness to blood was so horrifying.

Now they had come across the first huddled bodies and carrion circled above them, wheeling and cawing ever lower and lower. Most had been abandoned, even despoiled already by their own companions or by jubilant Yorkists, others were guarded by some wary camp follower or comrade, who cowered at the sight of the newcomers and moved in protectively. The ground here had been savagely churned by the horses in the pursuit and Elinor made, determinedly, for the meadow land near the river. Blaise had told her that the Duke of Gloucester had led the pursuit and where Gloucester was, Lord Gerard was certain to have been close by. He must have fallen here.

The bodies were certainly more thickly distributed here the river choked with them, the water muddied and red with blood. Elinor averted her eyes, trying to ignore the tortured voices which pleaded for water. Someone had lit a torch ahead of them and she saw two squires tending the body of their injured master. Elinor looked impatiently at the devices on their surcoats and hastened on. Jeannine caught at her arm and she saw in the distance the grey, indistinct forms of those who moved amongst the dead. A hoarse cry sounded close by and she stood stockstill, the hairs on the nape of her neck rising.

"My Lady, My Lady?"

She turned instantly, hunting desperately for the source of that voice, undoubtedly Simon's.

"Here, My Lady."

He was standing up, waving a rag of a scarf to attract her attention. Exhausted and heart-sick though she was, she half flew the distance between them, dropping to her knees beside the armoured form that Simon had been so resolutely guarding. The squire had lifted free Lord Gerard's helmet and Elinor gave a sharp cry at sight of his pale face, marred by a massive bruise which shadowed his left cheek and temple.

"He's not dead, My Lady," Simon reassured her. "He suffered a wound in the arm between the vambrace and couter, but he was also struck on the face, as you see, a massive head wound delivered by a mace. It must have wrenched him right out of the saddle."

Elinor touched Lord Gerard's cold cheek. The pulse at his temple beat true and sound and she gave a great sob of relief.

"How long has he been like this?"

"He was unconscious when Ralf Brent and I found him. He came to, for a moment, but he didn't know me."

"Ralf?" Elinor stared distractedly round the deserted field. "Where is he? Why did he leave his master?"

"He's gone to fetch a litter, My Lady. His Grace of Gloucester gave instructions that we were not to move My Lord. He will make arrangements in the town for lodgings and for a surgeon to tend him."

"How long must we wait?" Elinor raged. "He may die, now, while we delay, and those fiends are drawing nearer all the time. Jeannine, can Blaise come and help carry My Lord to the cart?"

The lute player was already closely examining the injured knight.

"Simon has done well," she said in French. "He has staunched the bleeding of the arm wound. As for the head blow, like Simon's, that may well take some time to heal. I don't think it too serious. He's breathing normally and since he came to a while ago, that is good. It might be better to keep him quite still and mount guard. Help cannot be long in coming. Le Vicomte is an important man."

Elinor's watchful gaze had caught the movement of what had appeared to be shadows, pressing ever nearer, and once she thought she glimpsed a flash as if someone wielded a dagger.

"Simon," she commanded, "get Blaise. If it isn't safe to move My Lord at least we should have a better guard. I fear those jackals — "

"My Lady, I should not leave him. His Grace of Gloucester ordered me — "

"I will stay with Jeannine. She can check the bandaging. Go, Simon." Her eyes flashed golden fire at him and he dared not disobey.

He rose reluctantly. "My Lord wouldn't wish me to leave you two unprotected."

"But you can go and be back quickly. It's not far. Hurry, man."

Elinor sat on the spoiled earth and lifted her husband's head and shoulders upon her lap. Jeannine was already busied with the stained rag of bandaging on Lord Gerard's arm. His vambrace lay discarded where Simon had thrown it after undoing the leather straps to get at his wound.

Simon waited for no more. Jeannine gave him instructions as to where he would most likely find Blaise and he took off at once.

Elinor fixed her eyes hungrily upon her husband's loved face. It had been so long. From the moment she had reached Amboise she had known of her mistake, then he had come to her and she had dared to hope again. There could be no happiness for her without Gerard Cranley. She blinked back angry tears as she remembered the hours she had spent within his arms. He had brought her patiently to the brink of fulfilment. Even the fear-crazed experience following his discovery of her second betrayal could not blind her to her longing for him. Jeannine had said his wounds were not mortal. A cold paralysing fear swept through her. Suppose Jeannine was wrong. Her hope of happiness could not be destroyed on this Tewkesbury field.

He stirred and moaned. Jeannine looked up and nodded. "It is as I said. He will soon be himself again. There is a brook nearby. I'll fetch some water."

432

Elinor snatched up a wineskin negligently discarded by some fleeing soldier. "Yes, be quick, Jeannine. I shall be safe enough. Simon will hasten back with Blaise."

She kept her eyes fixed on Lord Gerard's closed ones as she heard the light patter of Jeannine's bare feet as she ran off. His black lashes flickered and she prayed that he would open his eyes, look up, know her. Again that little heartstirring moan and his shoulders moved slightly upon her knees. She bent and kissed him upon the mouth.

"Hush, my love, there will be help for you soon. Ralf has gone for a litter and Simon is close by with a cart. Whichever comes first will take you to the town. Keep very still now. I am close, your wife, Elinor."

At first she thought it was Blaise who came up behind her, casting a shadow upon Lord Gerard's pale face as she held him tight pressed to her heart.

"Elinor."

She went suddenly cold at the familiar voice and her dread for Lord Gerard caused her to clutch at his shoulder more tightly.

"Father?" she said doubtfully.

"You must come with us, at once." His tone was curt, peremptory. "Why did you leave the nunnery? We've been searching for you."

She looked up to see Reginald, grim-faced, behind him. Both men had discarded most of their armour. Their faces were strained, showing utter exhaustion and a wariness which betrayed their fear of being taken prisoner, but neither showed sign of injury.

"Go, Father," she said hurriedly. "If you are taken, the King will show no mercy. Make for the abbey or cut across country to Gloucester."

"Not without you," Sir Thomas said shortly. "We cannot desert the Queen. She must be got safely across the river."

"I'll not leave My Lord," Elinor said quietly.

"What nonsense is this?" Sir Thomas bent and thrust his face close to hers. She saw that his lips were drawn back from his teeth in a snarl. "The man is your enemy. Do you think he will cherish the bride who deserted him, made him the laughing stock of the King's army?"

434

She blanched at his plain speaking. "I — I love him," she whispered piteously.

Sir Thomas turned abruptly from her and spoke sharply to his nephew. Elinor turned back to her husband.

Before she was aware of his intentions, Reginald had brutally kicked her husband's body clear of her, reached down and forcibly drawn her to her feet. She screamed shrilly and pummelled at him with her fists. He gave a muttered oath and there came a second command from her father, the words not clear enough for her to catch. Reginald Beckwith's fist caught her a hard blow beneath the chin, the pain stunning her into silence.

Vainly she fought against the blackness which engulfed her.

13

TO the sound of trumpets and clarion, battle standards floating free to the brilliant blue of the May sky, King Edward entered London through lines of cheering citizens. Duke Richard of Gloucester led the triumphant procession, then came Lord Hastings's contingent and, riding alone, unhelmed, the sun glinting upon that glorious fair hair, came the King, his hand raised in salute to his doting, joycrazed subjects. At the rear rode the Duke of Clarence guarding a chariot in which sat the black-clad, pitiful form of the defeated Margaret of Anjou. Behind that lumbered a second chariot bearing the widowed Princess of Wales and, finally, a cart carrying the Queen's ladies, Elinor amongst them.

As the Queen was pulled by in the King's Roman triumph, the fair mood of the crowd changed. Howls of derision and catcalls were levelled at her and her ladies and one or two clods of earth and dung were flung, the filth splattering the women's garments. The younger ladies were openly terrified and in tears. Elinor was determined to keep up a brave front. She stood, clinging desperately to the rough wooden rail of the cart, the splinters working into her fingers. She did not heed the pain. She was deaf and blind to everything about her. All that had happened since she had been torn from her lord's side had left her numbed and tearless.

She had come to her senses within a litter borne by her father's retainers. She had felt sick and bruised and lain quiescent, knowing it pointless to rebel against his authority. The company had halted at Bushley across the Avon and later Sir Thomas had conveyed his daughter to Payne's Place where the defeated Queen had taken refuge. The Lady Anne had tended Elinor, bleakly accepting the news of her young husband's death. Sobbing bitterly, Elinor had told of her brutal separation from Lord Gerard.

"Hush, hush now," Lady Anne soothed, "you know he will be lovingly tended.

Simon Radbourne was nearby and Blaise and your maid, Jeannine. He will come for you, the moment he is able to do so. Be very sure of that."

"My Lady, I — I fear that Reginald — he hates my husband so deeply — " Elinor could not frame her heart-stopping fear.

"They would not dare stay to harm him," the Lady Anne tried to reassure her, but Elinor could not be certain Lord Gerard still lived. How simple it would have been for her cousin to have ended her husband's life there and then. If only she had not led them to the battlefield. She should have waited patiently at the nunnery and they would then have had no need to search for her. Was she doomed, unwittingly, to bring disaster to the man she loved?

Next day the Queen's knights had escorted her to Worcester where they found shelter in a religious house. It was here that Lord William Stanley had taken her prisoner. Her household gentlemen had been hustled away, amongst them Elinor's father and Reginald. Sir William had informed the Queen of her son's end, which until now Lady Anne had felt unable to do. He had been trampled to death beneath the hoofs of the pursuing Yorkists. Margaret had given one cry and swooned, since then she had kept a dignified silence, refusing to allow Stanley the satisfaction of seeing her weep openly.

The cart jarred to a sudden halt. The jeering onlookers surged closer and the foot soldiers guarding the way appeared unable to hold them back. It was unbearably hot and the stinks of the city rose from the open kennels and Elinor gagged miserably. A stone caught her full on the cheek. She gave a little astonished cry at the sharp pain of it and lifted her hand wonderingly, to examine the wound, bringing it away wet with blood. She tried to staunch the flow but she had no kerchief and was unable to tear away a portion of her under kirtle. She was shaking uncontrollably. If the guards were unable to protect them they would be torn to pieces by the sheer ferocity of this mob.

There came a curt command and the crowd was forced back. The leading chariots had advanced again and the women in Elinor's cart looked frantically for some assistance. They were being left to the mercy of the townsfolk as the other vehicles creaked off ponderously ahead of them.

There was a jingle of harness, a loud neigh as a war horse closely pawed the ground impatiently. So a knight from the King's train had remained behind. To offer them protection? Elinor looked up, startled, into the cool blue eyes of her husband. If she had not gripped the bar so tightly that her knuckles gleamed white with the strain, she would have fainted ignominiously before him.

"Get these women clear. Keep that mob back." His words were harsh with temper and she could tell by the hard set of his mouth that he was angry. Spurring his mount closer, he leaned towards her.

"Put this cloak over your gown." He threw up the garment, his eyes dwelling contemptuously on her torn and mud-spattered clothing.

She took it with shaking fingers and obeyed him. She could not trust her senses. All these weary days she had so longed for a sight of him and, he was well, strong, and here, by her side. She found herself unable to greet him. He made no further comment while she adjusted the folds of the clean cloak about her, covering her soiled gown, then, abruptly ordered the guards as to the disposal of the cart with its remaining prisoners.

"See these women safely to the Tower. Double the guard round them. Cut down any fool who tries to harm them."

He held out a hand to Elinor. "Come."

Her limbs were stiff from the effort of balancing herself against the jolting of the cart and she moved only slowly to obey him. He eased his mount closer, bent and swept her up before his saddle pommel. She clung to him, terrified.

Hiding her face against his shoulder, she felt, rather than saw him, withdraw his mount from the crowd. His horse was forced to proceed at walking pace and it seemed hours before he spoke, his attention on controlling it.

"Are you hurt?"

She shook her head, her voice choked

with tears of mingled joy and fear at the grimness of his expression. "No, it was — rather alarming when those — people — pushed so close to the cart but — "

"Your cheek is bleeding."

"It — it is nothing, a chance stone, flung by a boy, I think."

"Animals," he grated, through clenched teeth. "There would be some excuse if the attackers had taken part in the actual fighting. They leave better men to do that, then vent their spite on the defenceless."

She braced herself as he drew rein. Strong hands reached up to lift her down. Wonderingly, she heard Simon Radbourne's voice.

"My Lady, thank God you are safe."

Lord Gerard dismounted and took Elinor from him. She tried to protest that she could walk, but he strode forward uncaring. They were in a street so narrow that the upper storeys almost met above their heads. It was deserted, the shopfronts shuttered. Either the townsfolk had gone to watch the triumphal procession or some more timid souls remained behind bolted doors, fearful of the possible damage to be perpetrated by excited crowds afterwards. Lord Gerard carried her through a door where an obsequious little man was waiting to greet him, then through a short corridor and up a flight of stairs. Moving into a room directly ahead, he laid her down upon a high-backed settle.

"Don't try to move. You are safe now in my lodging in the Chepe." She broke down and sobbed with reaction as she heard his firm tread on the stair as he left her.

"Madame la Vicomtesse, are you so badly hurt?"

Jeannine's voice speaking in French. Elinor gave a half cry of gladness and was gathered into the lute player's arms.

"There, there, it is over. Let me look at you. Simon told me you had been hurt, bleeding."

"It's nothing, nothing. Oh, Jeannine, how good it is to see you again. Tell me all that happened. My Lord looks well but — "

"Later, madame, I will tell you

everything, not now."

Gently she helped her from her soiled clothing. Suddenly Elinor felt the dull torpor of utter exhaustion. She was helped into a high-sided wooden tub. What bliss to feel the hot water wash over her. Jeannine soaped her hair and body, then, as she stood, Jeannine rinsed her in warm, scented water and patted her dry. She muttered something in her own southern patois and Elinor blushed.

"No, I have had no bleeding. I have been frantic with worry over My Lord and — and it was not pleasant in the escape with the Queen. I was afraid just now in that jeering crowd . . . Then, I am worried about the fates of my father and Reginald." She faced the grim fact that both men lay under guard and could soon die under the executioner's knife.

"You must not fret, Madame la Vicomtesse. Have I not promised you that all will be well?"

Elinor's eyes filled with tears of heart-felt relief. "Oh, Jeannine, is it really true? My Lord is completely well again?"

"*Certainement.*" Jeannine smiled reassuringly as she combed out Elinor's wet hair. "When I came back with the water, I found you gone. *Naturellement*, I was worried. I knew you would not have left your lord if someone had not forced you to do so. I could do nothing, not knowing where you had been taken and I thought you would wish me to guard Milord. When Blaise and Simon came back with the cart we carried Milord into the town to the abbey where the healing monks took care of him. Simon then reported to the Duke of Gloucester and we were allowed to camp with the Yorkist army and stay close to Milord Cranley. Simon fretted to go and search for you but Monsieur le Duc forbade it saying he believed you to be with the Lancastrian knights near the Queen, which proved correct. When Milord sent for us I went with Simon. I saw at once he was near to complete recovery."

"Did he — did he ask about me?"

"*Certainement* and enquiries were made for you. Milord ordered me to stay within his service and later brought us here to his lodging in London. Today he rode with the King in the procession. Simon says you were brought in a prisoner with the Queen's ladies. Milord must have taken steps to have you in his own keeping. I am commanded to see to your comfort and put you to bed."

"Does he know, about the child?"

"No, madame, that is for you to tell him."

For the first time Elinor felt clean and soothed, the nagging fear for Lord Gerard's safety at an end. Jeannine had wrapped her in a brocaded silk bed gown. For blessed moments she could relax, her guard down, for she trusted the lute player implicitly.

"Jeannine," she whispered, her cheeks crimsoning, "if — if My Lord should wish to take me to his bed, would it, would it harm the unborn child?"

The older woman was smiling broadly as she put down brush and comb. "*Non*, madame, not at this stage, but you should not delay long now before you tell your lord." She moved to the bed and drew back freshly laundered sheets. "Come and rest now as Milord commanded."

"Not yet, Jeannine. I am not prepared yet to be totally subservient to My Lord's wishes." She smiled faintly as she said the words.

"Then I'll bring you some food and you can rest here, on the settle."

"I don't think I could manage to eat it." Elinor touched her breast fleetingly. "It feels as if I am full to the brim with uncertainties, excitement and — and an exhilarating feeling of — "

"Relief? Love?" Jeannine's brows arched upwards, enquiringly. Elinor lowered her gaze. Jeannine's brilliant green eyes saw far too much.

"Has My Lord spoken of me with tenderness?" She asked shyly.

Jeannine considered. "I do not think Milord is a man to reveal easily what is in his heart, certainly not to menials. I know he has searched unceasingly for news of you."

Elinor sighed. Was Lord Gerard's attitude towards her chiefly governed by a sense of pride in his possession, nothing else?

Jeannine stole from the chamber, murmuring that she would prepare something light and nourishing which Madame must try to eat. Elinor leaned her head tiredly against the back of the settle. She started to sudden alertness when Lord Gerard positioned himself before her, in familiar stance, right thumb hooked aggressively into the gilded and jewelled belt he wore. Her eyes passed over him longingly. Like the others of the King's gentlemen he was dressed splendidly in a doublet of cloth of gold and blue weave over darker blue hose, so that the deep blue of his eyes seemed the more striking in that tanned face crowned by a mass of thick, curling dark hair. She was touched by the sight of the now fading bruise on his temple. It was so faint that none but the eyes of love would have noticed it at all.

A rush of joy went through her. He was unharmed, master of his own lands again. It was swiftly followed by a cold trickle of doubt. He no longer had need of her. Would he fret against the necessity of harbouring a wife whom he'd been forced to wed as hostage for all he held dear? He could not easily rid himself of her, especially now that she was to bear his child. The marriage could not be annulled. He could banish her, of course, to Cranley or to some other manor where her presence could not trouble him. He would then be free to take noble lady or strumpet to his bed, whichever pleased him. She found herself thinking with grim satisfaction, no strumpet however well born, can give him a legitimate heir, that only I can do. Yet this secret she would keep to herself for some little time yet.

"Jeannine tells me you rebel against the need to rest in bed."

She inclined her head, hiding her eyes from him.

"After the ordeal it would be best for you to sleep awhile after you've eaten, of course."

"Forgive me, My Lord, but I could not do that — yet." She hesitated then brought it out in a rush. "I must thank you for coming to my assistance. I was becoming frightened, I confess. Those townsfolk were so hostile. I find it hard to believe that we helpless women could have aroused such bitter hatred."

He hooked forward a stool with one booted foot and seated himself opposite.

"They feared Margaret's attack on the city. Her mercenaries have not been noted for their good behaviour." She lowered her gaze shyly as he continued to stare at her with those bright blue eyes, never wavering for a moment in that intent, hard regard. Then he lifted one heavy damp strand of her brown hair and carried it to his lips.

"You are no less beautiful, my wife, despite your astounding adventures."

She felt herself melting with love for him. "You also, My Lord, seem none the worse for your activities."

"I've been fortunate, a few bruises and scratches, nothing serious. With the King and the Dukes of Gloucester and Clarence the Lord has preserved me from harm."

"And given the King the victory."

"Yes."

"Have you had word of my father and — and of my cousin?"

"They remain under close guard in the Tower with the remainder of the Queen's household."

Her bottom lip quivered uncertainly. "After Tewkesbury, did the King take summary vengeance on — on his enemies?"

"On Somerset and the rebel ringleaders, those who were guilty of deliberate treachery. All else went free."

"He tore them from sanctuary?"

"No, they gave themselves up after a night in the abbey and were judged by the Lord Constable of England, My Lord of Gloucester. Somerset died well, I am told. I was not present."

Elinor's thoughts raced. Her father could well be said to have committed deliberate treason to the King's cause. He had been Montecute's man and John Neville's allegiance had been sworn to York. How could she ask Lord Gerard to plead for him, after he and Reginald had been instrumental in the plan to trap him at Beckwith and used her for their purpose?

As if he read her thoughts he said, "I have asked Gloucester to plead with the King for Sir Thomas's life. It was from Gloucester, of course, that I obtained the authority to take you from that cart into my own custody."

Mentally she blessed the kindness

the young duke had more than once shown her. How would the Lady Anne fare now, fatherless, widowed, captured within the household of the enemy? Could Gloucester's love save her from the consequences of her father's folly?

"Sir, I thank you for your good offices for my father. I know he has shown himself your enemy, but I believe he did so out of his belief in the injustice shown to My Lord Marquess of Montecute."

"Do you?" Lord Gerard said shortly. Dull crimson flooded her cheeks. In her heart she knew it was not so. Her father and Reginald had both wished to profit from this war. Reginald had spoken bluntly of his intention to destroy her husband. Yet they were her kinsmen. How could she not do her utmost now to save their lives, if not their lands?

Jeannine entered with a tray laden with food for Elinor. Elinor demurred but Lord Gerard waved aside her objections.

"You must eat. I'll stand over you and see that you take some of this chicken breast and a manchet of bread, yes, and take some of this good wine to hearten you." His lips curved in a half smile as Jeannine left the chamber. "Come, Elinor, you'll not want me to force you." He poured wine for them both and she took the cup from his hand, her fingers tingling at the touch of his flesh on hers.

Under his stern gaze she reluctantly took some nourishment. At last he nodded and thrust aside the tray. He stood watching her, his head slightly on one side, then he gave a little inarticulate cry and drew her up and into his arms.

"Elinor, my love, my sweet, I thought you were lost to me."

Was she hearing true, this proud, unyielding man confessing his love for her? Tears of joy rained unrestrained down her cheeks.

"I thought, feared, they had killed you there on the field or that you had fallen prey to those human jackals."

He put her from him at arm's length and tilted up her chin. "Beckwith drew you away?"

She nodded. "I stole from the nunnery with Jeannine and Blaise. Simon had heard your standard was down and we were afraid — " she drew a hard breath. "I don't know how they found me, Reginald must have had me followed. I cannot imagine why he should have wished to hold me prisoner when — when all was lost. I struggled with him. He — he hit me." She swallowed hard. "I can't remember anything more until I came to myself in a horse litter on the way to Bushley."

His arm stole around her waist and he led her towards the bed. "Nothing matters now. I have you safe and I'll see to it that you never escape from me again if I have to lock you up with fetters on wrists and ankles." There was a hint of amusement in his tone but an underlying grimness told her how deeply he meant the sentiment.

His lean, hard body was pressing against hers. Why should she wish to leave him — ever?

He reached out and drew the brocade bed gown from her shoulders so that the light from the window gleamed on her ivory shoulders and rounded breasts. Her nipples hardened with desire. Shamelessly she stepped free from the robe and kicked it from her. She saw his blue eyes flash

454

with the fire of longing and she was fiercely glad.

"My Lord?" she whispered huskily.

"You're so lovely, more beautiful than ever. At Grantham I held a girl in my arms, now I behold a woman."

She slipped into bed and laid back the sheets invitingly. It had been so long, so very long that she had been from him. "Why do you wait, My Lord? Does some urgent business for the King draw you from me now?"

"Nothing could draw me from you, except — " His voice was husky.

"Except?" Her brows flew up questioningly. "What is it, My Lord? Are you — are you still unfit — "

"No," he said, his lips twitching with amusement, "I'm fit enough, My Lady, as I could soon prove to you, but you, after all you have been through! I know I should be patient."

"After all I have been through, I need to have the comfort of being held in your arms, nothing less will serve to heal and comfort me, My Lord."

He gave a yelp of pure joy and turned from her to unrobe. She lay watching, her eyes dwelling lovingly on the hard leanness of his taut body. Bruises, purple and yellow, marred the flesh where heavy blows from mace and battle axe had dented the armour. Even his padded under-tunic had not been sufficient to protect him fully from those. As he joined her in the bed, her fingers touched the marks lovingly, tracing them, feeling the hurt of them in her own body.

Even now, when he was impatient to slake his passion, he was gentle with her. His hands wooed her to respond. As they moved across the soft smooth flesh of her belly she thought of the child. Afterwards, she must tell him, not yet. Jeannine had said it was safe, yet — and she had to be sure, know without a trace of doubt, that he loved her.

Her body arched to his with a little moan as he entered her. Her fingers caught and held him to her. He moved very gently, his lips caressing the cool softness of her breast, then excitement grew and hers with it.

She mounted on eagle's wings, soaring high above earth and waters, to the skies, falling to the deep depths of the seas, then mounting again on the crest of a wave. They were one, their bodies and souls fused, so that never again would they know that terrible loneliness of separation. Even when he was from her side, she would experience again this wild joy, this ecstasy, and remember.

He lay beside her, his arm tight, possessively close round her waist. She bent and kissed the dark hair curling upon his forehead. A line of sweat dewed his upper lip.

"So," he said softly, "my virgin bride has become a true woman."

"If that is so it is because you tutored me — and — and none other."

"Elinor, there was no thought of that in my heart."

"I was always yours," She whispered chokingly, "from the moment I saw you from the minstrels' gallery and then — then you were so loving and courteous until — until — "

"Think no more of that, my wife." His voice broke under the stress of his emotion.

"It seemed then that — that in spite of my love, you had become my enemy.

457

When — when you punished me for — for sending that letter — I still loved you but — but there was Simon — "

His head was turned from her and he did not speak. She waited in an agony of doubt.

"You do not still believe that Simon and I — "

Still he said nothing.

"I have love for Simon, not as you fear, but as for the brother I never had. He was good to me, My Lord, almost died to save me. He has never so much as touched me. You must believe that."

"I would willingly have strangled Simon with my own hands, watched the executioner tear at his vitals, and I, too, have loved Simon as a younger brother," he said slowly. "Understand this, Elinor, when a man is in love he does not think logically, not even sanely. I had seen him look at you and that was enough. When I saw that messenger wearing your necklace and guessed that Radbourne had been your go-between, I thought only the worst, that he had been paid — in coin to match his desire. He loves you, Elinor, you realize that?"

"Yes," she said soberly, "I wish it were not so, but he is young and there will be other women. I hope and pray he will learn to love one of them, truly."

"Amen to that," he echoed fervently.

"When the duke told me that Simon was free but that he refused to leave Bruges, I believed — " her voice broke oddly, "I believed that it was for me to see that he *did* go. He insisted on waiting till he knew I was safe. I was responsible for his peril. I had to make him go, and," she said awkwardly, "there was another reason."

He glanced at her sharply. "You feared I had heard the talk about you and Hastings."

She nodded, head lowered, lashes veiling her golden eyes from him.

"But Gloucester had told me the truth of that and — when I saw you at Amboise and, later — learned what you did to save me, could I doubt you, or fail to love you — with all my heart?"

She lay back against the pillows and watched the light outside the window pale from the apricot splendour of sunset to the purple shadows of twilight. Cocooned within this room, safe in her husband's arms, the world had seemed so very far away.

"My Lord," she said doubtfully, unsure if she had chosen the right moment to reveal her news, "I have to tell you — that — that I am to bear your child in October."

He sat up suddenly then bent his head down close to hers. She moved fearfully under that fierce regard. Did he doubt that the child was his?

"Elinor," he said, that harsh note sounding again and revealing his concern, for knowing him now as she did, she understood what that grimness betokened, "my love, you should not have endangered yourself."

"You wrong me, I would not have been so foolish as to risk your child," she said hurriedly. "Jeannine assured me that — that our love making could do no harm — "

He laughed heartily.

"Beautiful wanton, I was not thinking of this, but of all the travelling and hardships you've undergone and during those early months when, I understand,

460

things can go badly with a woman in your condition. Beckwith should have left you in France. How could he have been so thoughtless of your wellbeing?"

"He doesn't know. I did not tell my father — either."

She turned from him. Even now it hurt to know how her kinsmen had used her for their own ends.

"Well, we must take great care of you from now on," he said firmly, "no more riding or hectic travelling. Once the King has released me from service at Court I shall take you to Cranley." He laughed, deep in his throat, "But for now, since Jeannine assures you there can be no harm in it — "

She surrendered, laughing, into his embrace, until he brought her once more to the perfection of utter bliss and, later, her body aglow with the delicious aftermath of love, she slept in his arms.

14

THE interior of Lord Gerard's tent was pleasantly shaded. Elinor sat on a small folding camp stool while Simon armed his lord for the coming jousts. Outside the bright June sun blazed upon the emerald green of the lists and the colourful silks of the ladies' gowns where they sat in the specially erected stands to view the day's events. King Edward was celebrating his two great victories by a magnificent tournament held at Smithfield. The occasion was one of glitter and pomp. Knights had come from as far afield as Burgundy and even from France to take part.

Elinor watched fondly as Simon completed the strapping of Lord Gerard's right vambrace.

He smiled across at her. "Are you still concerned? There can be no possible risk. I am not to fight in the mêlée and we wield only blunted swords and wooden

462

maces. Come, sweetheart, bind on your favour."

She smiled resolutely but, in spite of all his reassurances, she regarded this coming encounter with decided alarm. She loved him so that every second he lived in danger she ached for him. Simon stood back so she might bind round Lord Gerard's right arm the white velvet sleeve cut from her betrothal gown. He had asked especially for that.

"It was the gown in which I first saw you. You were quite breathtaking, my wife, and remained so even after those first days we rode from Yorkshire."

He stooped and caught at her hand as she completed the task, covering it with kisses. She stood on tip-toe to kiss him upon the mouth, savouring the masculine smell of him, heightened by the acrid odours of tooled leather and metal oil.

"I love you, My Lord. Be very careful of your person. It is very precious to me, to both of us." It was an overt reminder of his responsibility to the coming child and he nodded happily.

Simon reached for the padded tilting helm, heavy, weighing almost twenty pounds, and surmounted with the gilded, forked tongued gryphon of Lord Gerard's device. His helm must be strapped firmly to back and breastplates in order to withstand the shock of encounter when lance or mace met helmet or breastplate in the charge. It was then that the knight was in the greatest peril for, if he were unhorsed in such heavy armour, he could fall with such force as to break his neck or back. Elinor's teeth worried her bottom lip. No one could convince her that today's activities would not endanger the life of the man she loved so dearly.

Simon escorted her out into the sunlight and she blinked, coming from the shaded dimness of the silken pavilion. The whole scene stretched before her like an illustration in the Book of Hours Lord Gerard had given to her as his betrothal gift. Like all the ladies of King Edward's Court, she was dressed extravagantly for the day's joyous celebration.

Her gown of apricot silk was embroidered with cloth of gold and her white silk modesty vest was laced with gilded strapping. Her butterfly head-dress was in the very latest fashion, the stiffly wired gauze veiling set back from a shortened cap covered in cloth of gold. Lord Gerard had insisted. Lady Cranley must not be outdone in splendour by any other lady seated in the royal stand. The Queen lolled in her cushioned chair, resplendent in scarlet brocade while the King, who was not to joust today, was in purple and cloth of gold weave, a jewelled chaplet encircling that gorgeous mane of red gold hair.

As Elinor emerged from the tent, she was saluted by Duke Richard of Gloucester who, attended by his squire, moved out from his own pavilion. She thought how remarkable it was that this slight, pale young man had already forged a warlike reputation on the fields of Barnet and Tewkesbury. Elinor gave no credence to the malicious rumour that the young duke was responsible for King Harry's murder. She knew Lord Gerard had been present with Gloucester on his visit to the Tower.

"His Grace was there only to inspect the armoury," Lord Gerard had snapped, furious at the vile insinuations. "I never once left his side. Neither he nor any one of his men paid a visit to poor, mad Harry's apartments. This is on a par with the lying tale that young Edward of Lancaster was done to death by the King and princes within the King's tent at Tewkesbury when everyone who was there knows the prince was mowed down in the pursuit. In all events, King Harry's servants were paid up to several days after Gloucester had left the city, proof positive that the King was still living that night."

Duke Richard's expression was grim though he smiled at sight of Elinor. If only the end of these wars could bring Gloucester his heart's desire. The Lady Anne was still denied him, though now a widow. His brother, Clarence, had taken her into his household, and though Clarence's wife, Isabel, was Lady Anne's sister, Elinor was uneasy about the situation. Anne was co-heiress with Isabel to all the Warwick riches. Clarence would not easily give her into his brother's keeping, since her dowry would be lost to him.

Jeannine fell into step behind her mistress and the soft folds of their gowns brushed the grass as they made their way towards the royal stand.

Elinor paused as they passed the site where the shields of today's participating knights were displayed. There shone the bright gold gryphon of Cranley and the argent silver bars of Beckwith. Even now, it disturbed her that Lord Gerard had so simply accepted Reginald's challenge.

Her father and cousin had been released into her husband's custody shortly after his return from Kent. A considerable fine had been levied, but the King had seen fit to be merciful. Sir Thomas had visited his daughter at Lord Gerard's lodging in the Chepe but Reginald had not been with him. Sir Thomas had been fulsome in his praise of Lord Gerard and his expressions of gratitude for his preservation, yet Elinor doubted his sincerity.

At the ceremony last night where good humoured challenges had been made and accepted, Reginald had touched the Cranley shield lightly with the blunted end of his sword. Elinor, standing beside her lord, had been bathed in a cold sweat as if suddenly douched in a can of ice cold water, despite the warm sultriness of the summer evening. Lord Gerard had smilingly nodded his acceptance, bending to pick up Reginald Beckwith's steel gauntlet. The two men had strode off in seeming friendship.

Later, at their lodging, her body still shivering with the unaccountable chill, huddled close to Lord Gerard in their bed, Elinor had spoken, haltingly, of her forebodings.

"I wish you two were not to fight. He wishes you no good. He is jealous of your good fortune and high standing at Court. Be very careful. Do not trust his overtures of friendship."

"Yet this bout is in the true chivalrous spirit of comradeship. He recognizes the service I did him and," Lord Gerard added, sardonically, "he knows he will need my further good offices if he is to be finally accepted at Court. He's your kinsman. I'd not be at enmity with the man nor with your father, sweetheart."

Elinor shivered. She remembered the cold-blooded fashion in which her cousin had spoken of benefiting from her husband's death. If she were now to be widowed and bear an heir the child would be at the mercy of her kinsmen during his minority, unless the King were to intervene.

She was being fearful and fanciful. Jeannine had told her that women with child were often so. This morning she could scarcely bear to leave her lord's side and had insisted on being present when Simon armed him.

She turned to Jeannine. "You would like to be with Blaise. Isn't he going to perform soon?"

"Before the King, madame. He will sing of the knighting of Arthur and the gift of the sacred sword Excalibur from the Lady of the Lake." Jeannine's green eyes were shadowed and Elinor touched her gently on her arm.

"What is it? Something is troubling you?"

The lute player smiled with rare sweetness. "Blaise has been offered a place in His Grace of Gloucester's household."

"I am happy for you both, Jeannine. He is a good lord and will give you due protection."

469

"I should not leave your service, now, while the child is coming."

"Oh, but you must. When these celebrations are over and My Lord feels free to ask leave of absence from Court, we shall go to Cranley. My old nurse, Alice, will come to me there. My father will be happy to allow it. I shall be in good hands and I am anxious for you and Blaise. Even here, in England, there are men who would strike you down if it were suspected — "

Jeannine looked full at her. "I believe le Duc suspects."

Elinor was shocked. "He cannot be a heretic."

"No, madame, but he understands true freedom of thought, even in religion."

"Jeannine, I shall miss you terribly. But my husband is one of the duke's gentlemen and we shall meet often. It is right that you should serve him. I shall never forget the kindness you showed to a stranger. I love you, Jeannine, as I did my own mother."

The lute player bent and kissed Elinor's fingers in homage. "Your God will protect you and give you the happiness you crave and deserve."

"You go now to Blaise. You will not want to miss the performance. I'm very close to my cousin's pavilion and my father is with him. He will escort me to the royal stand."

Jeannine dropped her that slow, grave curtsey which was never subservient and moved off in search of the troubadour. Elinor watched her thoughtfully. Now they were safe in England, she hoped Jeannine, too, would find fulfilment and bliss in Blaise's bed.

A page pushed back the flap of Reginald's tent. The Beckwith arms moved faintly in the summer breeze. Somehow she must impress upon her father the magnitude of the debt he owed Lord Cranley. Without Lord Gerard's pleas for clemency and his oath that he would stand surety for the conduct of his wife's kinsmen, neither Sir Thomas nor Reginald would be free men today. Behind her, near the royal stand, she heard the mellow plucking of lute strings and the moving beauty of Blaise's baritone voice. It would be still some time before the commencement of the individual jousts.

She halted, checked by the sound of her father's voice, his tone subdued, almost clandestine.

"We were right to take no risk. Cranley is skilful in the lists. It's unlikely you'll unhorse him. That man of mine can be trusted implicitly. It was a clever stroke to place him in Cranley's household. He is able to come and go in his lord's tent without question. He'll accompany that squire of Cranley's, Radbourne, to the steward's bench when the weapons are examined before the bouts. Together with your man, Green, who'll have the handling of your weapons from the moment they leave this pavilion until he places them in your hands, he'll keep an eye out for any problems which could arise."

Reginald's voice, low, spitting with menace. "I wish to see the man dead before the morning. Elinor will be distraught. The King will be able to deny her nothing. What more natural than she be placed within the care of her father and kinsman? Edward will be glad to have us all safely away from London where he cannot be pressed to involve himself in her affairs." There was a pause. "I'll manage to dispose of John Cranley, personally."

Elinor reeled on her feet and clutched blindly at the rough wood of the standard pole for support. Though she had heard their words plainly enough, she still could not fully take in their meaning.

Did they plot to murder her husband before the assembled Court, here, in the lists? How? They spoke of the weapons. Her thoughts flew to the dark-avised man, Withers, who had been laying out wine and food for her lord's refreshment following the bouts. She had seen him more than once about their lodging. Since he had not been in Lord Gerard's service prior to his arrival in London, she knew he was no man-at-arms and had believed him to have come from Cranley with others of My Lord's household. Her father had made it clear that the man had been placed in his present service with the intention of furthering his former master's plans, which were — to murder Lord Gerard? She repeated the words silently, mouthing them incredulously as if by doing so she would have the power to break the deadly nausea which assailed her at the thought of them. She was numbed, unable to move a muscle. The bright silks of the pavilions, the waving standards, the noise of men-at-arms, squires, attendant pages, clink of harness and weapons blurred, faded into a grey mist, all sounds deadened. She blinked rapidly as if to clear her eyes and ears. She must move, force her reluctant limbs to obey her, run to Lord Gerard, tell him all she had heard. No, he would not believe her or imagine she had misunderstood. Would it be wiser to make for the royal stand, appeal to the King for help? But he would not believe her either. He would soothe her, assure her there was nothing to fear from this mock combat. Oh yes, he would be unfailingly courteous but unwilling to halt the proceedings on the evidence offered by a distraught woman.

Dear God, what could she do? To whom should she turn? To Gloucester? He had come to her help before now. But he, too, was fighting today. He would be busied within his tent, his squire unwilling to allow her to disturb him.

The brilliant scene swam dizzily then righted itself. She stood upright letting go of her grasp at the standard pole. Lord Gerard *must* be faced. She must run to him now, fall upon her knees before him, weep, rage, anything to persuade him not to enter the lists today. She could not understand, even now, by what means he could be murdered, here before the assembled Court gathered as witnesses. Were Reginald's weapons poisoned? Withers, her father had said, was to see to it, with Reginald's squire, that his weapons remained untouched until they were to be used in the joust. Elinor had heard tales of the poisoning of enemies, particularly in France and Italy. Men and women too had died from the wearing of poisoned gloves, even the handling of poisoned letters. A rival wished a man dead and he perished horribly in agony. Jousting weapons were blunted and foiled. Lord Gerard could come to no harm by their use. The skill in the joust lay in unhorsing one's opponent, not by piercing his armour with lance or sword. What if the foils of Reginald's weapons had been so tampered with that they broke and proved deadly in the fray? Even so, Lord Gerard was an able fighter, he could parry such a blow. No, her father had intended to take no risks. Whether Reginald or Lord Gerard emerged from the joust the victor, it had been planned that Lord Gerard should die.

Disgust at her father's cowardly plan filled Elinor so that she almost gagged on it, black bile rising from her throat into her mouth.

She must move calmly. There would be no sense in running wildly across the grass. An hysterical woman would not be heeded, rather would Simon seek to keep her from her lord.

She covered half the distance towards the Cranley pavilion when a shadow darkened the grass before her, for she was moving with head lowered. Looking up, startled, she encountered the pale eyes of the manservant, Withers. She gave a little cry and, in doing so, gave herself away. His brows twitched together and, as she tried to avoid him, he adroitly tripped her. She stumbled and felt his arms round her, lifting, outwardly solicitous, conveying her back towards the Beckwith pavilion.

"It is nothing, sir, my mistress is faint from the heat and confusion of the crowds. Her father, Sir Thomas Beckwith, is close by and will see to her comfort."

Elinor tried to cry out a warning to the concerned bystander, but already Withers had hurried her by. His fingers gripped her arm mercilessly and swept her inexorably from any hope of assistance. The tent flap was thrust back and she found herself within the darkened interior. Reginald loomed before her, taller than usual in his plumed helm and armour, menacing. Her father's eyes snapped with fury at the manservant's presumption for he had thrust his hand over Elinor's mouth the moment they were safely clear of the onlookers.

"What is this, man? You had your orders. You should be with Radbourne at the steward's table."

Reginald appeared to take in the situation more quickly. He signalled to his man to hold Elinor fast and to continue to keep her silent.

"She knows?" The question was imperious and immediate.

"Aye, sir, I think so. She was coming from the direction of your tent. Her expression alarmed me. I acted fast. If she should alert My Lord Cranley — "

Reginald snatched up a linen kerchief on which his man had lain out his own refreshments and flung it at Withers.

"Gag her."

Elinor struggled frantically and her father made a half-hearted attempt to protest.

"Look at her, man," Reginald snapped, "her eyes tell the story. She knows what we intend. She must have been listening outside. She has to be kept from Cranley. Afterwards," he added, with grim irony, "it will not matter. What can she say? Who would believe her wild accusations against her own father? It will be safer if she disappears for a time."

"What?" Sir Thomas blustered, "how can that be managed? The King himself will note her absence to say nothing of that upstart, young Gloucester." Dispassionately, he watched his daughter's desperate struggles to free herself from the silken cords torn from the tent flaps, with which Withers was securing her wrists tightly behind her back. Her golden eyes blazed at him in anguished defiance above the linen gag.

Reginald shrugged. "She is known to have been wed to Cranley against her will. What if she has fled his unwanted attentions with a lover of her choice? She ran from him once before. There will be ugly talk, speculation, but we can keep her hidden somewhere until she has come round to our way of thinking."

Withers, at a nod from his master, had pushed Elinor down upon a folding stool at the back of the tent. To make doubly sure she would give no trouble, he tied her ankles firmly to the leg struts.

Sir Thomas eyed her moodily. "I can't see her ever accepting you, Reginald. I've been watching her. The girl's besotted with that husband of hers and it's my belief she's already breeding."

Reginald's eyes lit with some unholy glow, accentuated by the half darkness within the tent. Elinor could hardly believe that that genial countenance she had known and loved since early childhood could take on such an expression of pure malevolence. "Is she now?" he questioned softly. "Then we must find a way of dealing with that particular problem."

Sir Thomas worried at his thumb nail gloomily. "Well, it's plain to see she can't be allowed to get to Cranley or to the King. We'll face the other problems later." He glared at Withers. "You obeyed your instructions?"

"Aye, Sir Thomas." The man showed his yellow teeth in a wolfish grin. "Monkshood can be relied on, even better than belladonna and the symptoms are less obvious. You can be assured Lord Gerard'll not recover."

"And the source of the poison?"

"No need to let that worry you, Sir Reginald. The seller won't be around for questioning. I made sure of that."

Reginald grunted his approval. "Will can see all goes well before the joust. You'd best attend to My Lady. Sir Thomas and I must move towards the lists. The trumpets will soon sound the summons to arms." He reached for his mailed gauntlets from a trestle camp table near to Elinor and she shrank from him. He laughed as the little moaning sound reached him over the linen gag.

"Don't be afraid, cousin, we'll soon rid you of your noble husband."

Sir Thomas turned in his walk to the tent entrance. "If she is missing from the tournament, she might be held in suspicion of the crime we plan. I'll not have that, Reginald. Elinor is not to be harmed. God's Blood, she'd go to the fire."

"I've sworn to you I'll see to it. The squire, Radbourne, has every reason to be blamed. How do you think he received that scar which mars his handsome face? It's well known that Cranley tore his cheek apart with his riding whip, in a fit of jealous rage that Radbourne had shown particular attentions to his lady."

"But that ploy could involve Elinor, God damn it."

"Not if she's far from the scene when My Lord dies." Reginald chuckled, low in his throat. "And the boy will not see her accused. He'd go to his death without a word, if he thought that would save her."

Elinor's horror grew at the man's heartlessness. Not only was Lord Gerard doomed, but Simon threatened and herself ruined. She struggled once more ineffectually against her bonds.

"How will you carry her from the field, Withers?"

"Wrapped in the pavilion trappings, Sir. Once the jousts are underway, what more natural than we should begin stripping the tent? Like the Egyptian Queen Cleopatra she'll lie safe hidden within a silken binding until I get her on board a boat. The river ferrymen will keep their mouths tight shut if you pay them enough. She'll lie secure in some whorehouse on the South Wark until I hear from you."

Elinor's eyes followed her father imploringly as he went with her cousin from the tent. Withers assured himself that she was completely helpless then hastened out, presumably to make arrangements for the dismantling of the pavilion. The nauseating gag half choked her and she fought to free her mouth. It seemed an impossible task. Soon all the spectators would be moving into the wooden stands to see the contest, no one would hear her. At any moment Lord Gerard would ride into the lists all unsuspecting. It was likely that one of Reginald's weapons had been made to wound slightly or merely scratch his opponent. Who would suspect, if Lord Gerard were to die soon after, that he had not fallen a victim to some fever taken as a result of that accidental wounding? It could be weeks, months, before her father released her from some South Bank brothel, too late to save Lord Gerard or even to offer a word in Simon Radbourne's defence should he be accused of murdering his master. Should she accuse her own father, she would pityingly be considered mad from the loss of her husband, the more so when her condition became known. The King would be unlikely to concern himself over her welfare, he was far too busy rebuilding his trade and treaties. He would give her thankfully into the care of her father.

And her child, Lord Gerard's heir? Elinor froze as she recalled the gleam in Reginald's eyes when her father informed him that he suspected she was with child.

It would not be allowed to survive. She was sick with rage and frustration as she realized she could be so easily wed against her will to her cousin.

Her renewed struggle to untie her bonds caused the stool to fall, and her with it, in an untidy sprawl across the dirt floor. If only she could crawl towards the tent flap she might yet attract attention from some passer-by. That, too, seemed impossible for her limbs were entangled in her voluminous skirts and still firmly bound to the stool legs.

She would not give up. Sweat drenched her as the pain of her rubbed flesh made itself felt. She desisted for a moment, grunting, as she feared that her frantic struggles might harm the child.

A shrill trumpet call made her redouble her attempts. In a moment the King would ceremonially lift his ivory baton and the tournament would begin.

Then at last when she believed all hope lost she heard Jeannine's call, anxious, unusually high pitched. "Madame la Vicomtesse?"

Elinor sobbed aloud in helpless frustration. How could she summon

Jeannine who was so tantalizingly near to her. Again she jounced the stool along the floor, rubbing her knees raw. She had managed to get only a fraction nearer to the tent flap. Her knees were drawn up sideways and she set herself to crawl, crablike, some yards further. At any moment Withers would return and she would be carried secretly from the ground before her friends could help her.

There was a hurried pattering of feet outside and the tent flap was pushed aside. Elinor fell back exhausted, then gave a moan of relief as Blaise's spare form blocked out the sunlight. He turned at once to call to Jeannine some paces behind him. He reached her and his strong, brown fingers fumbled at the gag. She was able to breathe easily again, and croak to Jeannine who knelt by her side, pushing her gently back while she tackled the ankle thongs.

"*Doucement, doucement*, madame. You will be free very soon. We missed you and when your father appeared alone — "

Panting, Elinor tried to explain her need for urgency but her words were incoherent. She feared, even now, that her rescuers had come too late and that all three might be interrupted by Withers and the men summoned to dismantle the tent.

"My Lord, I — must get to him — or to the King. They mean to murder him — "

Blaise lifted her to her feet. She swayed with exhaustion and the blood raced agonizingly through her limbs now that her bonds had been released.

"Help me," she begged, "carry me. Blaise, I must get to Lord Gerard."

"But, madame, you say *le roi*, the King, is in danger."

"Not the King, my husband. My father — " Her face crumpled at the realization of Sir Thomas's intended foulness.

Blaise half carried her into the sunlight. This section of the enclosure was now deserted. Everyone had made his way to the lists to watch the jousts.

Once on her feet Elinor found herself able to walk, though Blaise kept a supporting arm round her waist. Her gown was stained with dust and grass, torn in places by her desperate efforts to free herself. Over the trampled grass they stumbled, every step an effort which brought her to the brink of utter collapse. Wisely Jeannine kept her fears concerning the unborn child to herself, though she exchanged some anxious glances with Blaise.

The participating knights were already mounted and were being handed their lances. Simon Radbourne was securing the chain of her husband's mace to the ring on the right of his breastplate. His destrier trampled the grass, impatient for the fray. Elinor lunged clumsily towards them. Lord Gerard had not yet lowered his visor. He let out a great roar of fury at sight of her.

"Elinor, God's Wounds, who has dared to harm you?"

Blaise had helped her to her lord's side and he leaned from the saddle to clasp her clawing fingers in his mailed hand.

"You must not fight Reginald," she panted. "He intends to kill you. The weapons he uses are — poisoned. Even with a blunted lance he could scratch you, pierce your armour between gorget and breastplate, or between vambrace and couter. My Lord, I beg of you, withdraw from the jousts. He must be accused and brought before the King."

"My Love, there is nothing to fear. You bring me fair warning. Simon, find My Lady's father. She must be escorted safely from Smithfield. Jeannine will attend her."

"No, My Lord, no. You must not trust my father. He and Reginald are plotting together."

Even beyond the shadowing of his jousting helmet, Elinor saw her husband's expression change, his blue eyes flash.

"So." He waved a mailed hand to Simon to approach. "I leave Lady Elinor in your care. Take her to the King. Later, after I have dealt with Beckwith, I'll settle accounts with Sir Thomas."

"My Lord, I should be close to you if you intend to enter the lists against Reginald Beckwith. Should you not," Simon eyed his master timidly, "reconsider? My Lady is distraught and — "

Lord Gerard's haughty features expressed fury at his squire's temerity. "You heard me. See to My Lady. Once she is safe, speak with Gloucester's squire. I would have audience with His Grace."

The herald was already announcing the bout. Elinor pleaded with her husband to ignore the summons.

He looked gravely down at her as Simon, at his signal, settled his lance. "Elinor, my heart's love, there is nothing to fear, I promise you. Now I am armed by your love, this man has no power to hurt me. I have this amulet." His fingers touched her favour, then he had set spurs to his mount, dust flew from his destrier's hoofs as he urged it into position on his side of the dividing wooden barrier.

Elinor allowed herself to be escorted to the royal stand. There came a concerted gasp as she made her appearance and her dishevelled state was noted. The babble of talk from the Queen's ladies was abruptly hushed as the King leaned to speak with her.

"Lady Cranley, I see some harm has befallen you. Are you badly hurt? Tell me who is responsible."

Elinor's lips trembled but she held her ground. "I — I overheard a plot to murder my husband, Your Grace. I have warned him but he insists on risking his life to avenge the insult shown to me. I beg you to forbid this contest."

There was a horrified silence as the spectators in the royal stand stared at her, wide-eyed, some with mouths half open in astonishment.

The King's blue eyes hardened as Lord Gerard's had done. He looked sternly across at the lists as the two mailed knights advanced to halt before the royal stand, their lances at rest, skilfully reining in their snorting, caparisoned destriers. The sun glinted on the sculptured form of the golden gryphon which surmounted Lord Gerard Cranley's helm and on the silver bars of the Beckwith arms displayed on Reginald's shield and surcoat.

The King acknowledged the salute from each of the knights as the lances were tipped before him. He raised his baton and the two turned and galloped to opposite ends of the lists. Eyes blurring with tears, Elinor watched along the line of the jousting barrier for her husband's loved form.

Out of the corner of her eye, she saw

the King gesture to an attendant and the man moved off in obedience to some instruction. In one heart-stopping moment, Elinor saw her father stare full at her from his vantage point at the right of the spectators' stand. Could she even now, reveal his part in this affair? One word from her and he would be arrested and returned to the Tower. She would condemn him to that barbarous traitor's death at Tyburn. She could not do it. Though Sir Thomas richly deserved to die, she could not be the instrument who would send him to such an end. The hideousness of it would lie like a menacing shadow between her love and her. She leaned forward slightly and inclined her chin. He rose and shouldered his way from the stand. No one stayed him. All were avidly intent on the commencement of the bout.

Elinor reached blindly for Jeannine's hand as the lute player took her place slightly behind her mistress.

The combatants thundered towards each other down the length of the lists. Dust flying upwards obscured her view. She prayed fervently that Reginald's wooden foils would not split and his lance blade wound some exposed place on her husband's body. There was a splintering of wood, a heavy thud, and the mounts sped on past each other. The dust cleared and she saw both men had remained in their saddles. A cheer went up from the massed spectators.

The knights settled fresh lances and once more rode towards each other, each thrusting hard at his opponent across the wooden barrier which separated them. One destrier gave a shrill neigh of outrage. Lord Gerard lurched in the saddle as Reginald Beckwith's lance caught him squarely upon the small, leather covered shield emblazoned with his coat of arms fastened upon his left breast. His lance had splintered and there was a gasp from the crowd then a hush as they waited breathlessly to see if he would fall from his horse. Elinor's mouth was dry as she saw him recover control of his mount and move him into position for the next encounter.

Confidently Reginald sat his mount, relinquished his lance, and the two men took their wooden jousting maces from their attendant squires. The horses advanced again at the gallop, there were ominous thuds as mace struck heavy plate armour and this time it was Reginald who was seen to stagger beneath his opponent's blow. A ragged cheer sounded and just as quickly was stilled. All eyes turned to the royal box where the King was leaning forward, one elbow supported upon the rail of the stand, his chin resting upon his hand. It was as if the spectators were suddenly made aware of a change in the atmosphere of these proceedings. There was a restlessness amongst them, a hushed murmuring. The Duke of Gloucester approached his brother and behind him Elinor caught the dull glint of raised pikes. So the King had taken her accusation seriously. But could Lord Gerard emerge from the lists alive? It mattered to her not one jot if Reginald was caught and paid the price for his treachery. All her concern was for her husband.

He was sitting tall in the saddle. Had he been hurt in that second encounter? He could emerge the victor only to fall dead at her feet, poisoned, or later, as

Reginald had implied, as if from a fever taken from his wound?

Again the two destriers advanced to the centre of the lists. Lord Gerard leaned well forward in the saddle and dealt his opponent a devastating blow which rocked Beckwith in his seat. This time there was no thundering off of the horses. The two reined in close, dealing hard blows at each other. The bout seemed, to the petrified Elinor, to be like the fight in the barn, unnaturally protracted; the slow lift and thrust forward of each man's weapon, the reiterated thuds, wood upon wood, wood upon metal. Then it was over. Reginald gave a gasping cry, reeled and fell heavily. Lord Gerard skilfully controlled his curvetting mount, waited for moments, then dismounted and bent over the fallen knight. Squires rushed to his assistance. The jubilation of the watching crowd was momentarily withheld as it became clear that the injured knight lay unmoving. Elinor's throat worked and she swallowed back the bitter, frightened tears.

The defeated knight was carried off on a wooden bier and Lord Cranley advanced on foot to the royal box. He raised his visor and saluted his King then dropped upon one knee before his wife. Trembling from reaction she extended her torn and scratched hand for him to kiss. He looked tired, the weight of the jousting armour was great and he was exhausted, breathing hard but otherwise unscathed. Reginald had spoken of monkshood as being deadlier than belladonna. Could she dare to hope that he would not fall a victim to that venom which might merely have entered a light scratch on his flesh?

Already he was leaving the lists and the herald was summoning participating knights to the following bout. Elinor requested leave of the Queen to withdraw from the royal presence. She would have Simon examine every inch of Lord Gerard's body. Jeannine was skilled in herbal lore. Surely she must know of some antidote.

As they crossed the grass between the royal stand and Lord Gerard's pavilion she told Jeannine of her fear, what she had overheard. The lute player stopped dead in her tracks.

"Your cousin, he spoke of monkshood, what we call aconite, *oui*, madame?"

"Yes, smeared upon his weapons. This is why I begged My Lord not to endanger himself. Jeannine, if he is scratched, can he be saved?"

Jeannine's green eyes flickered uncertainly. Doubt was mirrored on her habitually serene features. Elinor went cold with dread.

"There is no known antidote?"

"Madame la Vicomtesse, I do not understand. If these men planned to poison Milord it could not have been on the weapons. It is not possible to kill so. The poison, it would lose its power in the air. So much would have had to be induced into a deep wound. You cannot have heard correctly."

"But men have died so in Italy and France — "

"There is no truth in such tales, madame. Such men must have taken poison in food or drink. Milord can be in no danger from a wound taken in the joust, I assure you."

"But I heard my cousin order his servant to ensure that his weapons were well guarded. He said quite distinctly that monkshood is more deadly than deadly nightshade and less easy to detect the symptoms."

Jeannine considered, her eyes hooded. "It may be that the weapons were tampered with, the foils weakened on Messire Beckwith's blade, or Milord's lance made so it would splinter easily in the first shock of encounter. That would be possible?"

Elinor was rapidly becoming more afraid. "Yes, that might be managed, though the stewards examine all weapons carefully. But, Jeannine, if the poison was not to be induced into a wound, then — " her voice tailed off uncertainly.

"Aconite can be given only in strongly tasting food or drink. The concentration can then be controlled by the poisoner and could well prove fatal."

They stood, staring into each other's eyes as the horrifying suggestion struck them both at the very same moment.

"In My Lord's tent, the meat, bread and wine. Withers could have tampered with that. Even now he will be in danger. He will be exhausted after the bout, sweating. He'll take wine."

Slipping and lurching, her heart pumping wildly, Elinor raced across the grass. The gryphon device waved on its standard pole outside Lord Gerard's tent. Gasping for breath, Jeannine hard on her heels, Elinor dashed aside the tent flap and burst in.

Simon had already divested his lord of most of his armour. Lord Gerard stood in his padded under-tunic, a cup of wine half-way to his lips. With an inarticulate cry, Elinor launched herself at him and dashed the cup to the ground. Seizing his sleeve she shook him fiercely. "Did you drink any of it, any of it at all? Tell me?"

Momentarily taken off balance he stood unresisting, his lips parted in astonishment. Had she taken leave of her senses?

"Drink?" He gave a little harsh chuckle. "My dear Elinor, you gave me no opportunity to do so."

"Did you so much as set your lips to the cup? *Did* you?"

"No," he shrugged helplessly. "I've said as much."

"And you, Simon, have you eaten or drunk of any of the food and wine set out in this tent?"

The squire's face whitened. "No, My Lady, I would not presume — "

"Thank God! Oh thank God," Elinor stumbled against her husband in the first relief of realization. He lifted her from her feet and, unmindful of the others within the tent, pressed his lips hard upon her lips and throat. Gently he set her down upon the stool on which she had formerly sat and watched him arm, then he knelt and caught her hands tight within his own grasp.

Her lips worked. "My cousin, Reginald?"

His blue eyes clouded. "Piers Langham has just brought us the news. He is dead. I am sorry, sweeting. His back was broken. Had he lived — "

"It is better so." Her voice was very low, "Had he lived he would have died a traitor's death."

His fingers tightened on her imprisoned hands. "Tell me all," he commanded.

Jeannine signed to Simon to withdraw from the tent and followed him. Her lord and lady would need refreshment later which she would allow no one but herself to provide. For the moment they needed only to be alone together.

Haltingly Elinor told Lord Gerard of her abduction by Withers and all she had heard within her cousin's tent.

"In Amboise he — " she gulped hastily, "he made no secret of his lust for wealth and power. Had you — died, my father would have been my only protector and guardian. He and Reginald would have administered my — the child's estates."

"The child would not have been allowed to live," he finished grimly. "It was a well designed plot, as well planned as the one which trapped me at Beckwith. And I believed you had a hand in that. Elinor, my love, how can I make up to you for all you have suffered?"

She clung to him, speaking no words, only needing the comfort of his nearness.

"War or no war, I will never again let you out of my sight. Tomorrow we leave for Cranley."

"But the King may have need of you still and the Duke of Gloucester. I hear

500

he is still kept from the Lady Anne. Should you not stay near him? He has helped us so many times."

"Gloucester has great reserves of strength and courage. He will win his bride whatever it costs, as I have won mine."

He drew her to her feet, his lips scorching hers. His power and strength flowed into her so that she felt no longer drained. Her body glowed and vibrated. In his arms she was safe at last, and she believed his assurance that he would not leave her. When the time came for him to return to Court he would take her with him.

A tingle ran through her as she thought how close she had been to losing him. Reginald was dead. She could not find it in her heart to grieve. The kindly, jovial cousin whom she had loved in childhood had died at Amboise when she had seen him stripped of his outward show of chivalry towards her. She was sure that her father would make good his escape. His fate would not shadow her happiness with her husband and, from exile, he had no power to harm them.

Lord Gerard held her from him, his

blue eyes shining with love as they lingered over her body. She stepped back, freeing herself, and made him a low curtsey. He took her hand and pressed it gallantly against his mouth.

It was over, the King's war with Lancaster.

And she and Lord Gerard were no longer enemies.

THE END

TO FIGHT THE WILD
Rod Ansell and Rachel Percy

Lost in uncharted Australian bush, Rod Ansell survived by hunting and trapping wild animals, improvising shelter and using all the bushman's skills he knew.

COROMANDEL
Pat Barr

India in the 1830s is a hot, uncomfortable place, where the East India Company still rules. Amelia and her new husband find themselves caught up in the animosities which seethe between the old order and the new.

THE SMALL PARTY
Lillian Beckwith

A frightening journey to safety begins for Ruth and her small party as their island is caught up in the dangers of armed insurrection.

THE WILDERNESS WALK
Sheila Bishop

Stifling unpleasant memories of a misbegotten romance in Cleave with Lord Francis Aubrey, Lavinia goes on holiday there with her sister. The two women are thrust into a romantic intrigue involving none other than Lord Francis.

THE RELUCTANT GUEST
Rosalind Brett

Ann Calvert went to spend a month on a South African farm with Theo Borland and his sister. They both proved to be different from her first idea of them, and there was Storr Peterson — the most disturbing man she had ever met.

ONE ENCHANTED SUMMER
Anne Tedlock Brooks

A tale of mystery and romance and a girl who found both during one enchanted summer.

CLOUD OVER MALVERTON
Nancy Buckingham

Dulcie soon realises that something is seriously wrong at Malverton, and when violence strikes she is horrified to find herself under suspicion of murder.

AFTER THOUGHTS
Max Bygraves

The Cockney entertainer tells stories of his East End childhood, of his RAF days, and his post-war showbusiness successes and friendships with fellow comedians.

MOONLIGHT
AND MARCH ROSES
D. Y. Cameron

Lynn's search to trace a missing girl takes her to Spain, where she meets Clive Hendon. While untangling the situation, she untangles her emotions and decides on her own future.

NURSE ALICE IN LOVE
Theresa Charles

Accepting the post of nurse to little Fernie Sherrod, Alice Everton could not guess at the romance, suspense and danger which lay ahead at the Sherrod's isolated estate.

POIROT INVESTIGATES
Agatha Christie

Two things bind these eleven stories together — the brilliance and uncanny skill of the diminutive Belgian detective, and the stupidity of his Watson-like partner, Captain Hastings.

LET LOOSE THE TIGERS
Josephine Cox

Queenie promised to find the long-lost son of the frail, elderly murderess, Hannah Jason. But her enquiries threatened to unlock the cage where crucial secrets had long been held captive.